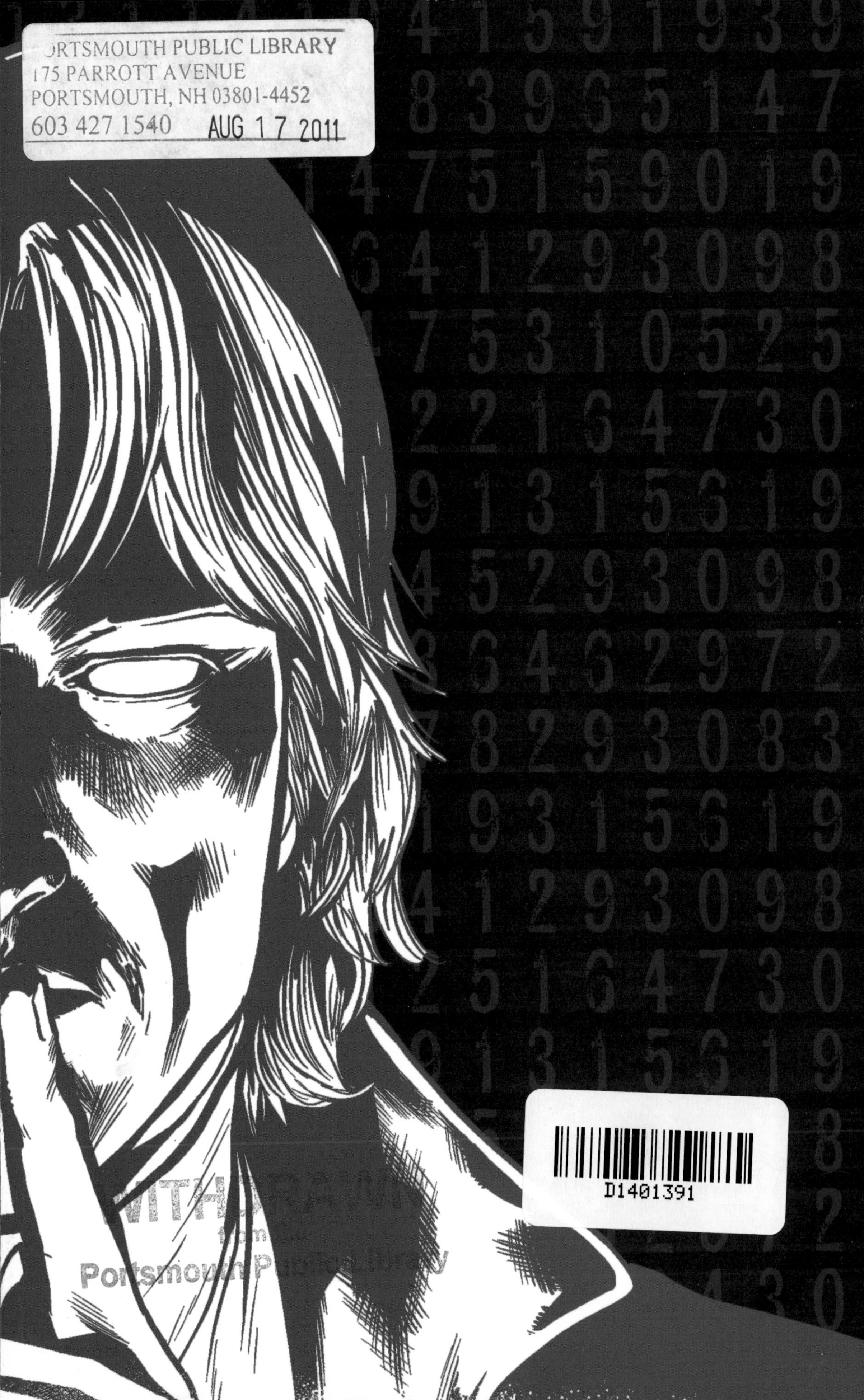

RODDENBERRY PRESENTS

9 DAYS 1939514350

MIS51NG 318408

KESTUS

Archaia Entertainment LLC
WWW.ARCHAIA.COM

RODDENBERRY
WWW.RODDENBERRY.COM

RODDENBERRY PRESENTS

19 DAYS 19395 14350
518 MIS51NG 318408
KESTUS

Written by **Phil Hester**
Art by **David Marquez**
Cover by **Alex Ross**

First Fold Written by **Trevor Roth**
Colors by **Digikore & Rachelle Rosenberg**
Letters by **Troy Peteri**

Series Covers by **Alex Ross, Jorge Molina, Ryan Benjamin,
David Mack & Dale Keown**

Edited by **Paul Morrissey**
Executive Editors **Trevor Roth & Eugene Roddenberry**

Created by **Trevor Roth**

Published by **Archaia**

Archaia Entertainment LLC
1680 Vine Street, Suite 912
Los Angeles, California, 90028, USA
www.archaia.com

Roddenberry Productions

Tory Ireland Mell, *Production Supervisor*
Brent Beaudette, *E-Commerce Manager*
Ryan Harvie, *Executive Assistant*

www.daysmissing.com
www.roddenberry.com

DAYS MISSING ® VOLUME TWO **KESTUS** Hardcover.

May 2011. FIRST PRINTING.

10 9 8 7 6 5 4 3 2 1

ISBN: 1-936393-10-7
ISBN 13: 978-1-936393-10-7

ARCHAIA
BLACK LABEL ™

RODDENBERRY ®

1 3 1 1 4 1 9 4 1

9 1 0 2 1 5 1 8 1

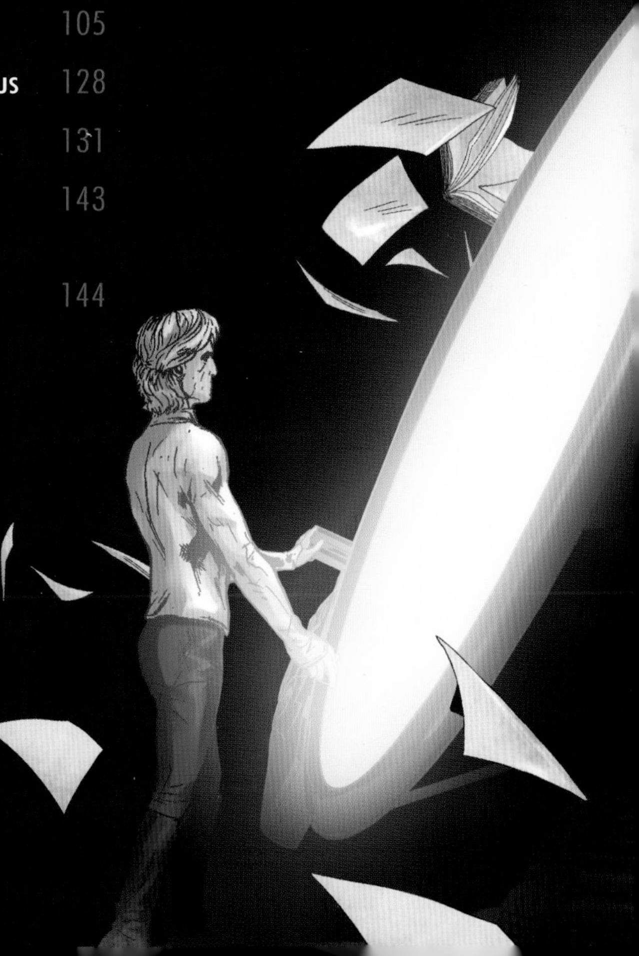

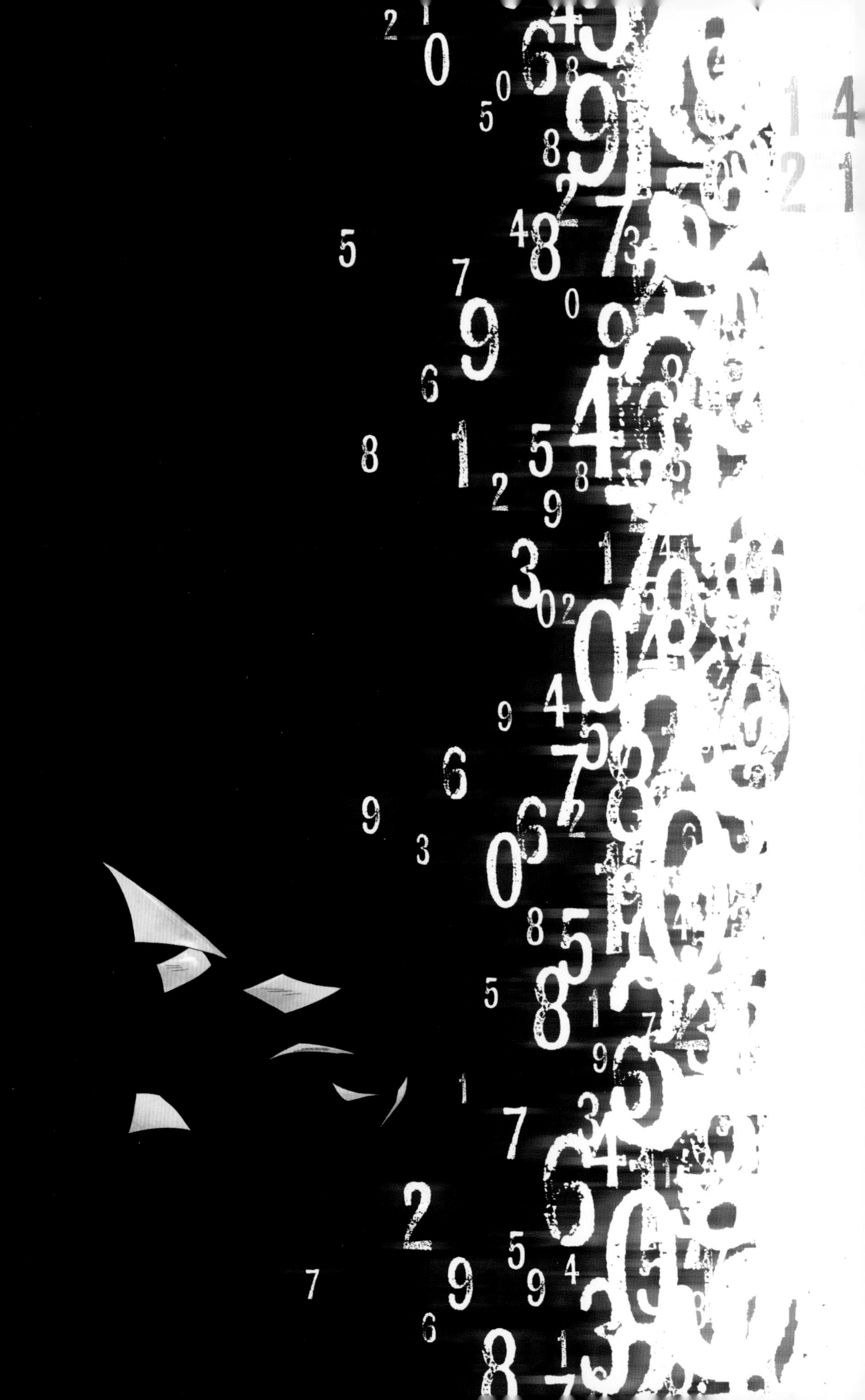

FOREWORD | WIL **WHEATON**

When I was in my early 20s, I flew halfway across the world, alone, to work on a movie in France. I expected a grand adventure (and eventually, it was), but when I got to Nice after a long and turbulent flight, I realized that I was going to be the apocryphal Stranger in a Strange Land for the next three months. I sat on the edge of my bed, thousands of miles away from everyone and everything I knew, and felt as alone as I've ever felt in my life, before or since.

I took a long nap, and, jetlagged, slept through most of my first day there. When I woke up, I took a walk along the Bord De Mer. It was absolutely beautiful, bathed in golden, late afternoon sunlight that glittered in the Mediterranean Sea. A few dozen people walked along the seaside, and the constant din of pedestrian and vehicle traffic filled the air. Though I was surrounded by other people, I felt isolated and lonely. I cut my walk short and retreated to my hotel room where I could wrap myself in the familiar comfort of an English-language television station.

While I was reading Days Missing, I thought about that production for the first time in over 15 years. In my own imagination-fueled artist's way, I could relate to The Steward, surrounded by a billion people, yet feeling utterly and completely alone. At least I didn't have a responsibility – self-imposed or otherwise – to care for an entire species.

Before I get out of your way and let you get into this book, I want you to use your imagination for a minute: Imagine what it must be like to be The Steward. Imagine how it would feel to live for tens of thousands of years, surrounded by a species you're responsible for protecting from themselves, like they're some kind of giant self-destructive ant farm. No matter what you do, no matter how many times you do good, they can't truly thank you, because they're simply not able. You will go to bed alone every night and wake up alone every morning, because in the entire universe, there is no other being that is anything like you.

Until one day, suddenly and unexpectedly, there is. Finally, there is someone else in the universe who can relate to you. Finally, you can have a friend, and possibly a lover.

Except this other person, who you've waited your entire impossibly long life to meet, embodies everything you despise. Everything you've dedicated your existence to fighting against, she embraces. You haven't met a friend; you've met your greatest enemy.

Imagine, then, how you would feel. Despondent? Defeated? More alone than ever before? Or would you feel resolved? There is no correct answer, just an honest one. Now, take a moment to think about it. Let yourself feel it.

Okay. Now you're ready to meet Kestus.

— **Wil Wheaton**

Wil Wheaton's successful acting career began in 1986 with acclaimed roles in **Stand By Me** *and* **Toy Soldiers**. *He continued to build his resume through his teen years as series regular Wesley Crusher on* **Star Trek: The Next Generation**. *But Wil is much more than just an actor; he's an author, blogger, voice actor, widely-followed original Twitter user, and a champion of geek culture.*

"The meeting of two personalities is like the contact of two chemical substances: if there is any reaction, both are transformed."

— Carl Jung

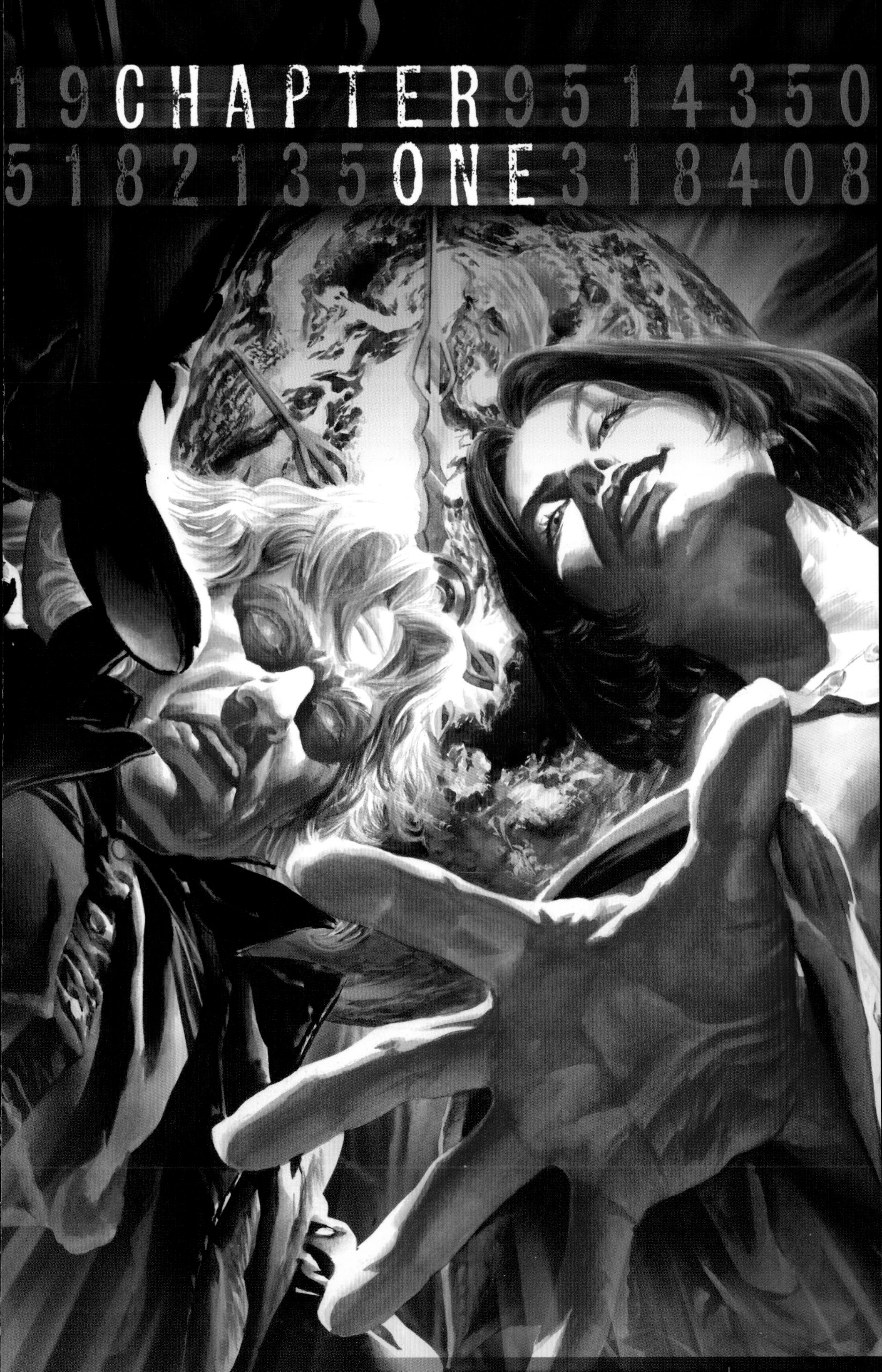
19CHAPTER9514350
518213 5ONE318408

CHAPTER ONE COVER ART | ALEX **ROSS**

531 BCE

THE SWORD

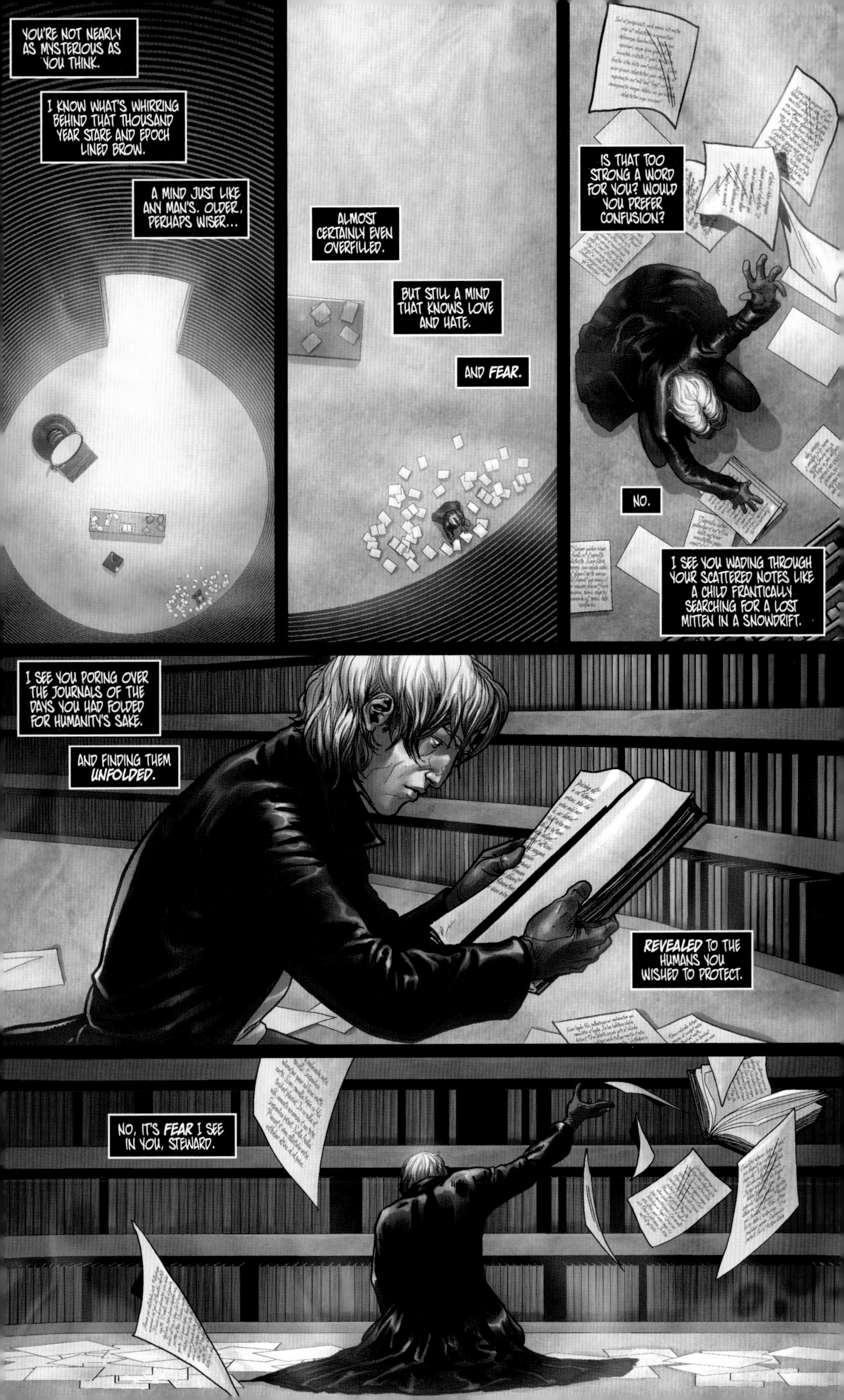
YOU'RE NOT NEARLY AS MYSTERIOUS AS YOU THINK.
I KNOW WHAT'S WHIRRING BEHIND THAT THOUSAND YEAR STARE AND EPOCH LINED BROW.
A MIND JUST LIKE ANY MAN'S. OLDER, PERHAPS WISER...
ALMOST CERTAINLY EVEN OVERFILLED.
BUT STILL A MIND THAT KNOWS LOVE AND HATE.
AND FEAR.
IS THAT TOO STRONG A WORD FOR YOU? WOULD YOU PREFER CONFUSION?
NO.
I SEE YOU WADING THROUGH YOUR SCATTERED NOTES LIKE A CHILD FRANTICALLY SEARCHING FOR A LOST MITTEN IN A SNOWDRIFT.
I SEE YOU PORING OVER THE JOURNALS OF THE DAYS YOU HAD FOLDED FOR HUMANITY'S SAKE.
AND FINDING THEM UNFOLDED.
REVEALED TO THE HUMANS YOU WISHED TO PROTECT.
NO, IT'S FEAR I SEE IN YOU, STEWARD.

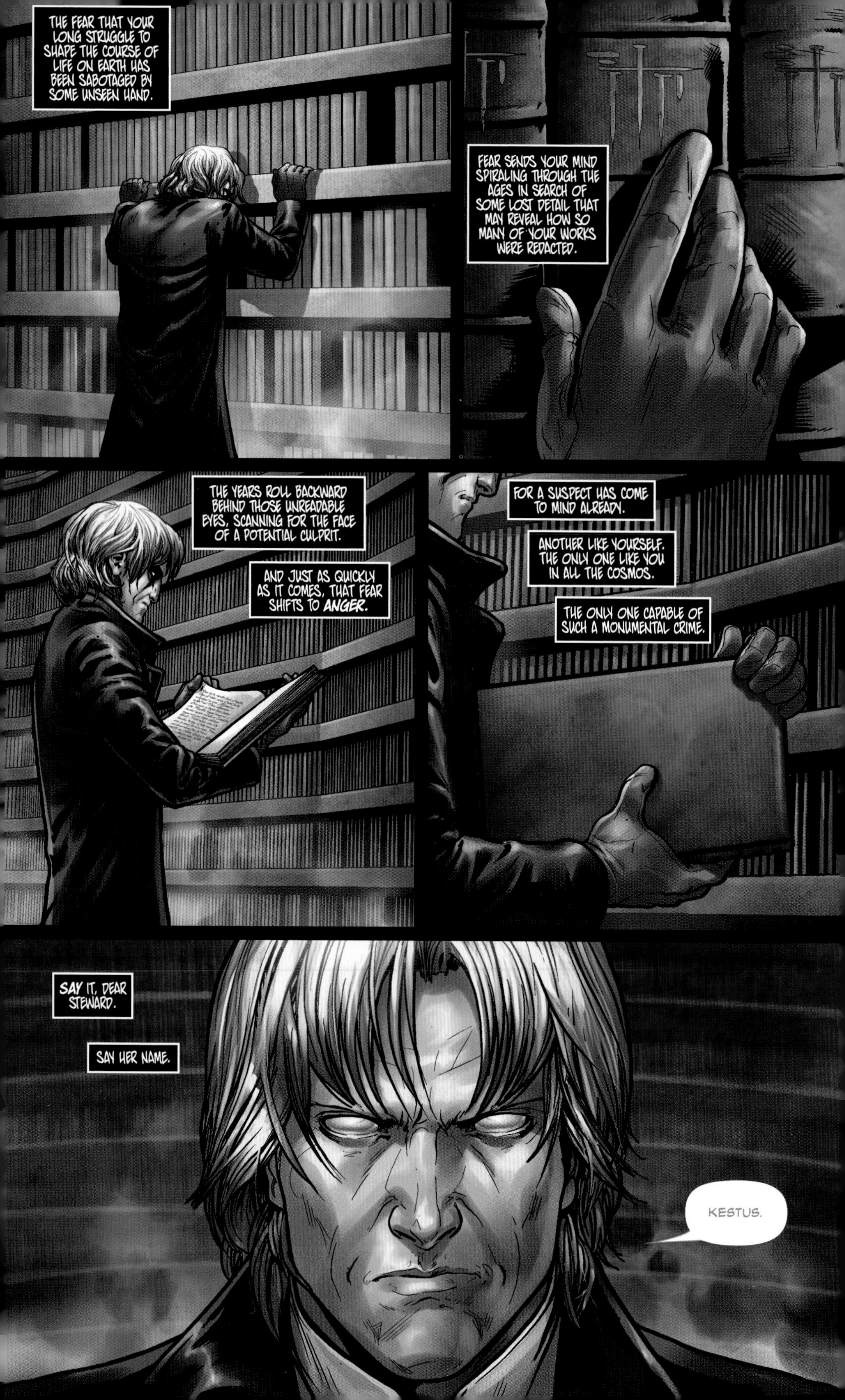
THE FEAR THAT YOUR LONG STRUGGLE TO SHAPE THE COURSE OF LIFE ON EARTH HAS BEEN SABOTAGED BY SOME UNSEEN HAND.
FEAR SENDS YOUR MIND SPIRALING THROUGH THE AGES IN SEARCH OF SOME LOST DETAIL THAT MAY REVEAL HOW SO MANY OF YOUR WORKS WERE REDACTED.
THE YEARS ROLL BACKWARD BEHIND THOSE UNREADABLE EYES, SCANNING FOR THE FACE OF A POTENTIAL CULPRIT.
AND JUST AS QUICKLY AS IT COMES, THAT FEAR SHIFTS TO ANGER.
FOR A SUSPECT HAS COME TO MIND ALREADY.
ANOTHER LIKE YOURSELF. THE ONLY ONE LIKE YOU IN ALL THE COSMOS.
THE ONLY ONE CAPABLE OF SUCH A MONUMENTAL CRIME.
SAY IT, DEAR STEWARD.
SAY HER NAME.
KESTUS.

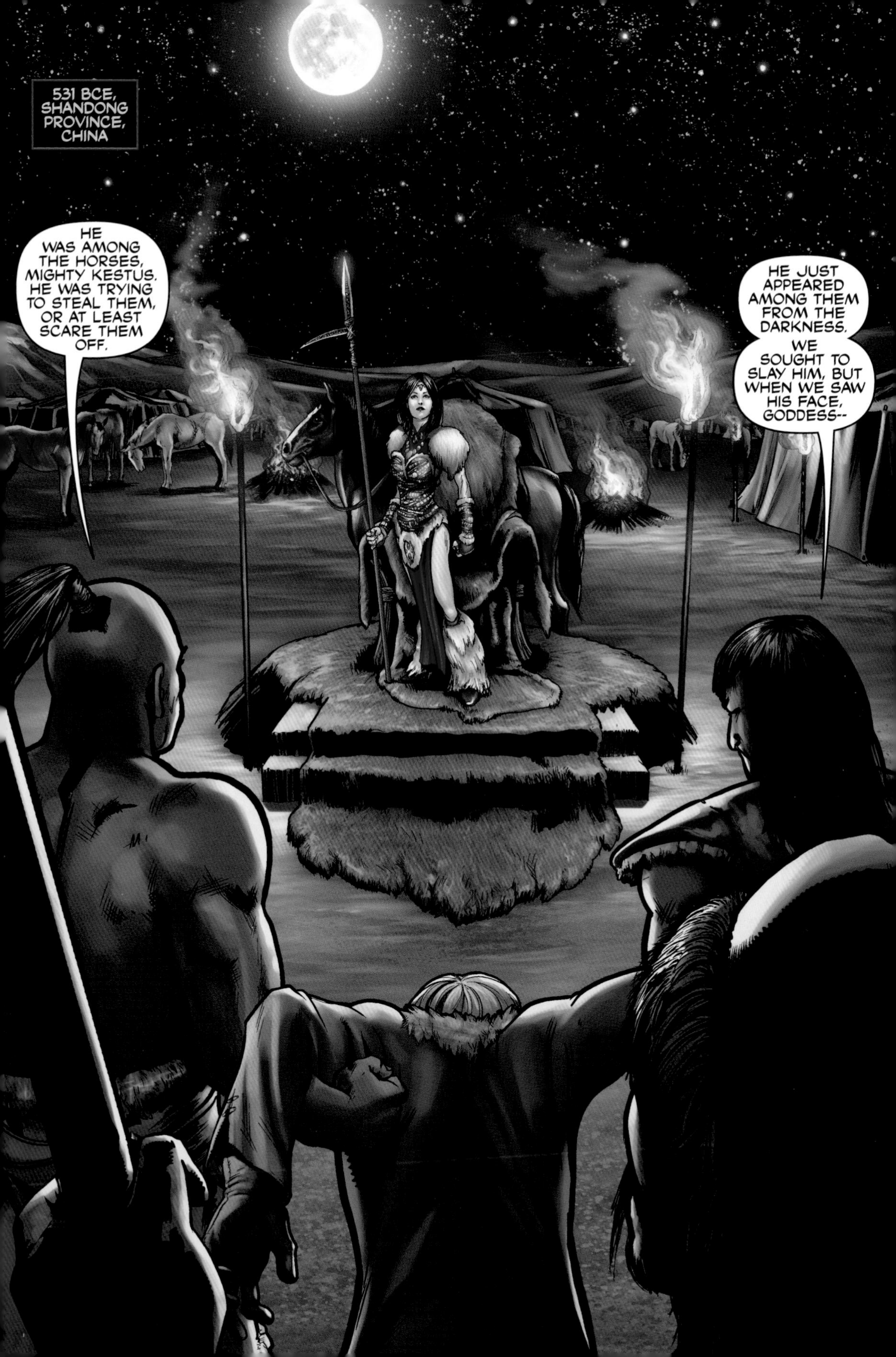
531 BCE, SHANDONG PROVINCE, CHINA
HE WAS AMONG THE HORSES, MIGHTY KESTUS. HE WAS TRYING TO STEAL THEM, OR AT LEAST SCARE THEM OFF.
HE JUST APPEARED AMONG THEM FROM THE DARKNESS.
WE SOUGHT TO SLAY HIM, BUT WHEN WE SAW HIS FACE, GODDESS--

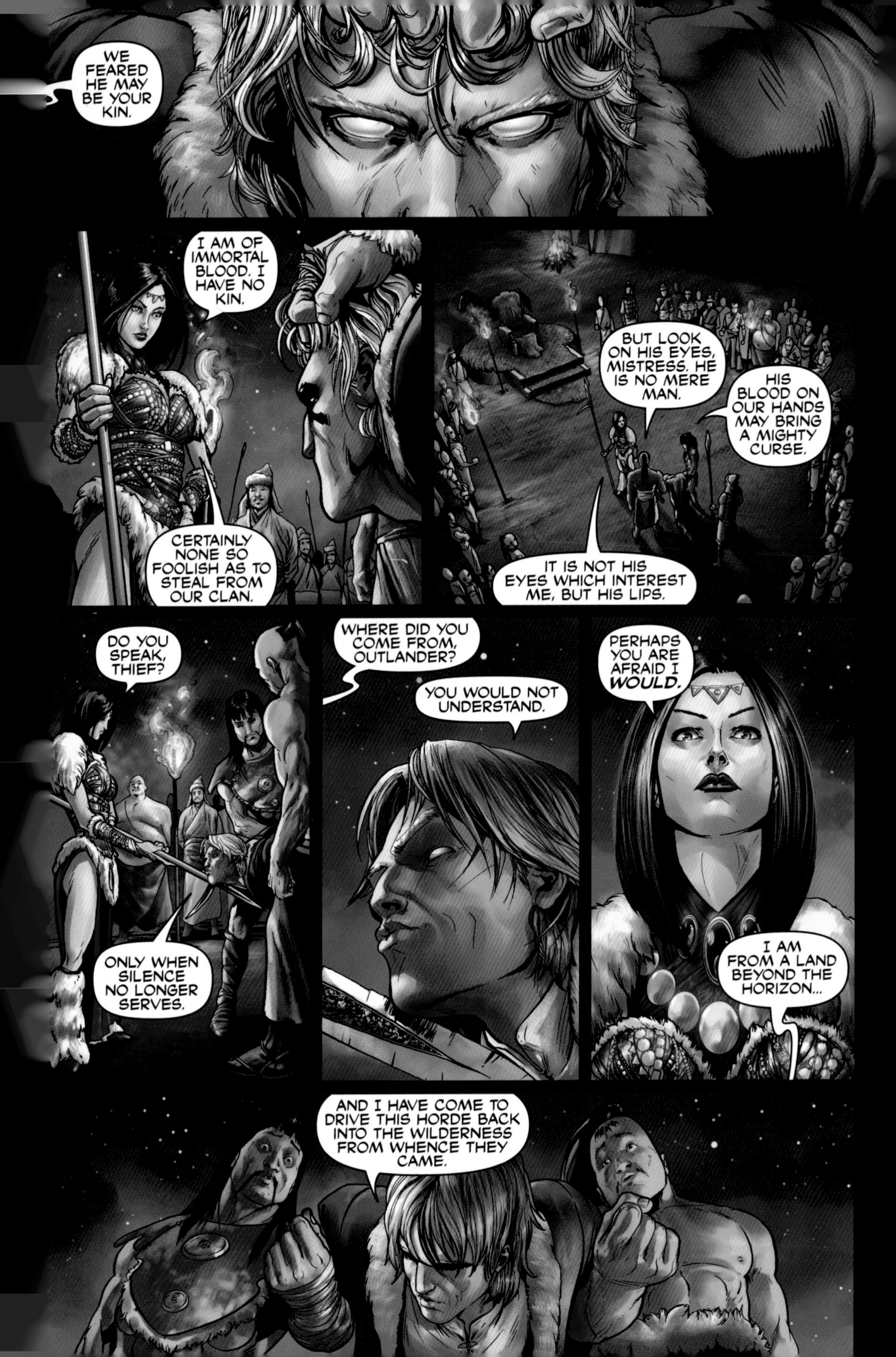
WE FEARED HE MAY BE YOUR KIN.
I AM OF IMMORTAL BLOOD. I HAVE NO KIN.
CERTAINLY NONE SO FOOLISH AS TO STEAL FROM OUR CLAN.
BUT LOOK ON HIS EYES, MISTRESS. HE IS NO MERE MAN.
HIS BLOOD ON OUR HANDS MAY BRING A MIGHTY CURSE.
IT IS NOT HIS EYES WHICH INTEREST ME, BUT HIS LIPS.
DO YOU SPEAK, THIEF?
ONLY WHEN SILENCE NO LONGER SERVES.
WHERE DID YOU COME FROM, OUTLANDER?
YOU WOULD NOT UNDERSTAND.
PERHAPS YOU ARE AFRAID I *WOULD.*
I AM FROM A LAND BEYOND THE HORIZON...
AND I HAVE COME TO DRIVE THIS HORDE BACK INTO THE WILDERNESS FROM WHENCE THEY CAME.

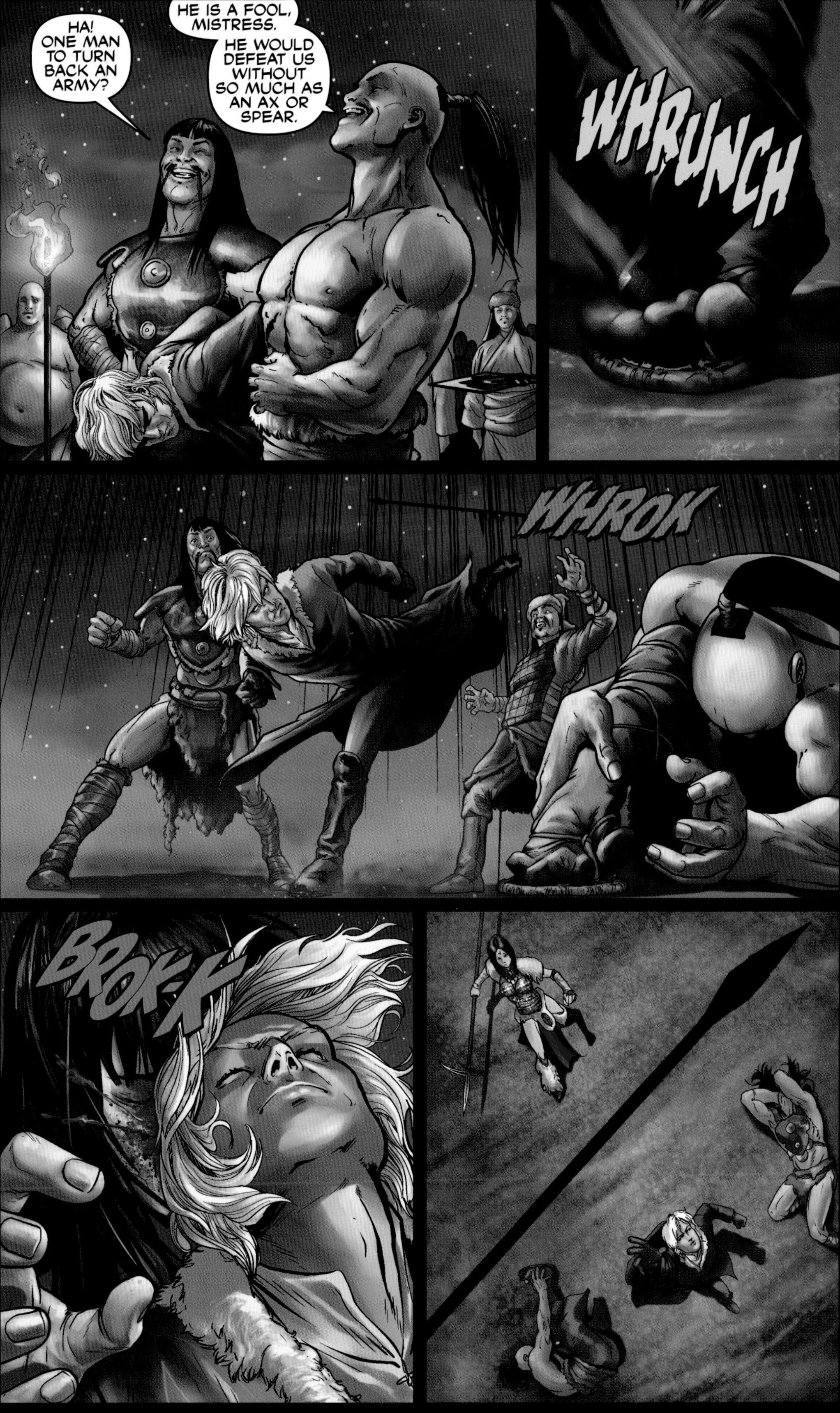
HA! ONE MAN TO TURN BACK AN ARMY?
HE IS A FOOL, MISTRESS.
HE WOULD DEFEAT US WITHOUT SO MUCH AS AN AX OR SPEAR.
WHRUNCH
WHROK
BROK-K

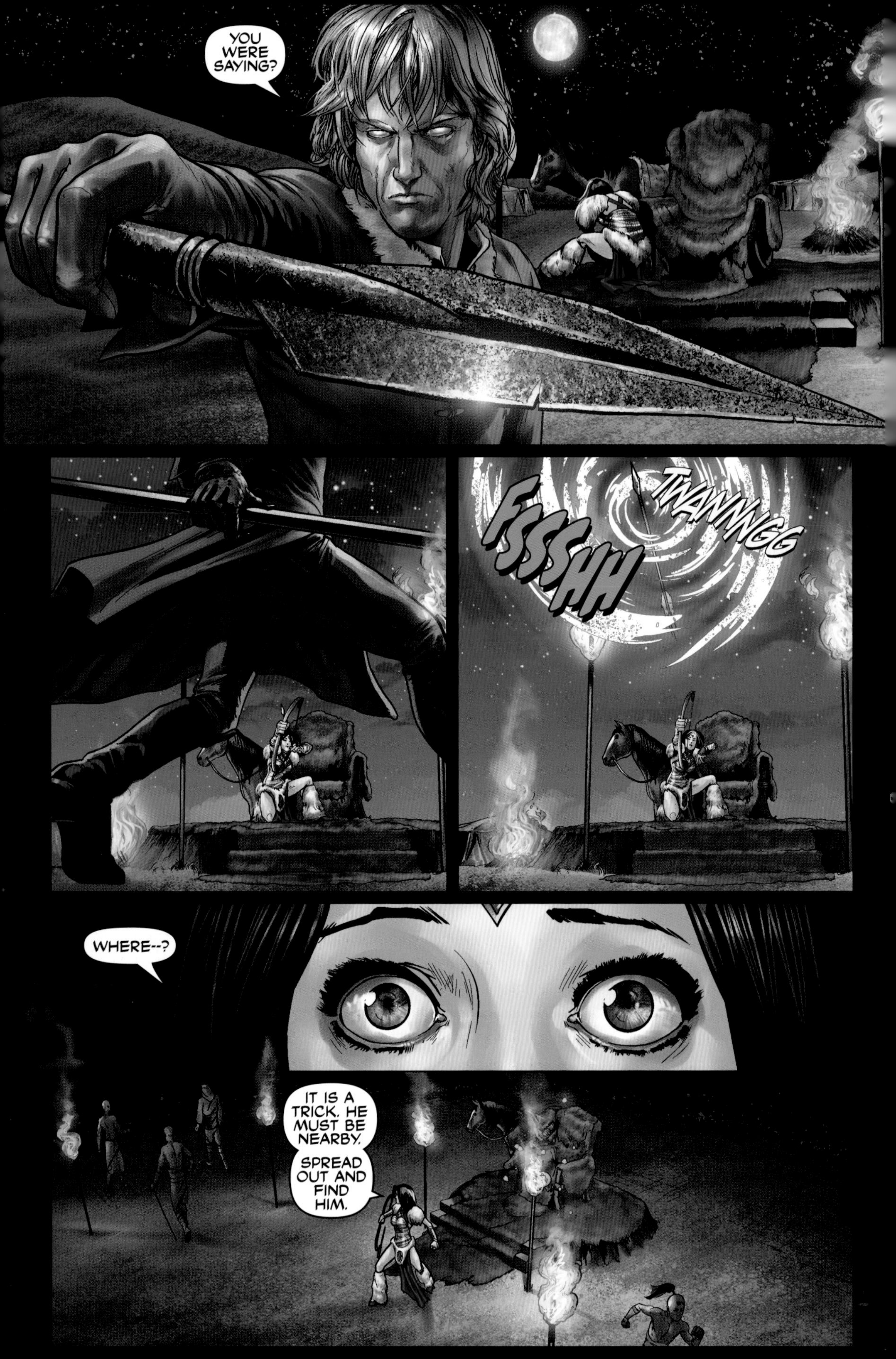
YOU WERE SAYING?
FSSSHH
TWANNNGG
WHERE--?
IT IS A TRICK. HE MUST BE NEARBY.
SPREAD OUT AND FIND HIM.

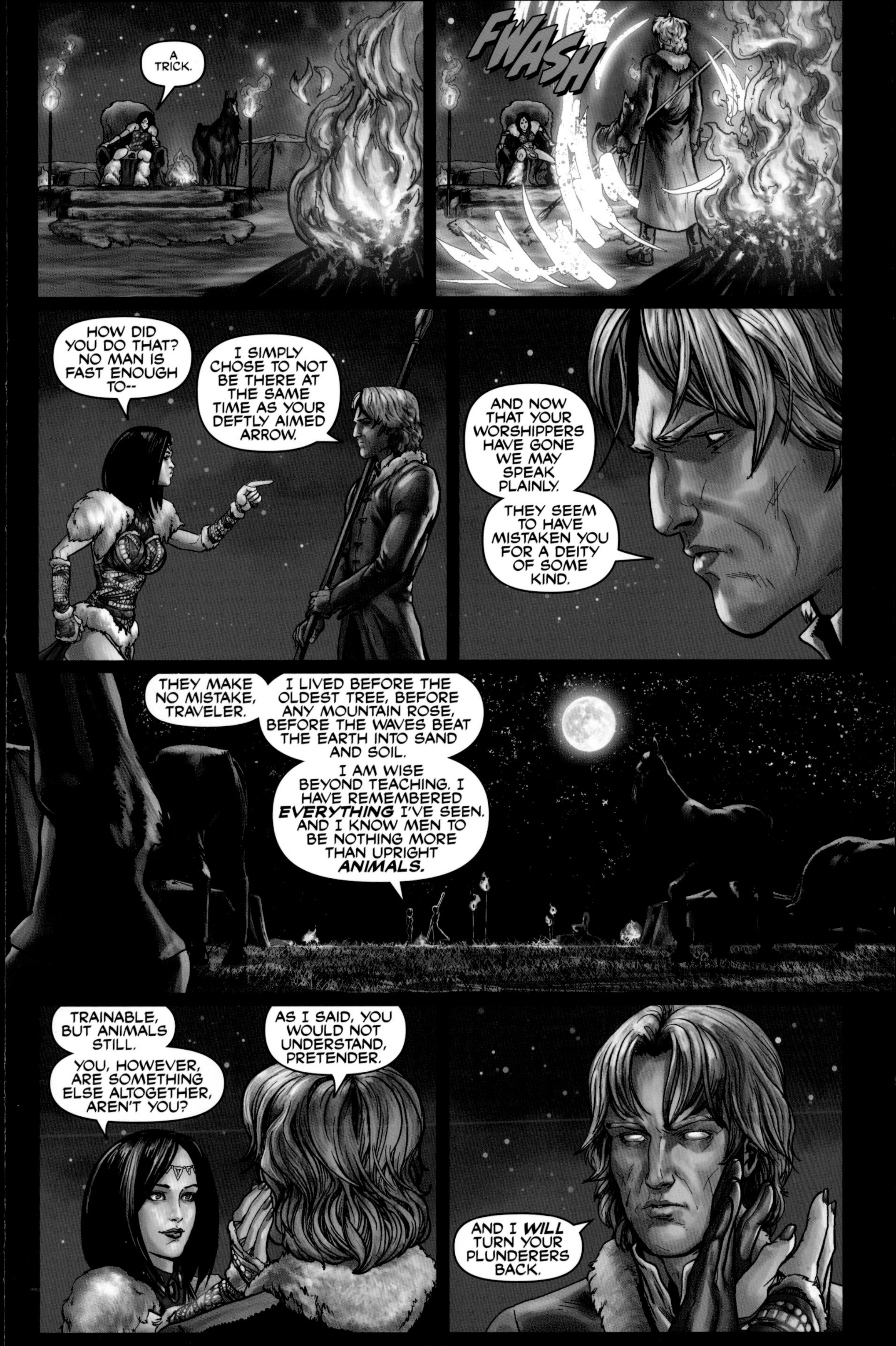
A TRICK.
FWASH
HOW DID YOU DO THAT? NO MAN IS FAST ENOUGH TO--
I SIMPLY CHOSE TO NOT BE THERE AT THE SAME TIME AS YOUR DEFTLY AIMED ARROW.
AND NOW THAT YOUR WORSHIPPERS HAVE GONE WE MAY SPEAK PLAINLY.
THEY SEEM TO HAVE MISTAKEN YOU FOR A DEITY OF SOME KIND.
THEY MAKE NO MISTAKE, TRAVELER.
I LIVED BEFORE THE OLDEST TREE, BEFORE ANY MOUNTAIN ROSE, BEFORE THE WAVES BEAT THE EARTH INTO SAND AND SOIL.
I AM WISE BEYOND TEACHING. I HAVE REMEMBERED EVERYTHING I'VE SEEN. AND I KNOW MEN TO BE NOTHING MORE THAN UPRIGHT ANIMALS.
TRAINABLE, BUT ANIMALS STILL.
YOU, HOWEVER, ARE SOMETHING ELSE ALTOGETHER, AREN'T YOU?
AS I SAID, YOU WOULD NOT UNDERSTAND, PRETENDER.
AND I WILL TURN YOUR PLUNDERERS BACK.

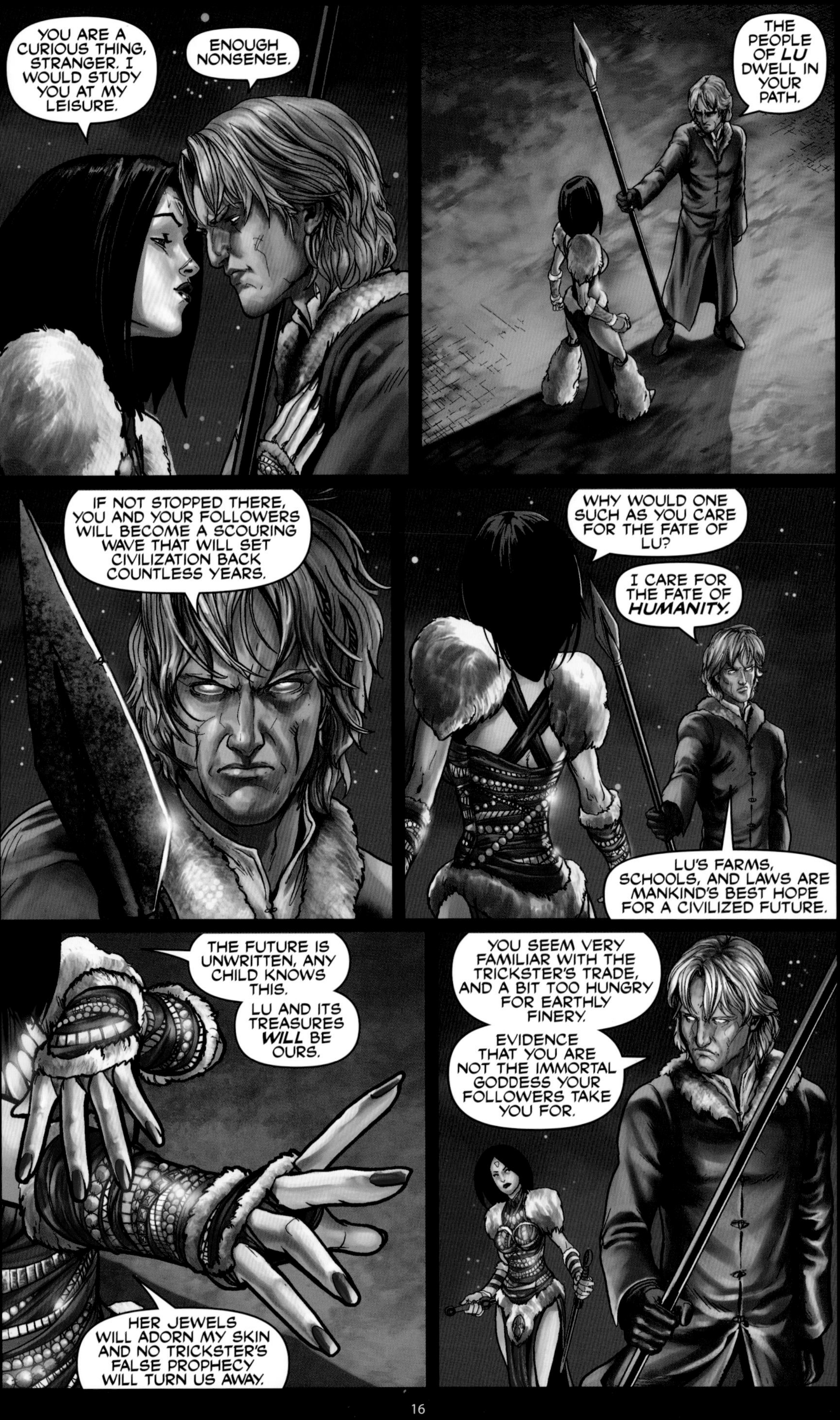

YOU ARE A CURIOUS THING, STRANGER. I WOULD STUDY YOU AT MY LEISURE.
ENOUGH NONSENSE.
THE PEOPLE OF LU DWELL IN YOUR PATH.
IF NOT STOPPED THERE, YOU AND YOUR FOLLOWERS WILL BECOME A SCOURING WAVE THAT WILL SET CIVILIZATION BACK COUNTLESS YEARS.
WHY WOULD ONE SUCH AS YOU CARE FOR THE FATE OF LU?
I CARE FOR THE FATE OF HUMANITY.
LU'S FARMS, SCHOOLS, AND LAWS ARE MANKIND'S BEST HOPE FOR A CIVILIZED FUTURE.
THE FUTURE IS UNWRITTEN, ANY CHILD KNOWS THIS.
LU AND ITS TREASURES WILL BE OURS.
HER JEWELS WILL ADORN MY SKIN AND NO TRICKSTER'S FALSE PROPHECY WILL TURN US AWAY.
YOU SEEM VERY FAMILIAR WITH THE TRICKSTER'S TRADE, AND A BIT TOO HUNGRY FOR EARTHLY FINERY.
EVIDENCE THAT YOU ARE NOT THE IMMORTAL GODDESS YOUR FOLLOWERS TAKE YOU FOR.

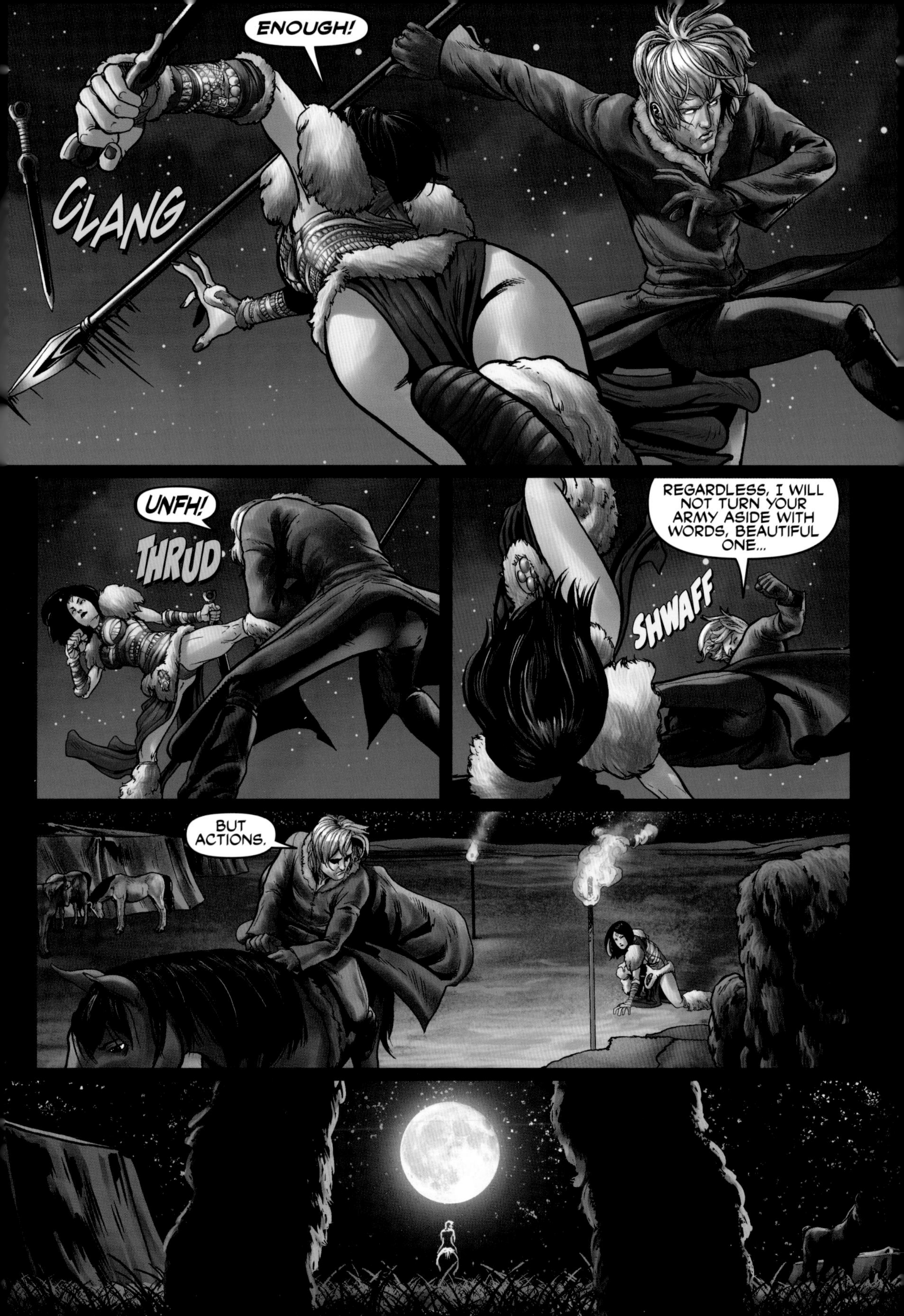
ENOUGH!
CLANG
UNFH!
THRUD
REGARDLESS, I WILL NOT TURN YOUR ARMY ASIDE WITH WORDS, BEAUTIFUL ONE...
SHWAFF
BUT ACTIONS.

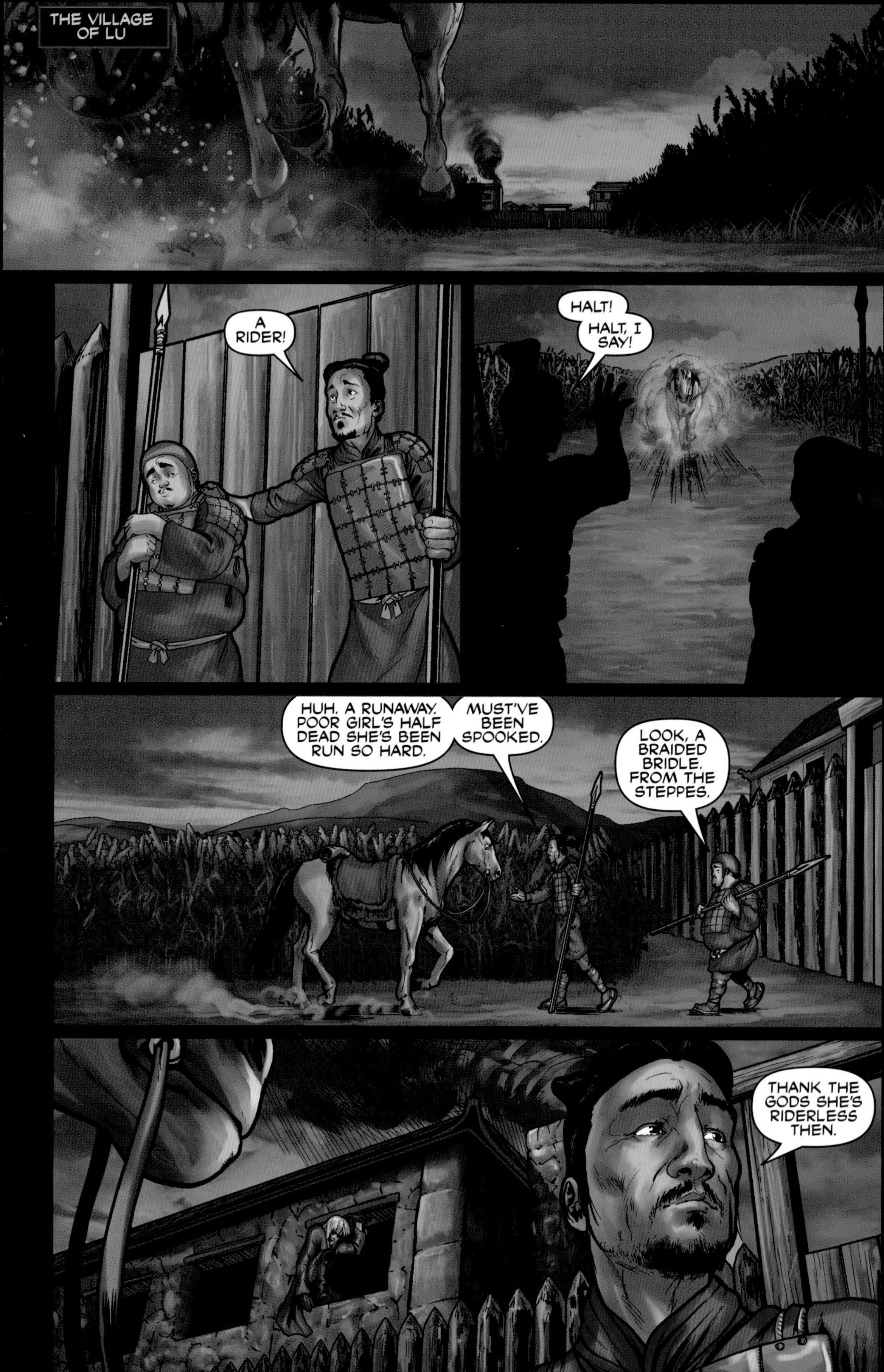
THE VILLAGE OF LU
A RIDER!
HALT!
HALT, I SAY!
HUH. A RUNAWAY. POOR GIRL'S HALF DEAD SHE'S BEEN RUN SO HARD.
MUST'VE BEEN SPOOKED.
LOOK, A BRAIDED BRIDLE. FROM THE STEPPES.
THANK THE GODS SHE'S RIDERLESS THEN.

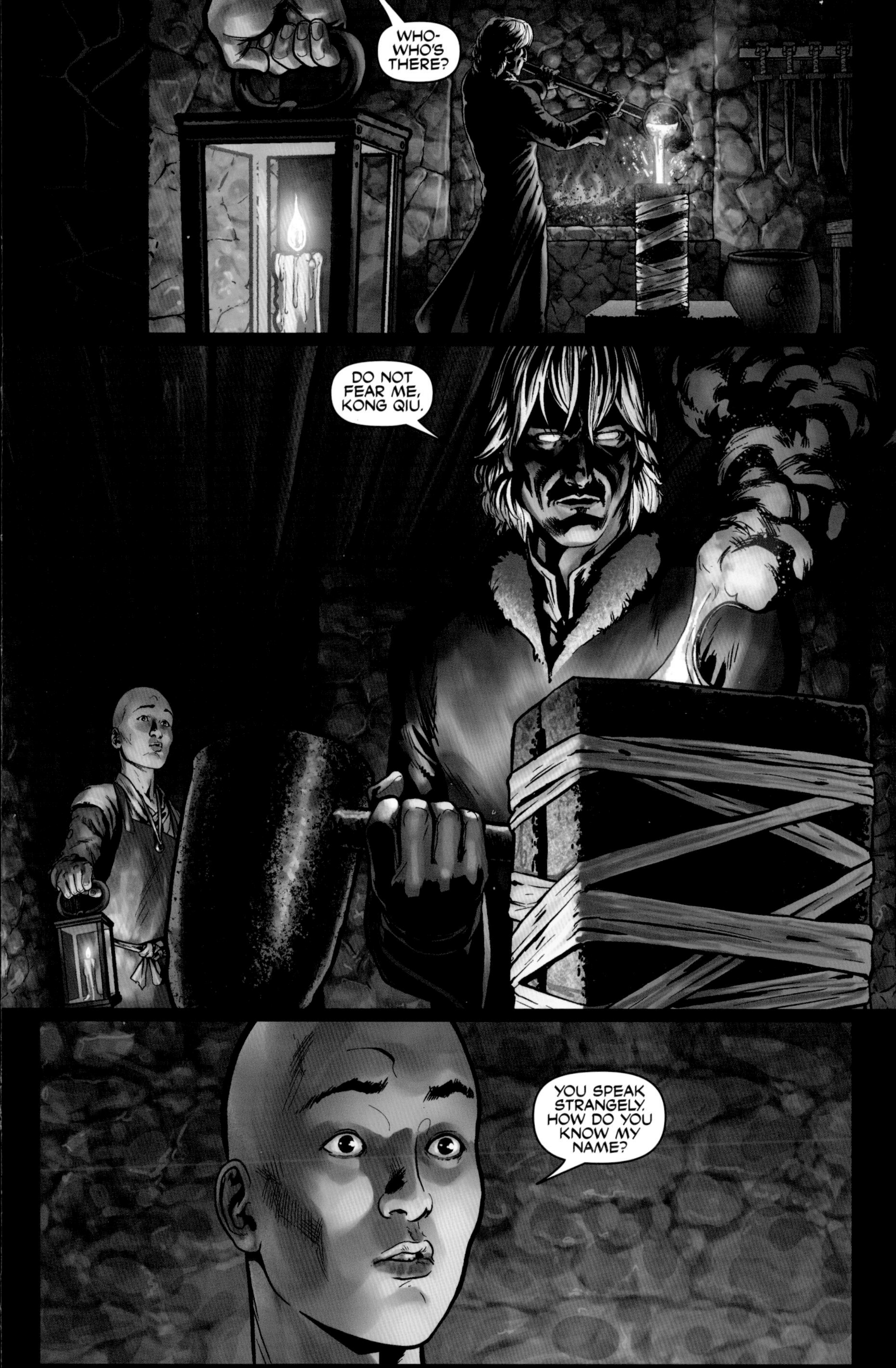
WHO-WHO'S THERE?
DO NOT FEAR ME, KONG QIU.
YOU SPEAK STRANGELY. HOW DO YOU KNOW MY NAME?

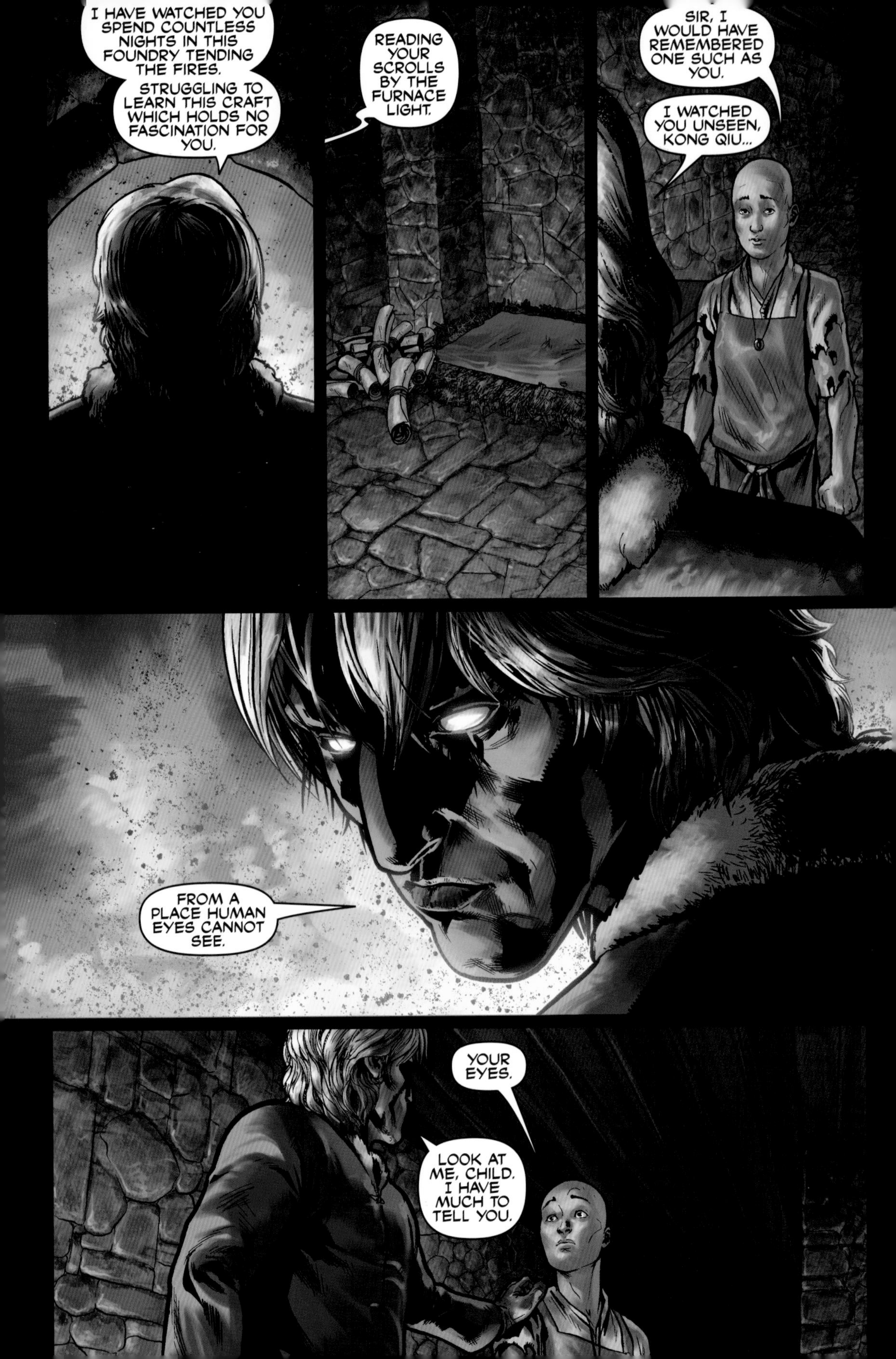
I HAVE WATCHED YOU SPEND COUNTLESS NIGHTS IN THIS FOUNDRY TENDING THE FIRES.
STRUGGLING TO LEARN THIS CRAFT WHICH HOLDS NO FASCINATION FOR YOU.
READING YOUR SCROLLS BY THE FURNACE LIGHT.
SIR, I WOULD HAVE REMEMBERED ONE SUCH AS YOU.
I WATCHED YOU UNSEEN, KONG QIU...
FROM A PLACE HUMAN EYES CANNOT SEE.
YOUR EYES.
LOOK AT ME, CHILD. I HAVE MUCH TO TELL YOU.

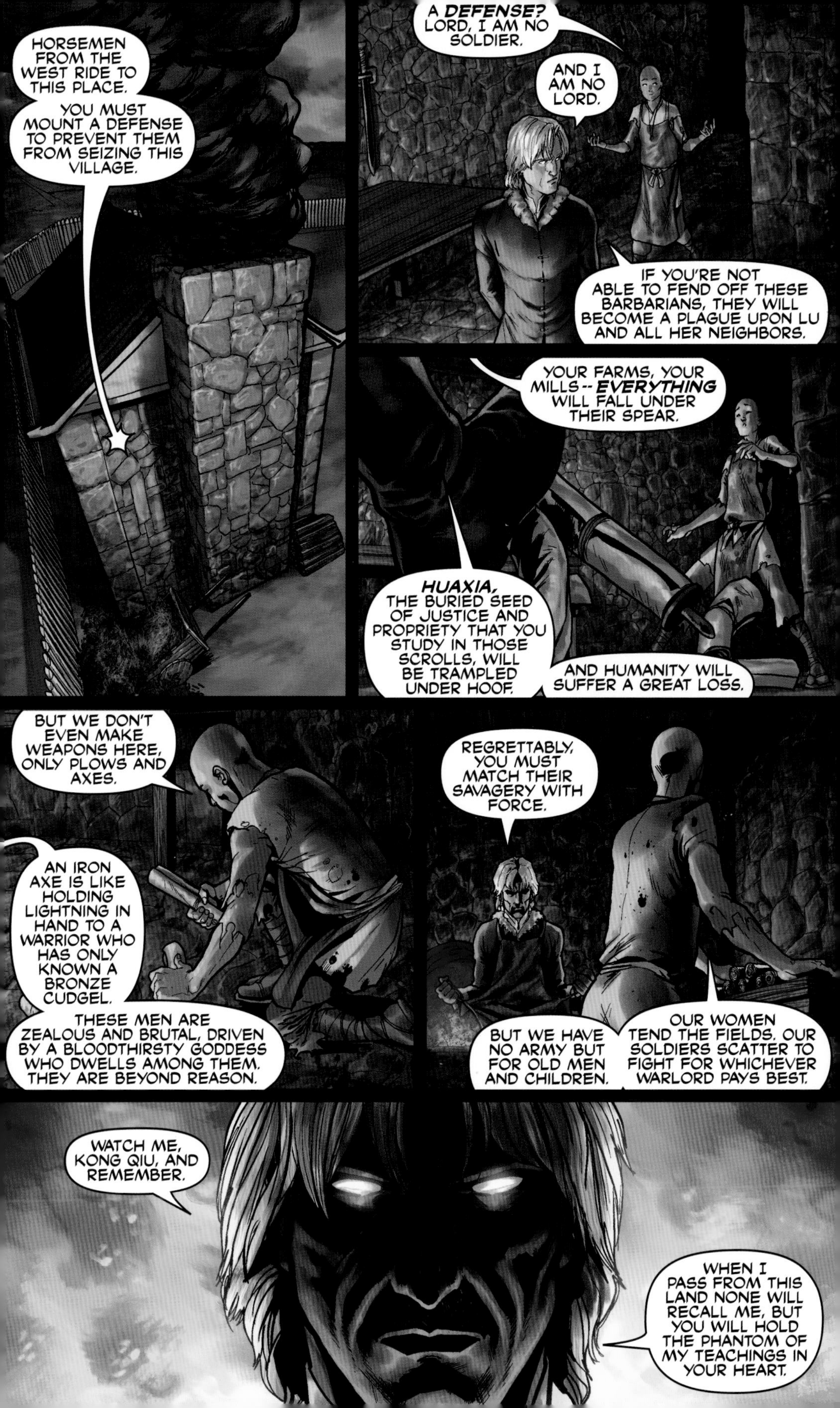
HORSEMEN FROM THE WEST RIDE TO THIS PLACE.
YOU MUST MOUNT A DEFENSE TO PREVENT THEM FROM SEIZING THIS VILLAGE.
A *DEFENSE?* LORD, I AM NO SOLDIER.
AND I AM NO LORD.
IF YOU'RE NOT ABLE TO FEND OFF THESE BARBARIANS, THEY WILL BECOME A PLAGUE UPON LU AND ALL HER NEIGHBORS.
YOUR FARMS, YOUR MILLS--*EVERYTHING* WILL FALL UNDER THEIR SPEAR.
HUAXIA, THE BURIED SEED OF JUSTICE AND PROPRIETY THAT YOU STUDY IN THOSE SCROLLS, WILL BE TRAMPLED UNDER HOOF.
AND HUMANITY WILL SUFFER A GREAT LOSS.
BUT WE DON'T EVEN MAKE WEAPONS HERE, ONLY PLOWS AND AXES.
AN IRON AXE IS LIKE HOLDING LIGHTNING IN HAND TO A WARRIOR WHO HAS ONLY KNOWN A BRONZE CUDGEL.
THESE MEN ARE ZEALOUS AND BRUTAL, DRIVEN BY A BLOODTHIRSTY GODDESS WHO DWELLS AMONG THEM. THEY ARE BEYOND REASON.
REGRETTABLY, YOU MUST MATCH THEIR SAVAGERY WITH FORCE.
BUT WE HAVE NO ARMY BUT FOR OLD MEN AND CHILDREN.
OUR WOMEN TEND THE FIELDS. OUR SOLDIERS SCATTER TO FIGHT FOR WHICHEVER WARLORD PAYS BEST.
WATCH ME, KONG QIU, AND REMEMBER.
WHEN I PASS FROM THIS LAND NONE WILL RECALL ME, BUT YOU WILL HOLD THE PHANTOM OF MY TEACHINGS IN YOUR HEART.

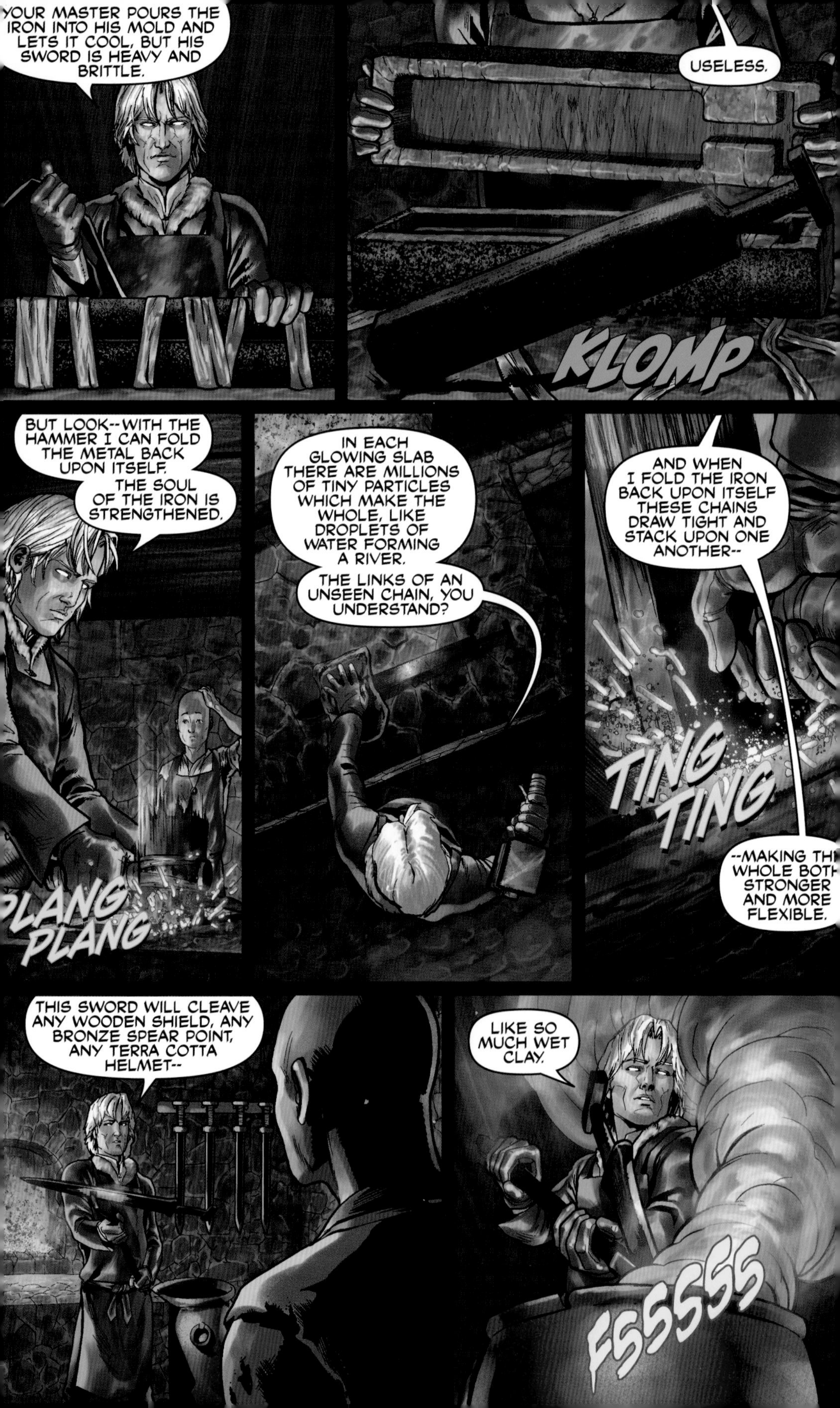
YOUR MASTER POURS THE IRON INTO HIS MOLD AND LETS IT COOL, BUT HIS SWORD IS HEAVY AND BRITTLE.
USELESS.
KLOMP
BUT LOOK--WITH THE HAMMER I CAN FOLD THE METAL BACK UPON ITSELF.
THE SOUL OF THE IRON IS STRENGTHENED.
PLANG PLANG
IN EACH GLOWING SLAB THERE ARE MILLIONS OF TINY PARTICLES WHICH MAKE THE WHOLE, LIKE DROPLETS OF WATER FORMING A RIVER.
THE LINKS OF AN UNSEEN CHAIN, YOU UNDERSTAND?
AND WHEN I FOLD THE IRON BACK UPON ITSELF THESE CHAINS DRAW TIGHT AND STACK UPON ONE ANOTHER--
TING TING
--MAKING THE WHOLE BOTH STRONGER AND MORE FLEXIBLE.
THIS SWORD WILL CLEAVE ANY WOODEN SHIELD, ANY BRONZE SPEAR POINT, ANY TERRA COTTA HELMET--
LIKE SO MUCH WET CLAY.
FSSSSS

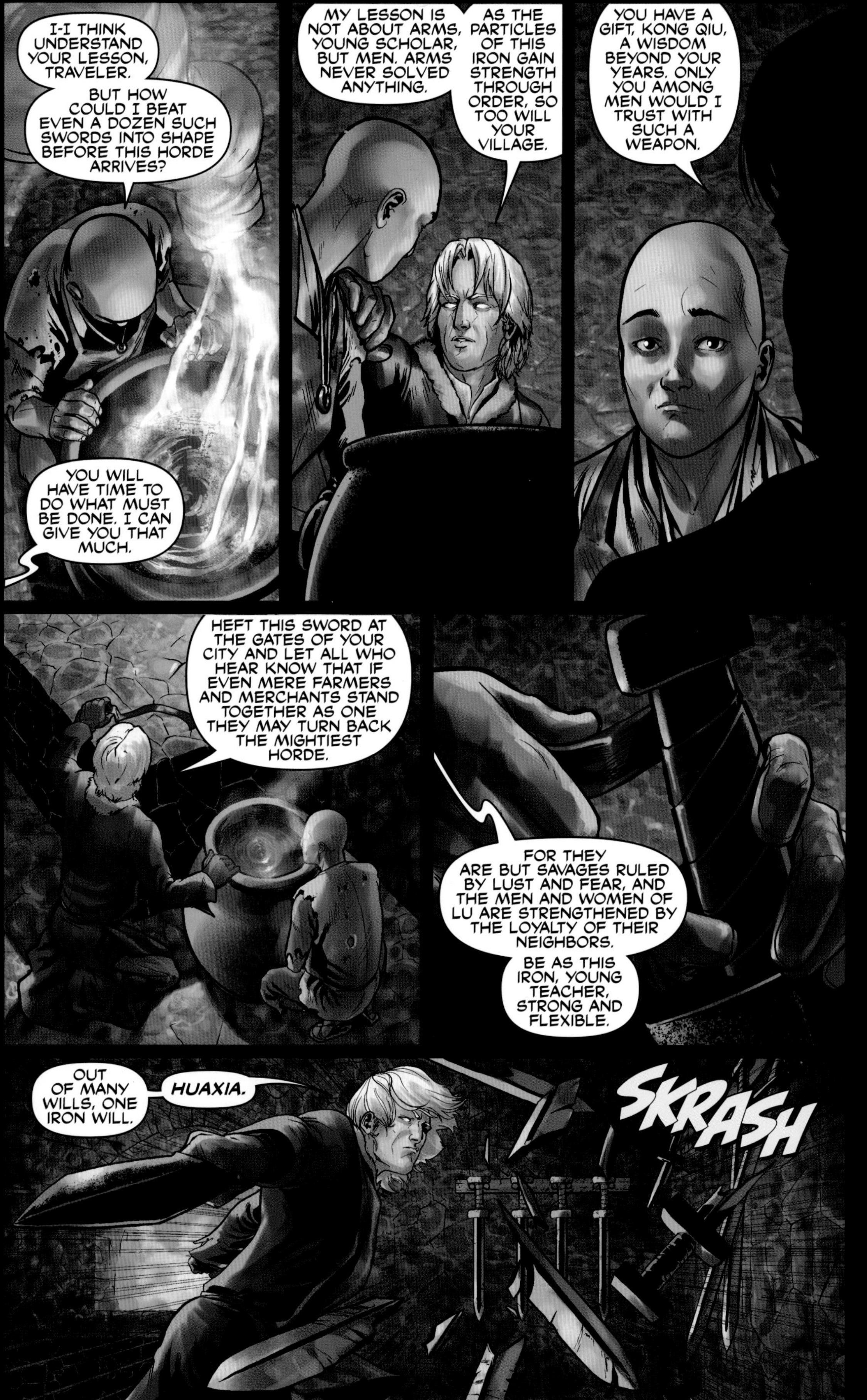

I-I THINK UNDERSTAND YOUR LESSON, TRAVELER.
BUT HOW COULD I BEAT EVEN A DOZEN SUCH SWORDS INTO SHAPE BEFORE THIS HORDE ARRIVES?
YOU WILL HAVE TIME TO DO WHAT MUST BE DONE. I CAN GIVE YOU THAT MUCH.
MY LESSON IS NOT ABOUT ARMS, YOUNG SCHOLAR, BUT MEN. ARMS NEVER SOLVED ANYTHING.
AS THE PARTICLES OF THIS IRON GAIN STRENGTH THROUGH ORDER, SO TOO WILL YOUR VILLAGE.
YOU HAVE A GIFT, KONG QIU, A WISDOM BEYOND YOUR YEARS. ONLY YOU AMONG MEN WOULD I TRUST WITH SUCH A WEAPON.
HEFT THIS SWORD AT THE GATES OF YOUR CITY AND LET ALL WHO HEAR KNOW THAT IF EVEN MERE FARMERS AND MERCHANTS STAND TOGETHER AS ONE THEY MAY TURN BACK THE MIGHTIEST HORDE.
FOR THEY ARE BUT SAVAGES RULED BY LUST AND FEAR, AND THE MEN AND WOMEN OF LU ARE STRENGTHENED BY THE LOYALTY OF THEIR NEIGHBORS.
BE AS THIS IRON, YOUNG TEACHER, STRONG AND FLEXIBLE.
OUT OF MANY WILLS, ONE IRON WILL.
HUAXIA.
SKRASH

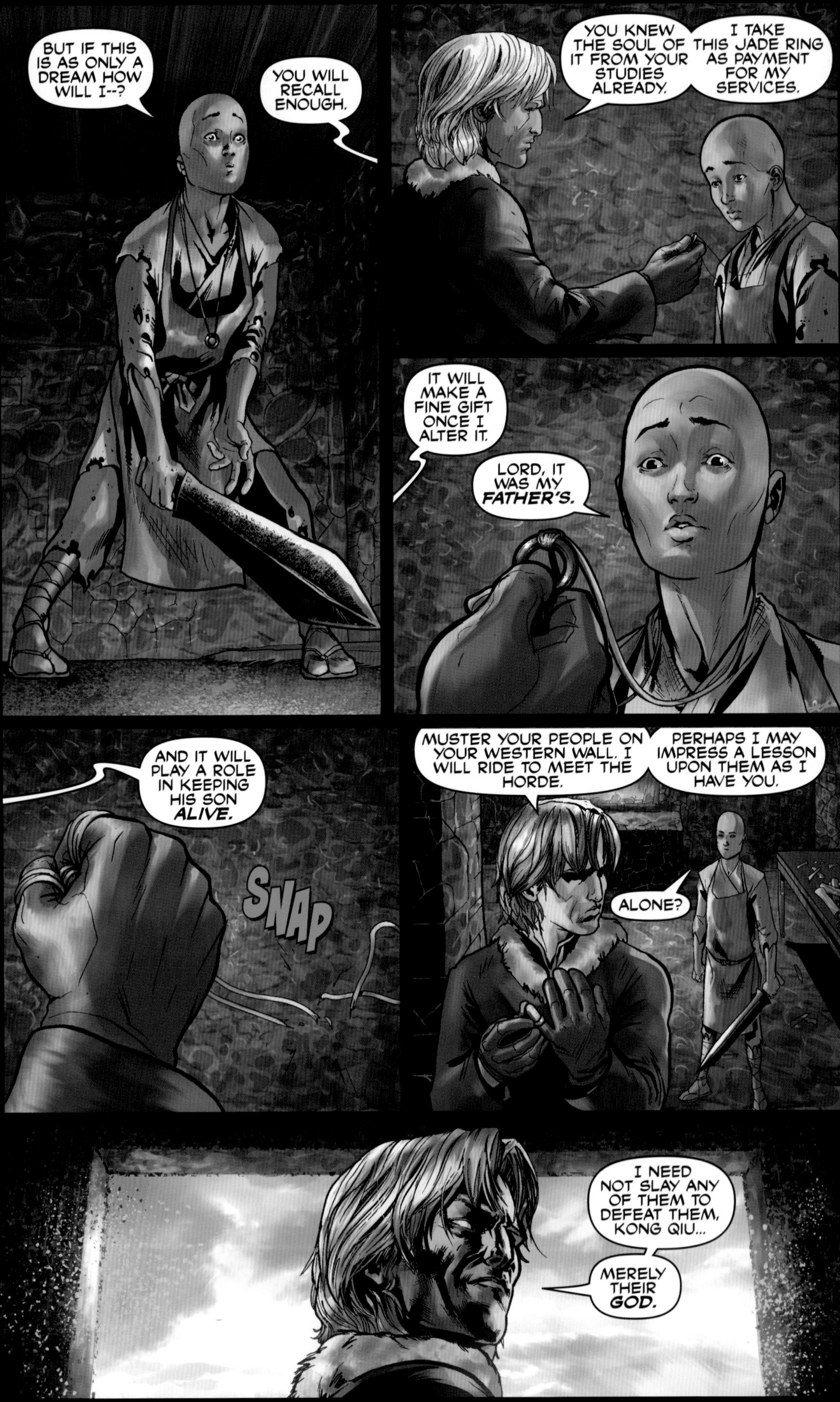
BUT IF THIS IS AS ONLY A DREAM HOW WILL I--?
YOU WILL RECALL ENOUGH.
YOU KNEW THE SOUL OF IT FROM YOUR STUDIES ALREADY.
I TAKE THIS JADE RING AS PAYMENT FOR MY SERVICES.
IT WILL MAKE A FINE GIFT ONCE I ALTER IT.
LORD, IT WAS MY FATHER'S.
AND IT WILL PLAY A ROLE IN KEEPING HIS SON ALIVE.
SNAP
MUSTER YOUR PEOPLE ON YOUR WESTERN WALL. I WILL RIDE TO MEET THE HORDE.
PERHAPS I MAY IMPRESS A LESSON UPON THEM AS I HAVE YOU.
ALONE?
I NEED NOT SLAY ANY OF THEM TO DEFEAT THEM, KONG QIU...
MERELY THEIR GOD.

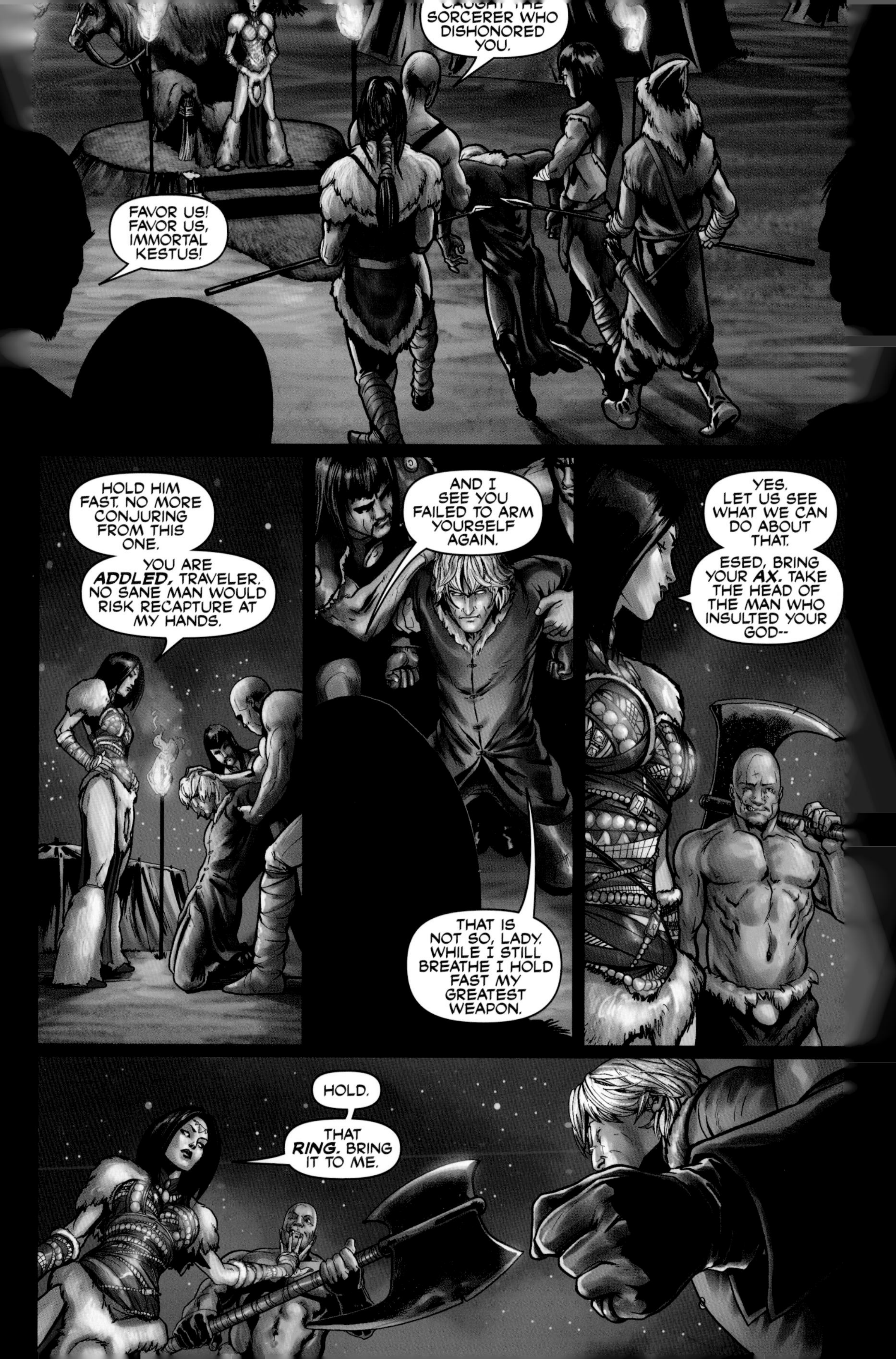
SORCERER WHO DISHONORED YOU.
FAVOR US! FAVOR US, IMMORTAL KESTUS!
HOLD HIM FAST. NO MORE CONJURING FROM THIS ONE.
YOU ARE *ADDLED,* TRAVELER. NO SANE MAN WOULD RISK RECAPTURE AT MY HANDS.
AND I SEE YOU FAILED TO ARM YOURSELF AGAIN.
THAT IS NOT SO, LADY. WHILE I STILL BREATHE I HOLD FAST MY GREATEST WEAPON.
YES. LET US SEE WHAT WE CAN DO ABOUT THAT.
ESED, BRING YOUR *AX.* TAKE THE HEAD OF THE MAN WHO INSULTED YOUR GOD--
HOLD.
THAT *RING.* BRING IT TO ME.

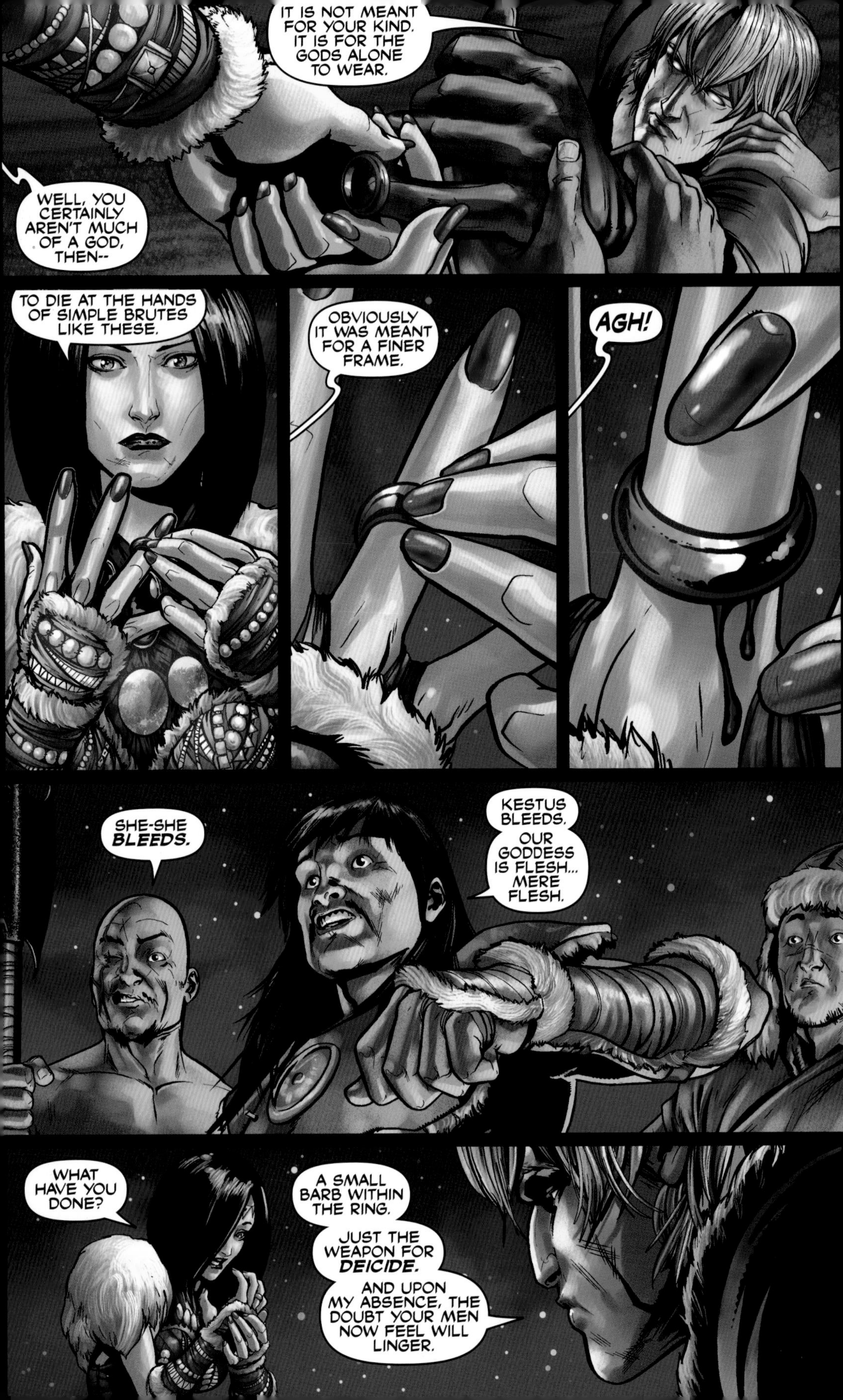

IT IS NOT MEANT FOR YOUR KIND. IT IS FOR THE GODS ALONE TO WEAR.
WELL, YOU CERTAINLY AREN'T MUCH OF A GOD, THEN--
TO DIE AT THE HANDS OF SIMPLE BRUTES LIKE THESE.
OBVIOUSLY IT WAS MEANT FOR A FINER FRAME.
AGH!
SHE-SHE BLEEDS.
KESTUS BLEEDS.
OUR GODDESS IS FLESH... MERE FLESH.
WHAT HAVE YOU DONE?
A SMALL BARB WITHIN THE RING.
JUST THE WEAPON FOR DEICIDE.
AND UPON MY ABSENCE, THE DOUBT YOUR MEN NOW FEEL WILL LINGER.

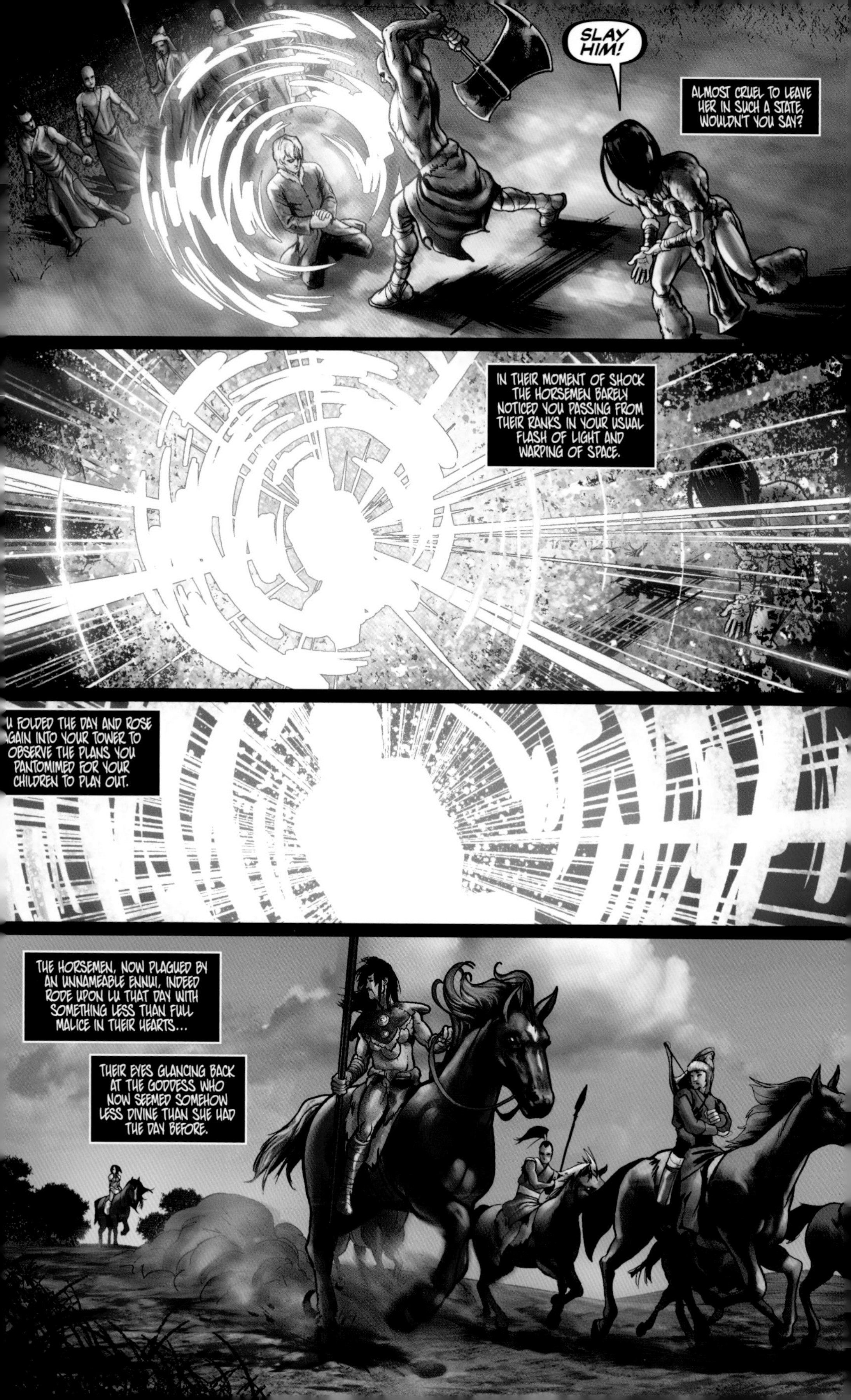
SLAY HIM!
ALMOST CRUEL TO LEAVE HER IN SUCH A STATE, WOULDN'T YOU SAY?
IN THEIR MOMENT OF SHOCK THE HORSEMEN BARELY NOTICED YOU PASSING FROM THEIR RANKS IN YOUR USUAL FLASH OF LIGHT AND WARPING OF SPACE.
U FOLDED THE DAY AND ROSE AGAIN INTO YOUR TOWER TO OBSERVE THE PLANS YOU PANTOMIMED FOR YOUR CHILDREN TO PLAY OUT.
THE HORSEMEN, NOW PLAGUED BY AN UNNAMEABLE ENNUI, INDEED RODE UPON LU THAT DAY WITH SOMETHING LESS THAN FULL MALICE IN THEIR HEARTS…
THEIR EYES GLANCING BACK AT THE GODDESS WHO NOW SEEMED SOMEHOW LESS DIVINE THAN SHE HAD THE DAY BEFORE.

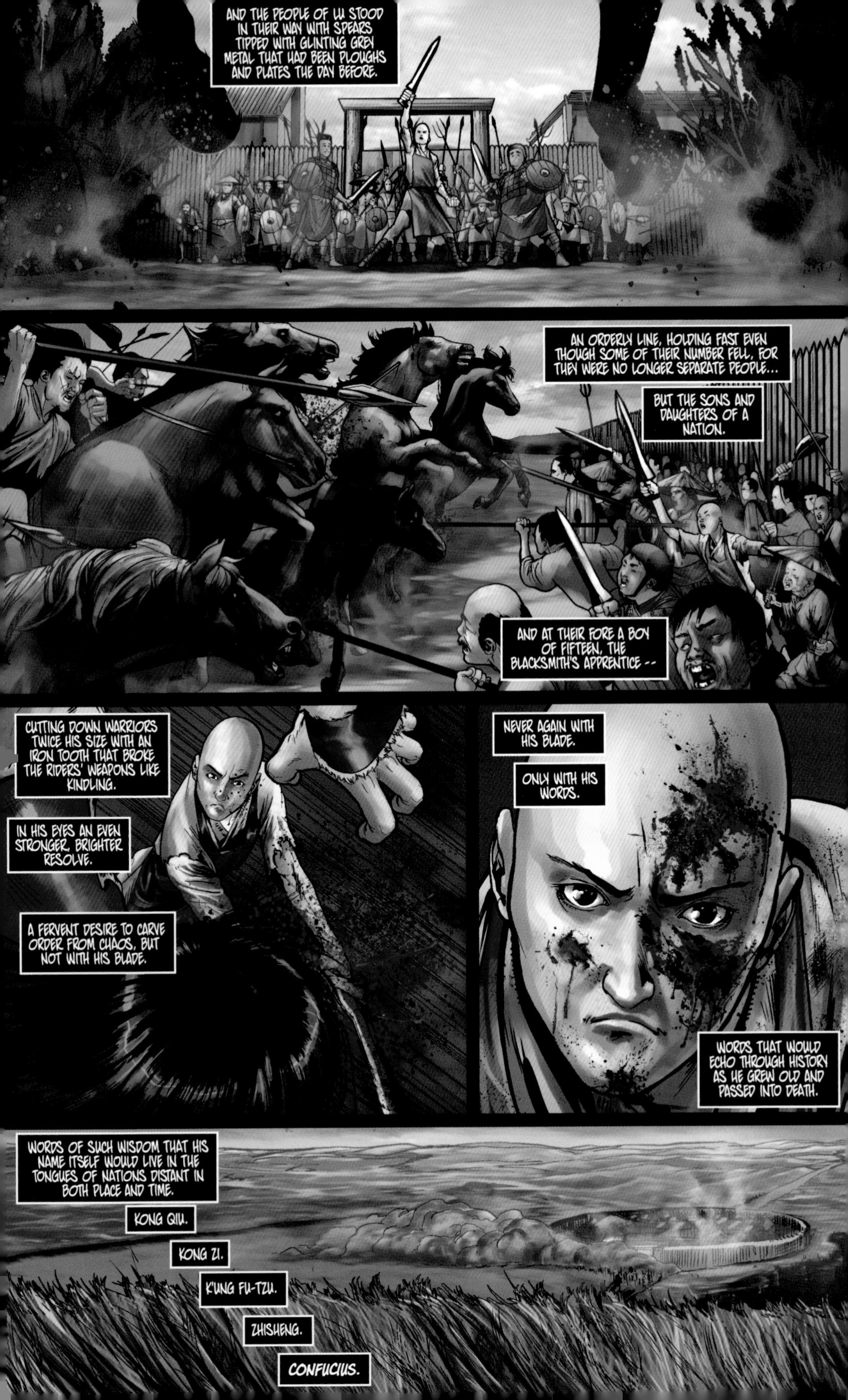
AND THE PEOPLE OF LU STOOD IN THEIR WAY WITH SPEARS TIPPED WITH GLINTING GREY METAL THAT HAD BEEN PLOUGHS AND PLATES THE DAY BEFORE.
AN ORDERLY LINE, HOLDING FAST EVEN THOUGH SOME OF THEIR NUMBER FELL, FOR THEY WERE NO LONGER SEPARATE PEOPLE...
BUT THE SONS AND DAUGHTERS OF A NATION.
AND AT THEIR FORE A BOY OF FIFTEEN, THE BLACKSMITH'S APPRENTICE --
CUTTING DOWN WARRIORS TWICE HIS SIZE WITH AN IRON TOOTH THAT BROKE THE RIDERS' WEAPONS LIKE KINDLING.
IN HIS EYES AN EVEN STRONGER, BRIGHTER RESOLVE.
A FERVENT DESIRE TO CARVE ORDER FROM CHAOS, BUT NOT WITH HIS BLADE.
NEVER AGAIN WITH HIS BLADE.
ONLY WITH HIS WORDS.
WORDS THAT WOULD ECHO THROUGH HISTORY AS HE GREW OLD AND PASSED INTO DEATH.
WORDS OF SUCH WISDOM THAT HIS NAME ITSELF WOULD LIVE IN THE TONGUES OF NATIONS DISTANT IN BOTH PLACE AND TIME.
KONG QIU.
KONG ZI.
K'UNG FU-TZU.
ZHISHENG.
CONFUCIUS.

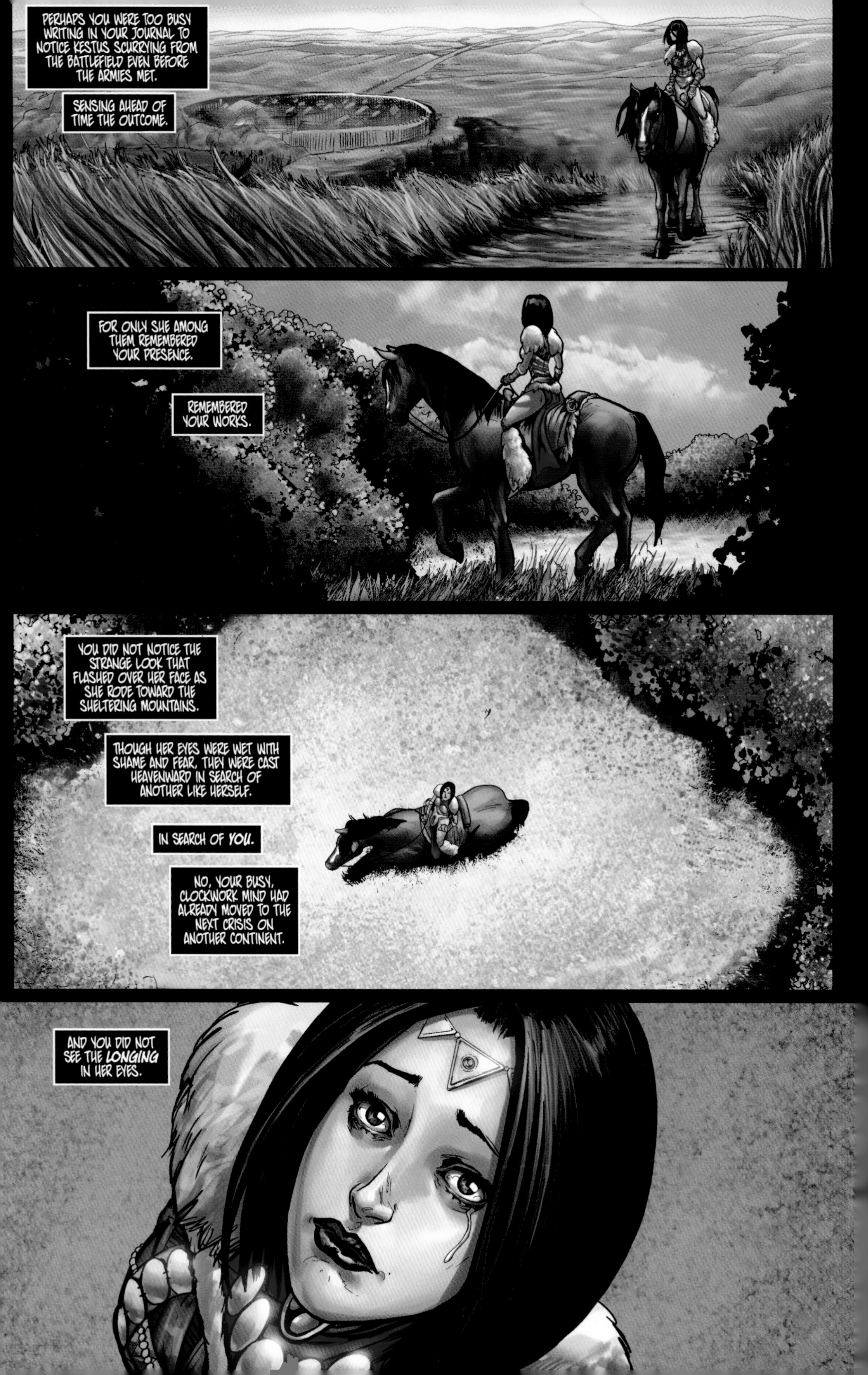
PERHAPS YOU WERE TOO BUSY WRITING IN YOUR JOURNAL TO NOTICE KESTUS SCURRYING FROM THE BATTLEFIELD EVEN BEFORE THE ARMIES MET.
SENSING AHEAD OF TIME THE OUTCOME.
FOR ONLY SHE AMONG THEM REMEMBERED YOUR PRESENCE.
REMEMBERED YOUR WORKS.
YOU DID NOT NOTICE THE STRANGE LOOK THAT FLASHED OVER HER FACE AS SHE RODE TOWARD THE SHELTERING MOUNTAINS.
THOUGH HER EYES WERE WET WITH SHAME AND FEAR, THEY WERE CAST HEAVENWARD IN SEARCH OF ANOTHER LIKE HERSELF.
IN SEARCH OF ***YOU***.
NO, YOUR BUSY, CLOCKWORK MIND HAD ALREADY MOVED TO THE NEXT CRISIS ON ANOTHER CONTINENT.
AND YOU DID NOT SEE THE ***LONGING*** IN HER EYES.

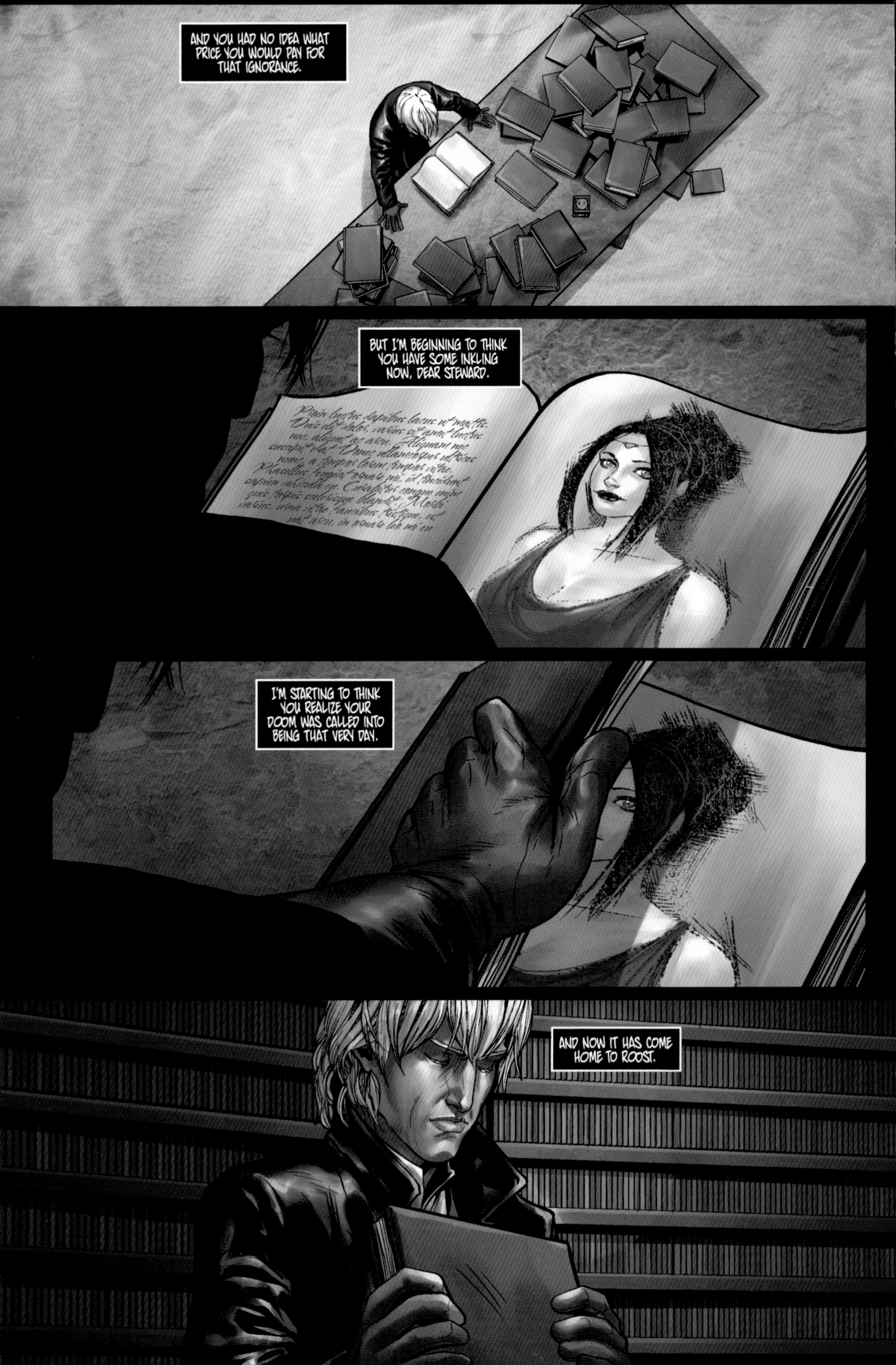
AND YOU HAD NO IDEA WHAT PRICE YOU WOULD PAY FOR THAT IGNORANCE.
BUT I'M BEGINNING TO THINK YOU HAVE SOME INKLING NOW, DEAR STEWARD.
I'M STARTING TO THINK YOU REALIZE YOUR DOOM WAS CALLED INTO BEING THAT VERY DAY.
AND NOW IT HAS COME HOME TO ROOST.

19 CHAPTER 9514350
5182135 TWO 318408

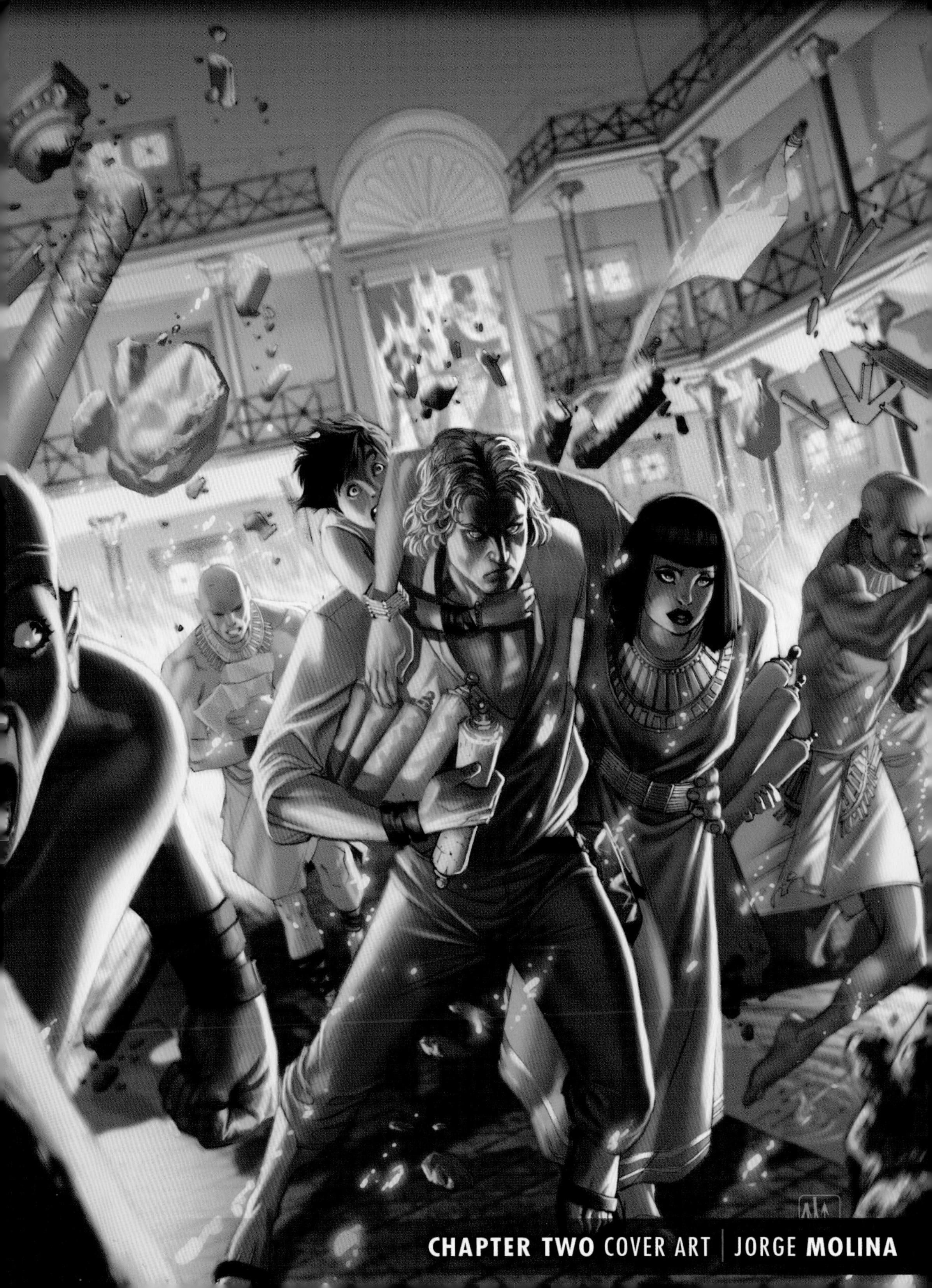

CHAPTER TWO COVER ART | JORGE **MOLINA**

48 BCE

THE BURNING OF ALEXANDRIA

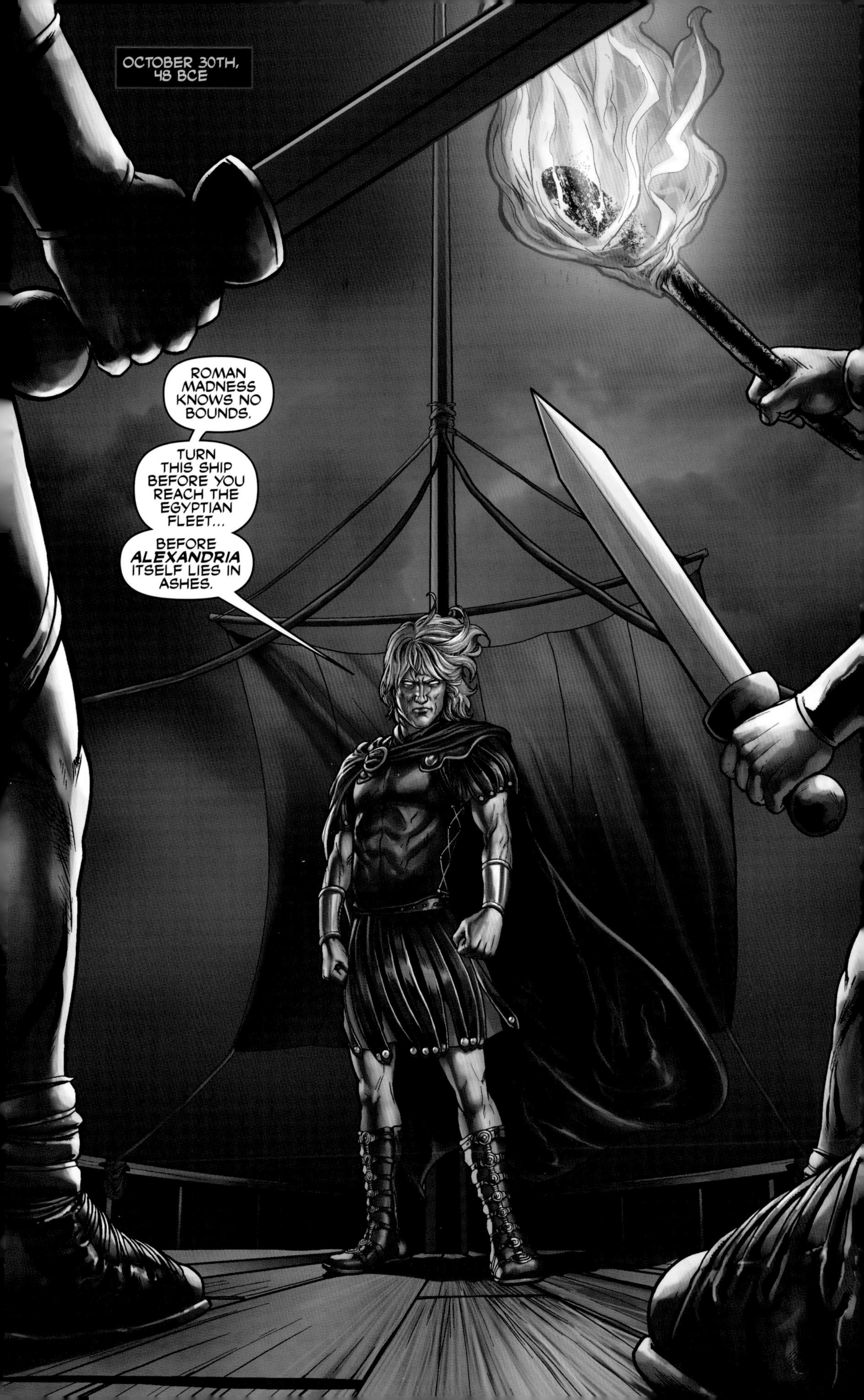
OCTOBER 30TH, 48 BCE
ROMAN MADNESS KNOWS NO BOUNDS.
TURN THIS SHIP BEFORE YOU REACH THE EGYPTIAN FLEET...
BEFORE ***ALEXANDRIA*** ITSELF LIES IN ASHES.

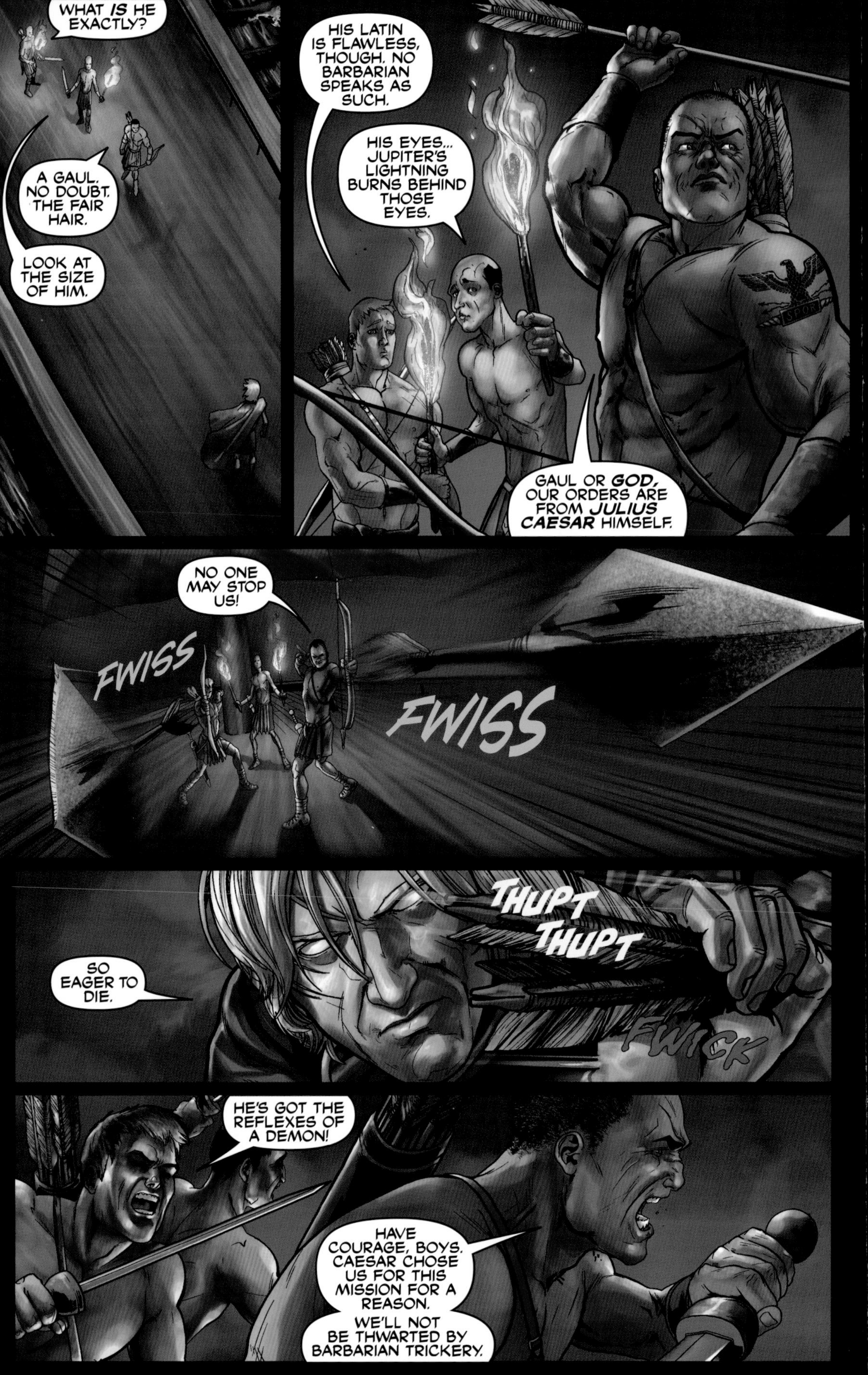
WHAT *IS* HE EXACTLY?
A GAUL. NO DOUBT. THE FAIR HAIR.
LOOK AT THE SIZE OF HIM.
HIS LATIN IS FLAWLESS, THOUGH. NO BARBARIAN SPEAKS AS SUCH.
HIS EYES... JUPITER'S LIGHTNING BURNS BEHIND THOSE EYES.
GAUL OR ***GOD***, OUR ORDERS ARE FROM ***JULIUS CAESAR*** HIMSELF.
NO ONE MAY STOP US!
FWISS
FWISS
THUPT
THUPT
SO EAGER TO DIE.
FWICK
HE'S GOT THE REFLEXES OF A DEMON!
HAVE COURAGE, BOYS. CAESAR CHOSE US FOR THIS MISSION FOR A REASON.
WE'LL NOT BE THWARTED BY BARBARIAN TRICKERY.

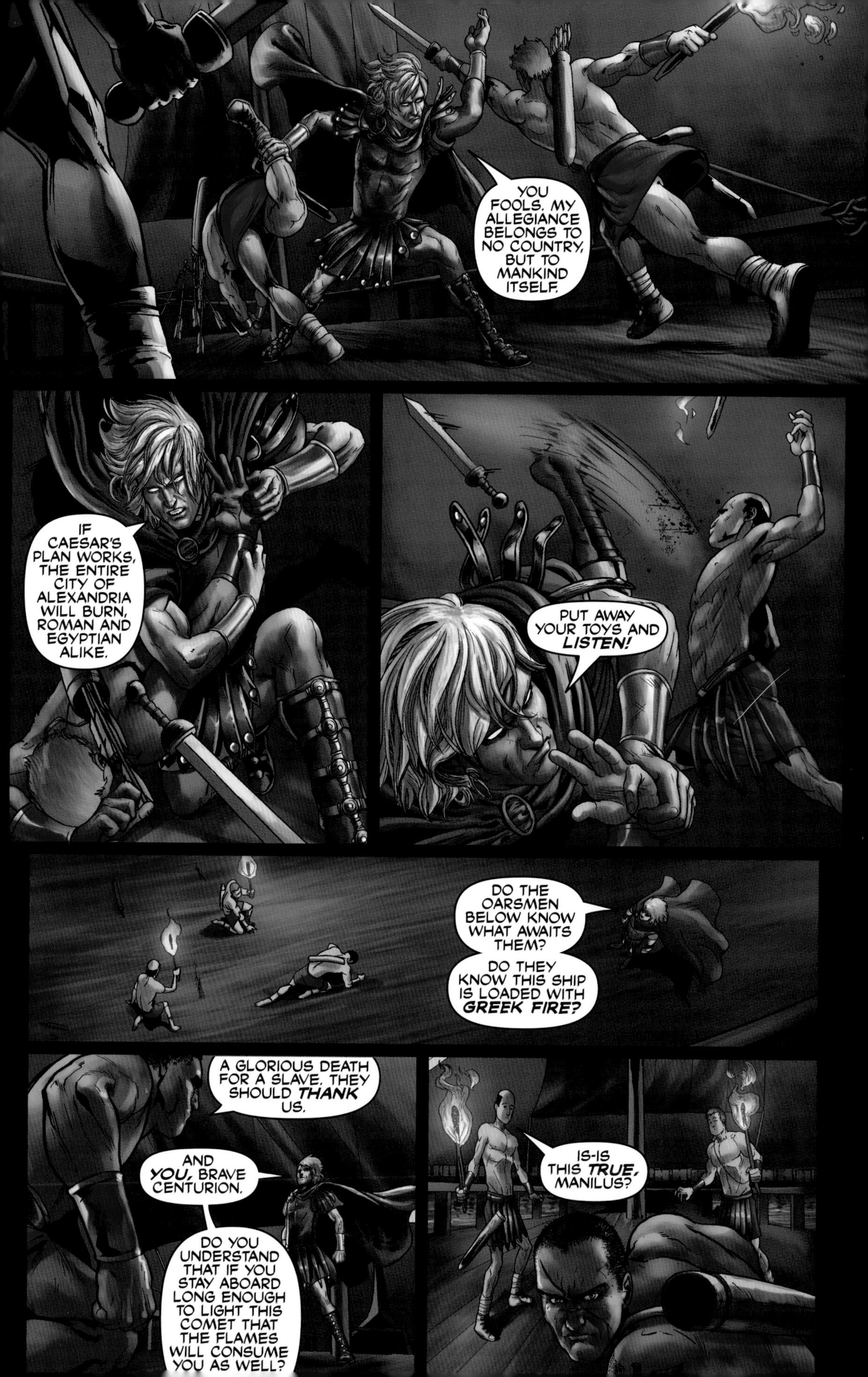
YOU FOOLS. MY ALLEGIANCE BELONGS TO NO COUNTRY, BUT TO MANKIND ITSELF.
IF CAESAR'S PLAN WORKS, THE ENTIRE CITY OF ALEXANDRIA WILL BURN, ROMAN AND EGYPTIAN ALIKE.
PUT AWAY YOUR TOYS AND LISTEN!
DO THE OARSMEN BELOW KNOW WHAT AWAITS THEM?
DO THEY KNOW THIS SHIP IS LOADED WITH GREEK FIRE?
A GLORIOUS DEATH FOR A SLAVE. THEY SHOULD THANK US.
AND YOU, BRAVE CENTURION.
DO YOU UNDERSTAND THAT IF YOU STAY ABOARD LONG ENOUGH TO LIGHT THIS COMET THAT THE FLAMES WILL CONSUME YOU AS WELL?
IS-IS THIS TRUE, MANILUS?

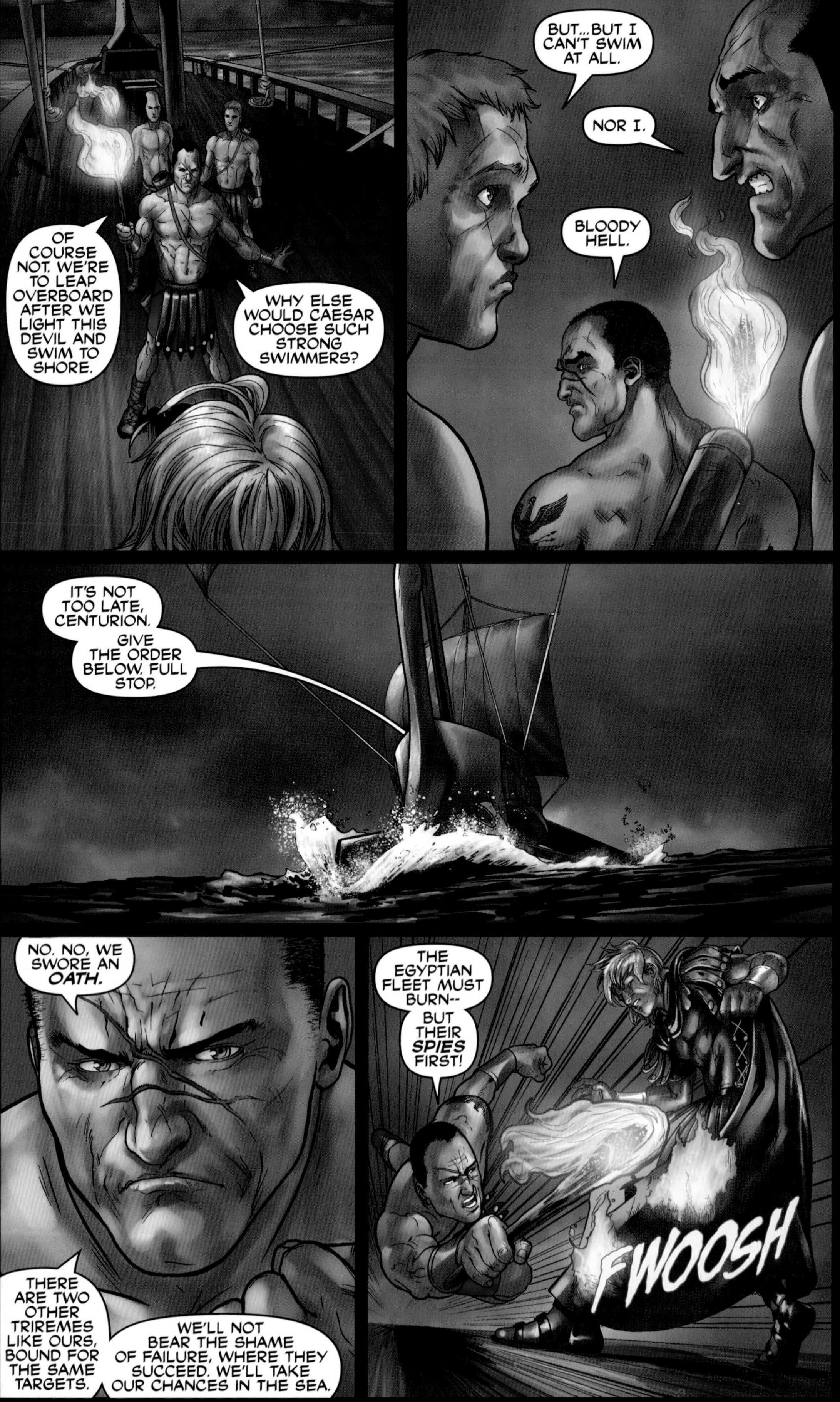
OF COURSE NOT. WE'RE TO LEAP OVERBOARD AFTER WE LIGHT THIS DEVIL AND SWIM TO SHORE.
WHY ELSE WOULD CAESAR CHOOSE SUCH STRONG SWIMMERS?
BUT...BUT I CAN'T SWIM AT ALL.
NOR I.
BLOODY HELL.
IT'S NOT TOO LATE, CENTURION.
GIVE THE ORDER BELOW. FULL STOP.
NO. NO, WE SWORE AN *OATH.*
THERE ARE TWO OTHER TRIREMES LIKE OURS, BOUND FOR THE SAME TARGETS.
WE'LL NOT BEAR THE SHAME OF FAILURE, WHERE THEY SUCCEED. WE'LL TAKE OUR CHANCES IN THE SEA.
THE EGYPTIAN FLEET MUST BURN--
BUT THEIR *SPIES* FIRST!
FWOOSH

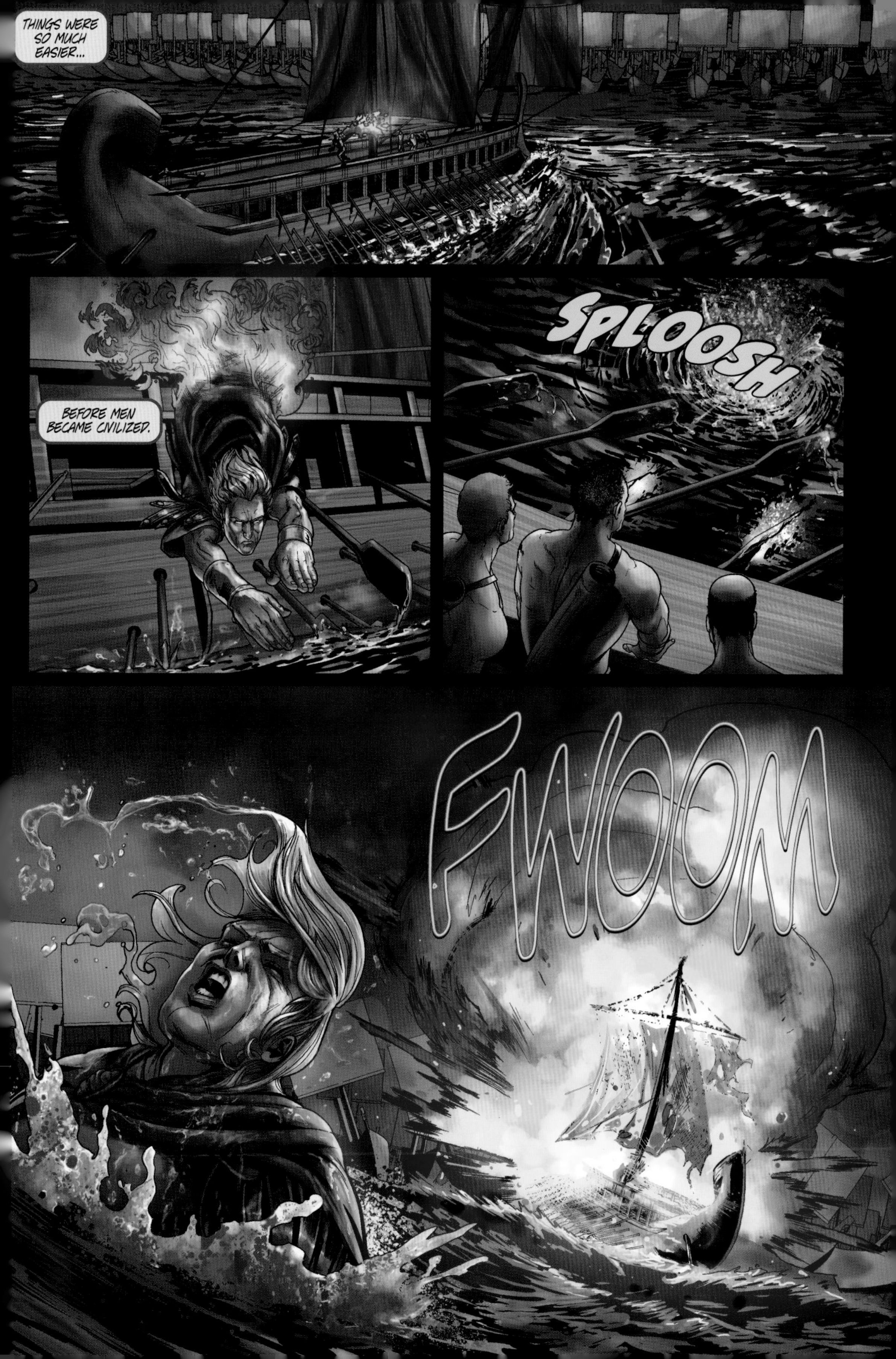
THINGS WERE SO MUCH EASIER...
BEFORE MEN BECAME CIVILIZED.
SPLOOSH
FWOOM

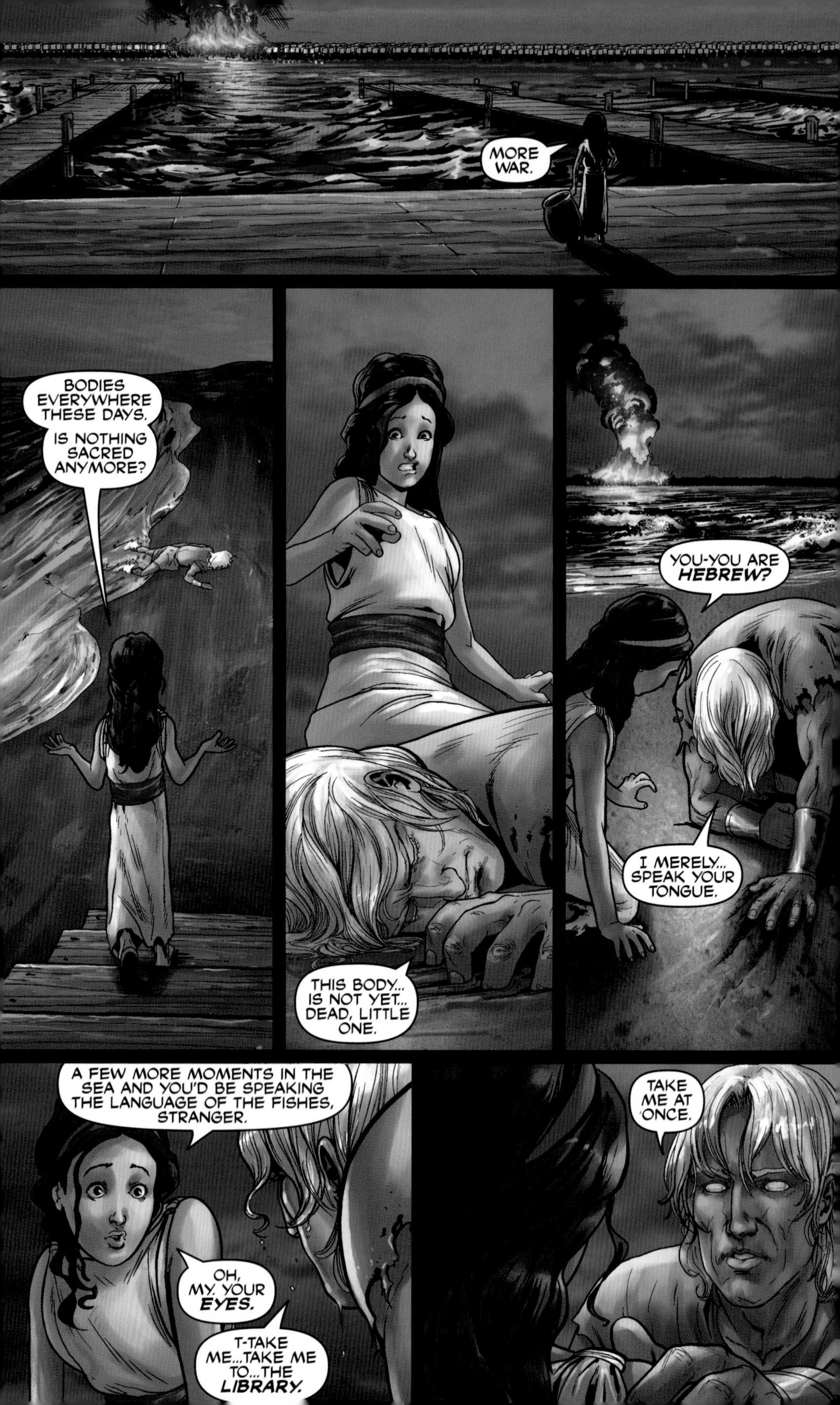
MORE WAR.
BODIES EVERYWHERE THESE DAYS.
IS NOTHING SACRED ANYMORE?
THIS BODY... IS NOT YET... DEAD, LITTLE ONE.
YOU-YOU ARE HEBREW?
I MERELY... SPEAK YOUR TONGUE.
A FEW MORE MOMENTS IN THE SEA AND YOU'D BE SPEAKING THE LANGUAGE OF THE FISHES, STRANGER.
OH, MY. YOUR EYES.
T-TAKE ME...TAKE ME TO...THE LIBRARY.
TAKE ME AT ONCE.

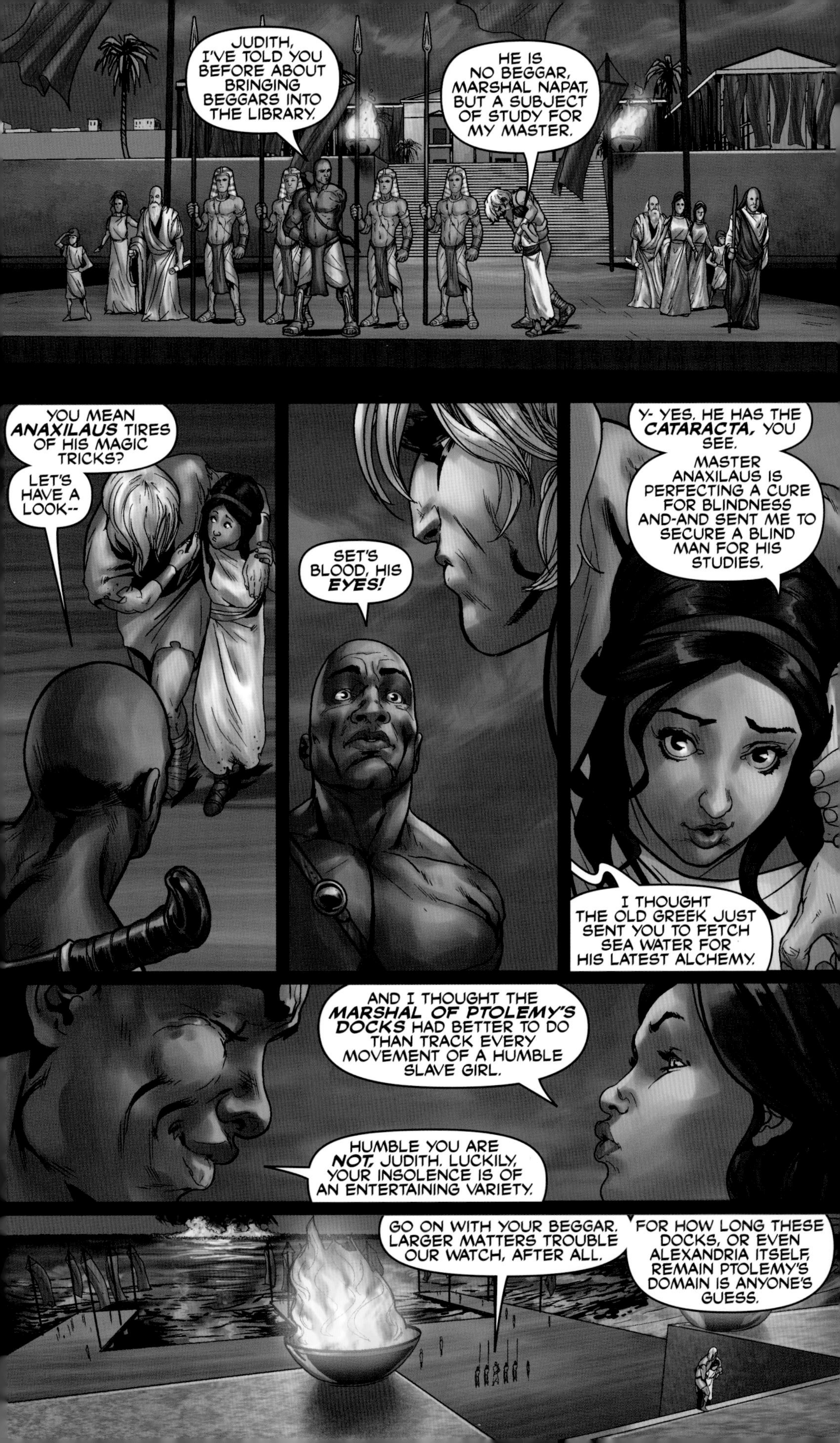
JUDITH, I'VE TOLD YOU BEFORE ABOUT BRINGING BEGGARS INTO THE LIBRARY.
HE IS NO BEGGAR, MARSHAL NAPAT, BUT A SUBJECT OF STUDY FOR MY MASTER.
YOU MEAN ANAXILAUS TIRES OF HIS MAGIC TRICKS?
LET'S HAVE A LOOK--
SET'S BLOOD, HIS EYES!
Y- YES. HE HAS THE CATARACTA, YOU SEE.
MASTER ANAXILAUS IS PERFECTING A CURE FOR BLINDNESS AND-AND SENT ME TO SECURE A BLIND MAN FOR HIS STUDIES.
I THOUGHT THE OLD GREEK JUST SENT YOU TO FETCH SEA WATER FOR HIS LATEST ALCHEMY.
AND I THOUGHT THE MARSHAL OF PTOLEMY'S DOCKS HAD BETTER TO DO THAN TRACK EVERY MOVEMENT OF A HUMBLE SLAVE GIRL.
HUMBLE YOU ARE NOT, JUDITH. LUCKILY, YOUR INSOLENCE IS OF AN ENTERTAINING VARIETY.
GO ON WITH YOUR BEGGAR. LARGER MATTERS TROUBLE OUR WATCH, AFTER ALL.
FOR HOW LONG THESE DOCKS, OR EVEN ALEXANDRIA ITSELF, REMAIN PTOLEMY'S DOMAIN IS ANYONE'S GUESS.

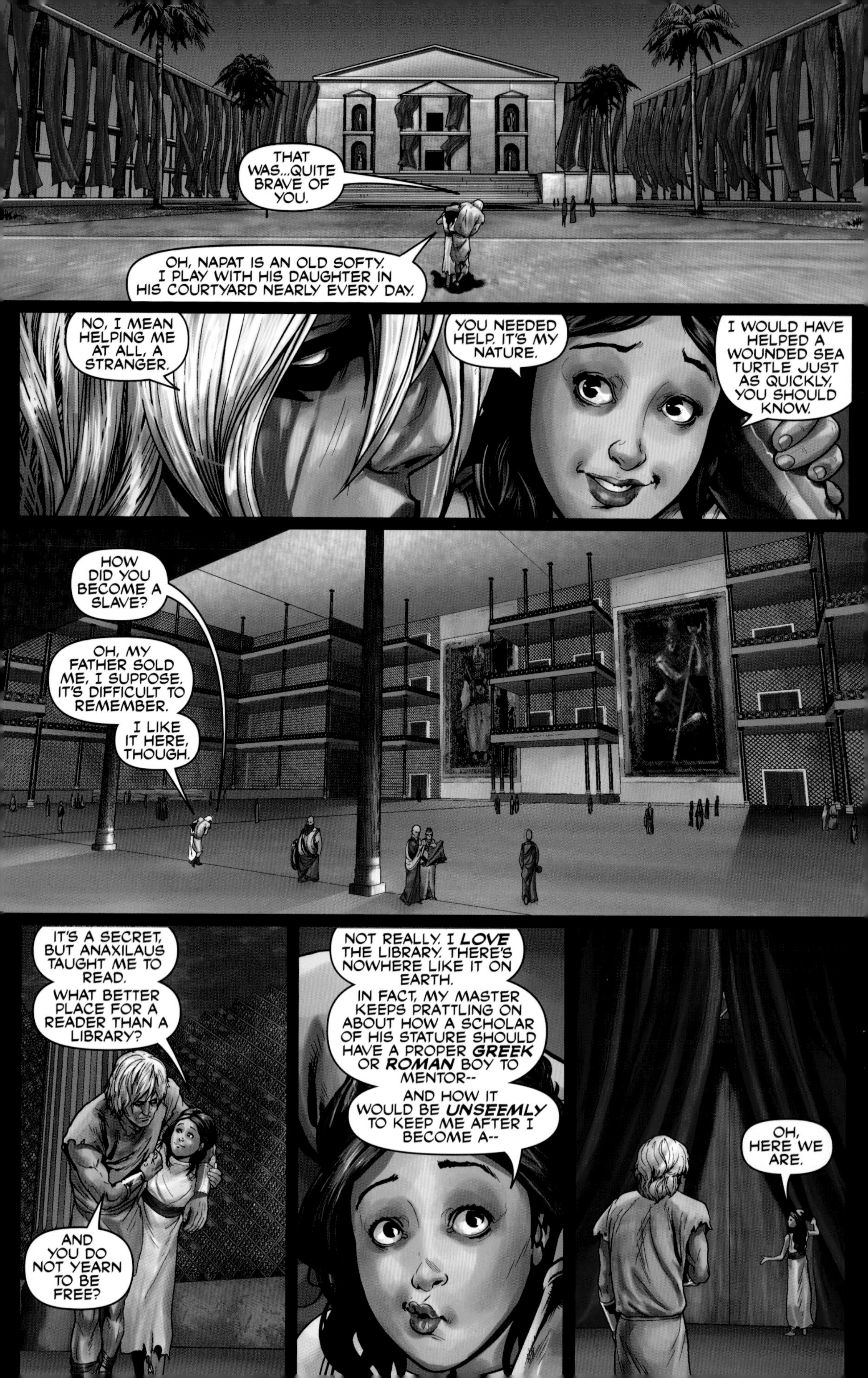
THAT WAS...QUITE BRAVE OF YOU.
OH, NAPAT IS AN OLD SOFTY. I PLAY WITH HIS DAUGHTER IN HIS COURTYARD NEARLY EVERY DAY.
NO, I MEAN HELPING ME AT ALL, A STRANGER.
YOU NEEDED HELP. IT'S MY NATURE.
I WOULD HAVE HELPED A WOUNDED SEA TURTLE JUST AS QUICKLY, YOU SHOULD KNOW.
HOW DID YOU BECOME A SLAVE?
OH, MY FATHER SOLD ME, I SUPPOSE. IT'S DIFFICULT TO REMEMBER.
I LIKE IT HERE, THOUGH.
IT'S A SECRET, BUT ANAXILAUS TAUGHT ME TO READ.
WHAT BETTER PLACE FOR A READER THAN A LIBRARY?
AND YOU DO NOT YEARN TO BE FREE?
NOT REALLY. I *LOVE* THE LIBRARY. THERE'S NOWHERE LIKE IT ON EARTH.
IN FACT, MY MASTER KEEPS PRATTLING ON ABOUT HOW A SCHOLAR OF HIS STATURE SHOULD HAVE A PROPER ***GREEK*** OR ***ROMAN*** BOY TO MENTOR--
AND HOW IT WOULD BE ***UNSEEMLY*** TO KEEP ME AFTER I BECOME A--
OH, HERE WE ARE.

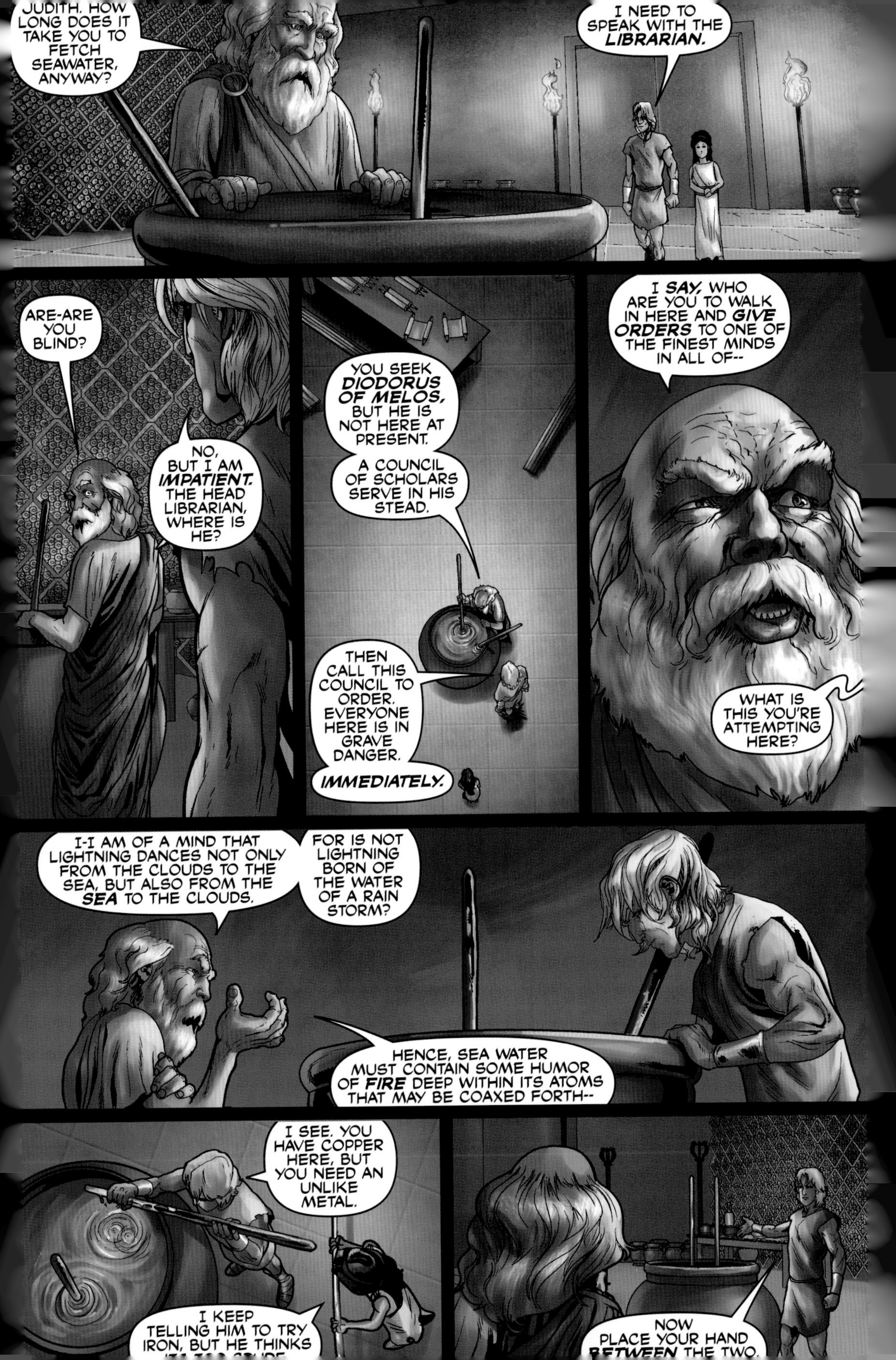
JUDITH, HOW LONG DOES IT TAKE YOU TO FETCH SEAWATER, ANYWAY?
I NEED TO SPEAK WITH THE LIBRARIAN.
ARE-ARE YOU BLIND?
NO, BUT I AM IMPATIENT. THE HEAD LIBRARIAN, WHERE IS HE?
YOU SEEK DIODORUS OF MELOS, BUT HE IS NOT HERE AT PRESENT.
A COUNCIL OF SCHOLARS SERVE IN HIS STEAD.
THEN CALL THIS COUNCIL TO ORDER. EVERYONE HERE IS IN GRAVE DANGER.
IMMEDIATELY.
I SAY, WHO ARE YOU TO WALK IN HERE AND GIVE ORDERS TO ONE OF THE FINEST MINDS IN ALL OF--
WHAT IS THIS YOU'RE ATTEMPTING HERE?
I-I AM OF A MIND THAT LIGHTNING DANCES NOT ONLY FROM THE CLOUDS TO THE SEA, BUT ALSO FROM THE SEA TO THE CLOUDS.
FOR IS NOT LIGHTNING BORN OF THE WATER OF A RAIN STORM?
HENCE, SEA WATER MUST CONTAIN SOME HUMOR OF FIRE DEEP WITHIN ITS ATOMS THAT MAY BE COAXED FORTH--
I SEE. YOU HAVE COPPER HERE, BUT YOU NEED AN UNLIKE METAL.
I KEEP TELLING HIM TO TRY IRON, BUT HE THINKS
NOW PLACE YOUR HAND BETWEEN THE TWO.

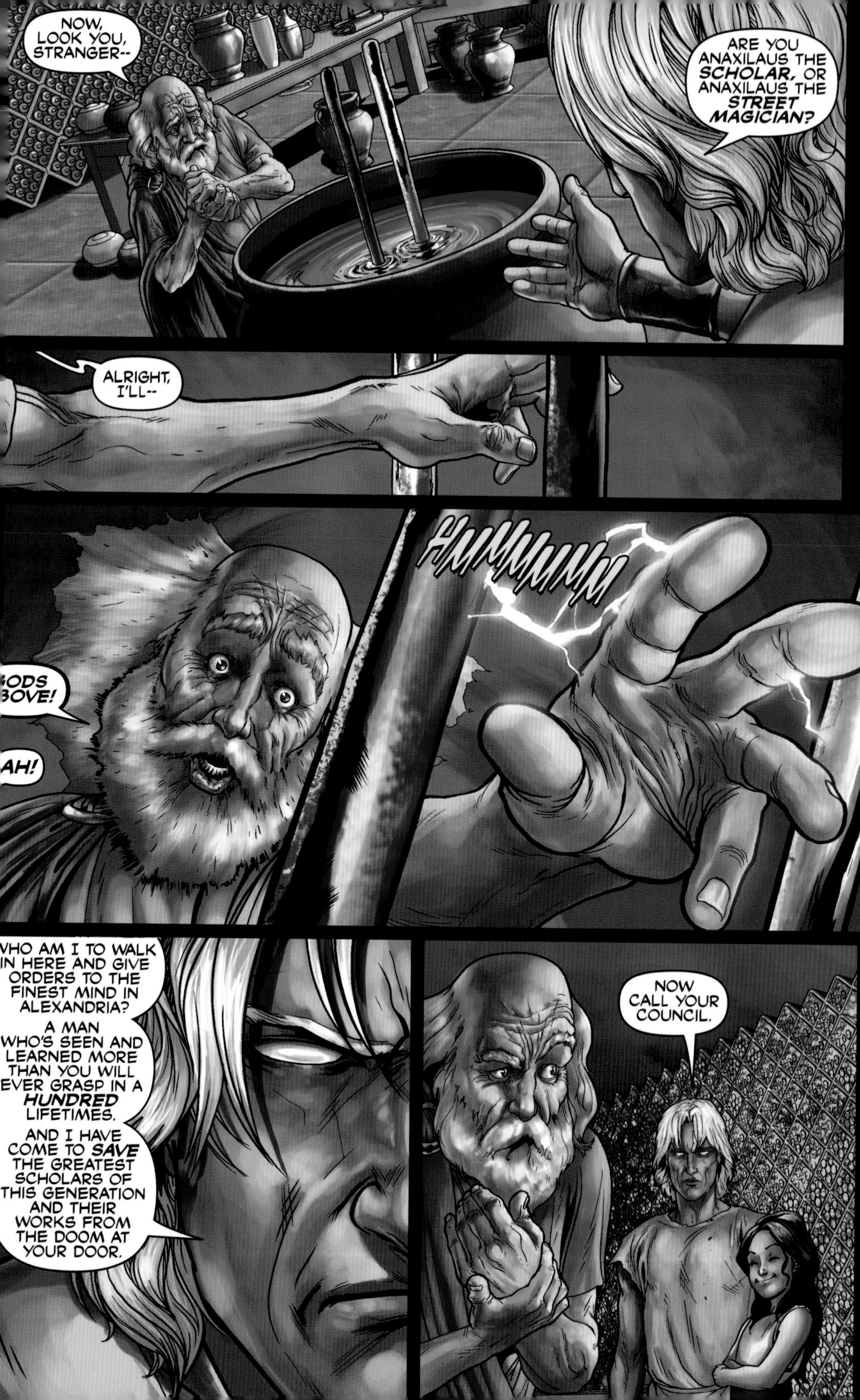
NOW, LOOK YOU, STRANGER--
ARE YOU ANAXILAUS THE *SCHOLAR,* OR ANAXILAUS THE *STREET MAGICIAN?*
ALRIGHT, I'LL--
HMMMMMM
ODS BOVE!
AH!
WHO AM I TO WALK IN HERE AND GIVE ORDERS TO THE FINEST MIND IN ALEXANDRIA?
A MAN WHO'S SEEN AND LEARNED MORE THAN YOU WILL EVER GRASP IN A *HUNDRED* LIFETIMES.
AND I HAVE COME TO *SAVE* THE GREATEST SCHOLARS OF THIS GENERATION AND THEIR WORKS FROM THE DOOM AT YOUR DOOR.
NOW CALL YOUR COUNCIL.

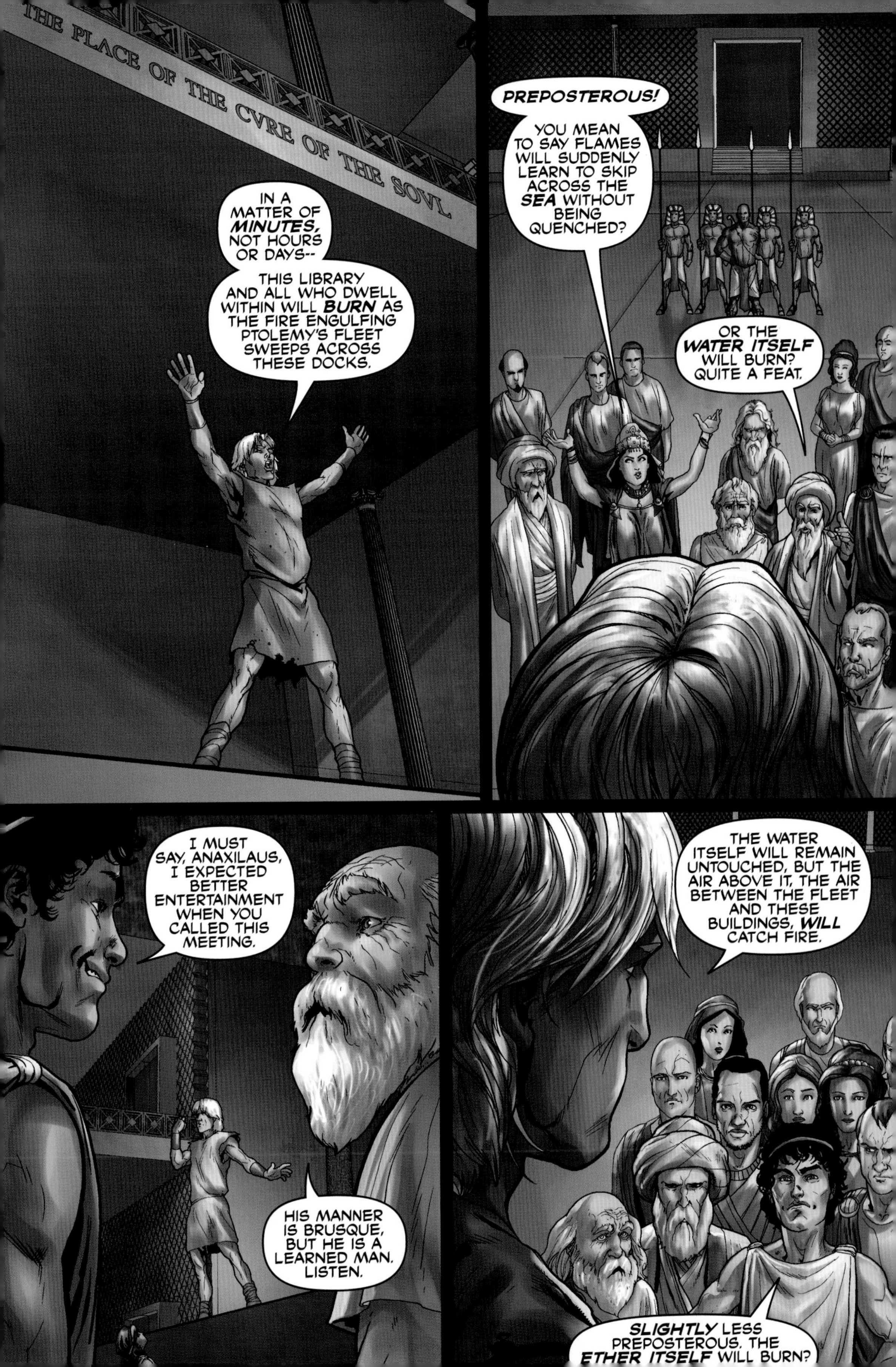
THE PLACE OF THE CVRE OF THE SOVL
IN A MATTER OF MINUTES, NOT HOURS OR DAYS--
THIS LIBRARY AND ALL WHO DWELL WITHIN WILL BURN AS THE FIRE ENGULFING PTOLEMY'S FLEET SWEEPS ACROSS THESE DOCKS.
PREPOSTEROUS!
YOU MEAN TO SAY FLAMES WILL SUDDENLY LEARN TO SKIP ACROSS THE SEA WITHOUT BEING QUENCHED?
OR THE WATER ITSELF WILL BURN? QUITE A FEAT.
I MUST SAY, ANAXILAUS, I EXPECTED BETTER ENTERTAINMENT WHEN YOU CALLED THIS MEETING.
HIS MANNER IS BRUSQUE, BUT HE IS A LEARNED MAN. LISTEN.
THE WATER ITSELF WILL REMAIN UNTOUCHED, BUT THE AIR ABOVE IT, THE AIR BETWEEN THE FLEET AND THESE BUILDINGS, WILL CATCH FIRE.
SLIGHTLY LESS PREPOSTEROUS. THE ETHER ITSELF WILL BURN?

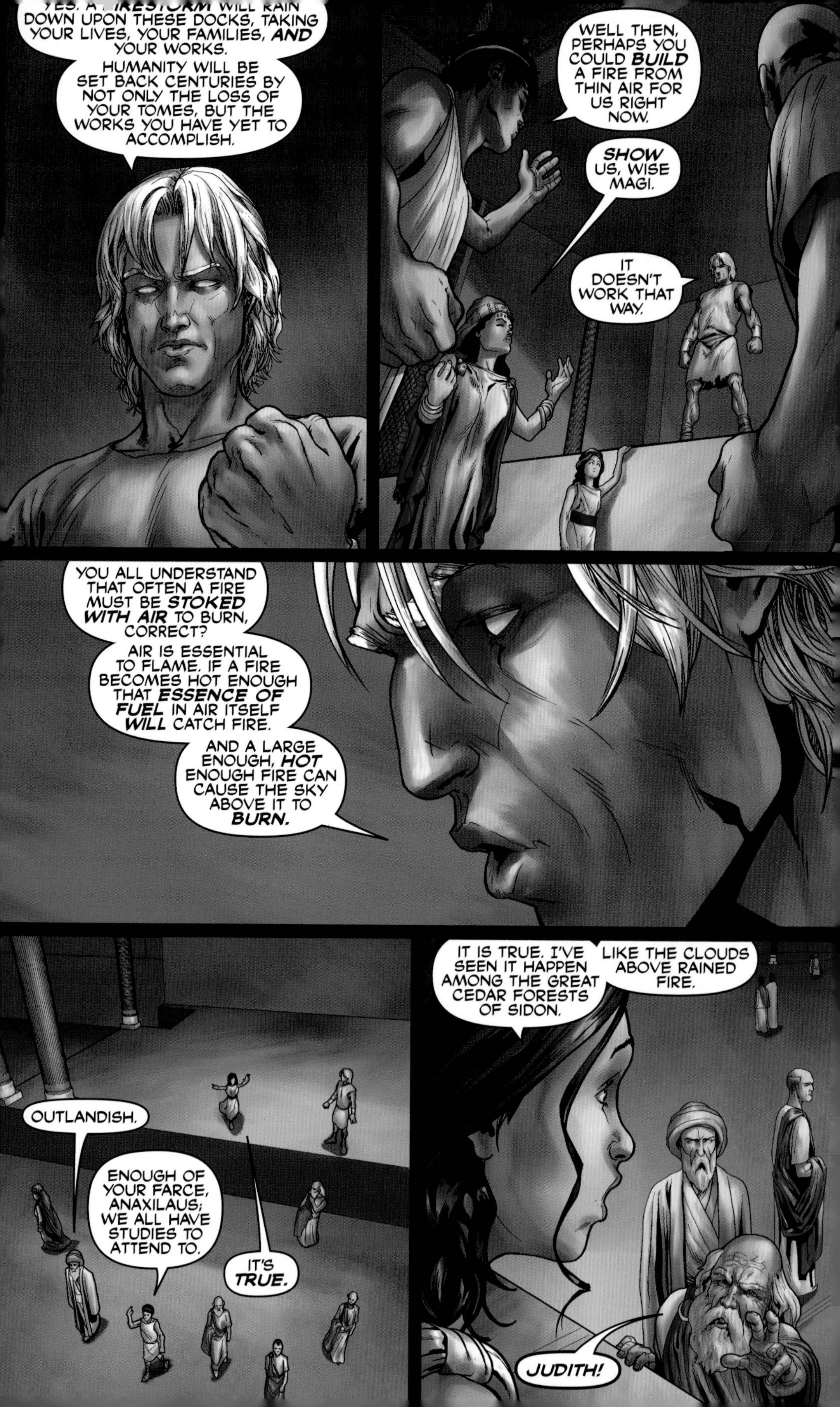
YES, A FIRESTORM WILL RAIN DOWN UPON THESE DOCKS, TAKING YOUR LIVES, YOUR FAMILIES, AND YOUR WORKS.
HUMANITY WILL BE SET BACK CENTURIES BY NOT ONLY THE LOSS OF YOUR TOMES, BUT THE WORKS YOU HAVE YET TO ACCOMPLISH.
WELL THEN, PERHAPS YOU COULD BUILD A FIRE FROM THIN AIR FOR US RIGHT NOW.
SHOW US, WISE MAGI.
IT DOESN'T WORK THAT WAY.
YOU ALL UNDERSTAND THAT OFTEN A FIRE MUST BE STOKED WITH AIR TO BURN, CORRECT?
AIR IS ESSENTIAL TO FLAME. IF A FIRE BECOMES HOT ENOUGH THAT ESSENCE OF FUEL IN AIR ITSELF WILL CATCH FIRE.
AND A LARGE ENOUGH, HOT ENOUGH FIRE CAN CAUSE THE SKY ABOVE IT TO BURN.
OUTLANDISH.
ENOUGH OF YOUR FARCE, ANAXILAUS; WE ALL HAVE STUDIES TO ATTEND TO.
IT'S TRUE.
IT IS TRUE. I'VE SEEN IT HAPPEN AMONG THE GREAT CEDAR FORESTS OF SIDON.
LIKE THE CLOUDS ABOVE RAINED FIRE.
JUDITH!

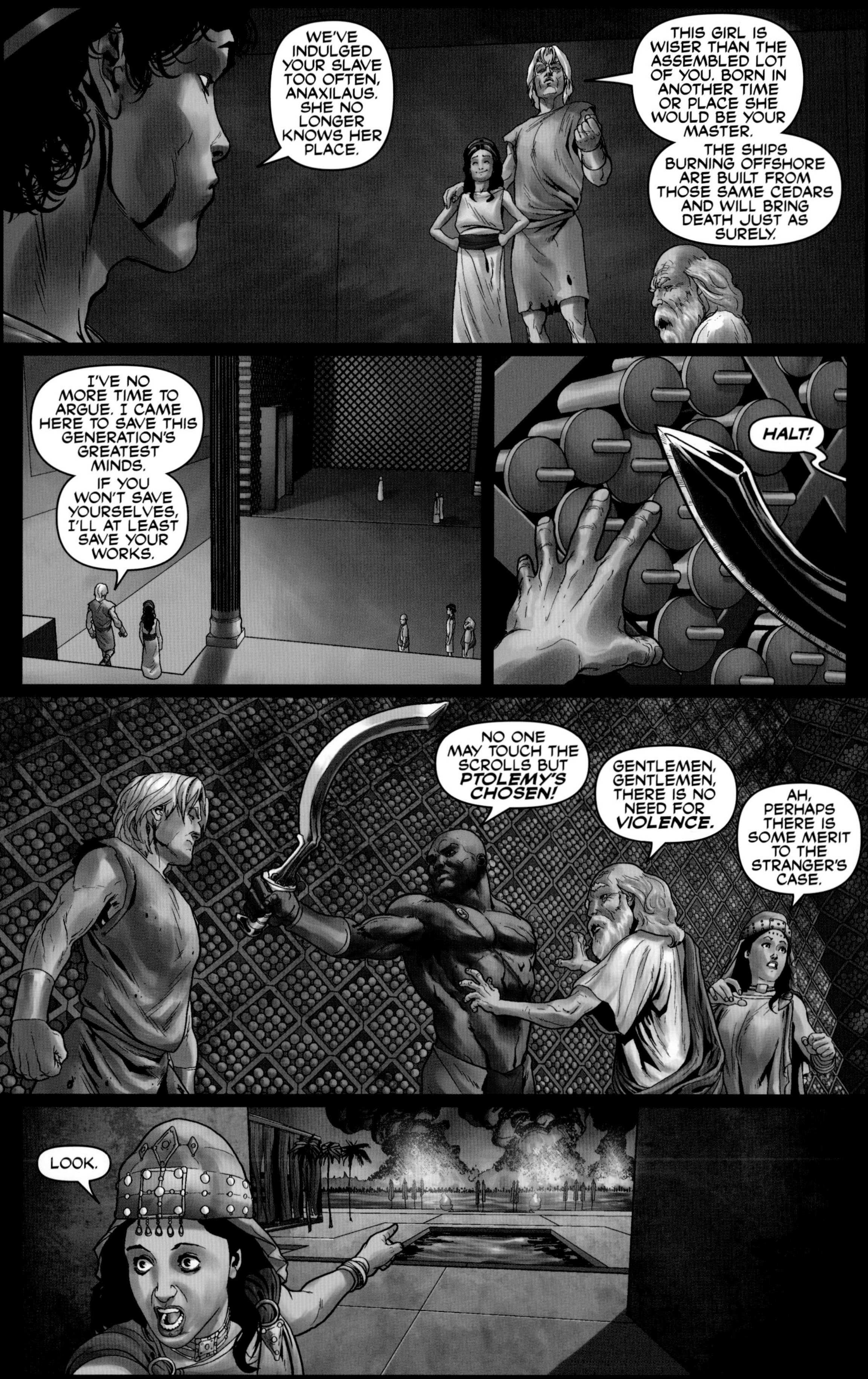
WE'VE INDULGED YOUR SLAVE TOO OFTEN, ANAXILAUS. SHE NO LONGER KNOWS HER PLACE.
THIS GIRL IS WISER THAN THE ASSEMBLED LOT OF YOU. BORN IN ANOTHER TIME OR PLACE SHE WOULD BE YOUR MASTER.
THE SHIPS BURNING OFFSHORE ARE BUILT FROM THOSE SAME CEDARS AND WILL BRING DEATH JUST AS SURELY.
I'VE NO MORE TIME TO ARGUE. I CAME HERE TO SAVE THIS GENERATION'S GREATEST MINDS.
IF YOU WON'T SAVE YOURSELVES, I'LL AT LEAST SAVE YOUR WORKS.
HALT!
NO ONE MAY TOUCH THE SCROLLS BUT PTOLEMY'S CHOSEN!
GENTLEMEN, GENTLEMEN, THERE IS NO NEED FOR VIOLENCE.
AH, PERHAPS THERE IS SOME MERIT TO THE STRANGER'S CASE.
LOOK.

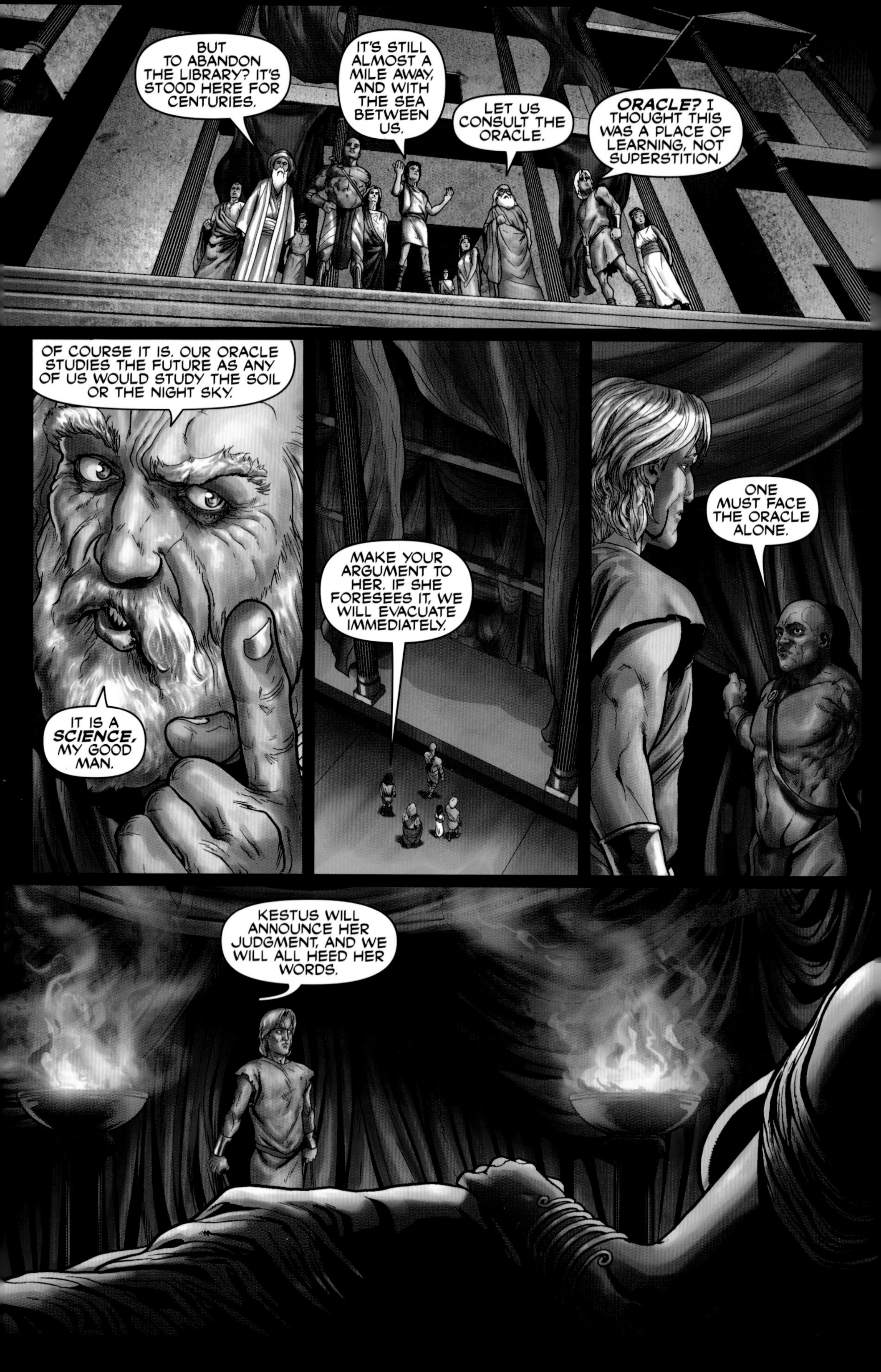

BUT TO ABANDON THE LIBRARY? IT'S STOOD HERE FOR CENTURIES.
IT'S STILL ALMOST A MILE AWAY, AND WITH THE SEA BETWEEN US.
LET US CONSULT THE ORACLE.
ORACLE? I THOUGHT THIS WAS A PLACE OF LEARNING, NOT SUPERSTITION.
OF COURSE IT IS. OUR ORACLE STUDIES THE FUTURE AS ANY OF US WOULD STUDY THE SOIL OR THE NIGHT SKY.
IT IS A SCIENCE, MY GOOD MAN.
MAKE YOUR ARGUMENT TO HER. IF SHE FORESEES IT, WE WILL EVACUATE IMMEDIATELY.
ONE MUST FACE THE ORACLE ALONE.
KESTUS WILL ANNOUNCE HER JUDGMENT, AND WE WILL ALL HEED HER WORDS.

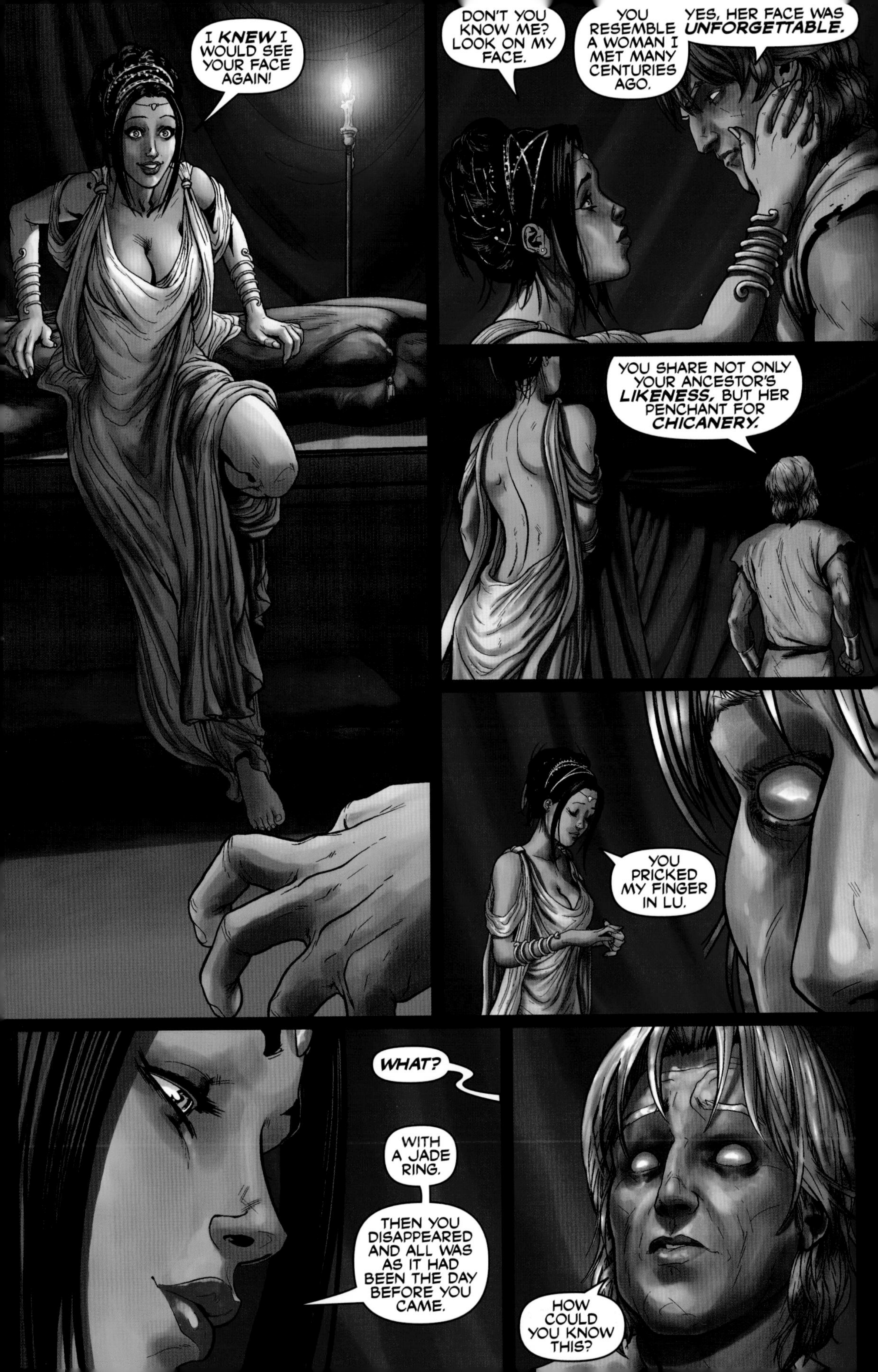

I **KNEW** I WOULD SEE YOUR FACE AGAIN!
DON'T YOU KNOW ME? LOOK ON MY FACE.
YOU RESEMBLE A WOMAN I MET MANY CENTURIES AGO.
YES, HER FACE WAS **UNFORGETTABLE.**
YOU SHARE NOT ONLY YOUR ANCESTOR'S **LIKENESS,** BUT HER PENCHANT FOR **CHICANERY.**
YOU PRICKED MY FINGER IN LU.
WHAT?
WITH A JADE RING.
THEN YOU DISAPPEARED AND ALL WAS AS IT HAD BEEN THE DAY BEFORE YOU CAME.
HOW COULD YOU KNOW THIS?

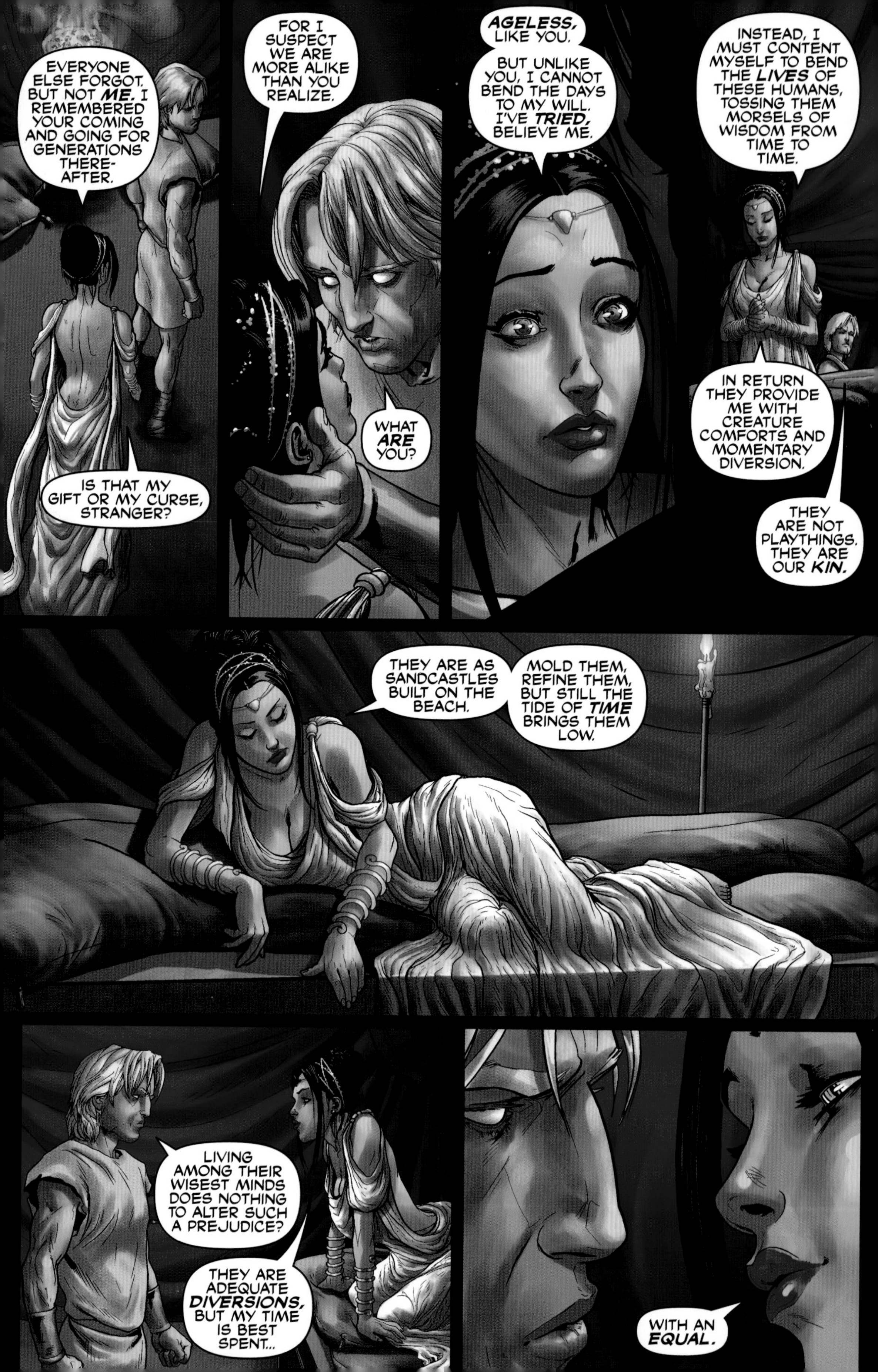
EVERYONE ELSE FORGOT, BUT NOT ME. I REMEMBERED YOUR COMING AND GOING FOR GENERATIONS THERE-AFTER.
IS THAT MY GIFT OR MY CURSE, STRANGER?
FOR I SUSPECT WE ARE MORE ALIKE THAN YOU REALIZE.
WHAT ARE YOU?
AGELESS, LIKE YOU.
BUT UNLIKE YOU, I CANNOT BEND THE DAYS TO MY WILL. I'VE TRIED, BELIEVE ME.
INSTEAD, I MUST CONTENT MYSELF TO BEND THE LIVES OF THESE HUMANS, TOSSING THEM MORSELS OF WISDOM FROM TIME TO TIME.
IN RETURN THEY PROVIDE ME WITH CREATURE COMFORTS AND MOMENTARY DIVERSION.
THEY ARE NOT PLAYTHINGS. THEY ARE OUR KIN.
THEY ARE AS SANDCASTLES BUILT ON THE BEACH.
MOLD THEM, REFINE THEM, BUT STILL THE TIDE OF TIME BRINGS THEM LOW.
LIVING AMONG THEIR WISEST MINDS DOES NOTHING TO ALTER SUCH A PREJUDICE?
THEY ARE ADEQUATE DIVERSIONS, BUT MY TIME IS BEST SPENT...
WITH AN EQUAL.

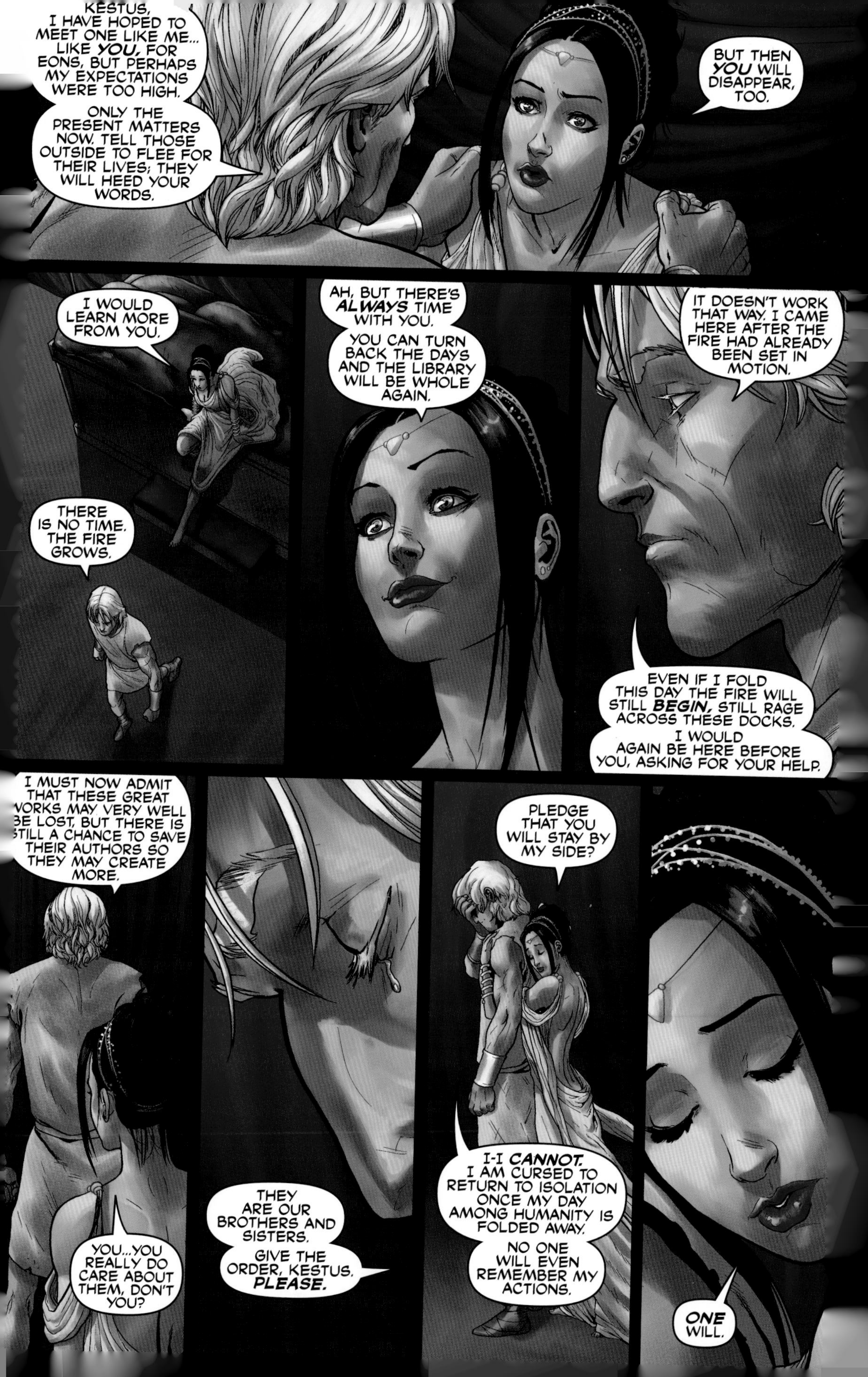
KESTUS, I HAVE HOPED TO MEET ONE LIKE ME... LIKE YOU, FOR EONS, BUT PERHAPS MY EXPECTATIONS WERE TOO HIGH.
ONLY THE PRESENT MATTERS NOW. TELL THOSE OUTSIDE TO FLEE FOR THEIR LIVES; THEY WILL HEED YOUR WORDS.
BUT THEN YOU WILL DISAPPEAR, TOO.
I WOULD LEARN MORE FROM YOU.
THERE IS NO TIME. THE FIRE GROWS.
AH, BUT THERE'S ALWAYS TIME WITH YOU.
YOU CAN TURN BACK THE DAYS AND THE LIBRARY WILL BE WHOLE AGAIN.
IT DOESN'T WORK THAT WAY. I CAME HERE AFTER THE FIRE HAD ALREADY BEEN SET IN MOTION.
EVEN IF I FOLD THIS DAY THE FIRE WILL STILL BEGIN, STILL RAGE ACROSS THESE DOCKS.
I WOULD AGAIN BE HERE BEFORE YOU, ASKING FOR YOUR HELP.
I MUST NOW ADMIT THAT THESE GREAT WORKS MAY VERY WELL BE LOST, BUT THERE IS STILL A CHANCE TO SAVE THEIR AUTHORS SO THEY MAY CREATE MORE.
YOU...YOU REALLY DO CARE ABOUT THEM, DON'T YOU?
THEY ARE OUR BROTHERS AND SISTERS.
GIVE THE ORDER, KESTUS, PLEASE.
PLEDGE THAT YOU WILL STAY BY MY SIDE?
I-I CANNOT. I AM CURSED TO RETURN TO ISOLATION ONCE MY DAY AMONG HUMANITY IS FOLDED AWAY.
NO ONE WILL EVEN REMEMBER MY ACTIONS.
ONE WILL.

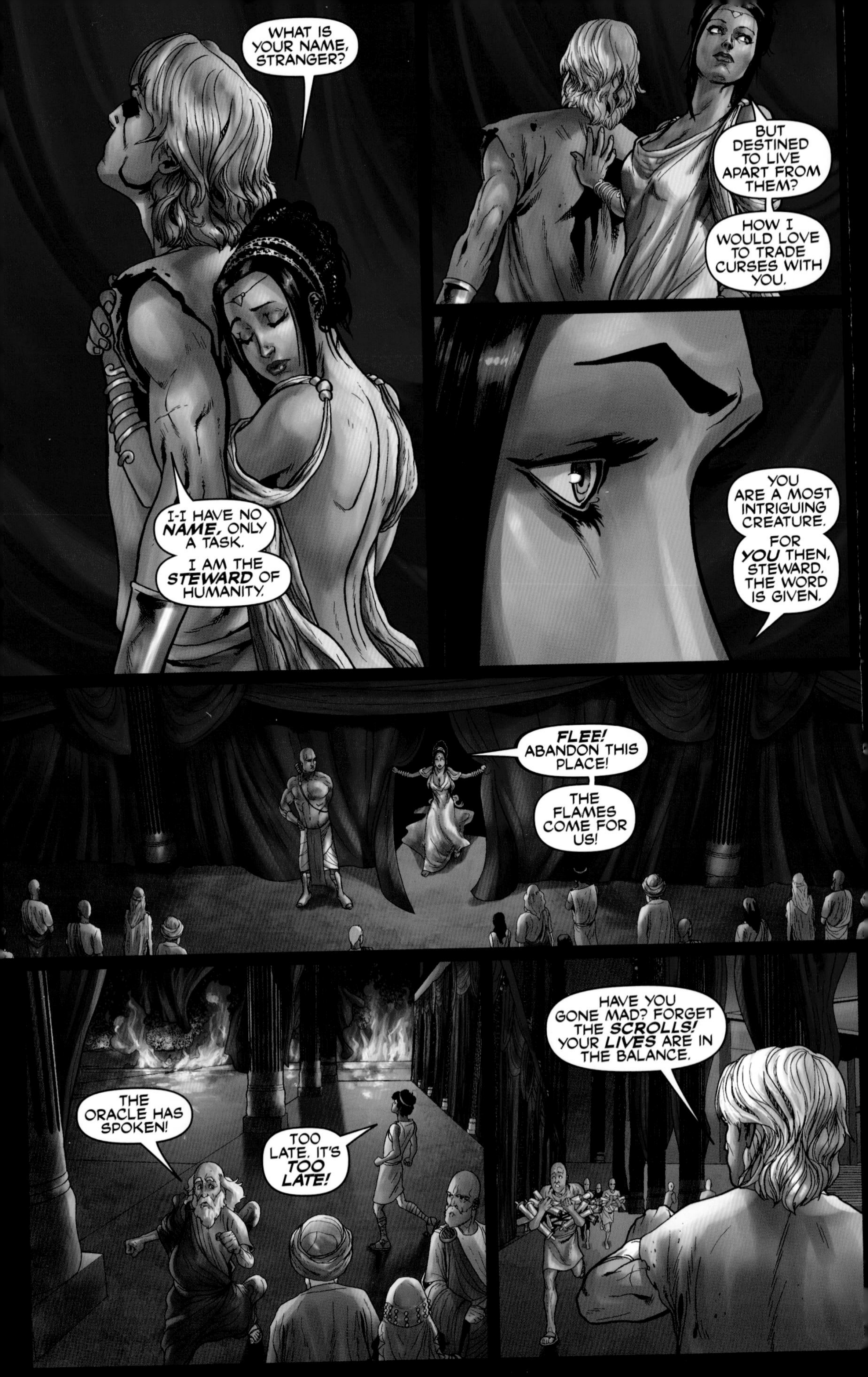
WHAT IS YOUR NAME, STRANGER?
I-I HAVE NO NAME, ONLY A TASK.
I AM THE STEWARD OF HUMANITY.
BUT DESTINED TO LIVE APART FROM THEM?
HOW I WOULD LOVE TO TRADE CURSES WITH YOU.
YOU ARE A MOST INTRIGUING CREATURE.
FOR YOU THEN, STEWARD, THE WORD IS GIVEN.
FLEE! ABANDON THIS PLACE!
THE FLAMES COME FOR US!
THE ORACLE HAS SPOKEN!
TOO LATE. IT'S TOO LATE!
HAVE YOU GONE MAD? FORGET THE SCROLLS! YOUR LIVES ARE IN THE BALANCE.

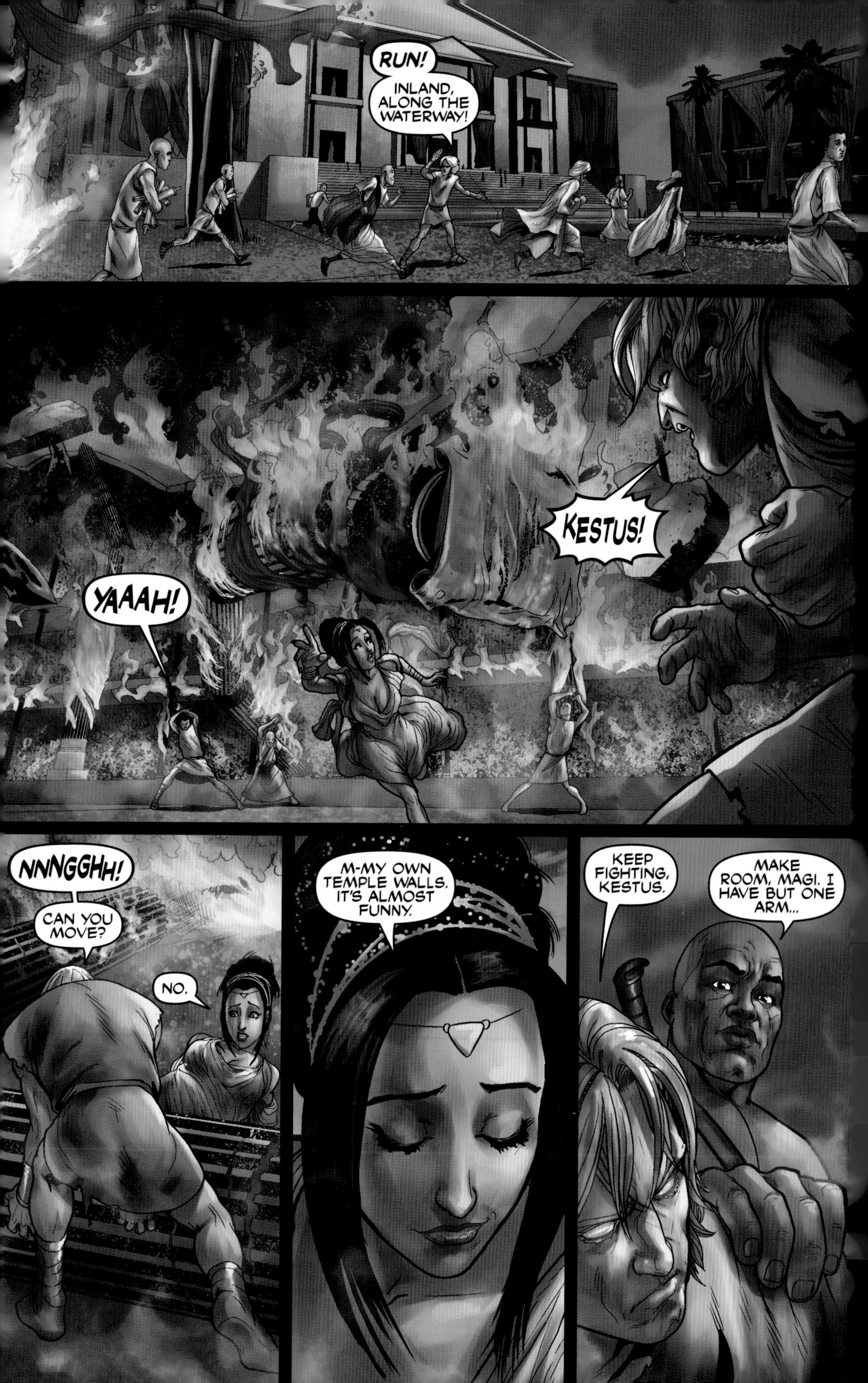
RUN!
INLAND, ALONG THE WATERWAY!
KESTUS!
YAAAH!
NNNGGHH!
CAN YOU MOVE?
NO.
M-MY OWN TEMPLE WALLS. IT'S ALMOST FUNNY.
KEEP FIGHTING, KESTUS.
MAKE ROOM, MAGI. I HAVE BUT ONE ARM...

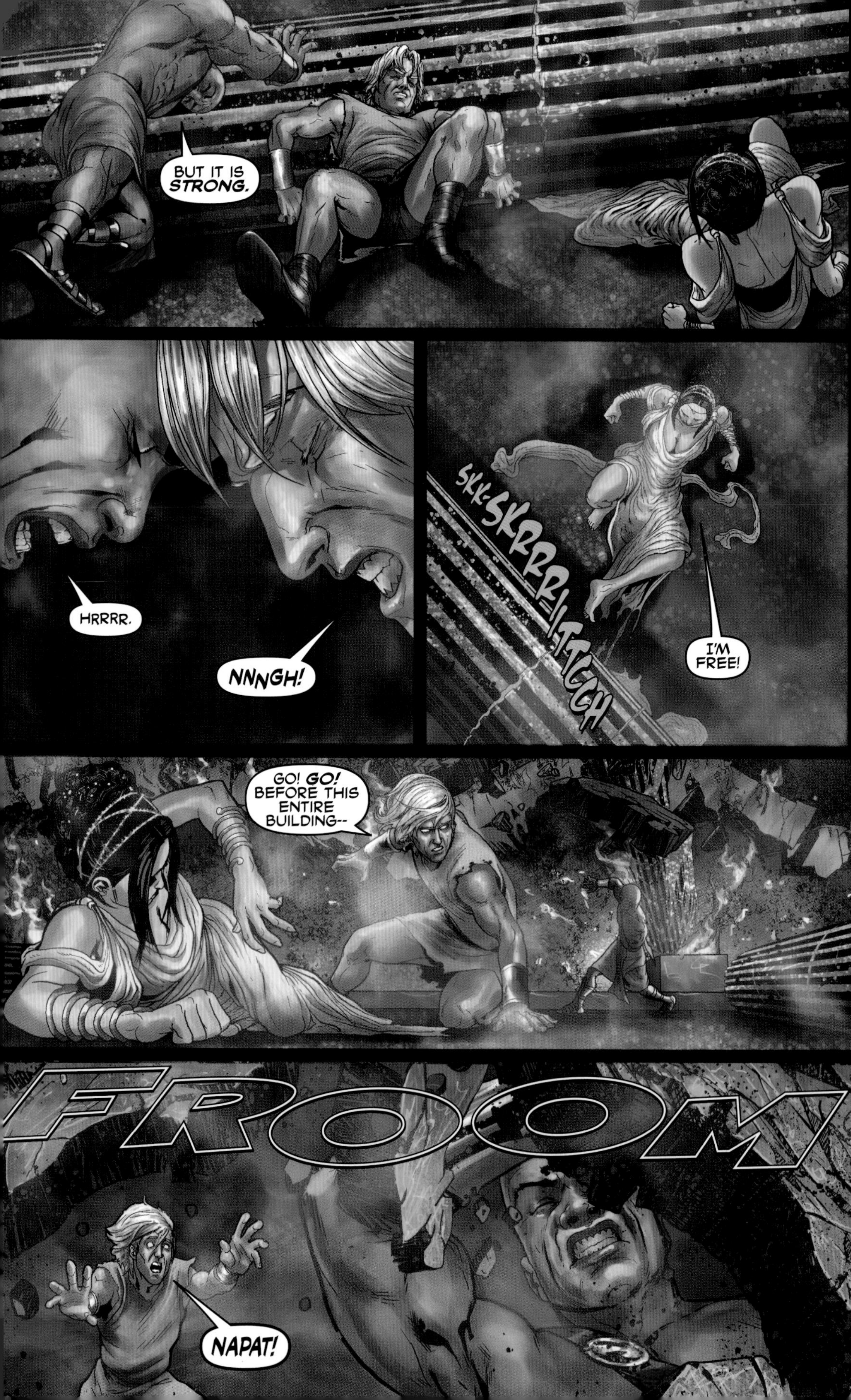

BUT IT IS STRONG.
HRRRR.
NNNGH!
SKK-SKRRRITTCCH
I'M FREE!
GO! GO! BEFORE THIS ENTIRE BUILDING--
FROOM
NAPAT!

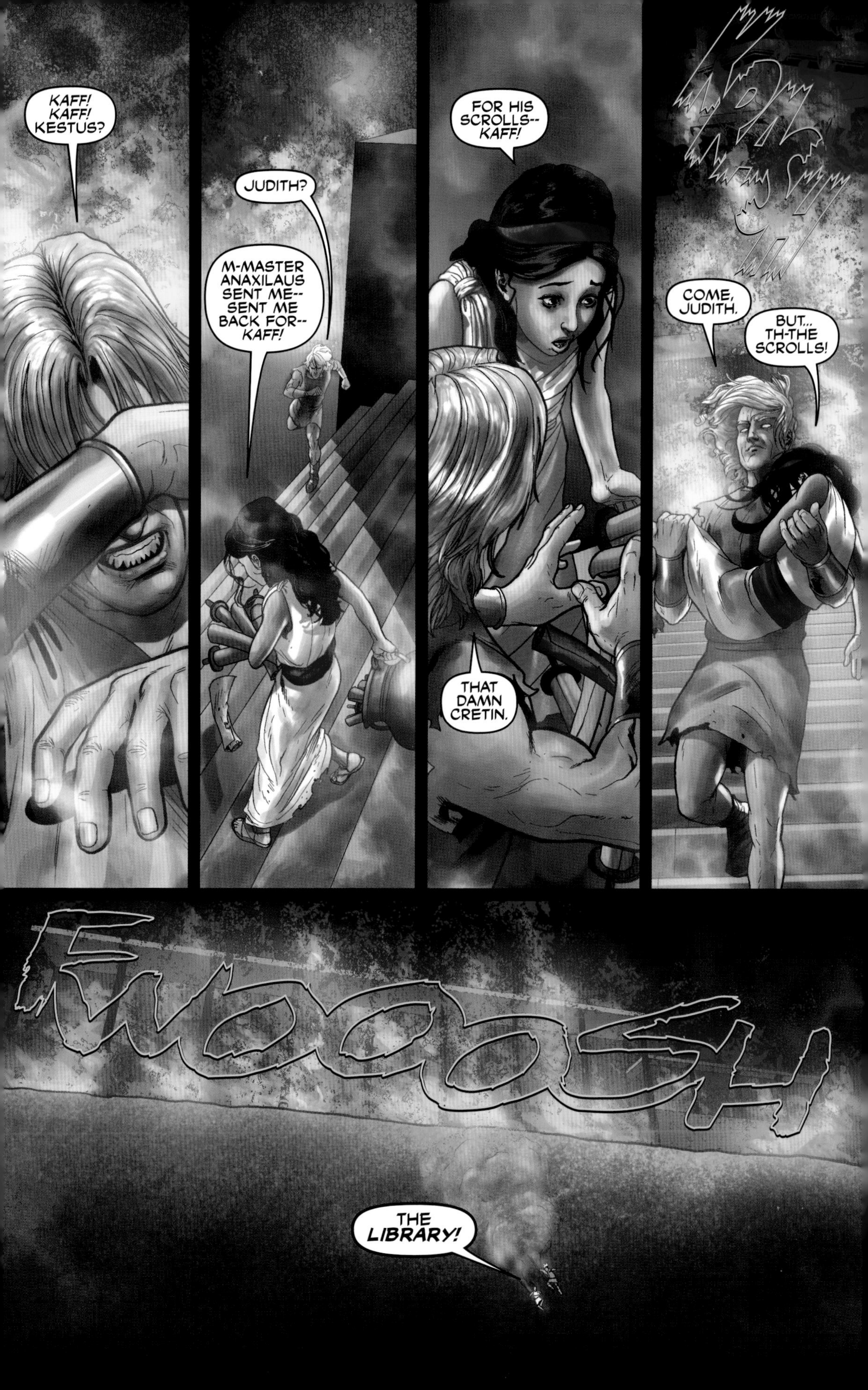
KAFF! KAFF! KESTUS?
JUDITH?
M-MASTER ANAXILAUS SENT ME-- SENT ME BACK FOR-- KAFF!
FOR HIS SCROLLS-- KAFF!
THAT DAMN CRETIN.
COME, JUDITH.
BUT... TH-THE SCROLLS!
THE LIBRARY!

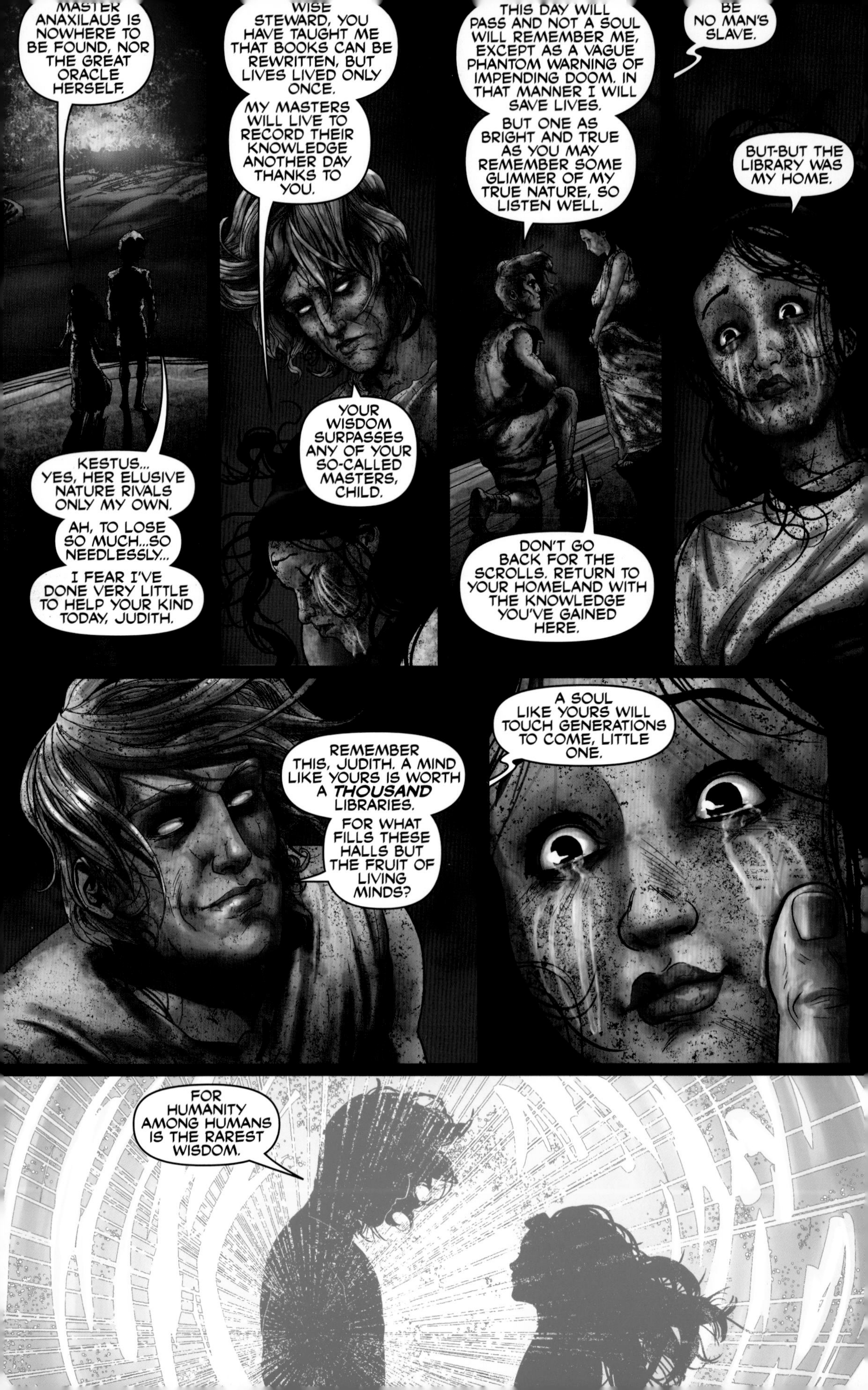
MASTER ANAXILAUS IS NOWHERE TO BE FOUND, NOR THE GREAT ORACLE HERSELF.
KESTUS... YES, HER ELUSIVE NATURE RIVALS ONLY MY OWN.
AH, TO LOSE SO MUCH...SO NEEDLESSLY...
I FEAR I'VE DONE VERY LITTLE TO HELP YOUR KIND TODAY, JUDITH.
WISE STEWARD, YOU HAVE TAUGHT ME THAT BOOKS CAN BE REWRITTEN, BUT LIVES LIVED ONLY ONCE.
MY MASTERS WILL LIVE TO RECORD THEIR KNOWLEDGE ANOTHER DAY THANKS TO YOU.
YOUR WISDOM SURPASSES ANY OF YOUR SO-CALLED MASTERS, CHILD.
THIS DAY WILL PASS AND NOT A SOUL WILL REMEMBER ME, EXCEPT AS A VAGUE PHANTOM WARNING OF IMPENDING DOOM. IN THAT MANNER I WILL SAVE LIVES.
BUT ONE AS BRIGHT AND TRUE AS YOU MAY REMEMBER SOME GLIMMER OF MY TRUE NATURE, SO LISTEN WELL.
DON'T GO BACK FOR THE SCROLLS. RETURN TO YOUR HOMELAND WITH THE KNOWLEDGE YOU'VE GAINED HERE.
BE NO MAN'S SLAVE.
BUT-BUT THE LIBRARY WAS MY HOME.
REMEMBER THIS, JUDITH. A MIND LIKE YOURS IS WORTH A *THOUSAND* LIBRARIES.
FOR WHAT FILLS THESE HALLS BUT THE FRUIT OF LIVING MINDS?
A SOUL LIKE YOURS WILL TOUCH GENERATIONS TO COME, LITTLE ONE.
FOR HUMANITY AMONG HUMANS IS THE RAREST WISDOM.

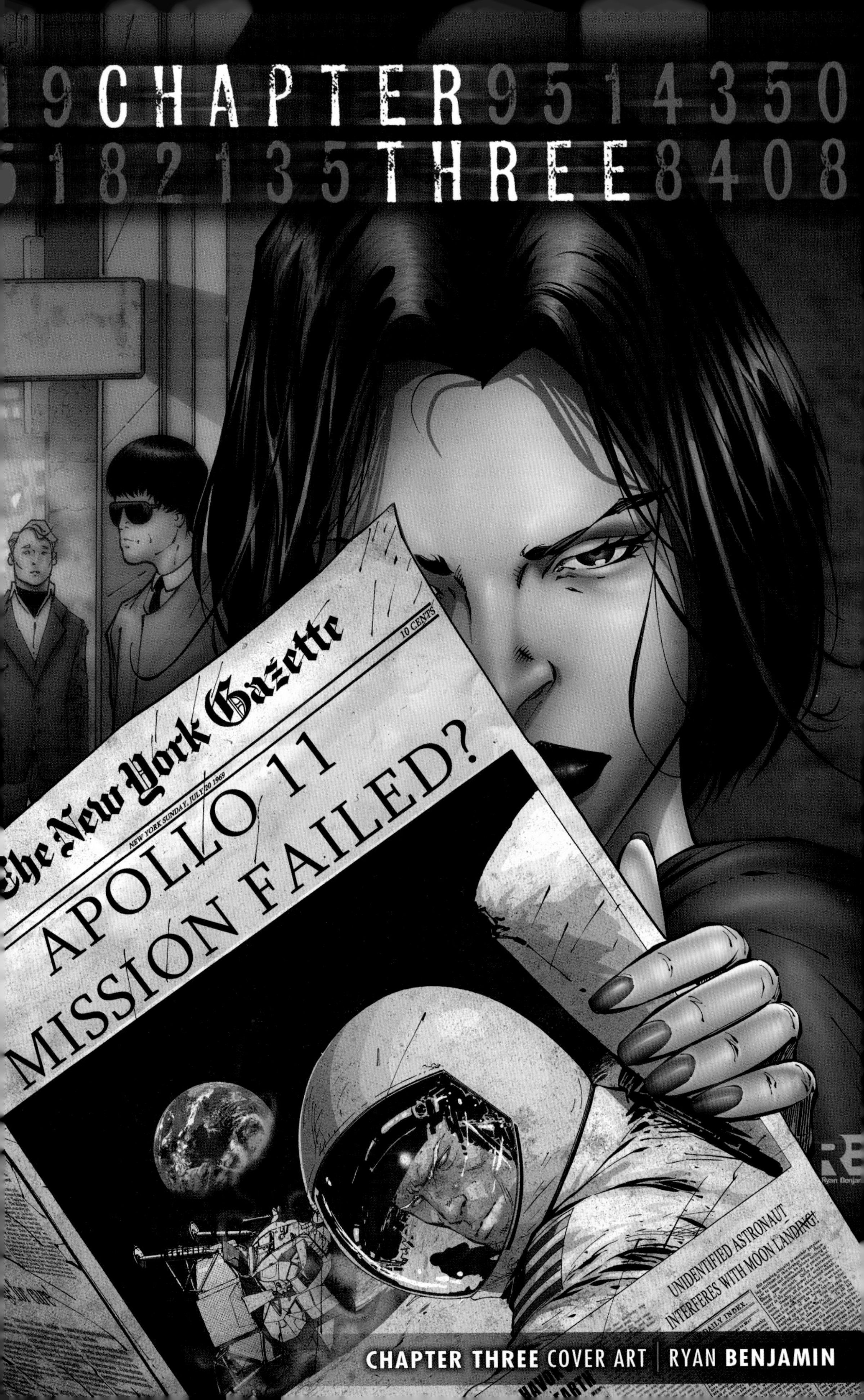

CHAPTER
THREE
The New York Gazette
10 CENTS
NEW YORK SUNDAY, JULY 20 1969
APOLLO 11
MISSION FAILED?
UNIDENTIFIED ASTRONAUT
INTERFERES WITH MOON LANDING!

CHAPTER THREE COVER ART | RYAN BENJAMIN

JULY 16 1969

ONE GIANT LEAP

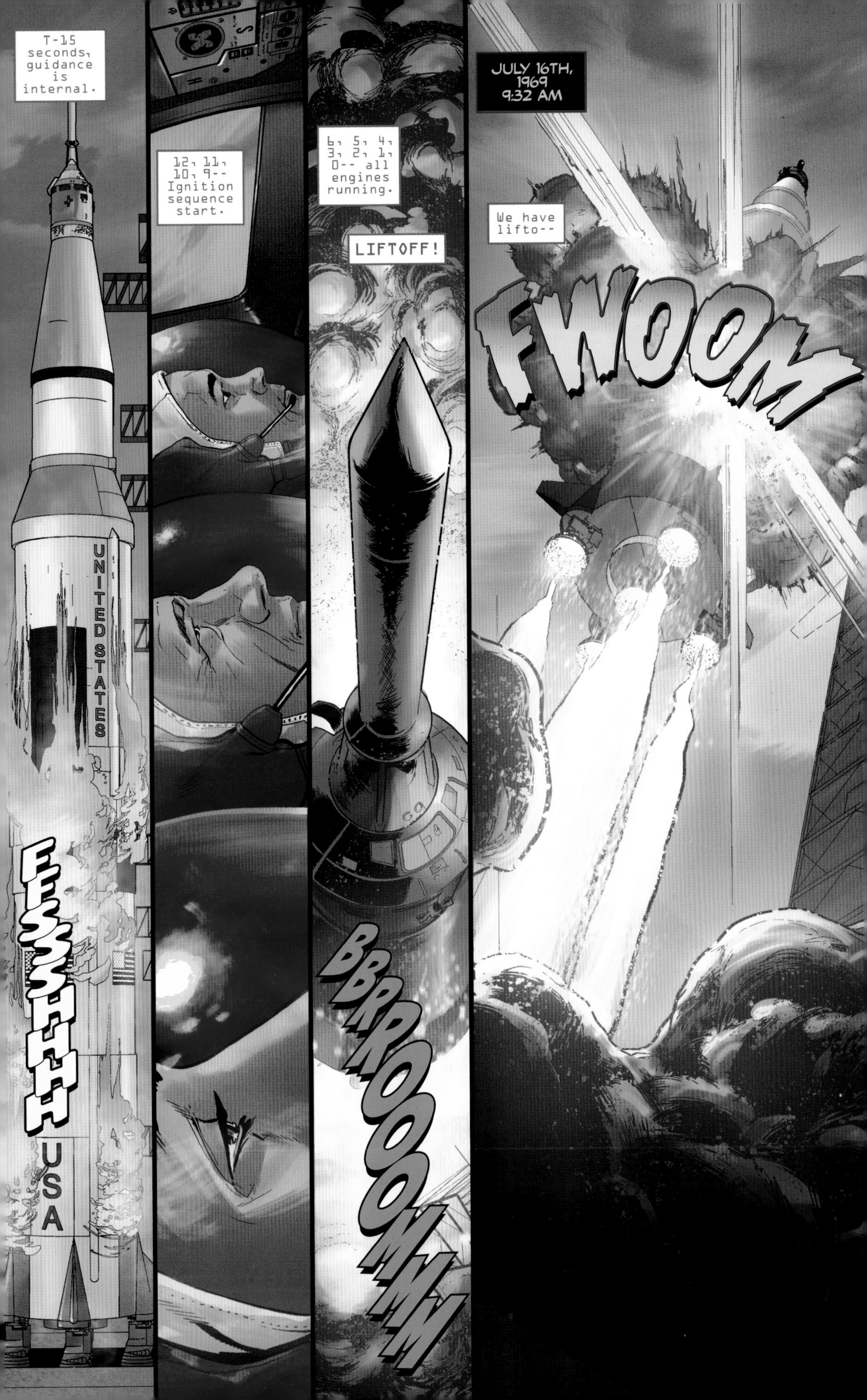
T-15 seconds, guidance is internal.
FFSSSHHHH
UNITED STATES
USA
12, 11, 10, 9-- Ignition sequence start.
6, 5, 4, 3, 2, 1, 0-- all engines running.
LIFTOFF!
BBRROOOOMMM
JULY 16TH, 1969 9:32 AM
We have lifto--
FWOOM

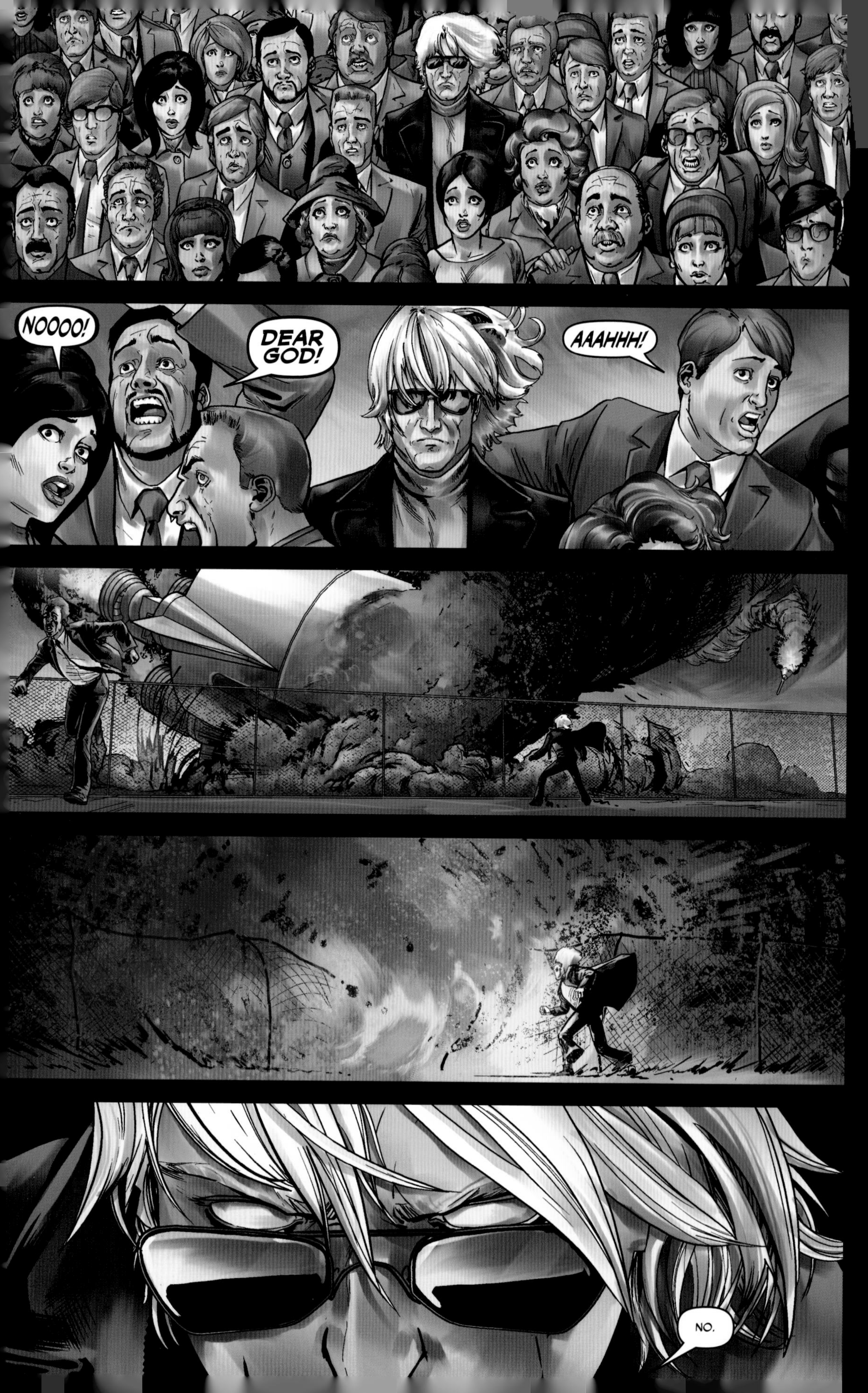
NOOOO!
DEAR GOD!
AAAHHH!
NO.

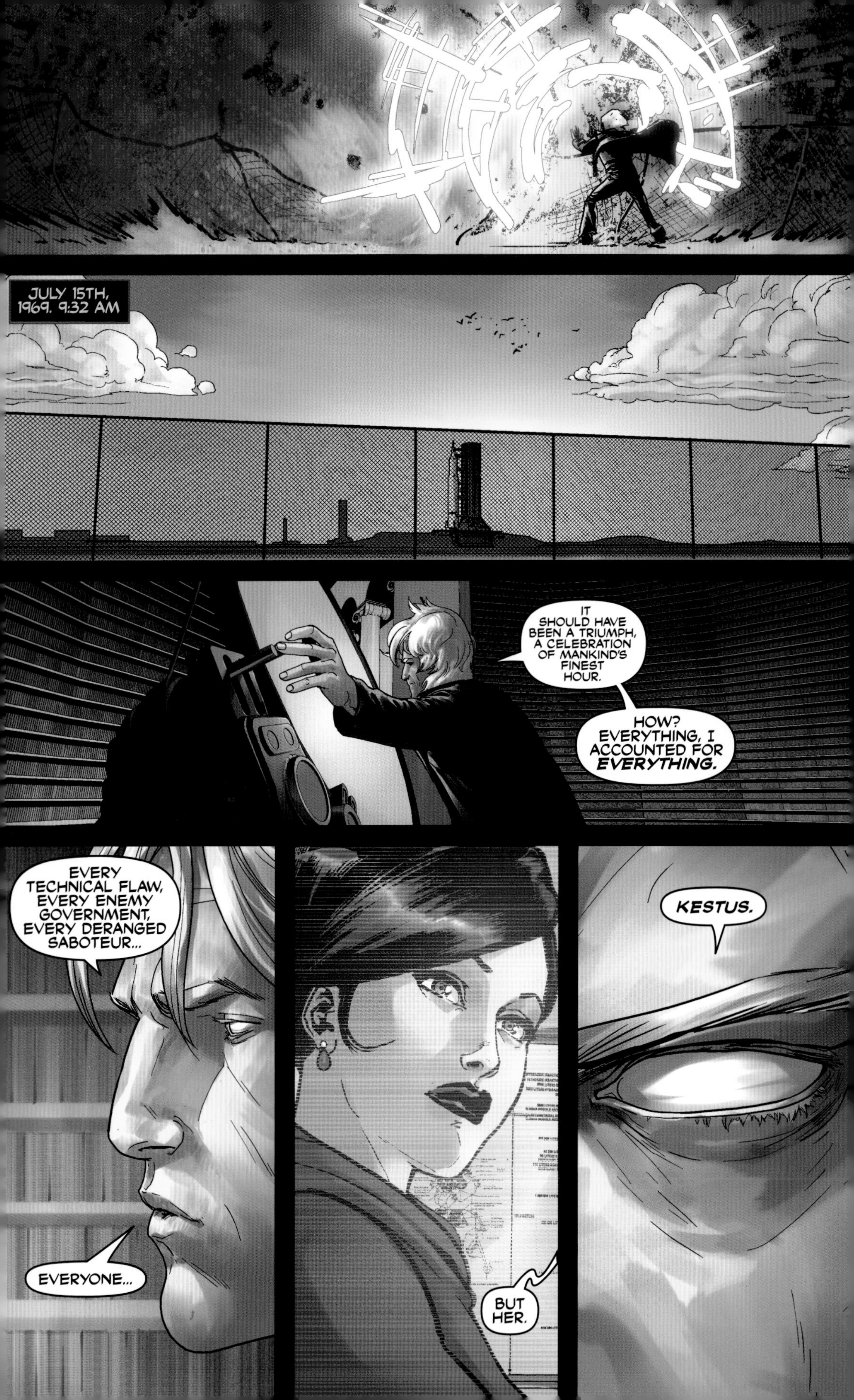
JULY 15TH, 1969, 9:32 AM
IT SHOULD HAVE BEEN A TRIUMPH, A CELEBRATION OF MANKIND'S FINEST HOUR.
HOW? EVERYTHING, I ACCOUNTED FOR EVERYTHING.
EVERY TECHNICAL FLAW, EVERY ENEMY GOVERNMENT, EVERY DERANGED SABOTEUR...
EVERYONE...
BUT HER.
KESTUS.

THERE YOU ARE.

KAREN, DID YOU HEAR A SINGLE WORD I JUST SAID?

SORRY. SUDDEN CASE OF DEJA VU.

COME ON, PEOPLE, THIS IS THE MOST IMPORTANT DAY IN **AMERICAN HISTORY** SINCE WORLD WAR II.

HELL, IT'S THE MOST IMPORTANT DAY IN **HUMAN** HISTORY SINCE WE STARTED PUTTING **BC'S** AND **AD'S** BEHIND THE DATELINE.

THIS COUNTRY HAS NO SHORTAGE OF SABOTEURS AND LUNATICS, INTERNAL AND EXTERNAL, WHO'D LOVE NOTHING BETTER THAN TO TURN THAT SATURN V INTO THE WORLD BIGGEST BONFIRE.

WE DO OUR JOB TODAY AND NO ONE EVER LEARNS ABOUT THIS SECRET CLUBHOUSE OF OURS. ALL GLORY TO THE SLIDE RULE BRIGADE.

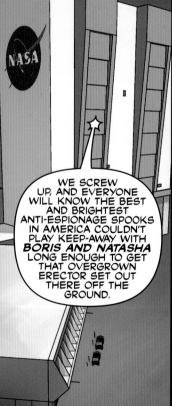

NASA

WE SCREW UP, AND EVERYONE WILL KNOW THE BEST AND BRIGHTEST ANTI-ESPIONAGE SPOOKS IN AMERICA COULDN'T PLAY KEEP-AWAY WITH **BORIS AND NATASHA** LONG ENOUGH TO GET THAT OVERGROWN ERECTOR SET OUT THERE OFF THE GROUND.

BEWARE OF FALLING IDIOMS.

HE'S ON A ROLL.

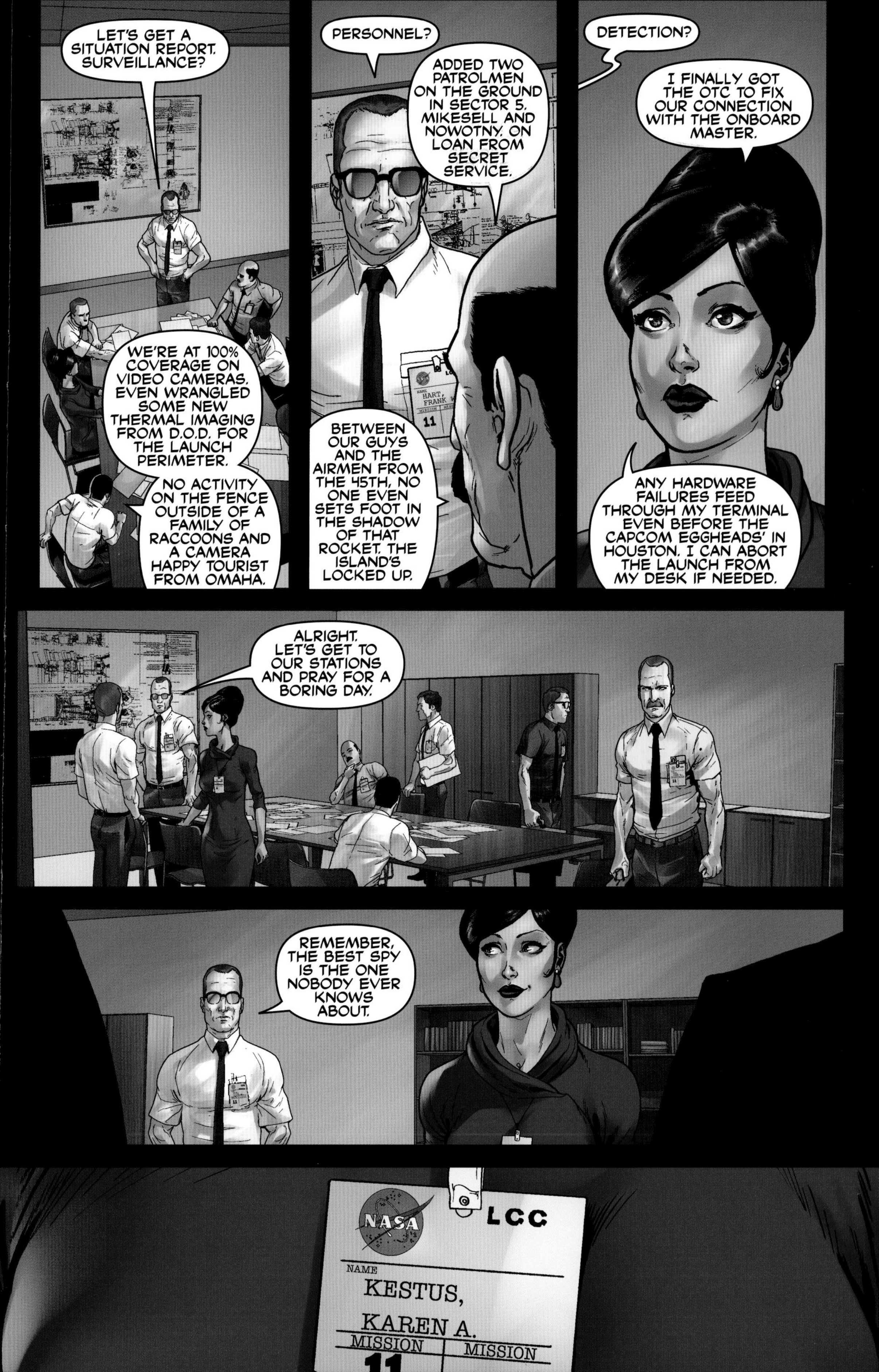
LET'S GET A SITUATION REPORT. SURVEILLANCE?
WE'RE AT 100% COVERAGE ON VIDEO CAMERAS. EVEN WRANGLED SOME NEW THERMAL IMAGING FROM D.O.D. FOR THE LAUNCH PERIMETER.
NO ACTIVITY ON THE FENCE OUTSIDE OF A FAMILY OF RACCOONS AND A CAMERA HAPPY TOURIST FROM OMAHA.
PERSONNEL?
ADDED TWO PATROLMEN ON THE GROUND IN SECTOR 5, MIKESELL AND NOWOTNY, ON LOAN FROM SECRET SERVICE.
NAME HART, FRANK
MISSION 11
BETWEEN OUR GUYS AND THE AIRMEN FROM THE 45TH, NO ONE EVEN SETS FOOT IN THE SHADOW OF THAT ROCKET. THE ISLAND'S LOCKED UP.
DETECTION?
I FINALLY GOT THE OTC TO FIX OUR CONNECTION WITH THE ONBOARD MASTER.
ANY HARDWARE FAILURES FEED THROUGH MY TERMINAL EVEN BEFORE THE CAPCOM EGGHEADS' IN HOUSTON. I CAN ABORT THE LAUNCH FROM MY DESK IF NEEDED.
ALRIGHT. LET'S GET TO OUR STATIONS AND PRAY FOR A BORING DAY.
REMEMBER, THE BEST SPY IS THE ONE NOBODY EVER KNOWS ABOUT.
NASA
LCC
NAME
KESTUS, KAREN A.
MISSION 11
MISSION

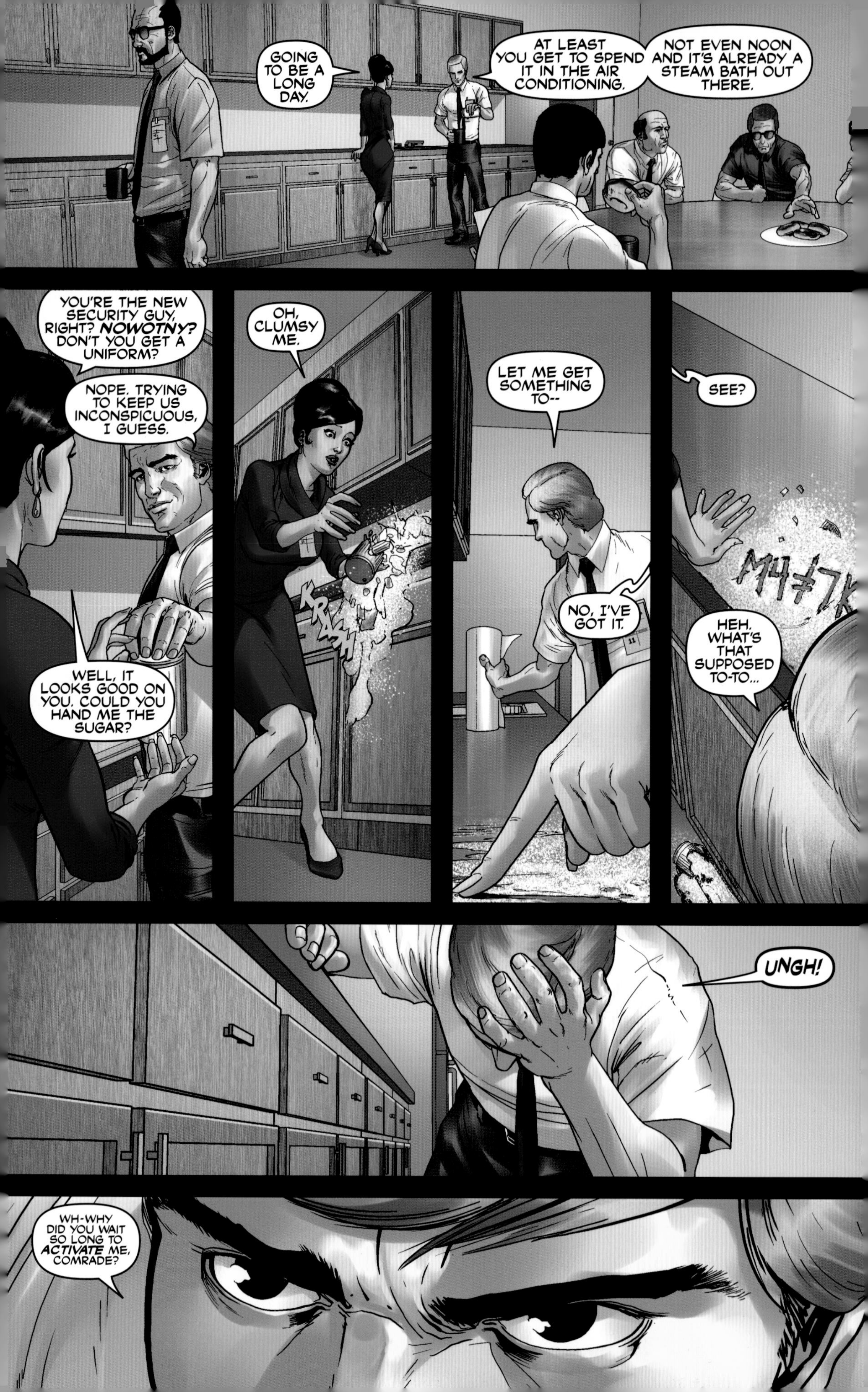
GOING TO BE A LONG DAY.
AT LEAST YOU GET TO SPEND IT IN THE AIR CONDITIONING.
NOT EVEN NOON AND IT'S ALREADY A STEAM BATH OUT THERE.
YOU'RE THE NEW SECURITY GUY, RIGHT? NOWOTNY? DON'T YOU GET A UNIFORM?
NOPE. TRYING TO KEEP US INCONSPICUOUS, I GUESS.
WELL, IT LOOKS GOOD ON YOU. COULD YOU HAND ME THE SUGAR?
OH, CLUMSY ME.
KRASH
LET ME GET SOMETHING TO--
NO, I'VE GOT IT.
SEE?
HEH. WHAT'S THAT SUPPOSED TO-TO...
UNGH!
WH-WHY DID YOU WAIT SO LONG TO ACTIVATE ME, COMRADE?

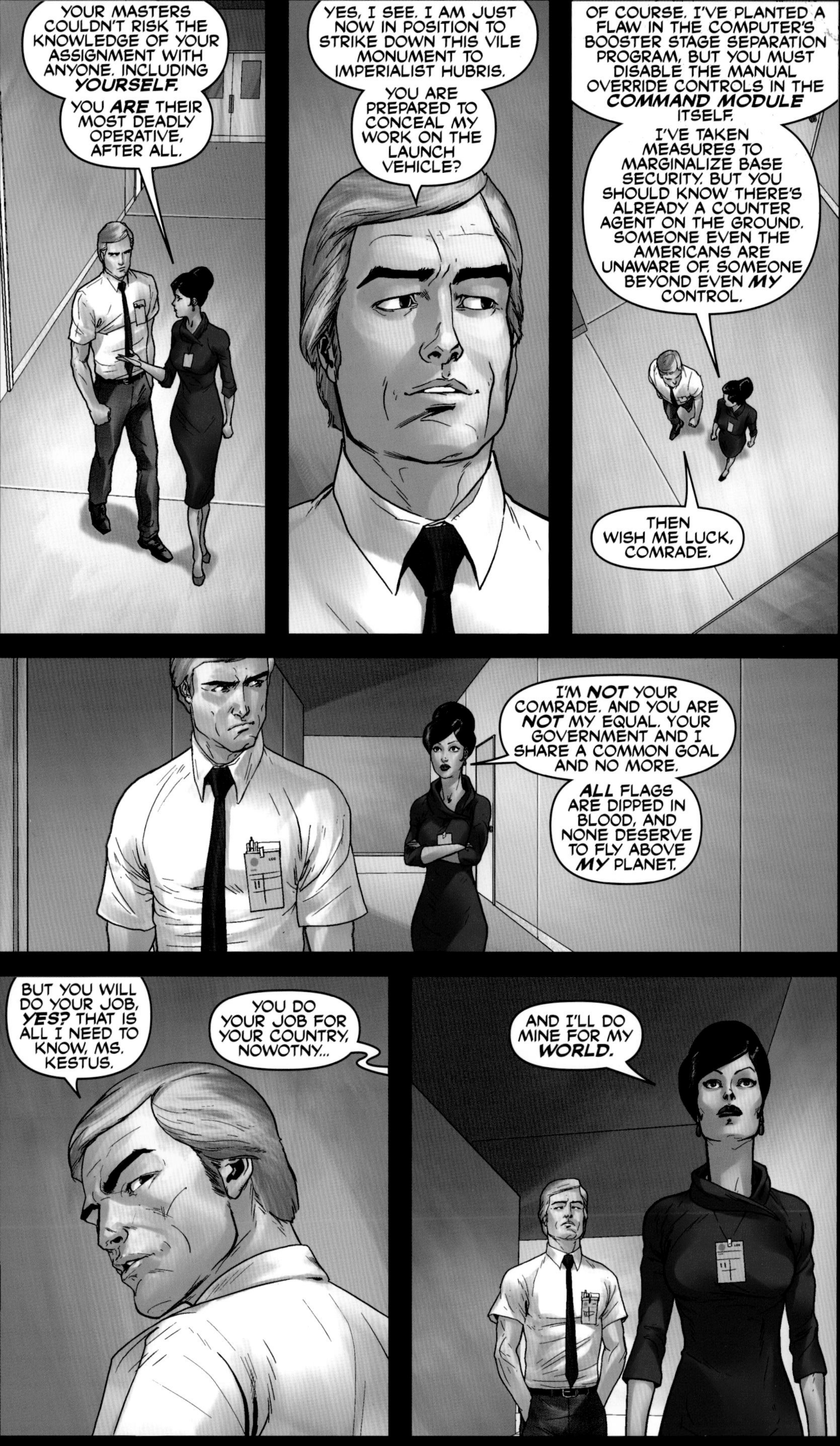

YOUR MASTERS COULDN'T RISK THE KNOWLEDGE OF YOUR ASSIGNMENT WITH ANYONE. INCLUDING YOURSELF.
YOU ARE THEIR MOST DEADLY OPERATIVE, AFTER ALL.
YES, I SEE. I AM JUST NOW IN POSITION TO STRIKE DOWN THIS VILE MONUMENT TO IMPERIALIST HUBRIS.
YOU ARE PREPARED TO CONCEAL MY WORK ON THE LAUNCH VEHICLE?
OF COURSE. I'VE PLANTED A FLAW IN THE COMPUTER'S BOOSTER STAGE SEPARATION PROGRAM, BUT YOU MUST DISABLE THE MANUAL OVERRIDE CONTROLS IN THE COMMAND MODULE ITSELF.
I'VE TAKEN MEASURES TO MARGINALIZE BASE SECURITY. BUT YOU SHOULD KNOW THERE'S ALREADY A COUNTER AGENT ON THE GROUND. SOMEONE EVEN THE AMERICANS ARE UNAWARE OF. SOMEONE BEYOND EVEN MY CONTROL.
THEN WISH ME LUCK, COMRADE.
I'M NOT YOUR COMRADE. AND YOU ARE NOT MY EQUAL. YOUR GOVERNMENT AND I SHARE A COMMON GOAL AND NO MORE.
ALL FLAGS ARE DIPPED IN BLOOD, AND NONE DESERVE TO FLY ABOVE MY PLANET.
BUT YOU WILL DO YOUR JOB, YES? THAT IS ALL I NEED TO KNOW, MS. KESTUS.
YOU DO YOUR JOB FOR YOUR COUNTRY, NOWOTNY...
AND I'LL DO MINE FOR MY WORLD.

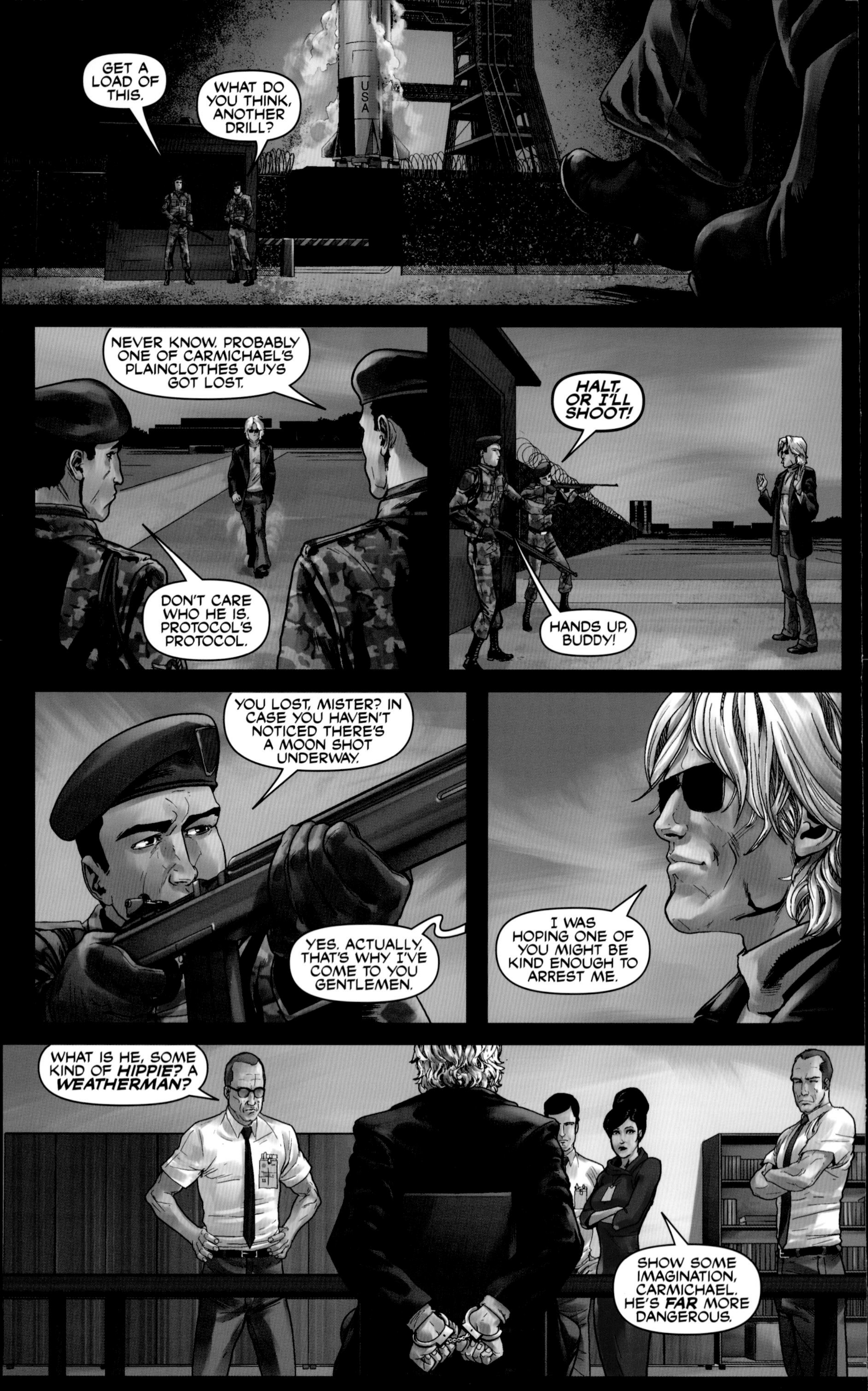
GET A LOAD OF THIS.
WHAT DO YOU THINK, ANOTHER DRILL?
NEVER KNOW. PROBABLY ONE OF CARMICHAEL'S PLAINCLOTHES GUYS GOT LOST.
DON'T CARE WHO HE IS. PROTOCOL'S PROTOCOL.
HALT, OR I'LL SHOOT!
HANDS UP, BUDDY!
YOU LOST, MISTER? IN CASE YOU HAVEN'T NOTICED THERE'S A MOON SHOT UNDERWAY.
YES. ACTUALLY, THAT'S WHY I'VE COME TO YOU GENTLEMEN.
I WAS HOPING ONE OF YOU MIGHT BE KIND ENOUGH TO ARREST ME.
WHAT IS HE, SOME KIND OF HIPPIE? A WEATHERMAN?
SHOW SOME IMAGINATION, CARMICHAEL. HE'S FAR MORE DANGEROUS.

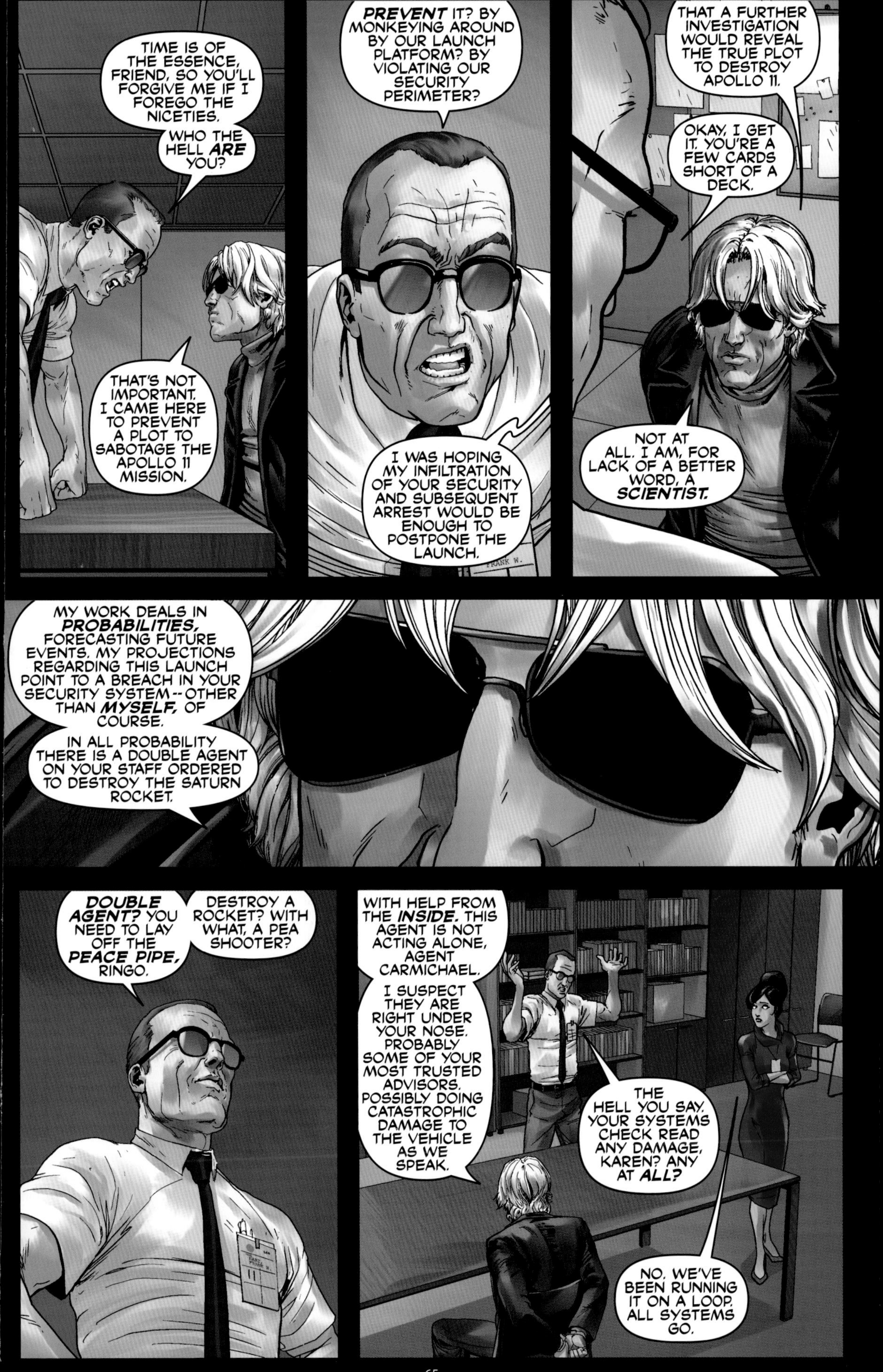
TIME IS OF THE ESSENCE, FRIEND, SO YOU'LL FORGIVE ME IF I FOREGO THE NICETIES.
WHO THE HELL ARE YOU?
THAT'S NOT IMPORTANT. I CAME HERE TO PREVENT A PLOT TO SABOTAGE THE APOLLO 11 MISSION.
PREVENT IT? BY MONKEYING AROUND BY OUR LAUNCH PLATFORM? BY VIOLATING OUR SECURITY PERIMETER?
I WAS HOPING MY INFILTRATION OF YOUR SECURITY AND SUBSEQUENT ARREST WOULD BE ENOUGH TO POSTPONE THE LAUNCH.
THAT A FURTHER INVESTIGATION WOULD REVEAL THE TRUE PLOT TO DESTROY APOLLO 11.
OKAY, I GET IT. YOU'RE A FEW CARDS SHORT OF A DECK.
NOT AT ALL. I AM, FOR LACK OF A BETTER WORD, A SCIENTIST.
MY WORK DEALS IN PROBABILITIES, FORECASTING FUTURE EVENTS. MY PROJECTIONS REGARDING THIS LAUNCH POINT TO A BREACH IN YOUR SECURITY SYSTEM--OTHER THAN MYSELF, OF COURSE.
IN ALL PROBABILITY THERE IS A DOUBLE AGENT ON YOUR STAFF ORDERED TO DESTROY THE SATURN ROCKET.
DOUBLE AGENT? YOU NEED TO LAY OFF THE PEACE PIPE, RINGO.
DESTROY A ROCKET? WITH WHAT, A PEA SHOOTER?
WITH HELP FROM THE INSIDE. THIS AGENT IS NOT ACTING ALONE, AGENT CARMICHAEL.
I SUSPECT THEY ARE RIGHT UNDER YOUR NOSE. PROBABLY SOME OF YOUR MOST TRUSTED ADVISORS. POSSIBLY DOING CATASTROPHIC DAMAGE TO THE VEHICLE AS WE SPEAK.
THE HELL YOU SAY. YOUR SYSTEMS CHECK READ ANY DAMAGE, KAREN? ANY AT ALL?
NO, WE'VE BEEN RUNNING IT ON A LOOP. ALL SYSTEMS GO.

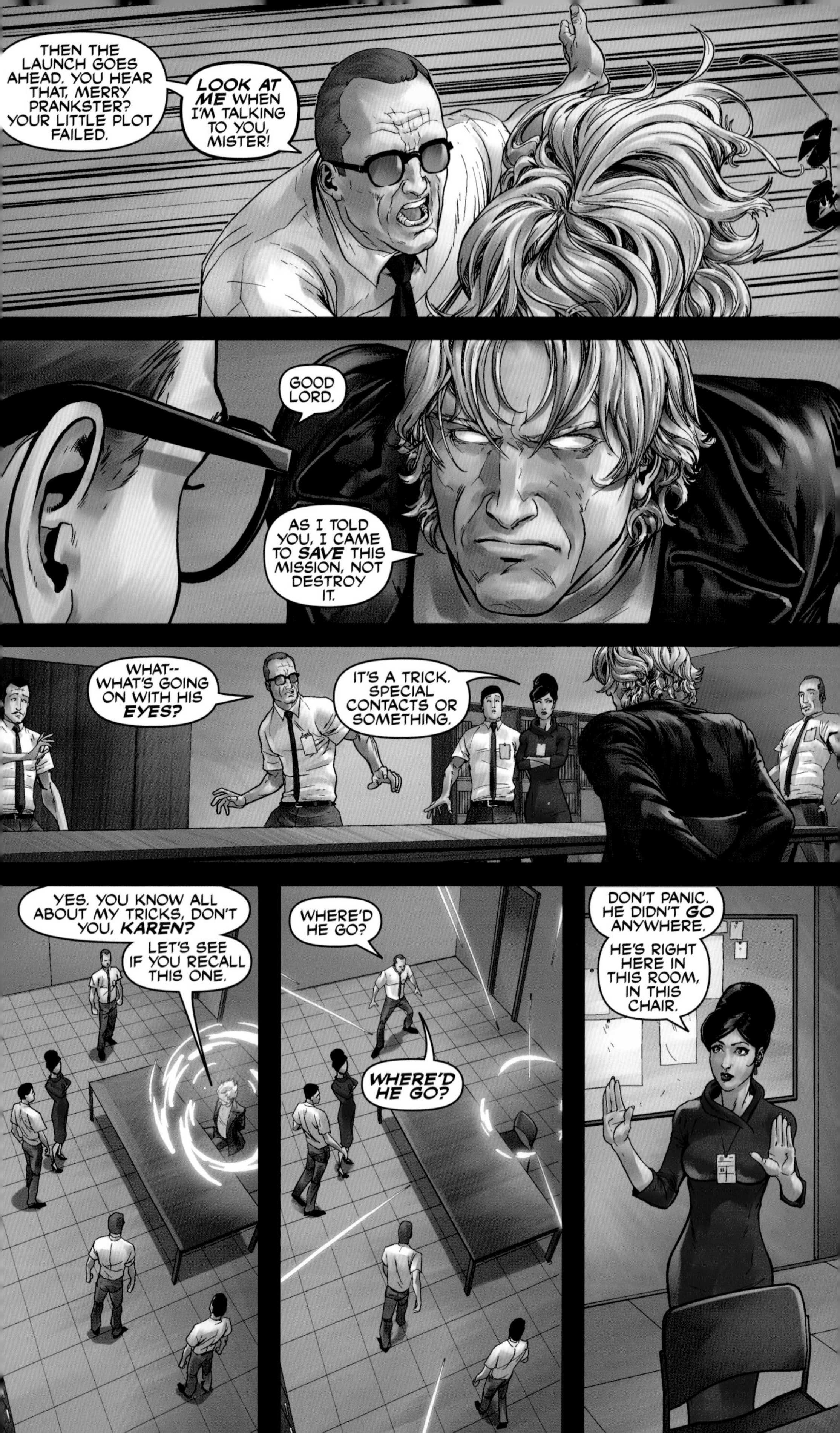
THEN THE LAUNCH GOES AHEAD. YOU HEAR THAT, MERRY PRANKSTER? YOUR LITTLE PLOT FAILED.
LOOK AT ME WHEN I'M TALKING TO YOU, MISTER!
GOOD LORD.
AS I TOLD YOU, I CAME TO SAVE THIS MISSION, NOT DESTROY IT.
WHAT-- WHAT'S GOING ON WITH HIS EYES?
IT'S A TRICK. SPECIAL CONTACTS OR SOMETHING.
YES. YOU KNOW ALL ABOUT MY TRICKS, DON'T YOU, KAREN?
LET'S SEE IF YOU RECALL THIS ONE.
WHERE'D HE GO?
WHERE'D HE GO?
DON'T PANIC, HE DIDN'T GO ANYWHERE.
HE'S RIGHT HERE IN THIS ROOM, IN THIS CHAIR.

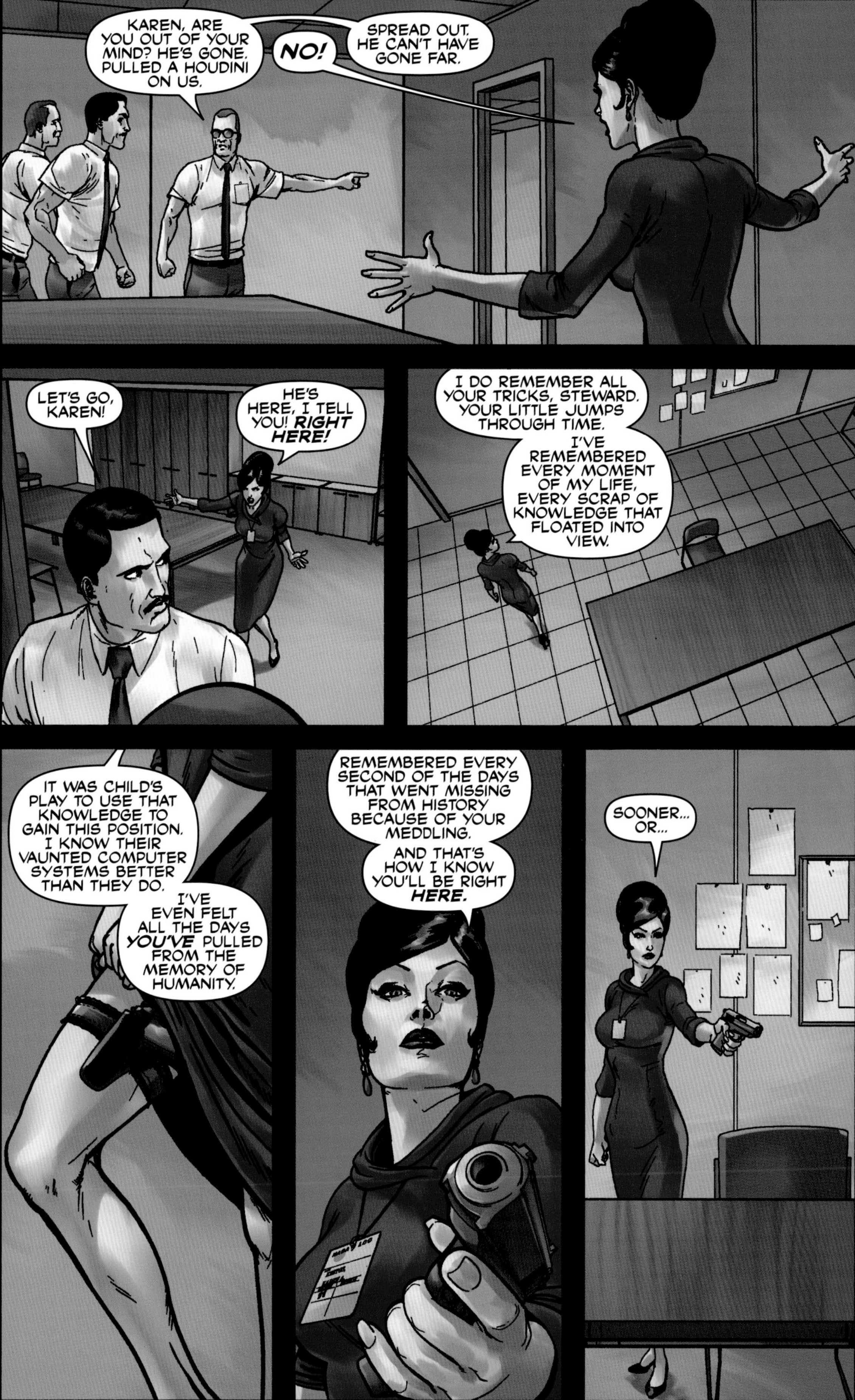
KAREN, ARE YOU OUT OF YOUR MIND? HE'S GONE. PULLED A HOUDINI ON US.
SPREAD OUT. HE CAN'T HAVE GONE FAR.
NO!
LET'S GO, KAREN!
HE'S HERE, I TELL YOU! RIGHT HERE!
I DO REMEMBER ALL YOUR TRICKS, STEWARD. YOUR LITTLE JUMPS THROUGH TIME.
I'VE REMEMBERED EVERY MOMENT OF MY LIFE, EVERY SCRAP OF KNOWLEDGE THAT FLOATED INTO VIEW.
IT WAS CHILD'S PLAY TO USE THAT KNOWLEDGE TO GAIN THIS POSITION. I KNOW THEIR VAUNTED COMPUTER SYSTEMS BETTER THAN THEY DO.
I'VE EVEN FELT ALL THE DAYS YOU'VE PULLED FROM THE MEMORY OF HUMANITY.
REMEMBERED EVERY SECOND OF THE DAYS THAT WENT MISSING FROM HISTORY BECAUSE OF YOUR MEDDLING.
AND THAT'S HOW I KNOW YOU'LL BE RIGHT HERE.
SOONER... OR...

HOW *DISAPPOINTING.*

THAT YOUR TRICK DIDN'T WORK?

NO, TO FIND YOU AT THE CENTER OF THIS *DESPICABLE* PLOT.

TO FIND *YOU* AMONG THOSE WHO WOULD BETRAY THEIR OWN SPECIES AT ITS FINEST HOUR.

AT THE HEIGHT OF ITS *HUBRIS,* RATHER.

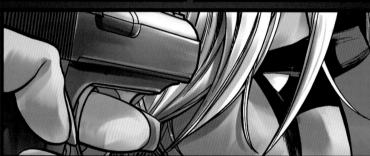

OPEN YOUR EYES, KESTUS.

JUST YESTERDAY THEY WERE WARRING WITH SPEARS AND STONES. TODAY THEY SET OFF FOR THE *STARS.*

LOOK CLOSER, STEWARD, AND YOU'LL SEE THEY'RE *STILL* FIGHTING WITH SPEARS AND STONES, ONLY BIGGER, MORE DEADLY ONES.

AND OVER THE SAME THINGS AS THEIR ANCESTORS; WATER, GOLD, GODS, LAND.

YOU WATCH THEM FROM AFAR, AS A SCIENTIST WOULD STUDY MICROBES, DUTIFULLY OBSERVING THEIR FITS OF PROGRESS.

BUT I LIVE AMONG THEM; I CANNOT ESCAPE THEM. I KNOW THEM AS YOU *NEVER* WILL.

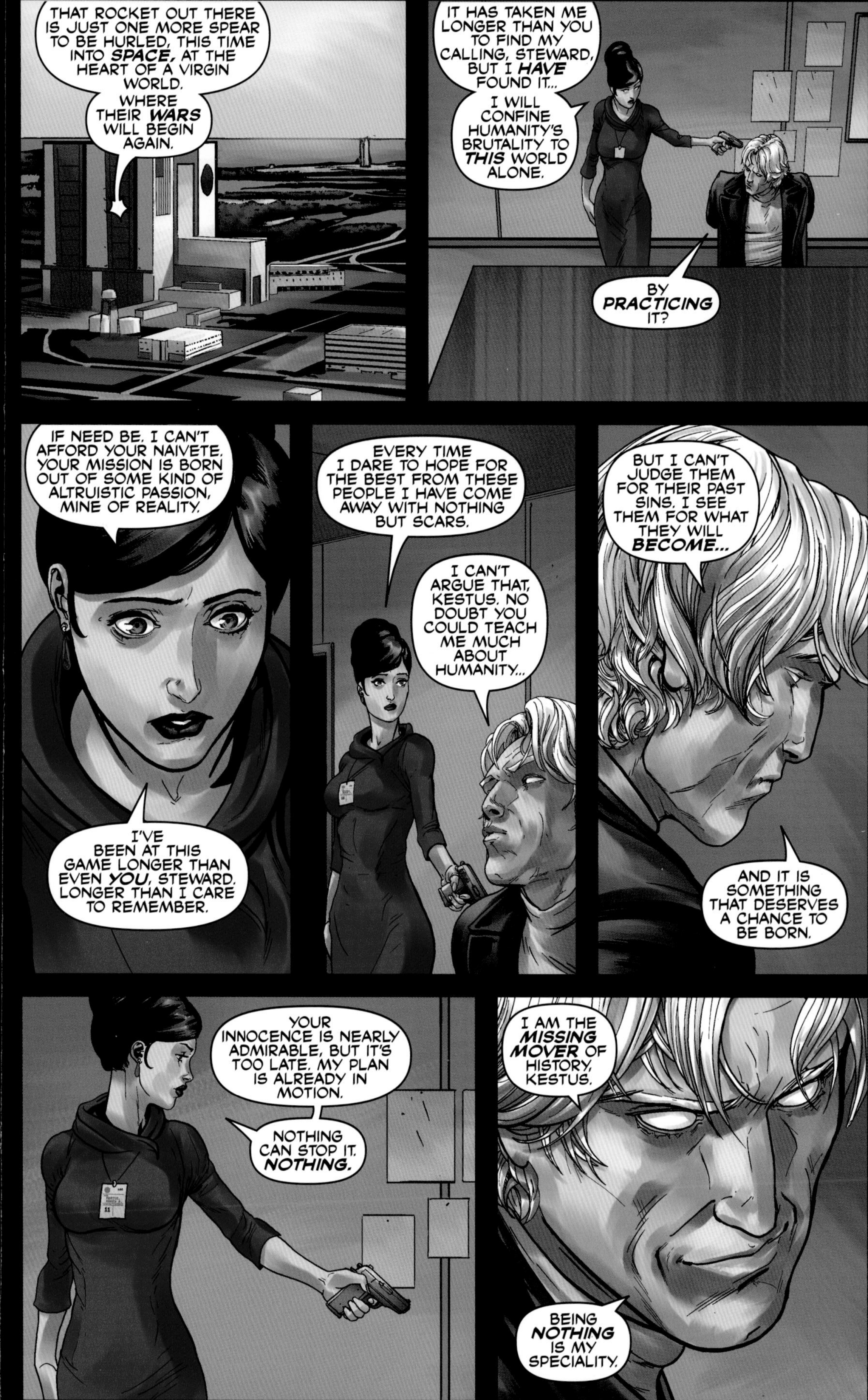
THAT ROCKET OUT THERE IS JUST ONE MORE SPEAR TO BE HURLED, THIS TIME INTO SPACE, AT THE HEART OF A VIRGIN WORLD.
WHERE THEIR WARS WILL BEGIN AGAIN.
IT HAS TAKEN ME LONGER THAN YOU TO FIND MY CALLING, STEWARD, BUT I HAVE FOUND IT...
I WILL CONFINE HUMANITY'S BRUTALITY TO THIS WORLD ALONE.
BY PRACTICING IT?
IF NEED BE. I CAN'T AFFORD YOUR NAIVETE. YOUR MISSION IS BORN OUT OF SOME KIND OF ALTRUISTIC PASSION, MINE OF REALITY.
I'VE BEEN AT THIS GAME LONGER THAN EVEN YOU, STEWARD. LONGER THAN I CARE TO REMEMBER.
EVERY TIME I DARE TO HOPE FOR THE BEST FROM THESE PEOPLE I HAVE COME AWAY WITH NOTHING BUT SCARS.
I CAN'T ARGUE THAT, KESTUS. NO DOUBT YOU COULD TEACH ME MUCH ABOUT HUMANITY...
BUT I CAN'T JUDGE THEM FOR THEIR PAST SINS. I SEE THEM FOR WHAT THEY WILL BECOME...
AND IT IS SOMETHING THAT DESERVES A CHANCE TO BE BORN.
YOUR INNOCENCE IS NEARLY ADMIRABLE, BUT IT'S TOO LATE. MY PLAN IS ALREADY IN MOTION.
NOTHING CAN STOP IT. NOTHING.
I AM THE MISSING MOVER OF HISTORY, KESTUS.
BEING NOTHING IS MY SPECIALITY.

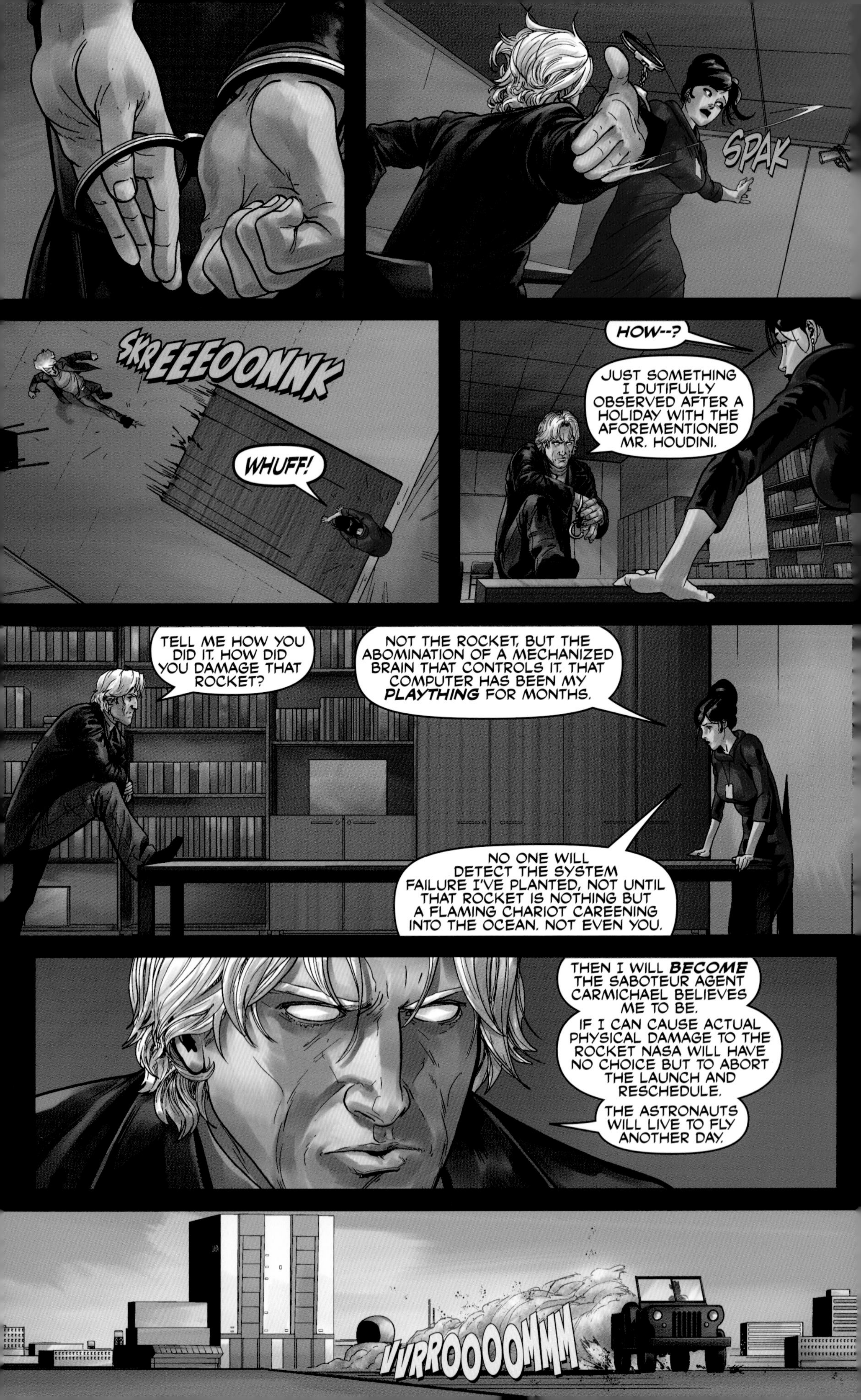

SPAK
SKREEEOONNK
WHUFF!
HOW--?
JUST SOMETHING I DUTIFULLY OBSERVED AFTER A HOLIDAY WITH THE AFOREMENTIONED MR. HOUDINI.
TELL ME HOW YOU DID IT. HOW DID YOU DAMAGE THAT ROCKET?
NOT THE ROCKET, BUT THE ABOMINATION OF A MECHANIZED BRAIN THAT CONTROLS IT. THAT COMPUTER HAS BEEN MY **PLAYTHING** FOR MONTHS.
NO ONE WILL DETECT THE SYSTEM FAILURE I'VE PLANTED, NOT UNTIL THAT ROCKET IS NOTHING BUT A FLAMING CHARIOT CAREENING INTO THE OCEAN. NOT EVEN YOU.
THEN I WILL **BECOME** THE SABOTEUR AGENT CARMICHAEL BELIEVES ME TO BE.
IF I CAN CAUSE ACTUAL PHYSICAL DAMAGE TO THE ROCKET NASA WILL HAVE NO CHOICE BUT TO ABORT THE LAUNCH AND RESCHEDULE.
THE ASTRONAUTS WILL LIVE TO FLY ANOTHER DAY.
VVRROOOOMMM

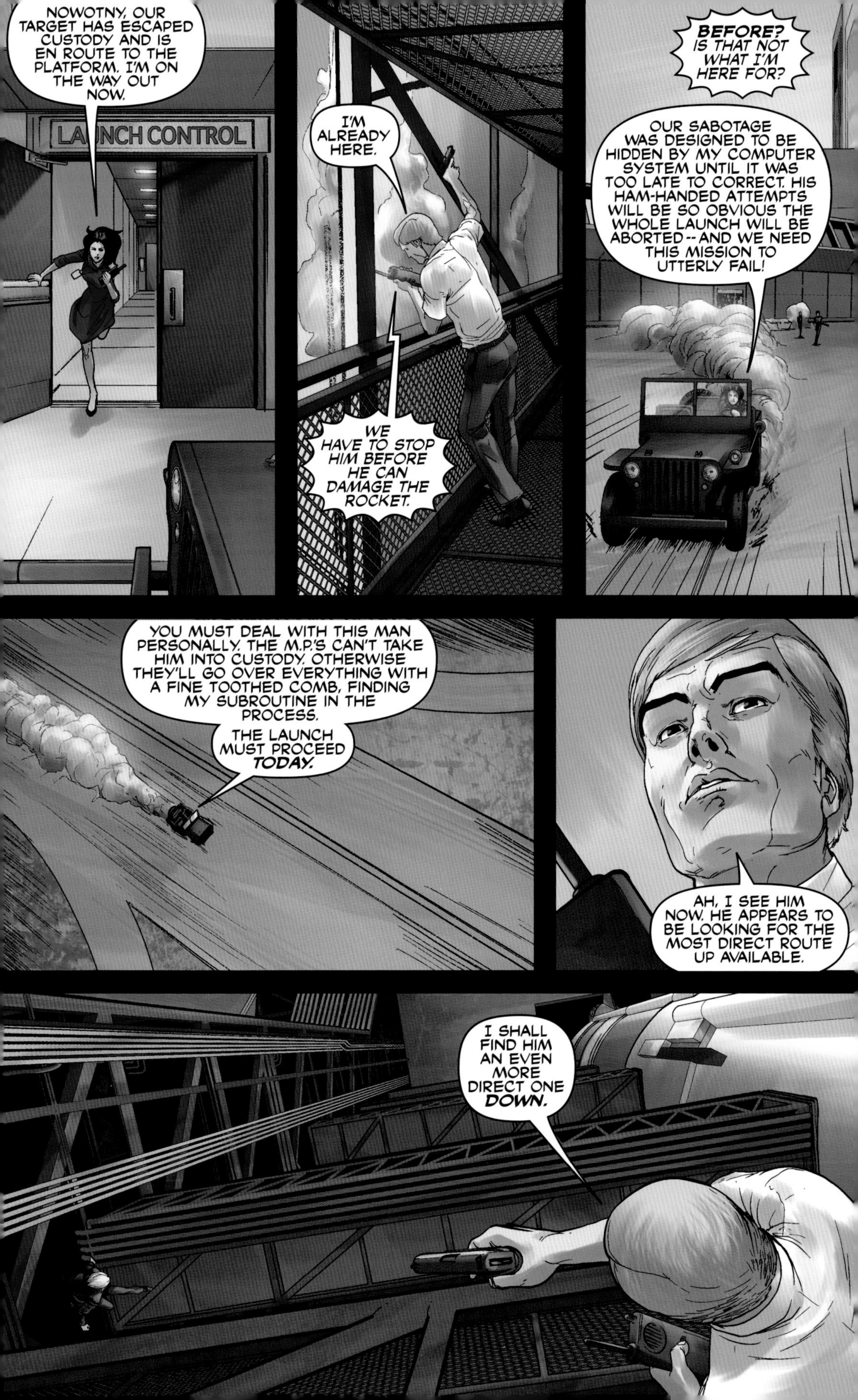
NOWOTNY, OUR TARGET HAS ESCAPED CUSTODY AND IS EN ROUTE TO THE PLATFORM. I'M ON THE WAY OUT NOW.
LAUNCH CONTROL
I'M ALREADY HERE.
WE HAVE TO STOP HIM BEFORE HE CAN DAMAGE THE ROCKET.
BEFORE? IS THAT NOT WHAT I'M HERE FOR?
OUR SABOTAGE WAS DESIGNED TO BE HIDDEN BY MY COMPUTER SYSTEM UNTIL IT WAS TOO LATE TO CORRECT. HIS HAM-HANDED ATTEMPTS WILL BE SO OBVIOUS THE WHOLE LAUNCH WILL BE ABORTED--AND WE NEED THIS MISSION TO UTTERLY FAIL!
YOU MUST DEAL WITH THIS MAN PERSONALLY. THE M.P.'S CAN'T TAKE HIM INTO CUSTODY. OTHERWISE THEY'LL GO OVER EVERYTHING WITH A FINE TOOTHED COMB, FINDING MY SUBROUTINE IN THE PROCESS.
THE LAUNCH MUST PROCEED TODAY.
AH, I SEE HIM NOW. HE APPEARS TO BE LOOKING FOR THE MOST DIRECT ROUTE UP AVAILABLE.
I SHALL FIND HIM AN EVEN MORE DIRECT ONE DOWN.

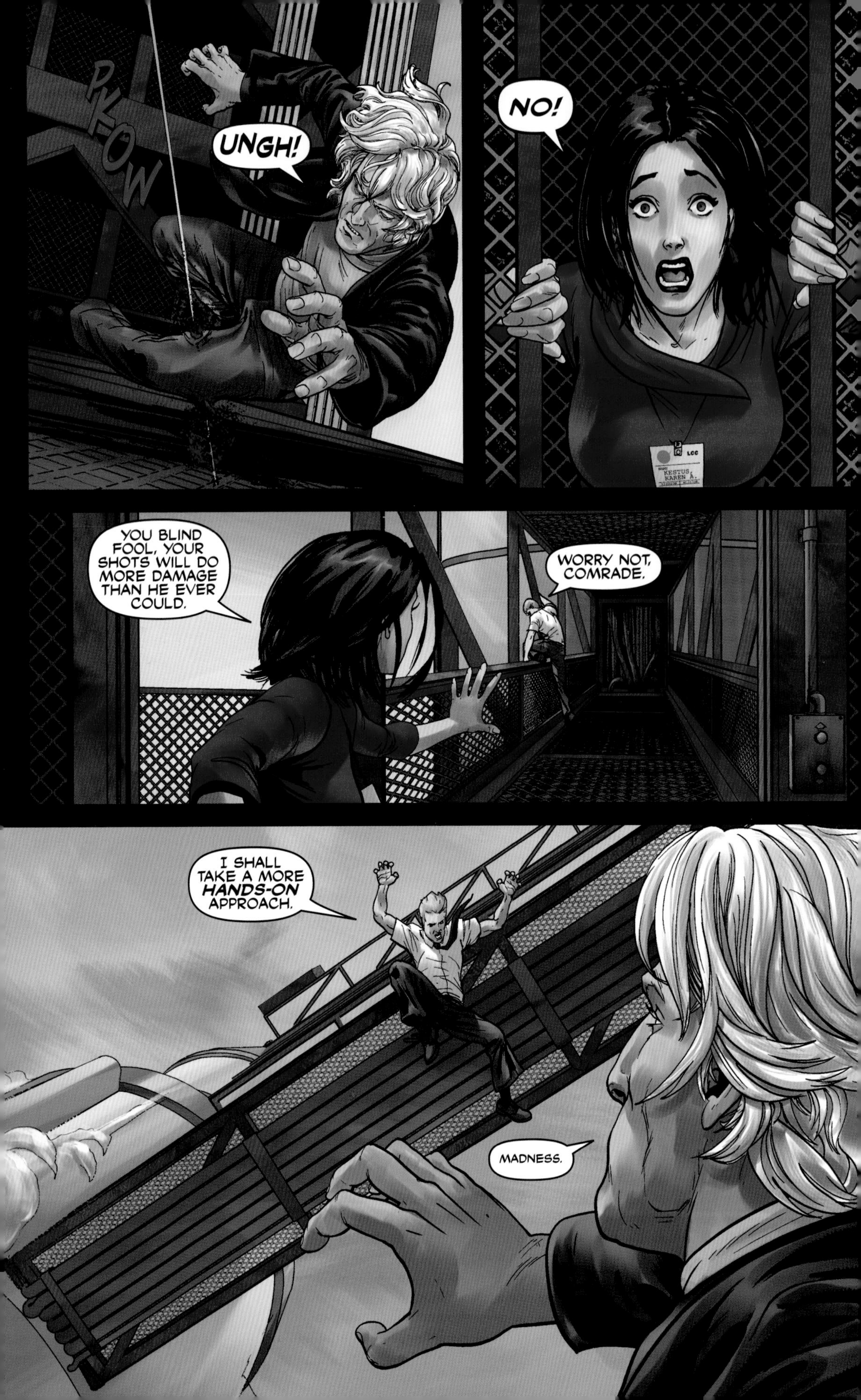
PKOW
UNGH!
NO!
LCC
KESTUS, KAREN A.
YOU BLIND FOOL, YOUR SHOTS WILL DO MORE DAMAGE THAN HE EVER COULD.
WORRY NOT, COMRADE.
I SHALL TAKE A MORE *HANDS-ON* APPROACH.
MADNESS.

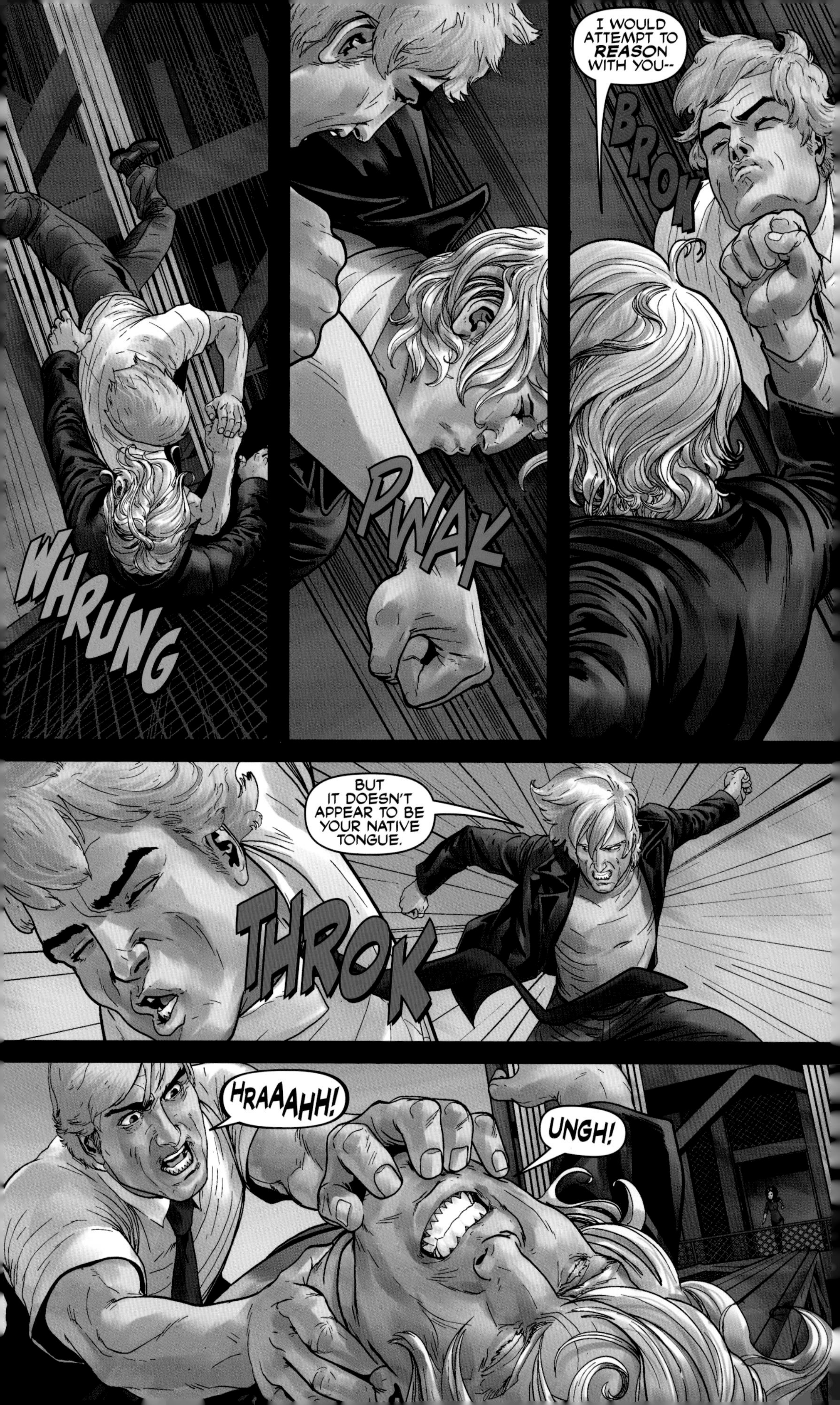
WHRUNG
PWAK
I WOULD ATTEMPT TO REASON WITH YOU--
BROK
BUT IT DOESN'T APPEAR TO BE YOUR NATIVE TONGUE.
THROK
HRAAAHH!
UNGH!

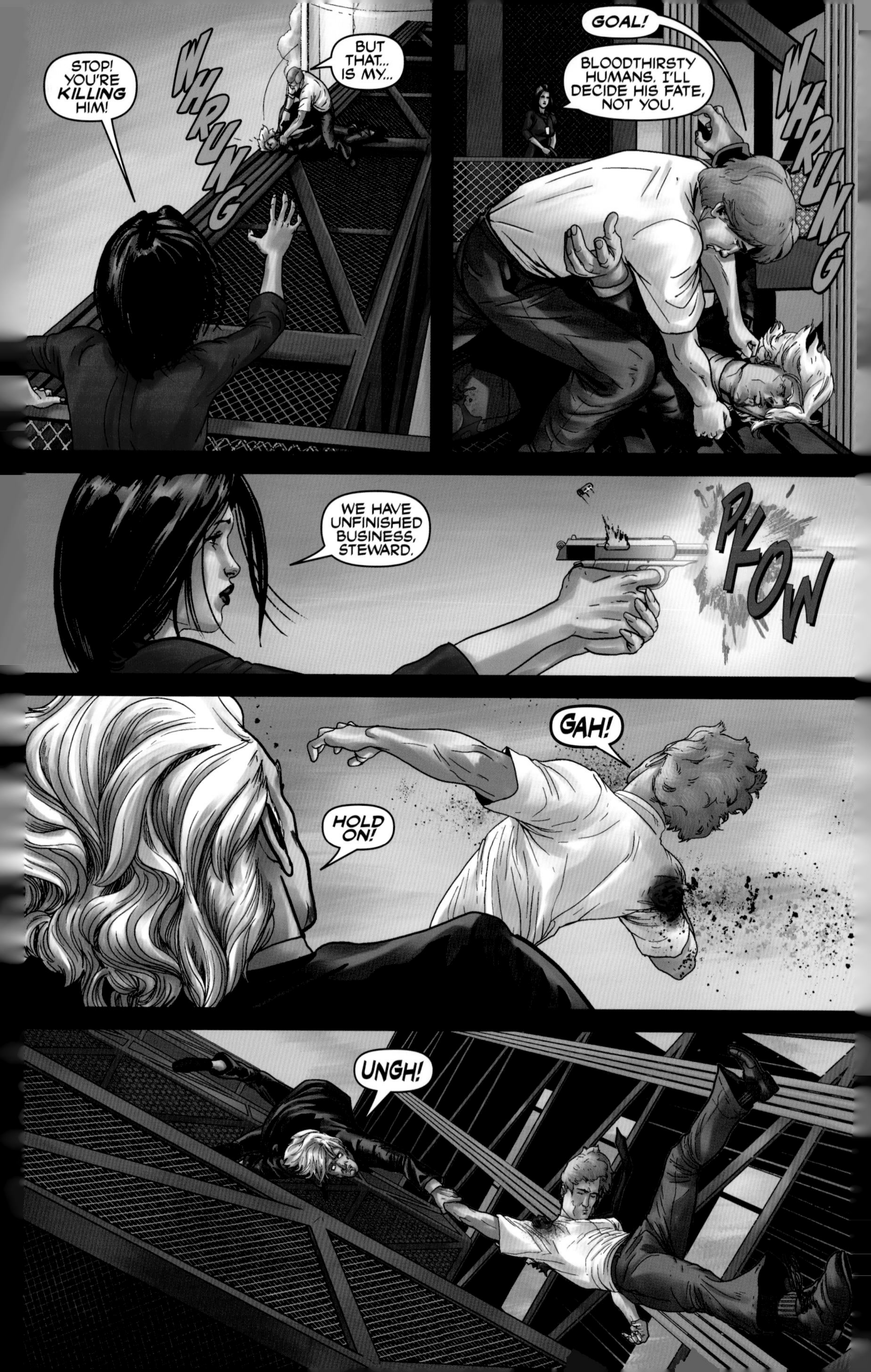
STOP! YOU'RE KILLING HIM!
WHRUNG
BUT THAT... IS MY...
GOAL!
BLOODTHIRSTY HUMANS, I'LL DECIDE HIS FATE, NOT YOU.
WHRUNG
WE HAVE UNFINISHED BUSINESS, STEWARD.
PKOW
GAH!
HOLD ON!
UNGH!

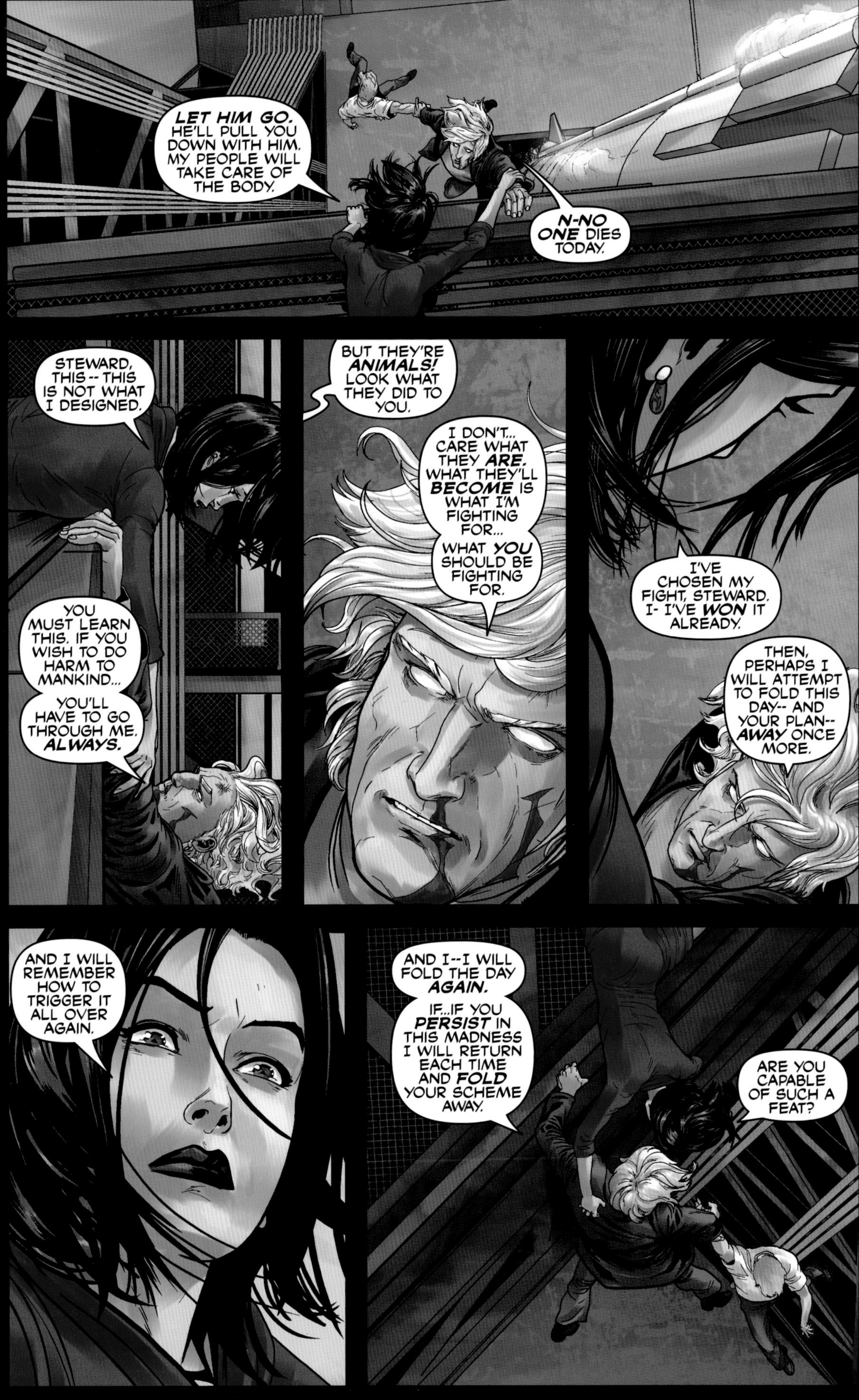
LET HIM GO. HE'LL PULL YOU DOWN WITH HIM. MY PEOPLE WILL TAKE CARE OF THE BODY.
N-NO ONE DIES TODAY.
STEWARD, THIS -- THIS IS NOT WHAT I DESIGNED.
YOU MUST LEARN THIS. IF YOU WISH TO DO HARM TO MANKIND...
YOU'LL HAVE TO GO THROUGH ME. ALWAYS.
BUT THEY'RE ANIMALS! LOOK WHAT THEY DID TO YOU.
I DON'T... CARE WHAT THEY ARE. WHAT THEY'LL BECOME IS WHAT I'M FIGHTING FOR...
WHAT YOU SHOULD BE FIGHTING FOR.
I'VE CHOSEN MY FIGHT, STEWARD. I- I'VE WON IT ALREADY.
THEN, PERHAPS I WILL ATTEMPT TO FOLD THIS DAY-- AND YOUR PLAN-- AWAY ONCE MORE.
AND I WILL REMEMBER HOW TO TRIGGER IT ALL OVER AGAIN.
AND I--I WILL FOLD THE DAY AGAIN.
IF...IF YOU PERSIST IN THIS MADNESS I WILL RETURN EACH TIME AND FOLD YOUR SCHEME AWAY.
ARE YOU CAPABLE OF SUCH A FEAT?

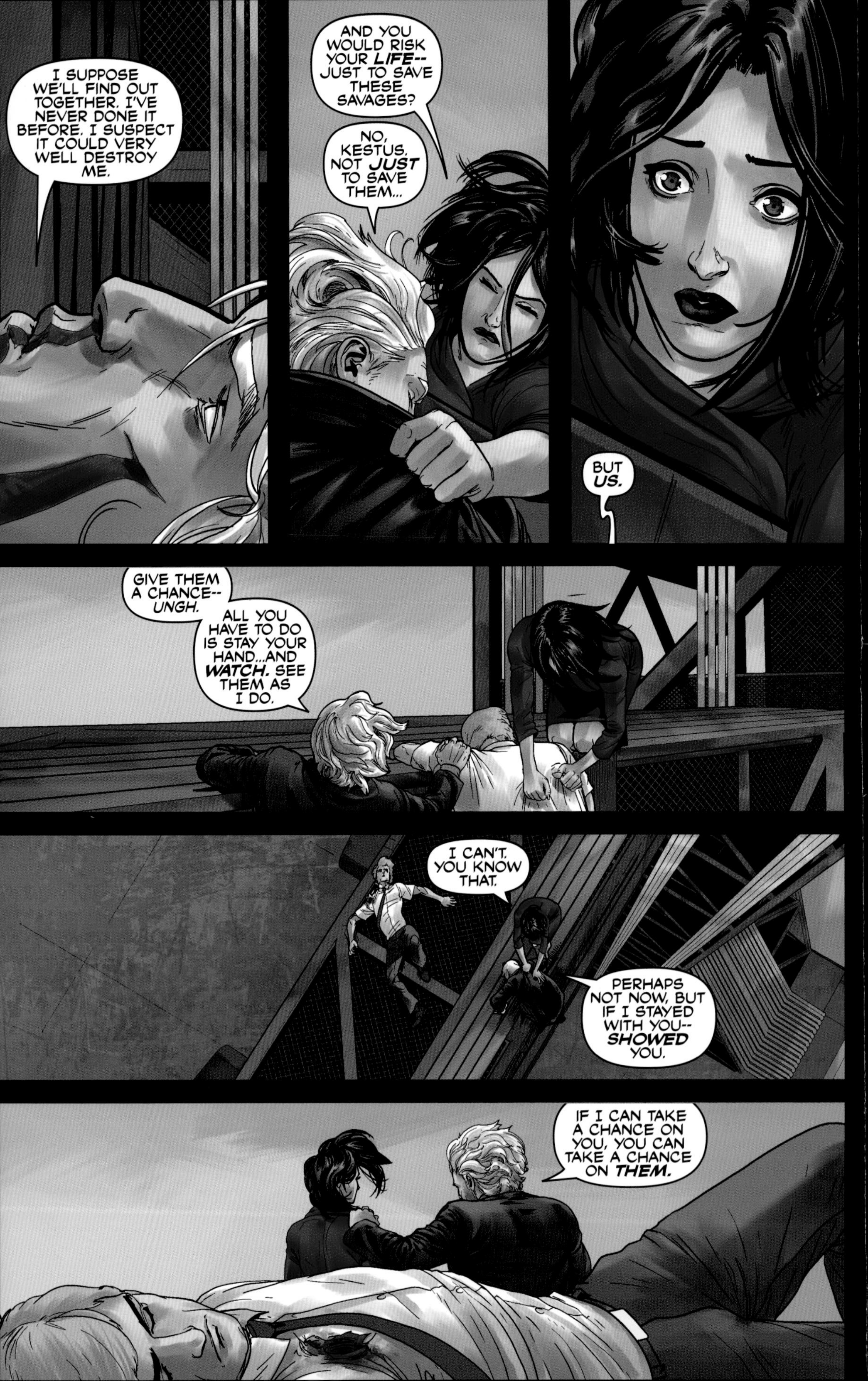
I SUPPOSE WE'LL FIND OUT TOGETHER. I'VE NEVER DONE IT BEFORE. I SUSPECT IT COULD VERY WELL DESTROY ME.
AND YOU WOULD RISK YOUR LIFE-- JUST TO SAVE THESE SAVAGES?
NO, KESTUS. NOT JUST TO SAVE THEM...
BUT US.
GIVE THEM A CHANCE-- UNGH.
ALL YOU HAVE TO DO IS STAY YOUR HAND...AND WATCH. SEE THEM AS I DO.
I CAN'T. YOU KNOW THAT.
PERHAPS NOT NOW, BUT IF I STAYED WITH YOU-- SHOWED YOU.
IF I CAN TAKE A CHANCE ON YOU, YOU CAN TAKE A CHANCE ON THEM.

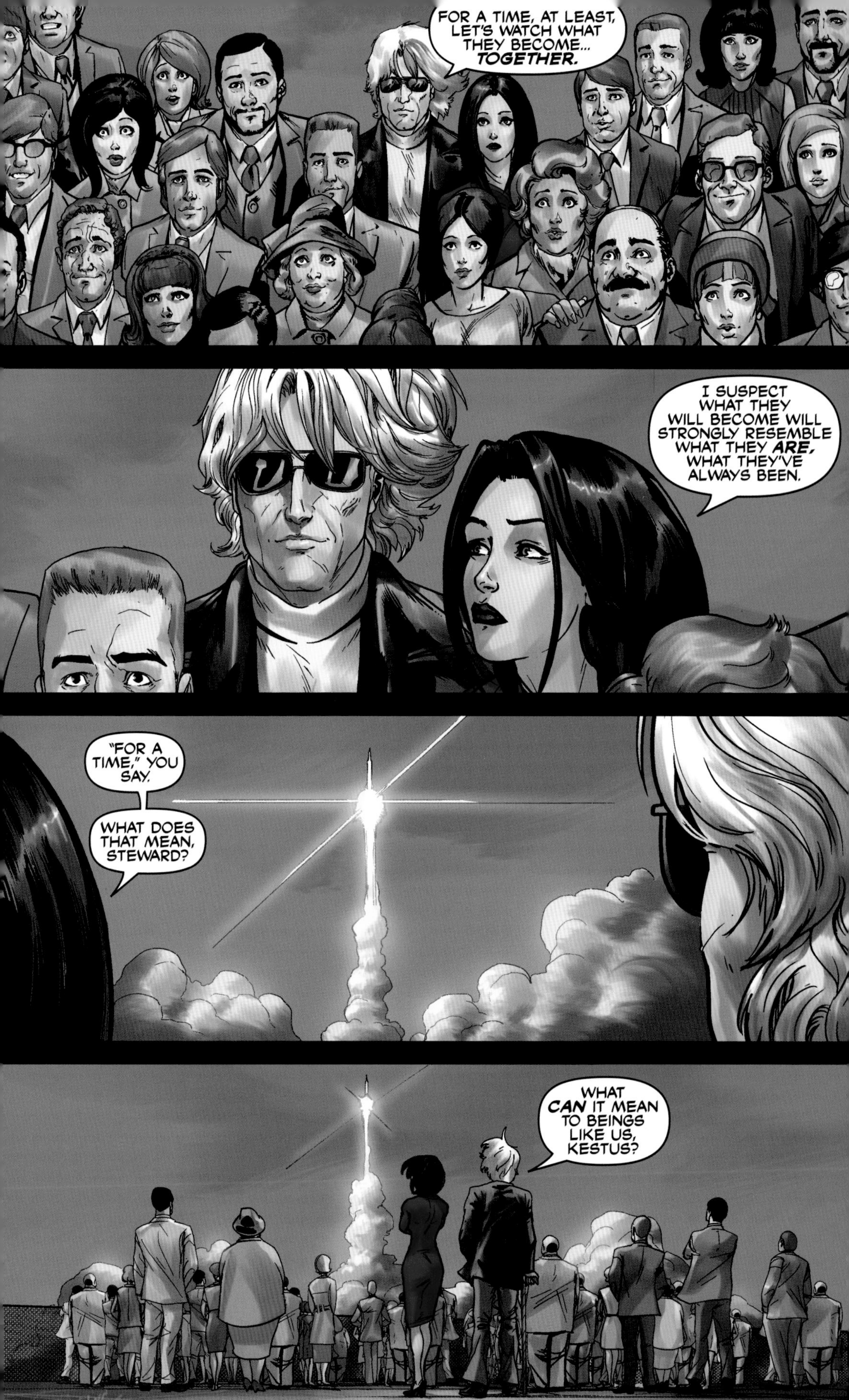
FOR A TIME, AT LEAST, LET'S WATCH WHAT THEY BECOME... TOGETHER.
I SUSPECT WHAT THEY WILL BECOME WILL STRONGLY RESEMBLE WHAT THEY ARE, WHAT THEY'VE ALWAYS BEEN.
"FOR A TIME," YOU SAY.
WHAT DOES THAT MEAN, STEWARD?
WHAT CAN IT MEAN TO BEINGS LIKE US, KESTUS?

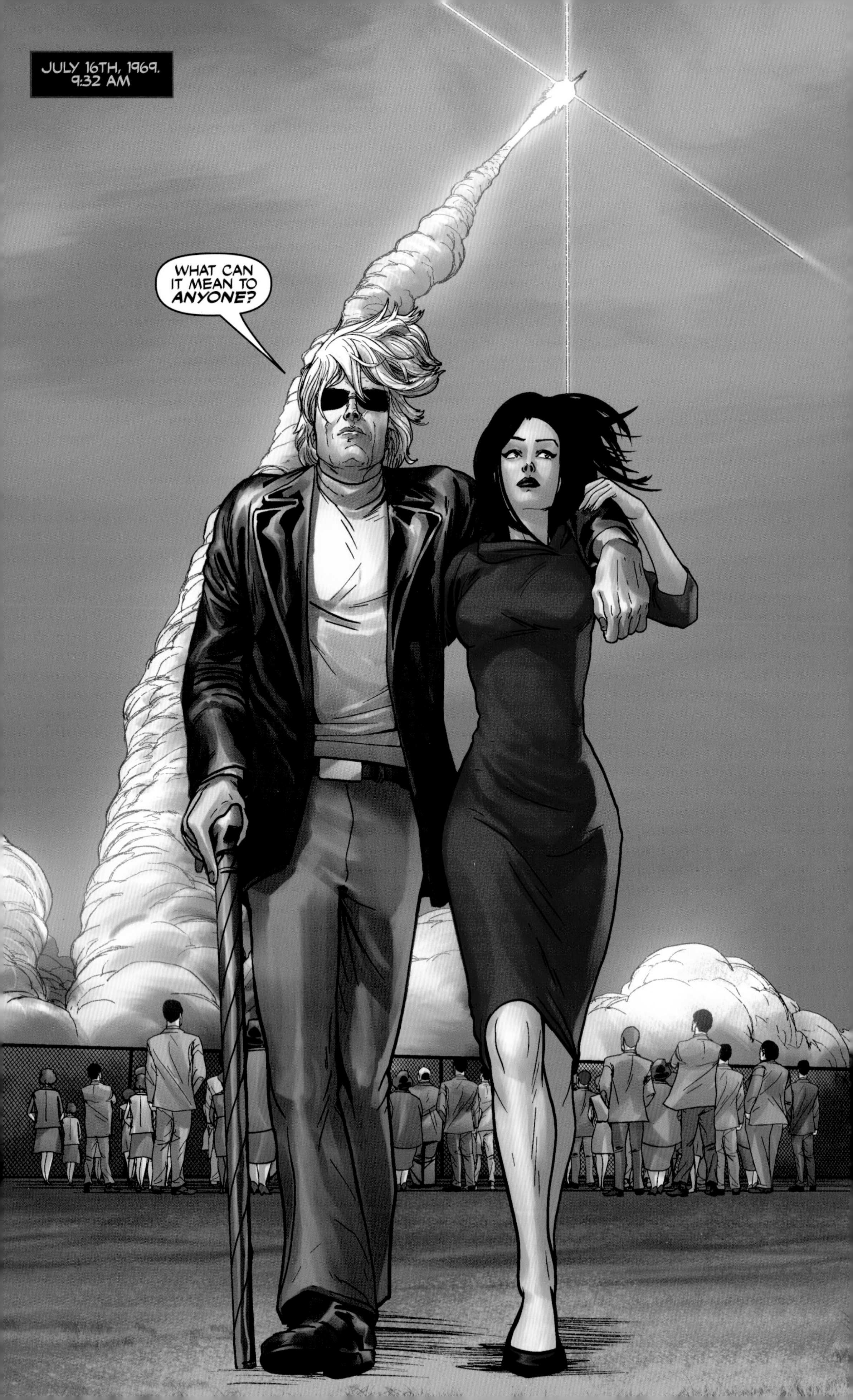
JULY 16TH, 1969.
9:32 AM
WHAT CAN IT MEAN TO ANYONE?

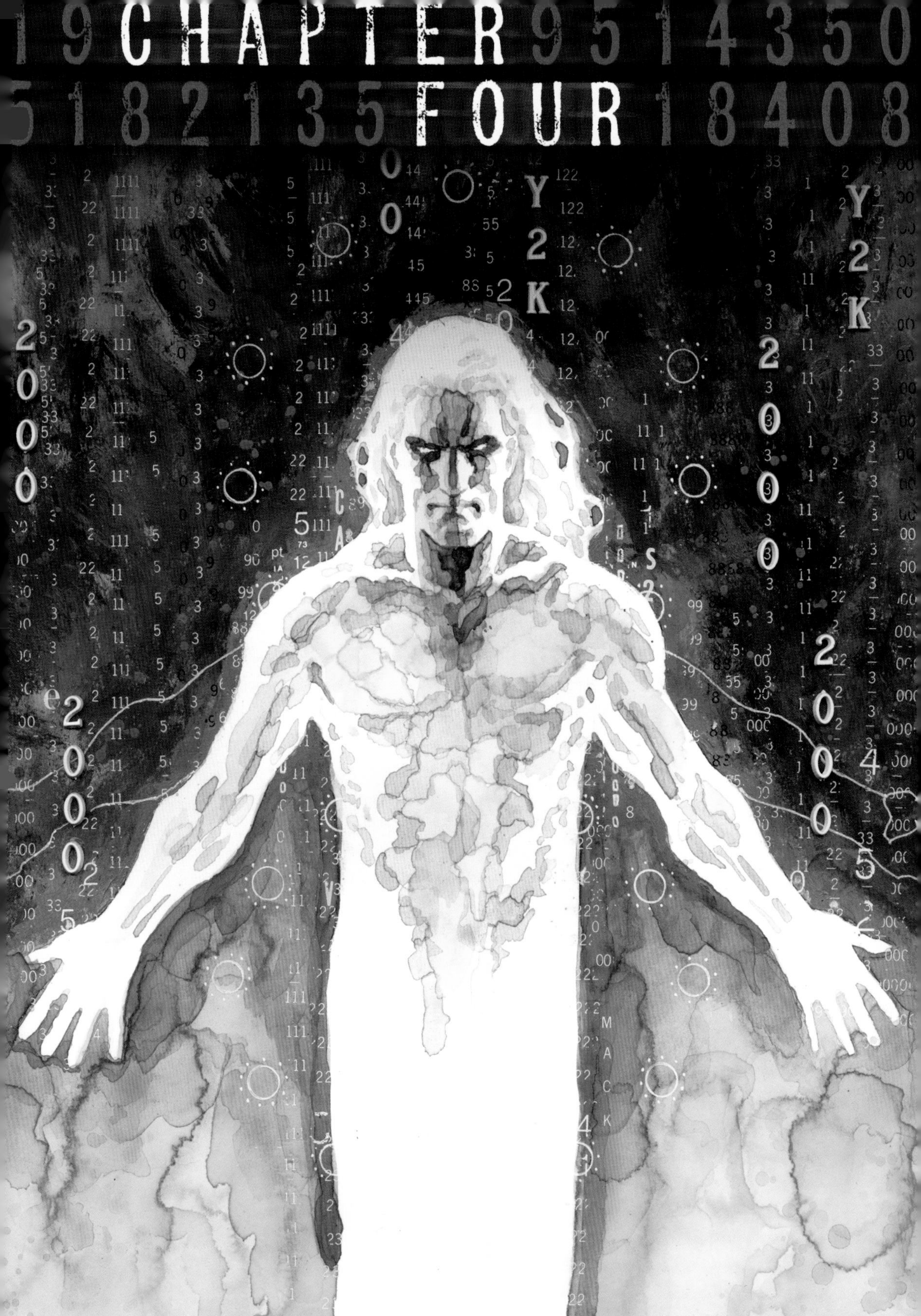
19CHAPTER9514350
5182135FOUR18408

CHAPTER FOUR COVER ART | DAVID **MACK**

JANUARY 2000

Y2K

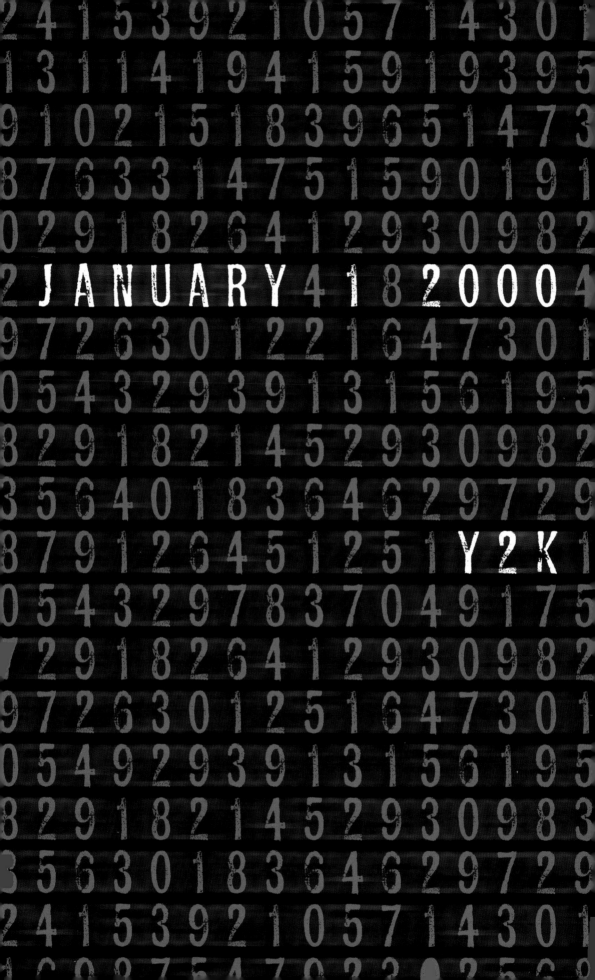

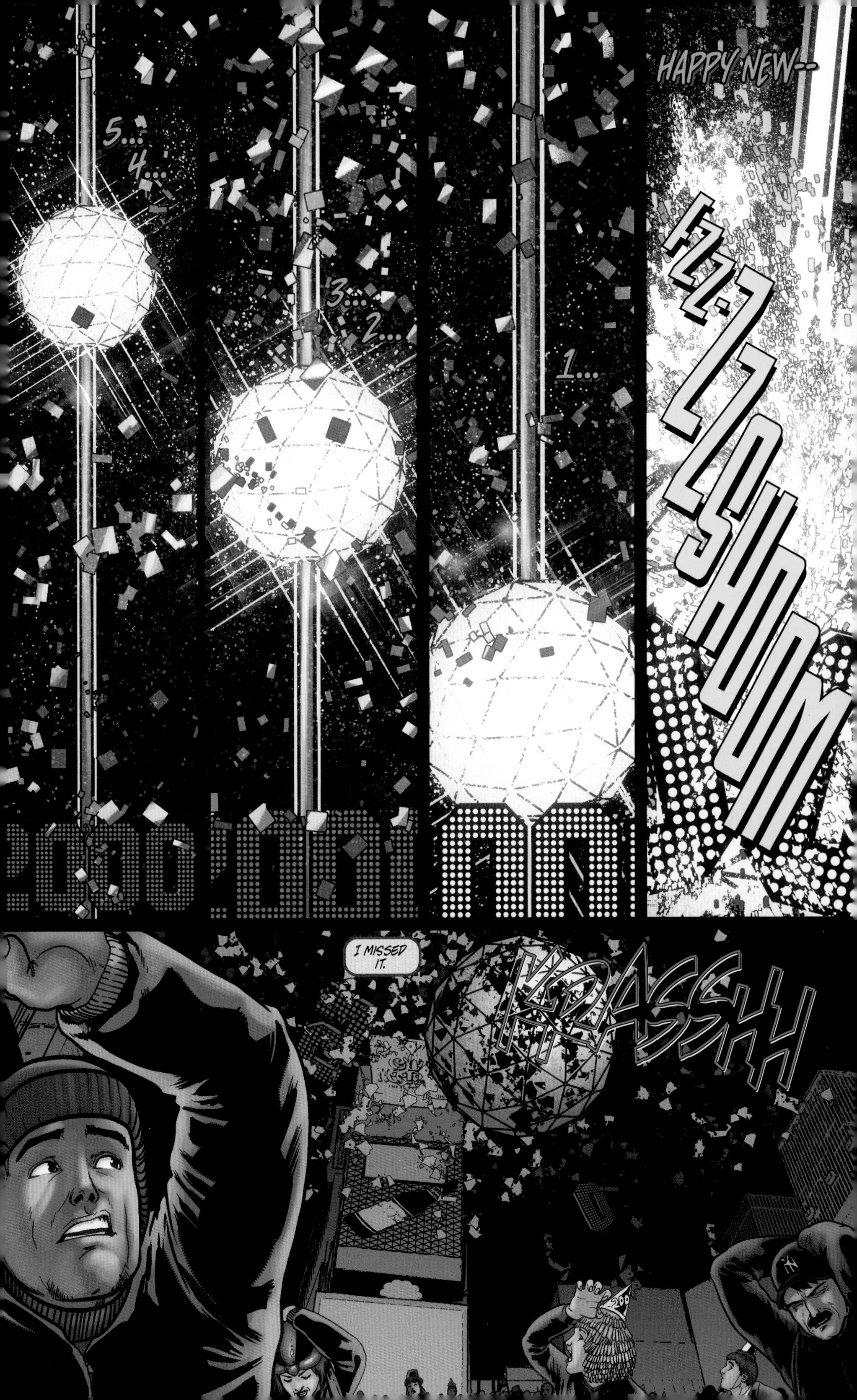
5...
4...
3...
2...
1...
HAPPY NEW--
FZZ-ZZSHOOM
2000
I MISSED IT.
KRASSHH

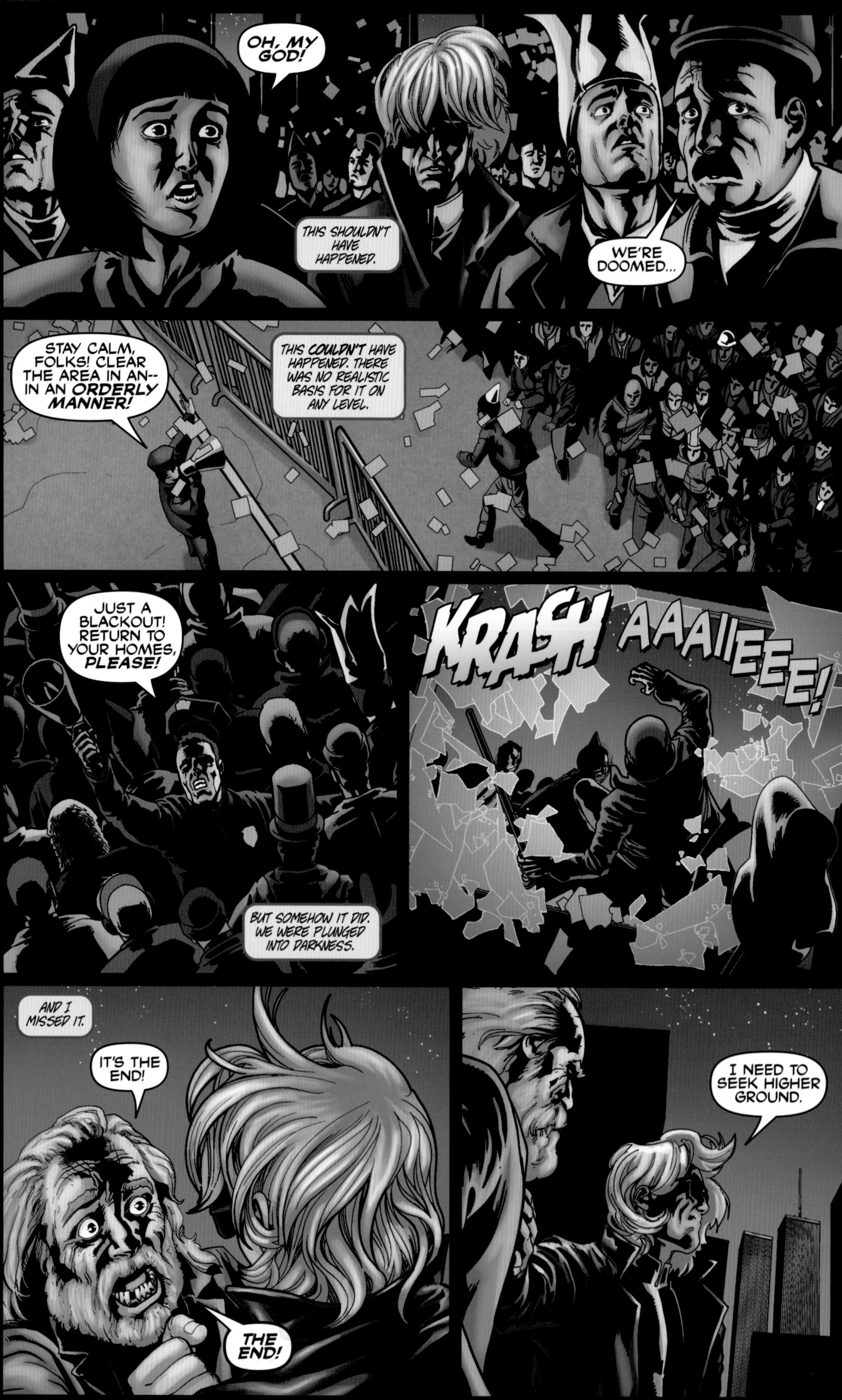
OH, MY GOD!
THIS SHOULDN'T HAVE HAPPENED.
WE'RE DOOMED...
STAY CALM, FOLKS! CLEAR THE AREA IN AN-- IN AN ORDERLY MANNER!
THIS COULDN'T HAVE HAPPENED. THERE WAS NO REALISTIC BASIS FOR IT ON ANY LEVEL.
JUST A BLACKOUT! RETURN TO YOUR HOMES, PLEASE!
BUT SOMEHOW IT DID. WE WERE PLUNGED INTO DARKNESS.
KRASH
AAAIIEEEE!
AND I MISSED IT.
IT'S THE END!
THE END!
I NEED TO SEEK HIGHER GROUND.

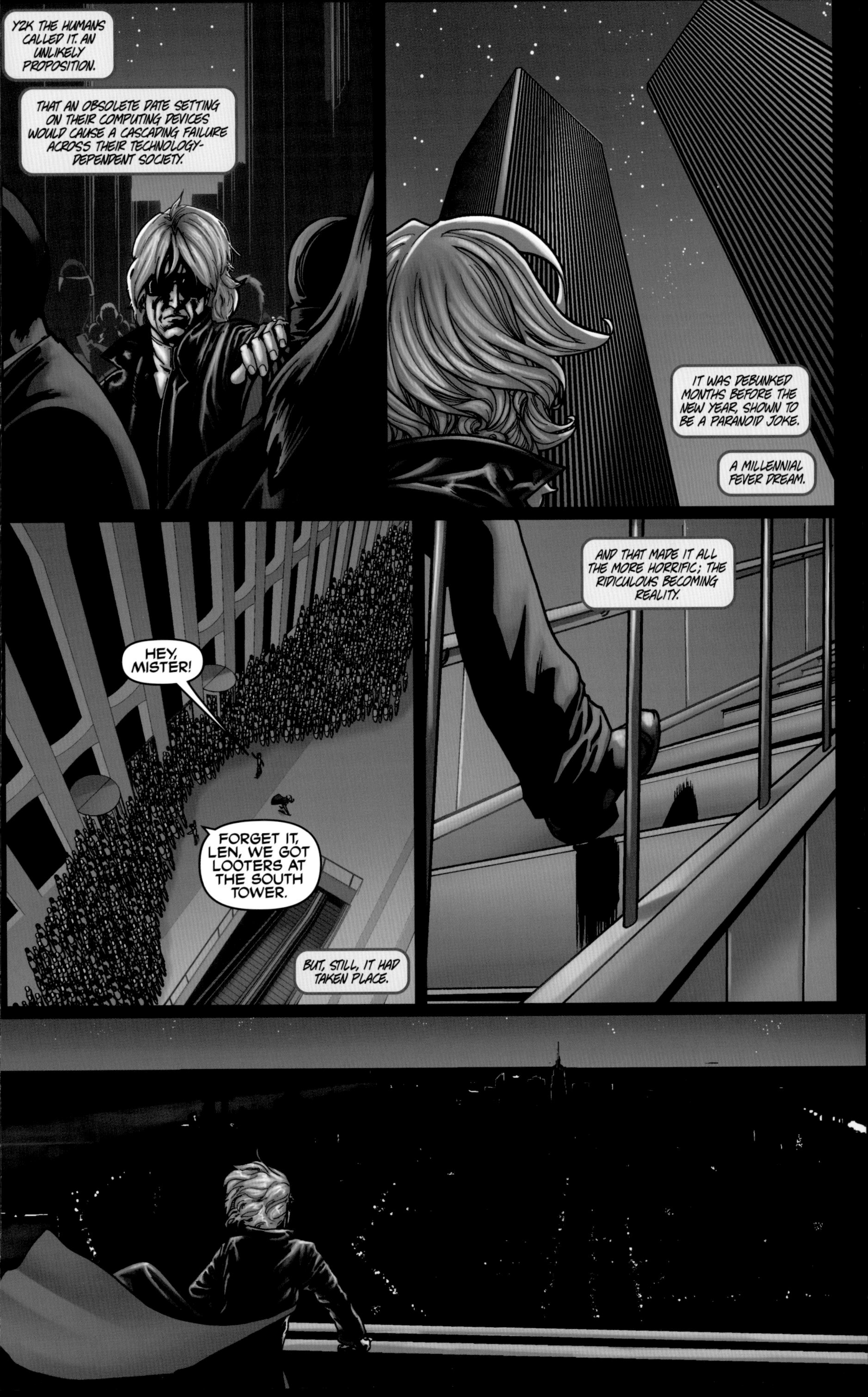
Y2K THE HUMANS CALLED IT. AN UNLIKELY PROPOSITION.
THAT AN OBSOLETE DATE SETTING ON THEIR COMPUTING DEVICES WOULD CAUSE A CASCADING FAILURE ACROSS THEIR TECHNOLOGY-DEPENDENT SOCIETY.
IT WAS DEBUNKED MONTHS BEFORE THE NEW YEAR, SHOWN TO BE A PARANOID JOKE.
A MILLENNIAL FEVER DREAM.
HEY, MISTER!
FORGET IT, LEN, WE GOT LOOTERS AT THE SOUTH TOWER.
BUT, STILL, IT HAD TAKEN PLACE.
AND THAT MADE IT ALL THE MORE HORRIFIC; THE RIDICULOUS BECOMING REALITY.

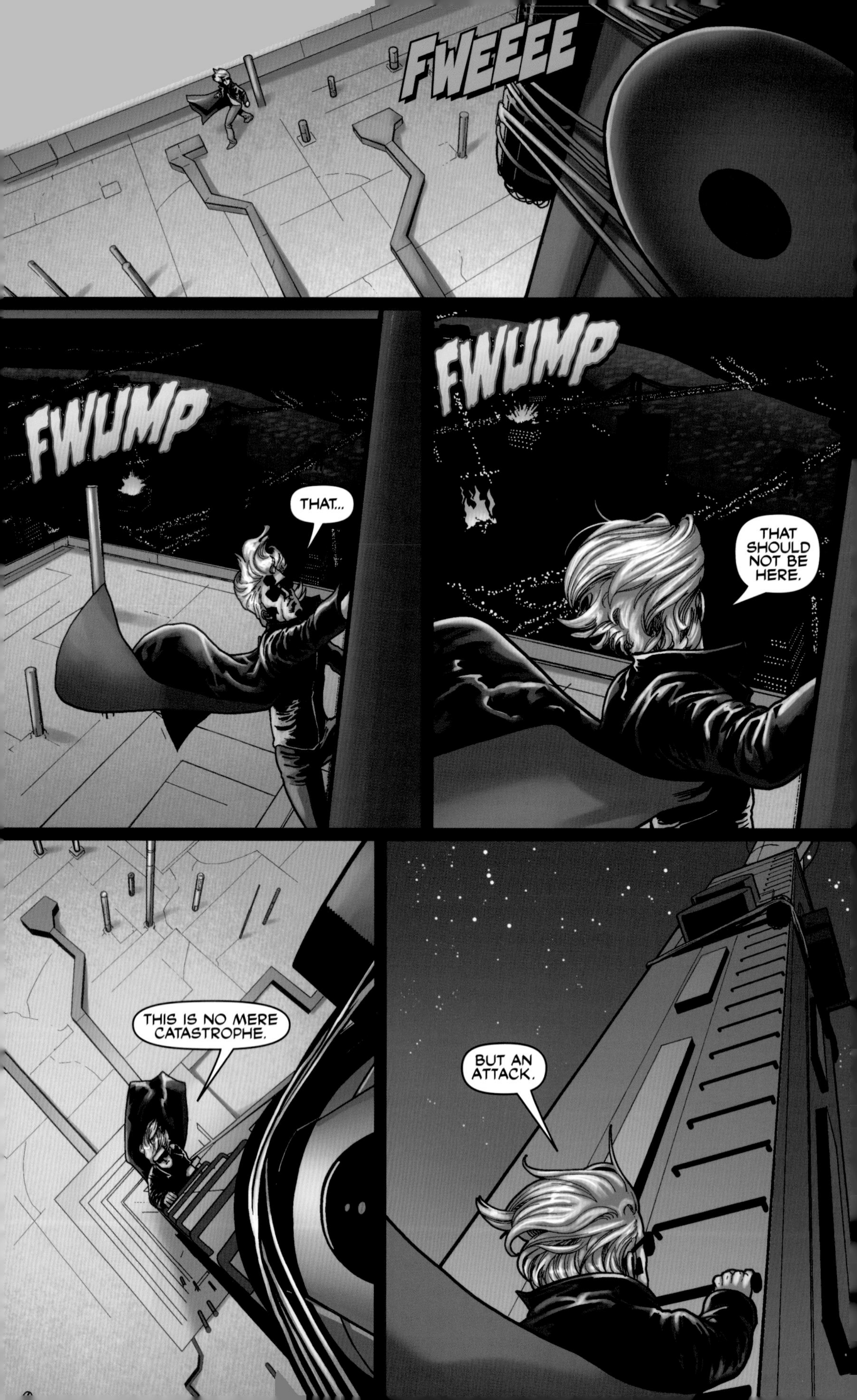
FWEEEE
FWUMP
THAT...
FWUMP
THAT SHOULD NOT BE HERE.
THIS IS NO MERE CATASTROPHE.
BUT AN ATTACK.

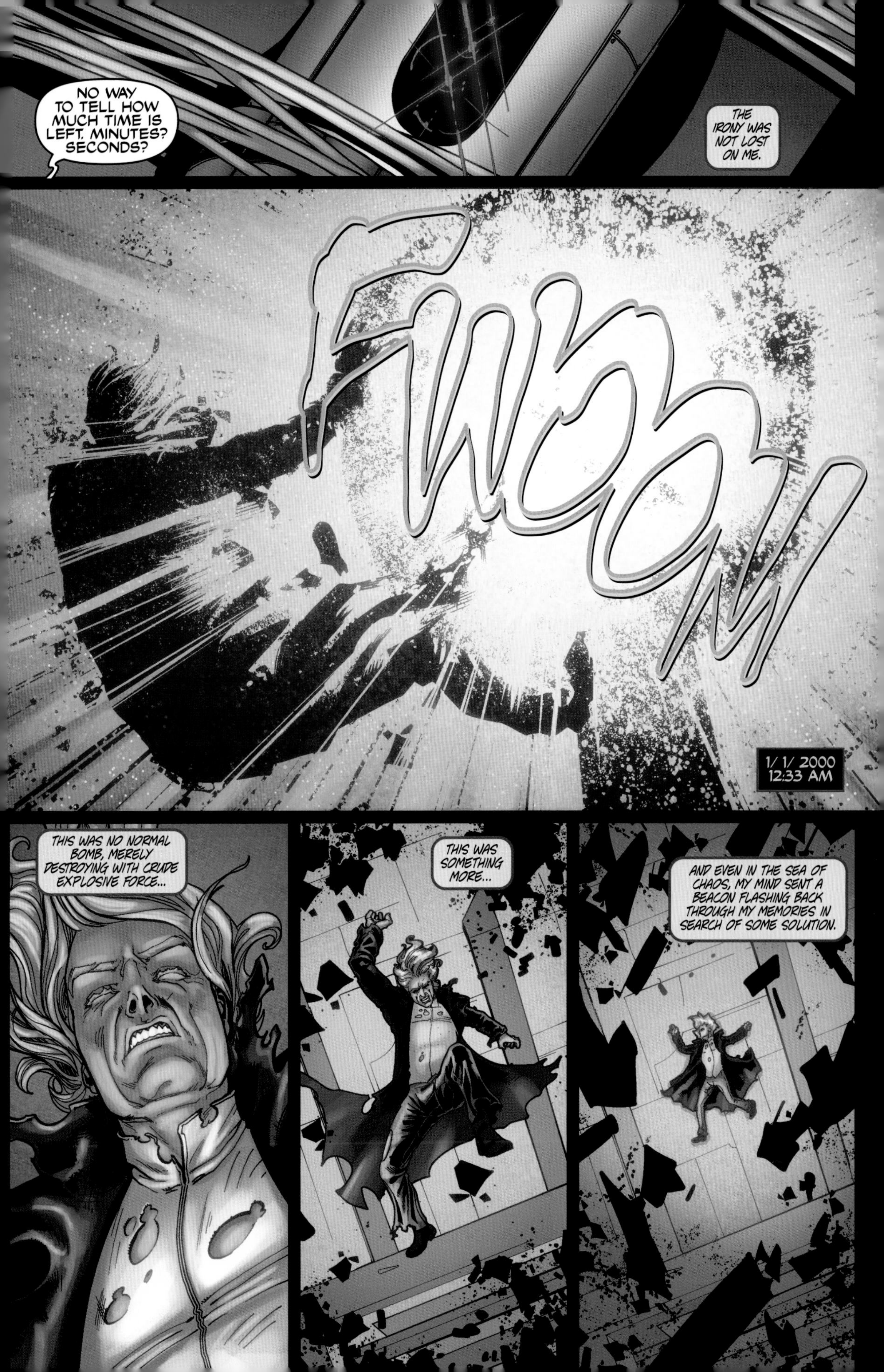
NO WAY TO TELL HOW MUCH TIME IS LEFT. MINUTES? SECONDS?
THE IRONY WAS NOT LOST ON ME.
FWOOM!
1/ 1/ 2000 12:33 AM
THIS WAS NO NORMAL BOMB, MERELY DESTROYING WITH CRUDE EXPLOSIVE FORCE...
THIS WAS SOMETHING MORE...
AND EVEN IN THE SEA OF CHAOS, MY MIND SENT A BEACON FLASHING BACK THROUGH MY MEMORIES IN SEARCH OF SOME SOLUTION.

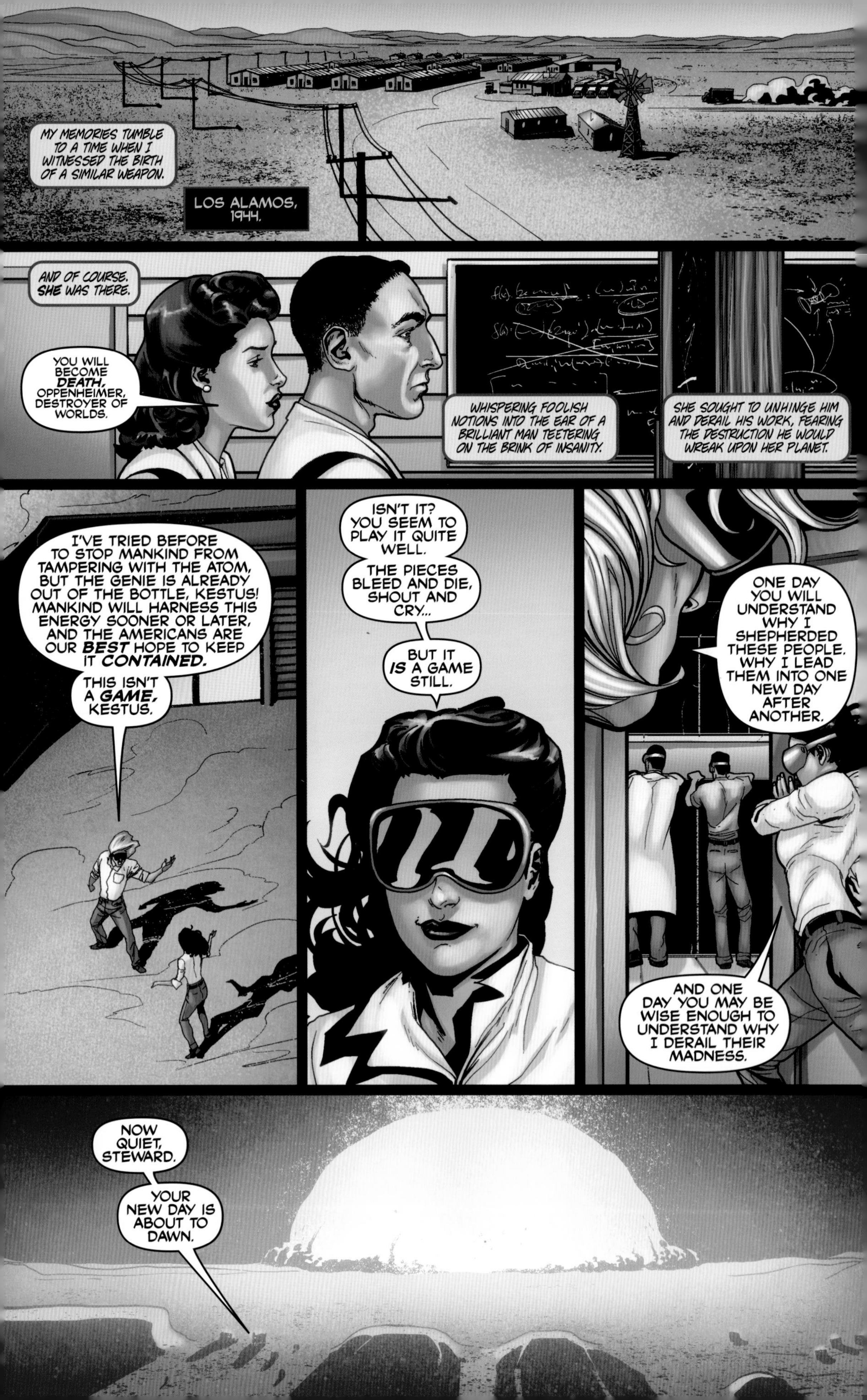

MY MEMORIES TUMBLE TO A TIME WHEN I WITNESSED THE BIRTH OF A SIMILAR WEAPON.
LOS ALAMOS, 1944.
AND OF COURSE. SHE WAS THERE.
YOU WILL BECOME DEATH, OPPENHEIMER, DESTROYER OF WORLDS.
WHISPERING FOOLISH NOTIONS INTO THE EAR OF A BRILLIANT MAN TEETERING ON THE BRINK OF INSANITY.
SHE SOUGHT TO UNHINGE HIM AND DERAIL HIS WORK, FEARING THE DESTRUCTION HE WOULD WREAK UPON HER PLANET.
I'VE TRIED BEFORE TO STOP MANKIND FROM TAMPERING WITH THE ATOM, BUT THE GENIE IS ALREADY OUT OF THE BOTTLE, KESTUS! MANKIND WILL HARNESS THIS ENERGY SOONER OR LATER, AND THE AMERICANS ARE OUR BEST HOPE TO KEEP IT CONTAINED.
THIS ISN'T A GAME, KESTUS.
ISN'T IT? YOU SEEM TO PLAY IT QUITE WELL.
THE PIECES BLEED AND DIE, SHOUT AND CRY...
BUT IT IS A GAME STILL.
ONE DAY YOU WILL UNDERSTAND WHY I SHEPHERDED THESE PEOPLE. WHY I LEAD THEM INTO ONE NEW DAY AFTER ANOTHER.
AND ONE DAY YOU MAY BE WISE ENOUGH TO UNDERSTAND WHY I DERAIL THEIR MADNESS.
NOW QUIET, STEWARD.
YOUR NEW DAY IS ABOUT TO DAWN.

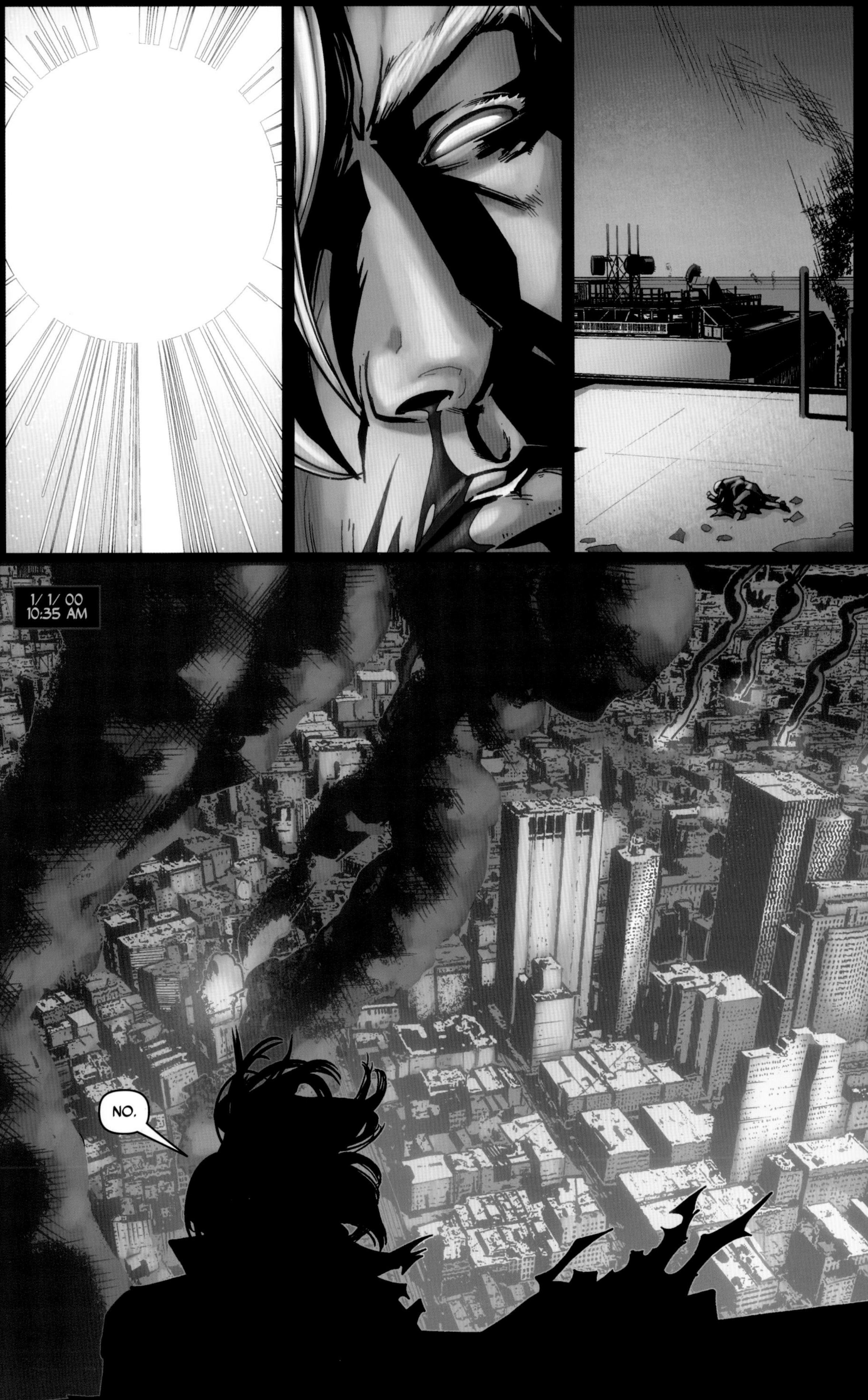
1/ 1/ 00
10:35 AM
NO.

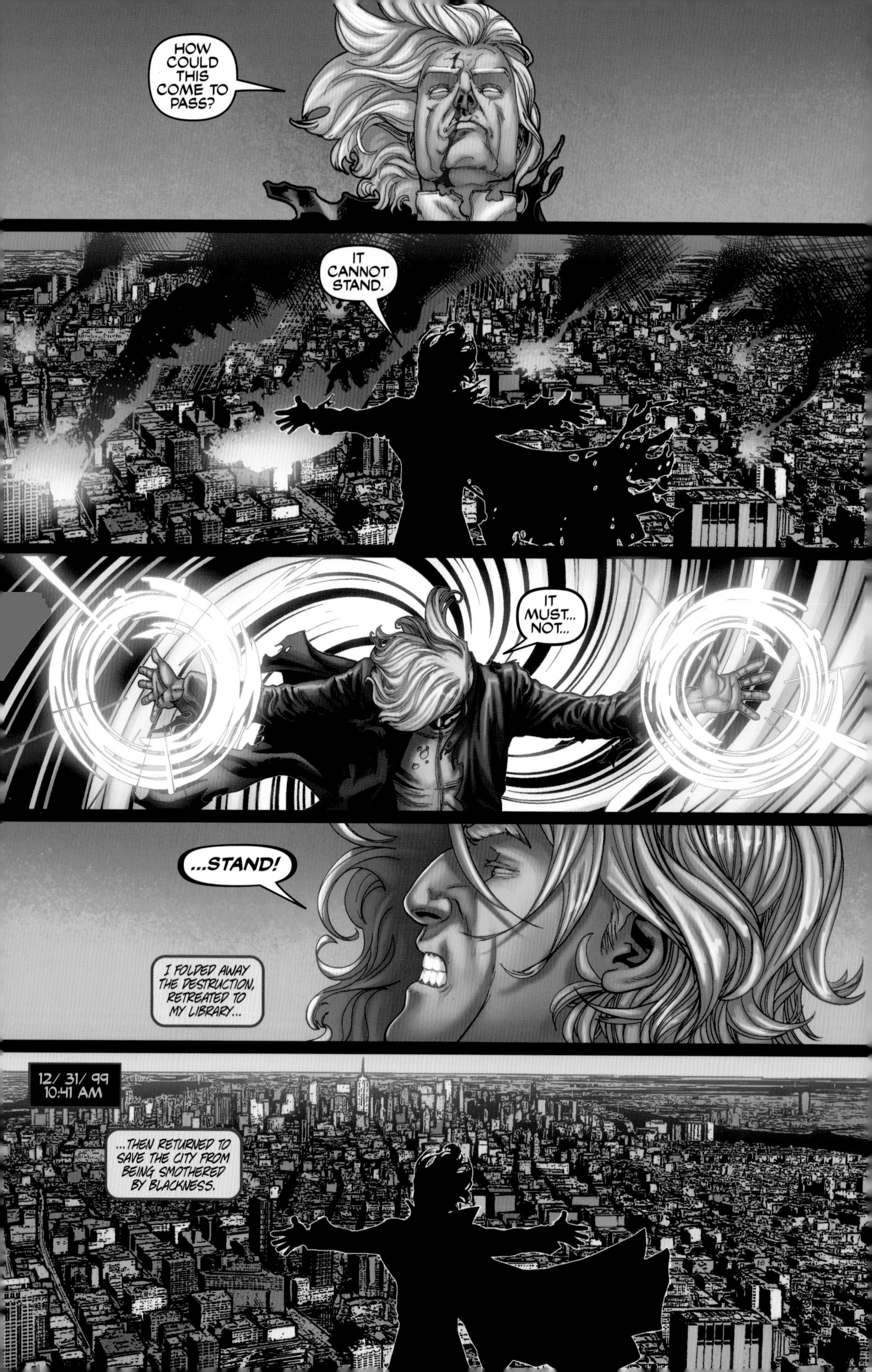
HOW COULD THIS COME TO PASS?
IT CANNOT STAND.
IT MUST... NOT...
...STAND!
I FOLDED AWAY THE DESTRUCTION, RETREATED TO MY LIBRARY...
12/ 31/ 99
10:41 AM
...THEN RETURNED TO SAVE THE CITY FROM BEING SMOTHERED BY BLACKNESS.

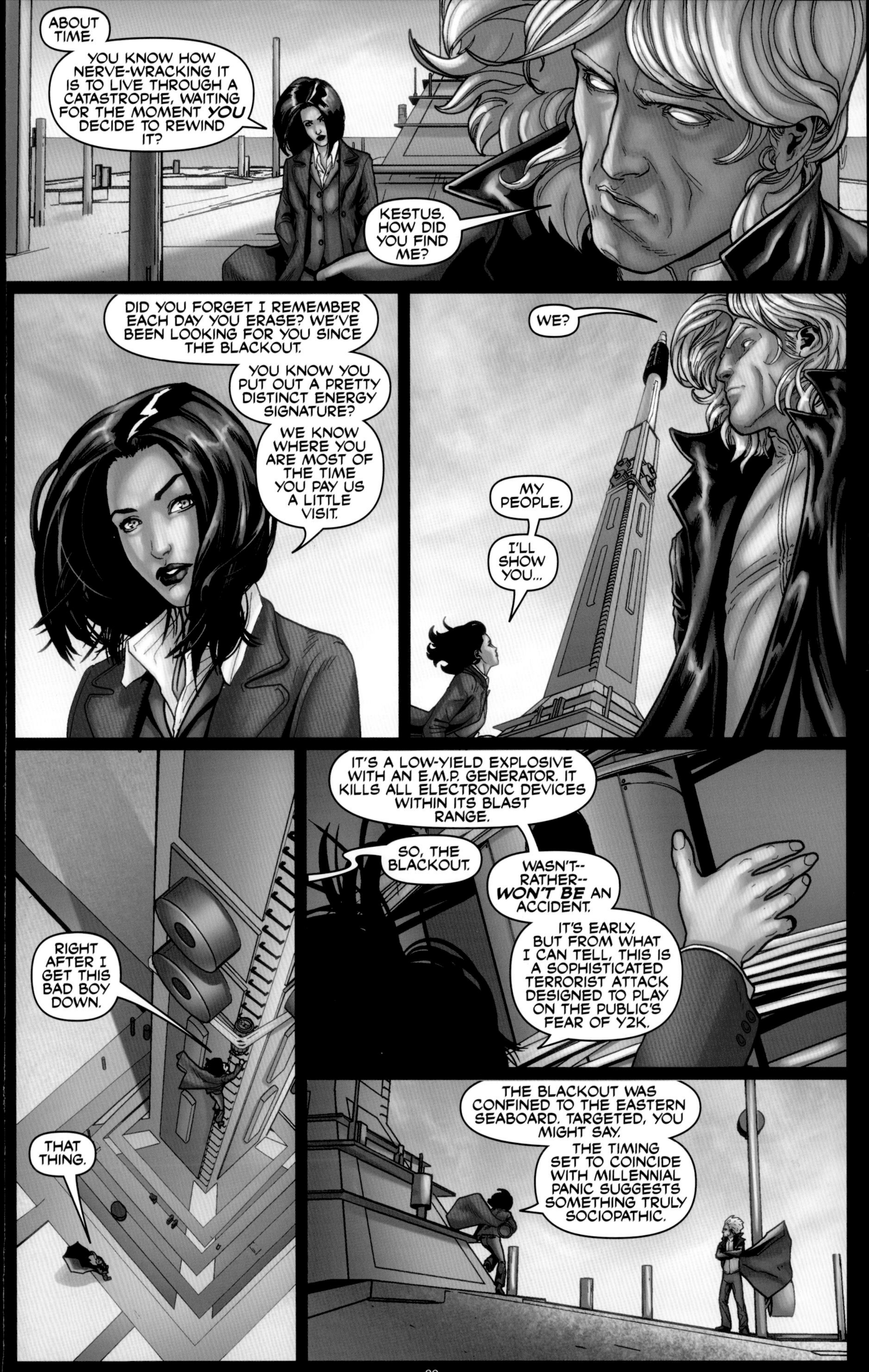
ABOUT TIME.
YOU KNOW HOW NERVE-WRACKING IT IS TO LIVE THROUGH A CATASTROPHE, WAITING FOR THE MOMENT YOU DECIDE TO REWIND IT?
KESTUS. HOW DID YOU FIND ME?
DID YOU FORGET I REMEMBER EACH DAY YOU ERASE? WE'VE BEEN LOOKING FOR YOU SINCE THE BLACKOUT.
YOU KNOW YOU PUT OUT A PRETTY DISTINCT ENERGY SIGNATURE?
WE KNOW WHERE YOU ARE MOST OF THE TIME YOU PAY US A LITTLE VISIT.
WE?
MY PEOPLE.
I'LL SHOW YOU...
RIGHT AFTER I GET THIS BAD BOY DOWN.
THAT THING.
IT'S A LOW-YIELD EXPLOSIVE WITH AN E.M.P. GENERATOR. IT KILLS ALL ELECTRONIC DEVICES WITHIN ITS BLAST RANGE.
SO, THE BLACKOUT.
WASN'T-- RATHER-- WON'T BE AN ACCIDENT.
IT'S EARLY, BUT FROM WHAT I CAN TELL, THIS IS A SOPHISTICATED TERRORIST ATTACK DESIGNED TO PLAY ON THE PUBLIC'S FEAR OF Y2K.
THE BLACKOUT WAS CONFINED TO THE EASTERN SEABOARD. TARGETED, YOU MIGHT SAY.
THE TIMING SET TO COINCIDE WITH MILLENNIAL PANIC SUGGESTS SOMETHING TRULY SOCIOPATHIC.

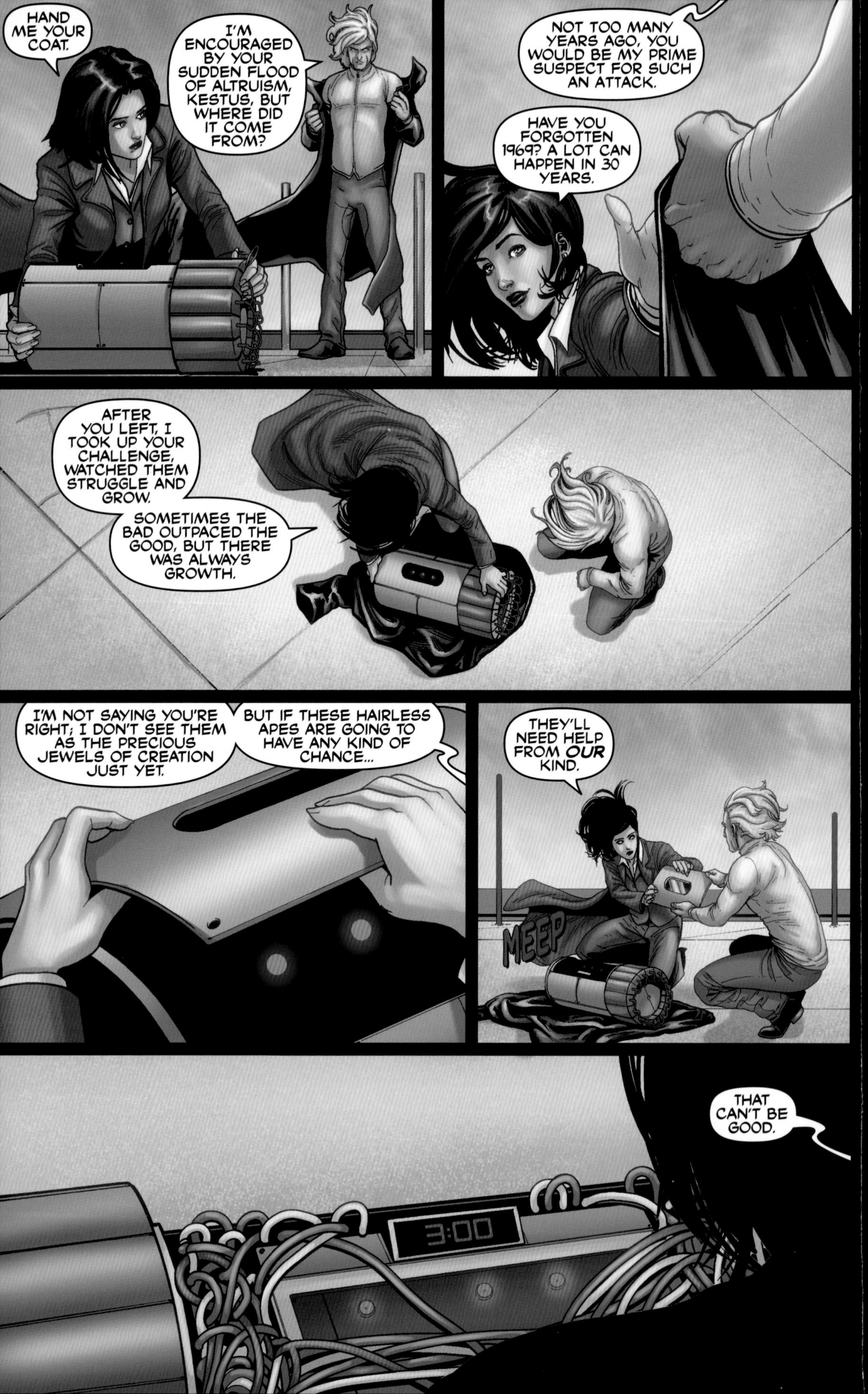
HAND ME YOUR COAT.
I'M ENCOURAGED BY YOUR SUDDEN FLOOD OF ALTRUISM, KESTUS, BUT WHERE DID IT COME FROM?
NOT TOO MANY YEARS AGO, YOU WOULD BE MY PRIME SUSPECT FOR SUCH AN ATTACK.
HAVE YOU FORGOTTEN 1969? A LOT CAN HAPPEN IN 30 YEARS.
AFTER YOU LEFT, I TOOK UP YOUR CHALLENGE, WATCHED THEM STRUGGLE AND GROW.
SOMETIMES THE BAD OUTPACED THE GOOD, BUT THERE WAS ALWAYS GROWTH.
I'M NOT SAYING YOU'RE RIGHT; I DON'T SEE THEM AS THE PRECIOUS JEWELS OF CREATION JUST YET.
BUT IF THESE HAIRLESS APES ARE GOING TO HAVE ANY KIND OF CHANCE...
THEY'LL NEED HELP FROM *OUR* KIND.
MEEP
THAT CAN'T BE GOOD.
3:00

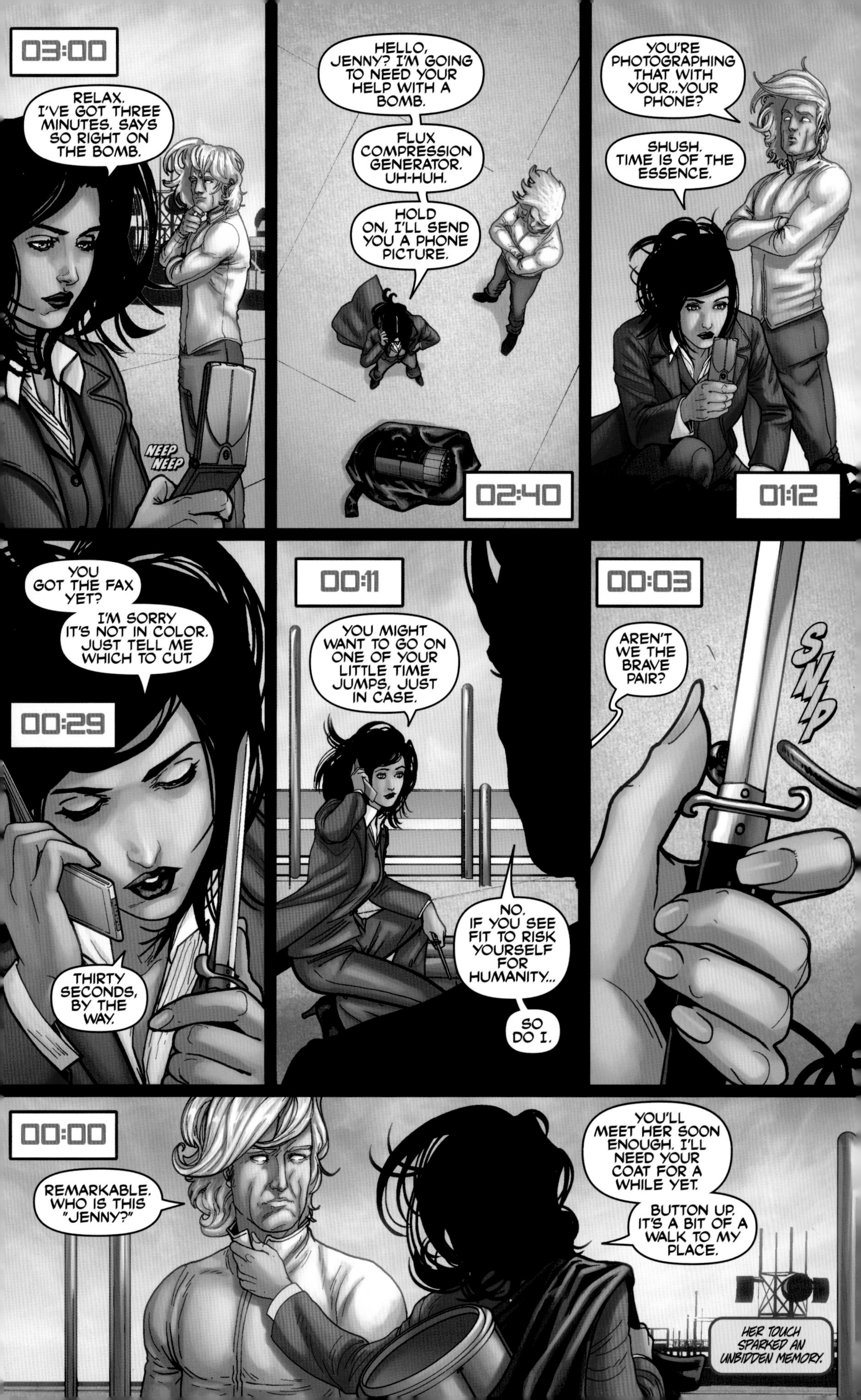
03:00
RELAX. I'VE GOT THREE MINUTES. SAYS SO RIGHT ON THE BOMB.
NEEP NEEP
HELLO, JENNY? I'M GOING TO NEED YOUR HELP WITH A BOMB.
FLUX COMPRESSION GENERATOR. UH-HUH.
HOLD ON, I'LL SEND YOU A PHONE PICTURE.
02:40
YOU'RE PHOTOGRAPHING THAT WITH YOUR...YOUR PHONE?
SHUSH. TIME IS OF THE ESSENCE.
01:12
YOU GOT THE FAX YET?
I'M SORRY IT'S NOT IN COLOR. JUST TELL ME WHICH TO CUT.
00:29
THIRTY SECONDS, BY THE WAY.
00:11
YOU MIGHT WANT TO GO ON ONE OF YOUR LITTLE TIME JUMPS, JUST IN CASE.
NO. IF YOU SEE FIT TO RISK YOURSELF FOR HUMANITY...
SO DO I.
00:03
AREN'T WE THE BRAVE PAIR?
SNIP
00:00
REMARKABLE. WHO IS THIS "JENNY?"
YOU'LL MEET HER SOON ENOUGH. I'LL NEED YOUR COAT FOR A WHILE YET.
BUTTON UP. IT'S A BIT OF A WALK TO MY PLACE.
HER TOUCH SPARKED AN UNBIDDEN MEMORY.

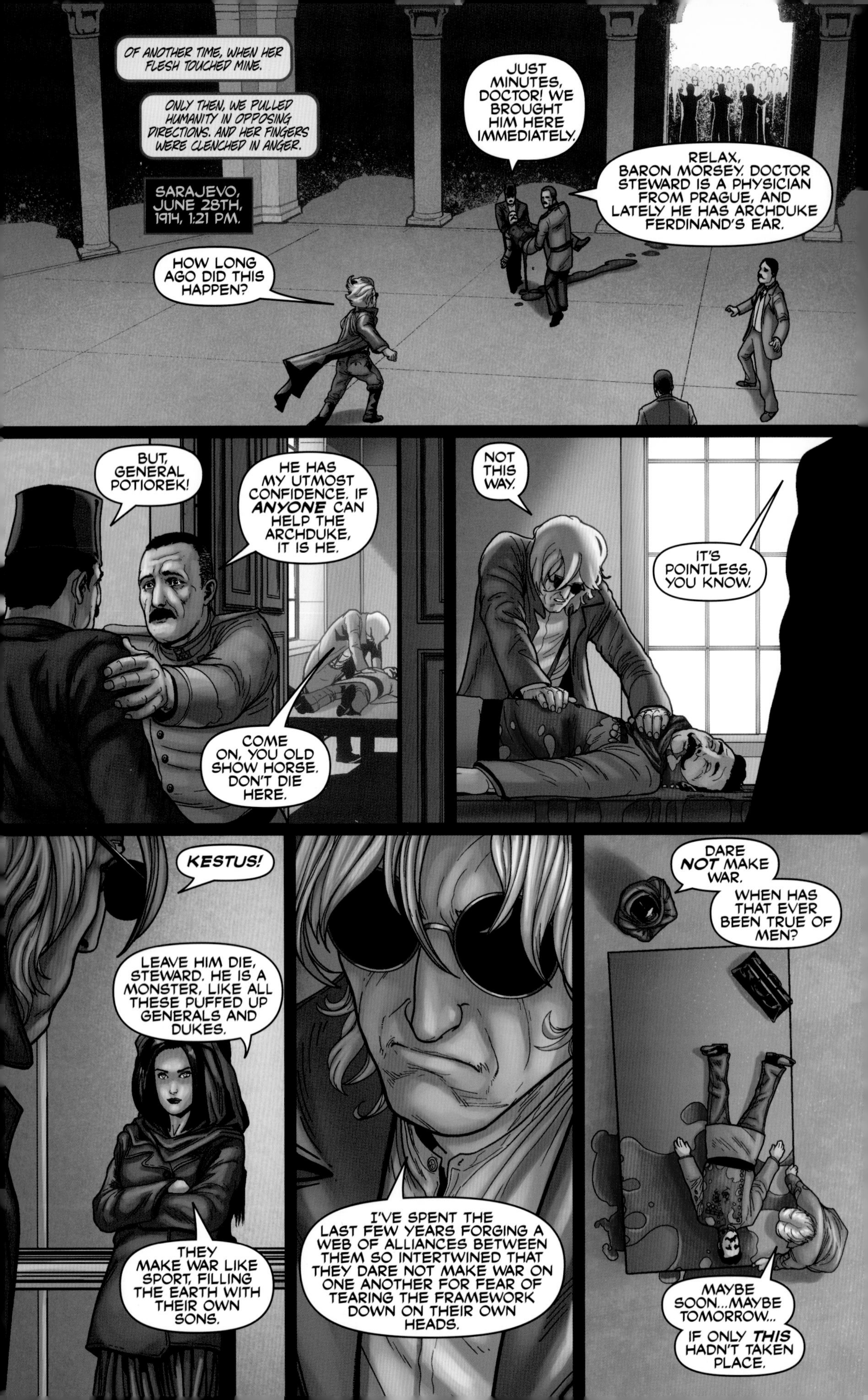
OF ANOTHER TIME, WHEN HER FLESH TOUCHED MINE.
ONLY THEN, WE PULLED HUMANITY IN OPPOSING DIRECTIONS. AND HER FINGERS WERE CLENCHED IN ANGER.
SARAJEVO, JUNE 28TH, 1914, 1:21 PM.
HOW LONG AGO DID THIS HAPPEN?
JUST MINUTES, DOCTOR! WE BROUGHT HIM HERE IMMEDIATELY.
RELAX, BARON MORSEY. DOCTOR STEWARD IS A PHYSICIAN FROM PRAGUE, AND LATELY HE HAS ARCHDUKE FERDINAND'S EAR.
BUT, GENERAL POTIOREK!
HE HAS MY UTMOST CONFIDENCE. IF *ANYONE* CAN HELP THE ARCHDUKE, IT IS HE.
COME ON, YOU OLD SHOW HORSE. DON'T DIE HERE.
NOT THIS WAY.
IT'S POINTLESS, YOU KNOW.
KESTUS!
LEAVE HIM DIE, STEWARD. HE IS A MONSTER, LIKE ALL THESE PUFFED UP GENERALS AND DUKES.
THEY MAKE WAR LIKE SPORT, FILLING THE EARTH WITH THEIR OWN SONS.
I'VE SPENT THE LAST FEW YEARS FORGING A WEB OF ALLIANCES BETWEEN THEM SO INTERTWINED THAT THEY DARE NOT MAKE WAR ON ONE ANOTHER FOR FEAR OF TEARING THE FRAMEWORK DOWN ON THEIR OWN HEADS.
DARE *NOT* MAKE WAR.
WHEN HAS THAT EVER BEEN TRUE OF MEN?
MAYBE SOON...MAYBE TOMORROW...
IF ONLY *THIS* HADN'T TAKEN PLACE.

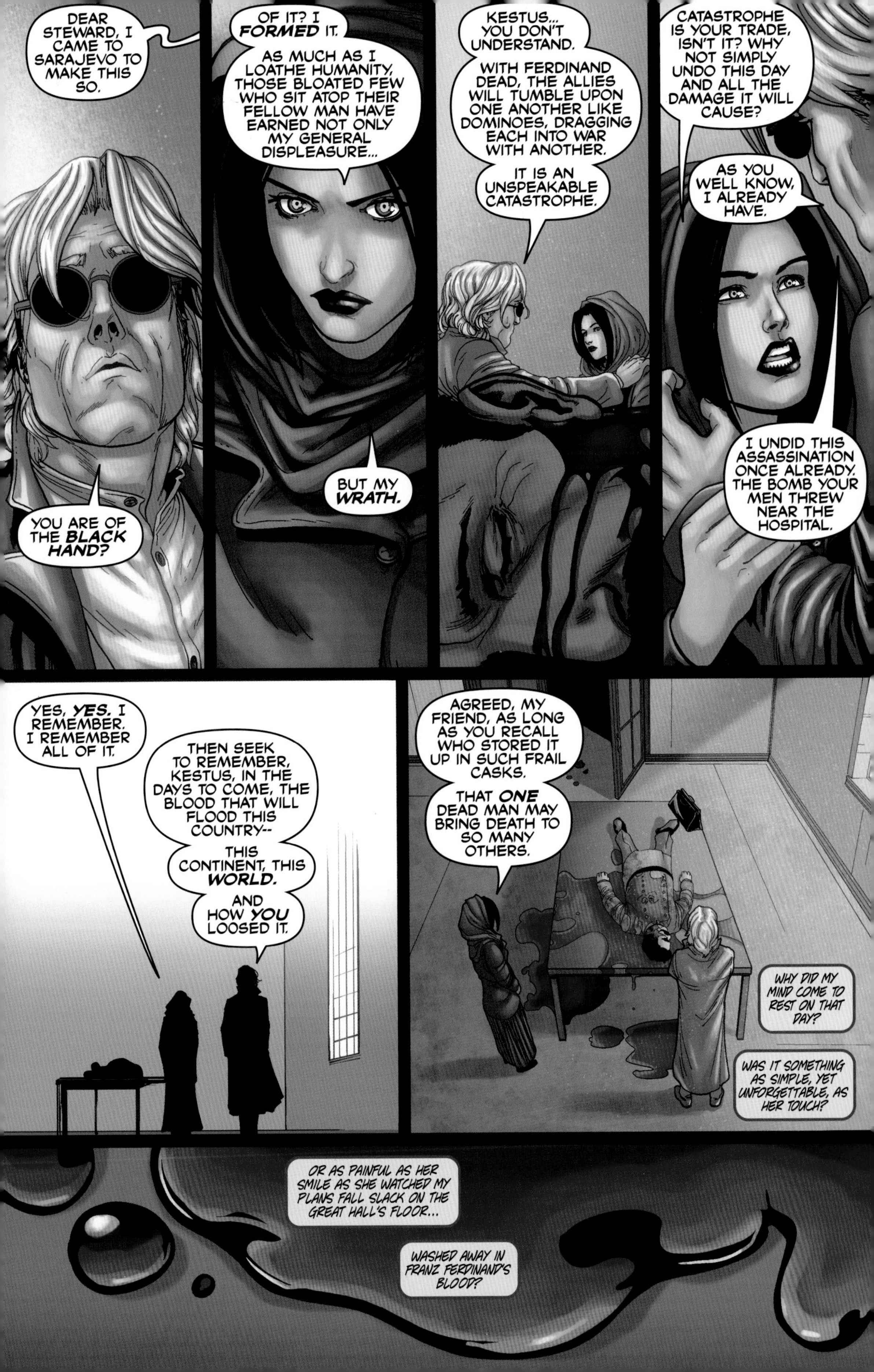
DEAR STEWARD, I CAME TO SARAJEVO TO MAKE THIS SO.
YOU ARE OF THE BLACK HAND?
OF IT? I FORMED IT.
AS MUCH AS I LOATHE HUMANITY, THOSE BLOATED FEW WHO SIT ATOP THEIR FELLOW MAN HAVE EARNED NOT ONLY MY GENERAL DISPLEASURE...
BUT MY WRATH.
KESTUS... YOU DON'T UNDERSTAND.
WITH FERDINAND DEAD, THE ALLIES WILL TUMBLE UPON ONE ANOTHER LIKE DOMINOES, DRAGGING EACH INTO WAR WITH ANOTHER.
IT IS AN UNSPEAKABLE CATASTROPHE.
CATASTROPHE IS YOUR TRADE, ISN'T IT? WHY NOT SIMPLY UNDO THIS DAY AND ALL THE DAMAGE IT WILL CAUSE?
AS YOU WELL KNOW, I ALREADY HAVE.
I UNDID THIS ASSASSINATION ONCE ALREADY. THE BOMB YOUR MEN THREW NEAR THE HOSPITAL.
YES, YES. I REMEMBER. I REMEMBER ALL OF IT.
THEN SEEK TO REMEMBER, KESTUS, IN THE DAYS TO COME, THE BLOOD THAT WILL FLOOD THIS COUNTRY--
THIS CONTINENT, THIS WORLD.
AND HOW YOU LOOSED IT.
AGREED, MY FRIEND, AS LONG AS YOU RECALL WHO STORED IT UP IN SUCH FRAIL CASKS.
THAT ONE DEAD MAN MAY BRING DEATH TO SO MANY OTHERS.
WHY DID MY MIND COME TO REST ON THAT DAY?
WAS IT SOMETHING AS SIMPLE, YET UNFORGETTABLE, AS HER TOUCH?
OR AS PAINFUL AS HER SMILE AS SHE WATCHED MY PLANS FALL SLACK ON THE GREAT HALL'S FLOOR...
WASHED AWAY IN FRANZ FERDINAND'S BLOOD?

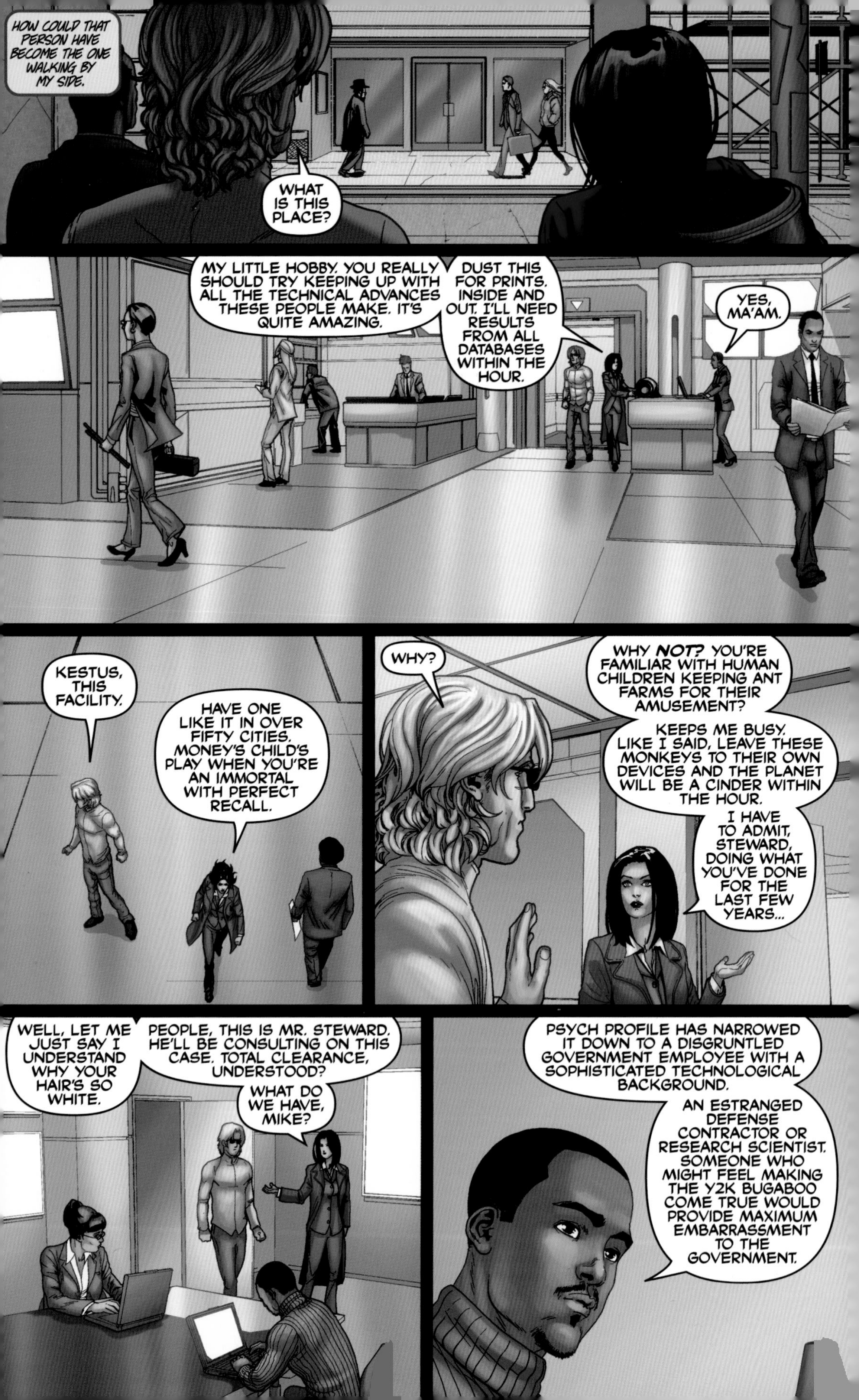
HOW COULD THAT PERSON HAVE BECOME THE ONE WALKING BY MY SIDE.
WHAT IS THIS PLACE?
MY LITTLE HOBBY. YOU REALLY SHOULD TRY KEEPING UP WITH ALL THE TECHNICAL ADVANCES THESE PEOPLE MAKE. IT'S QUITE AMAZING.
DUST THIS FOR PRINTS. INSIDE AND OUT. I'LL NEED RESULTS FROM ALL DATABASES WITHIN THE HOUR.
YES, MA'AM.
KESTUS, THIS FACILITY.
HAVE ONE LIKE IT IN OVER FIFTY CITIES. MONEY'S CHILD'S PLAY WHEN YOU'RE AN IMMORTAL WITH PERFECT RECALL.
WHY?
WHY NOT? YOU'RE FAMILIAR WITH HUMAN CHILDREN KEEPING ANT FARMS FOR THEIR AMUSEMENT?
KEEPS ME BUSY. LIKE I SAID, LEAVE THESE MONKEYS TO THEIR OWN DEVICES AND THE PLANET WILL BE A CINDER WITHIN THE HOUR.
I HAVE TO ADMIT, STEWARD, DOING WHAT YOU'VE DONE FOR THE LAST FEW YEARS...
WELL, LET ME JUST SAY I UNDERSTAND WHY YOUR HAIR'S SO WHITE.
PEOPLE, THIS IS MR. STEWARD. HE'LL BE CONSULTING ON THIS CASE. TOTAL CLEARANCE, UNDERSTOOD?
WHAT DO WE HAVE, MIKE?
PSYCH PROFILE HAS NARROWED IT DOWN TO A DISGRUNTLED GOVERNMENT EMPLOYEE WITH A SOPHISTICATED TECHNOLOGICAL BACKGROUND.
AN ESTRANGED DEFENSE CONTRACTOR OR RESEARCH SCIENTIST. SOMEONE WHO MIGHT FEEL MAKING THE Y2K BUGABOO COME TRUE WOULD PROVIDE MAXIMUM EMBARRASSMENT TO THE GOVERNMENT.

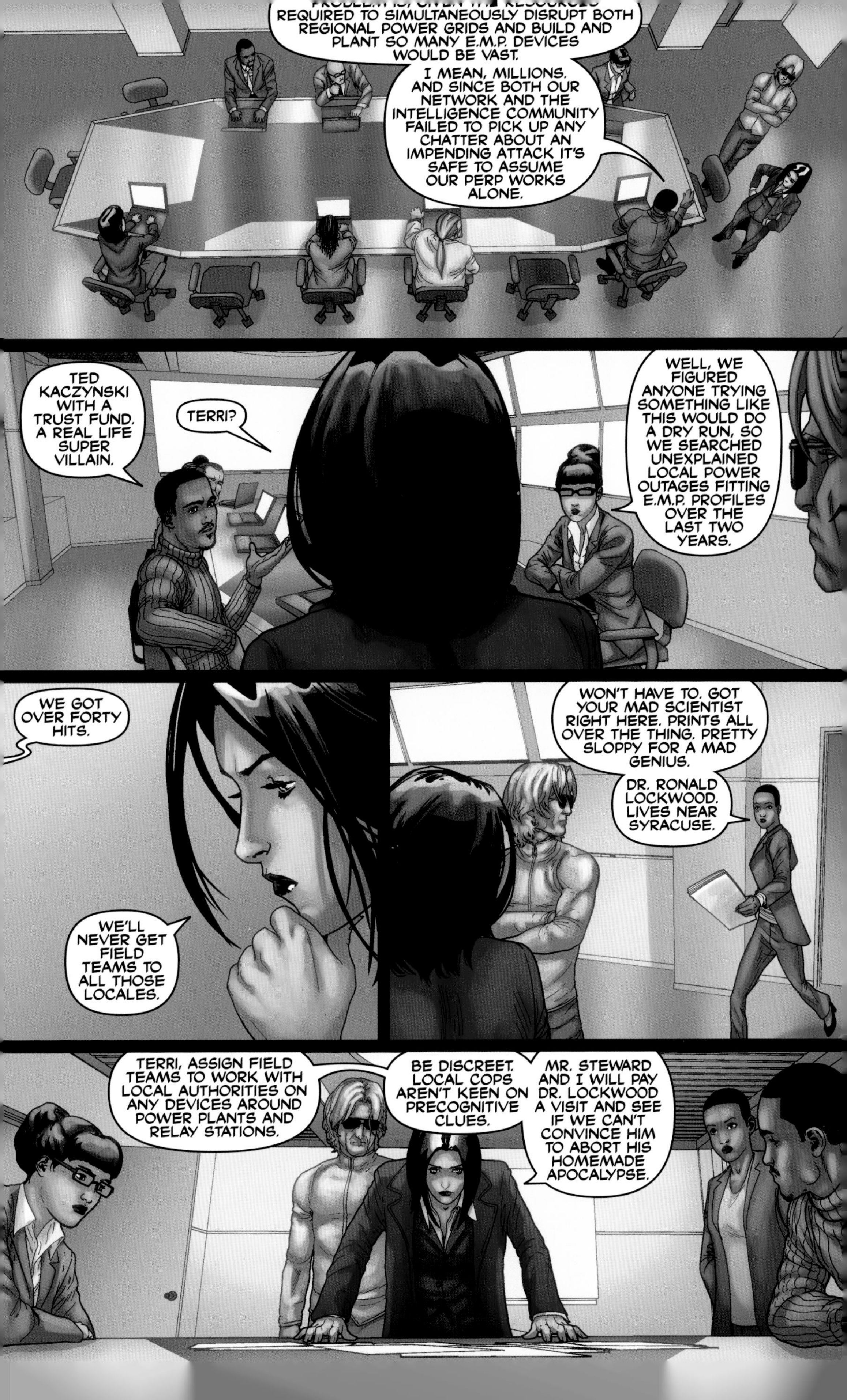
REQUIRED TO SIMULTANEOUSLY DISRUPT BOTH REGIONAL POWER GRIDS AND BUILD AND PLANT SO MANY E.M.P. DEVICES WOULD BE VAST.
I MEAN, MILLIONS. AND SINCE BOTH OUR NETWORK AND THE INTELLIGENCE COMMUNITY FAILED TO PICK UP ANY CHATTER ABOUT AN IMPENDING ATTACK IT'S SAFE TO ASSUME OUR PERP WORKS ALONE.
TED KACZYNSKI WITH A TRUST FUND. A REAL LIFE SUPER VILLAIN.
TERRI?
WELL, WE FIGURED ANYONE TRYING SOMETHING LIKE THIS WOULD DO A DRY RUN, SO WE SEARCHED UNEXPLAINED LOCAL POWER OUTAGES FITTING E.M.P. PROFILES OVER THE LAST TWO YEARS.
WE GOT OVER FORTY HITS.
WE'LL NEVER GET FIELD TEAMS TO ALL THOSE LOCALES.
WON'T HAVE TO. GOT YOUR MAD SCIENTIST RIGHT HERE. PRINTS ALL OVER THE THING. PRETTY SLOPPY FOR A MAD GENIUS.
DR. RONALD LOCKWOOD. LIVES NEAR SYRACUSE.
TERRI, ASSIGN FIELD TEAMS TO WORK WITH LOCAL AUTHORITIES ON ANY DEVICES AROUND POWER PLANTS AND RELAY STATIONS.
BE DISCREET. LOCAL COPS AREN'T KEEN ON PRECOGNITIVE CLUES.
MR. STEWARD AND I WILL PAY DR. LOCKWOOD A VISIT AND SEE IF WE CAN'T CONVINCE HIM TO ABORT HIS HOMEMADE APOCALYPSE.

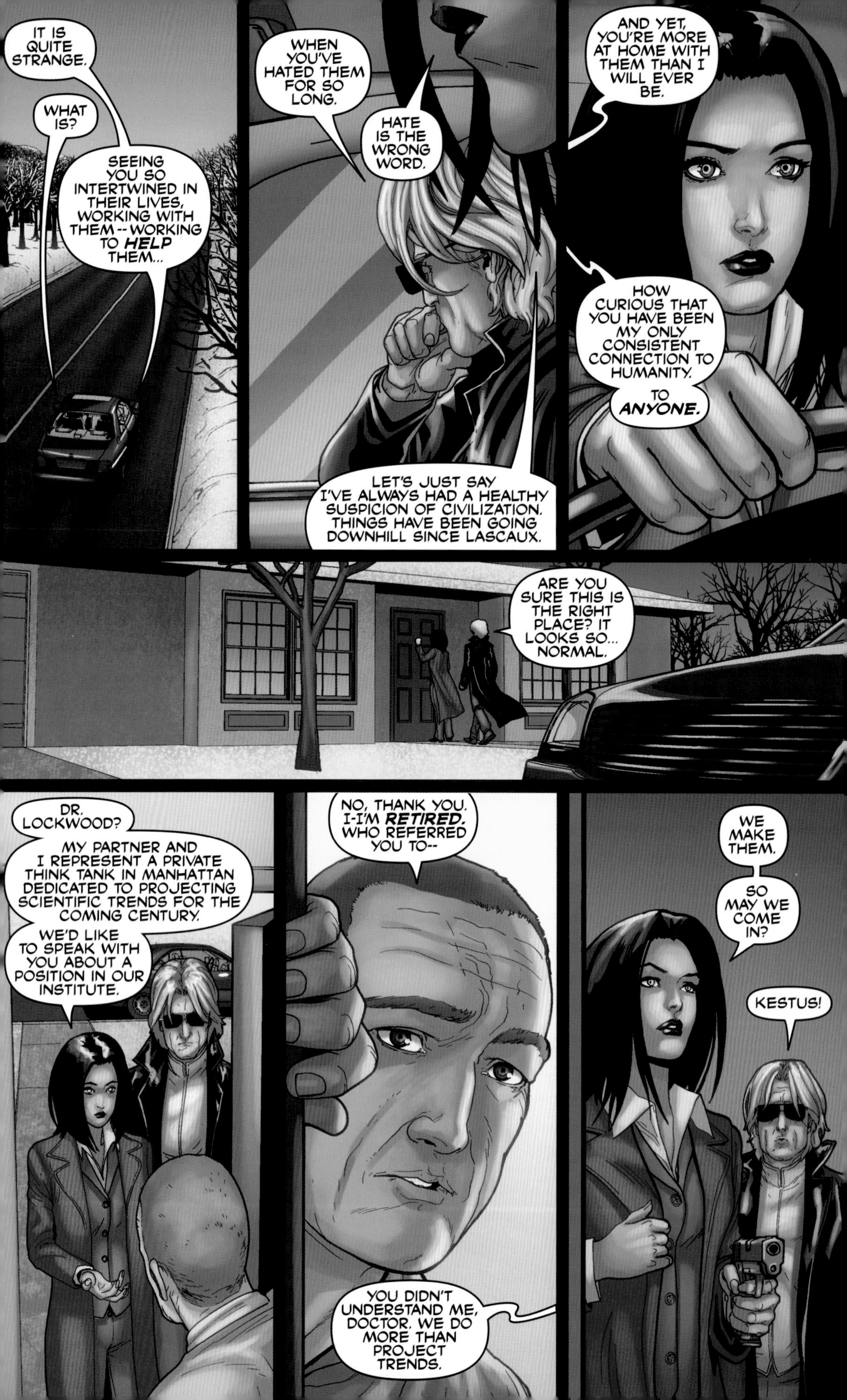
IT IS QUITE STRANGE.
WHAT IS?
SEEING YOU SO INTERTWINED IN THEIR LIVES, WORKING WITH THEM -- WORKING TO *HELP* THEM...
WHEN YOU'VE HATED THEM FOR SO LONG.
HATE IS THE WRONG WORD.
LET'S JUST SAY I'VE ALWAYS HAD A HEALTHY SUSPICION OF CIVILIZATION. THINGS HAVE BEEN GOING DOWNHILL SINCE LASCAUX.
AND YET, YOU'RE MORE AT HOME WITH THEM THAN I WILL EVER BE.
HOW CURIOUS THAT YOU HAVE BEEN MY ONLY CONSISTENT CONNECTION TO HUMANITY.
TO *ANYONE.*
ARE YOU SURE THIS IS THE RIGHT PLACE? IT LOOKS SO... NORMAL.
DR. LOCKWOOD?
MY PARTNER AND I REPRESENT A PRIVATE THINK TANK IN MANHATTAN DEDICATED TO PROJECTING SCIENTIFIC TRENDS FOR THE COMING CENTURY.
WE'D LIKE TO SPEAK WITH YOU ABOUT A POSITION IN OUR INSTITUTE.
NO, THANK YOU. I-I'M *RETIRED.* WHO REFERRED YOU TO--
YOU DIDN'T UNDERSTAND ME, DOCTOR. WE DO MORE THAN PROJECT TRENDS.
WE MAKE THEM.
SO MAY WE COME IN?
KESTUS!

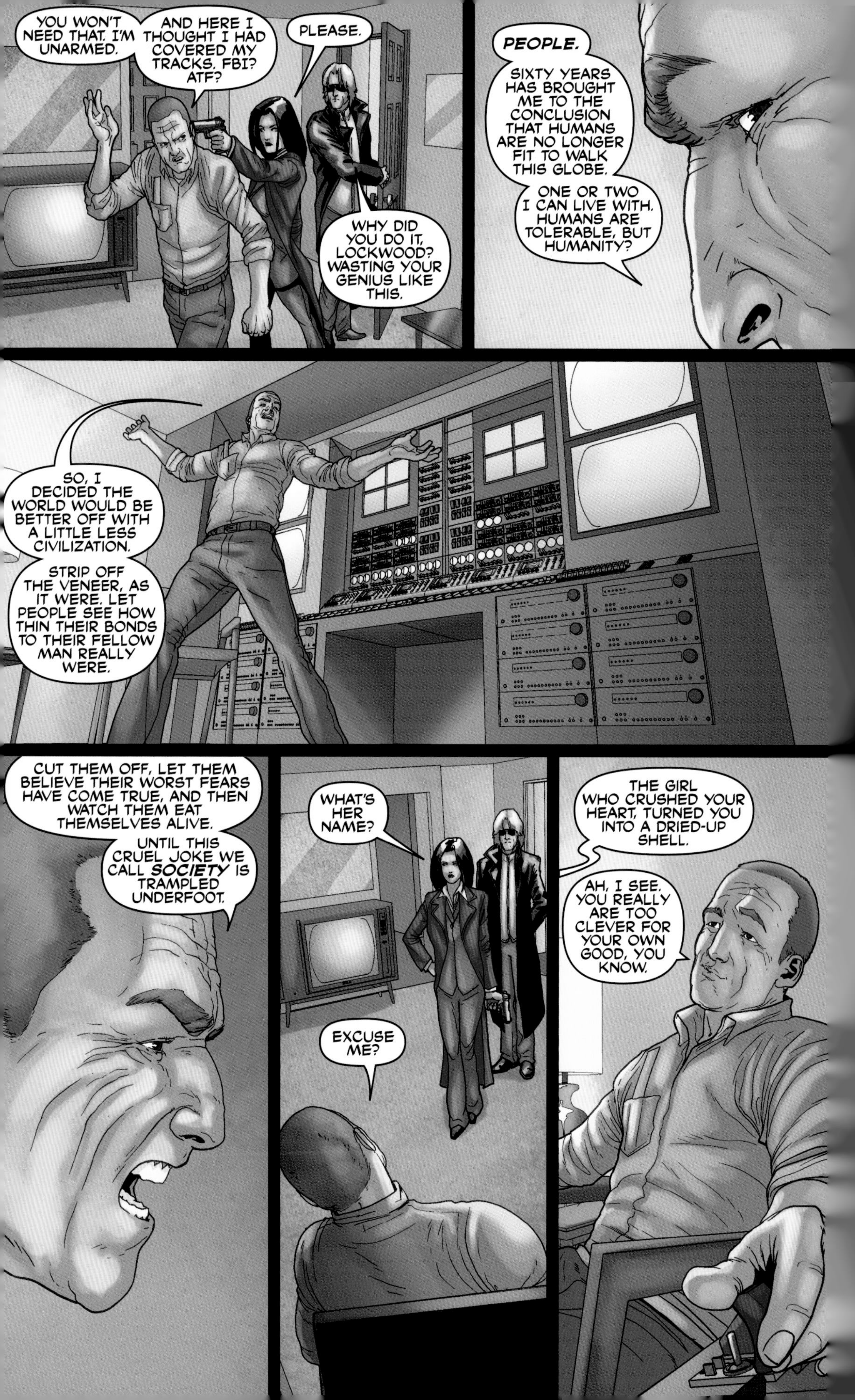
YOU WON'T NEED THAT. I'M UNARMED.
AND HERE I THOUGHT I HAD COVERED MY TRACKS. FBI? ATF?
PLEASE.
WHY DID YOU DO IT, LOCKWOOD? WASTING YOUR GENIUS LIKE THIS.
PEOPLE.
SIXTY YEARS HAS BROUGHT ME TO THE CONCLUSION THAT HUMANS ARE NO LONGER FIT TO WALK THIS GLOBE.
ONE OR TWO I CAN LIVE WITH. HUMANS ARE TOLERABLE, BUT HUMANITY?
SO, I DECIDED THE WORLD WOULD BE BETTER OFF WITH A LITTLE LESS CIVILIZATION.
STRIP OFF THE VENEER, AS IT WERE. LET PEOPLE SEE HOW THIN THEIR BONDS TO THEIR FELLOW MAN REALLY WERE.
CUT THEM OFF, LET THEM BELIEVE THEIR WORST FEARS HAVE COME TRUE, AND THEN WATCH THEM EAT THEMSELVES ALIVE.
UNTIL THIS CRUEL JOKE WE CALL SOCIETY IS TRAMPLED UNDERFOOT.
WHAT'S HER NAME?
EXCUSE ME?
THE GIRL WHO CRUSHED YOUR HEART, TURNED YOU INTO A DRIED-UP SHELL.
AH, I SEE. YOU REALLY ARE TOO CLEVER FOR YOUR OWN GOOD, YOU KNOW.

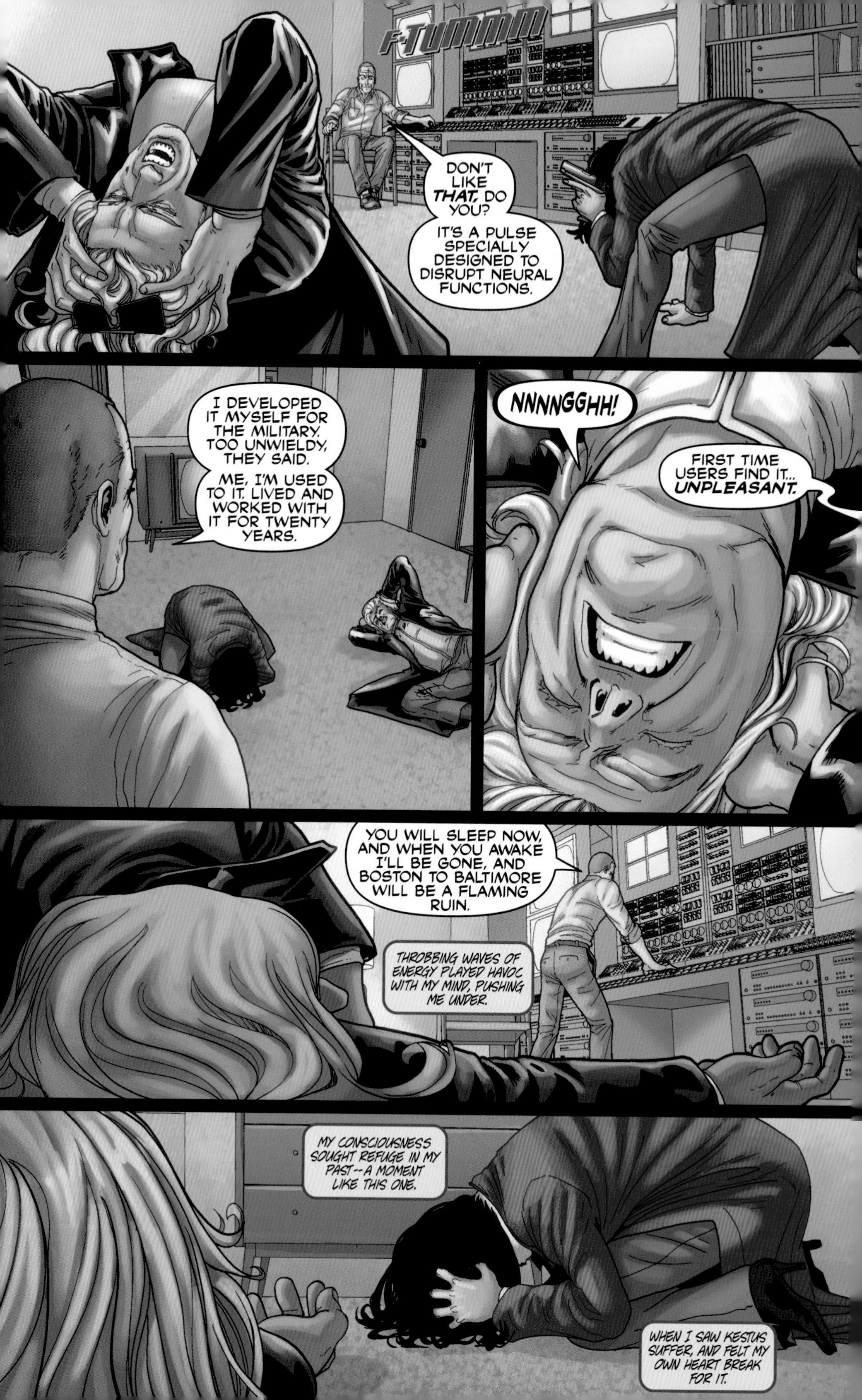
F-TUMMM
DON'T LIKE THAT, DO YOU?
IT'S A PULSE SPECIALLY DESIGNED TO DISRUPT NEURAL FUNCTIONS.
I DEVELOPED IT MYSELF FOR THE MILITARY. TOO UNWIELDY, THEY SAID.
ME, I'M USED TO IT. LIVED AND WORKED WITH IT FOR TWENTY YEARS.
NNNNGGHH!
FIRST TIME USERS FIND IT... UNPLEASANT.
YOU WILL SLEEP NOW, AND WHEN YOU AWAKE I'LL BE GONE, AND BOSTON TO BALTIMORE WILL BE A FLAMING RUIN.
THROBBING WAVES OF ENERGY PLAYED HAVOC WITH MY MIND, PUSHING ME UNDER.
MY CONSCIOUSNESS SOUGHT REFUGE IN MY PAST--A MOMENT LIKE THIS ONE.
WHEN I SAW KESTUS SUFFER, AND FELT MY OWN HEART BREAK FOR IT.

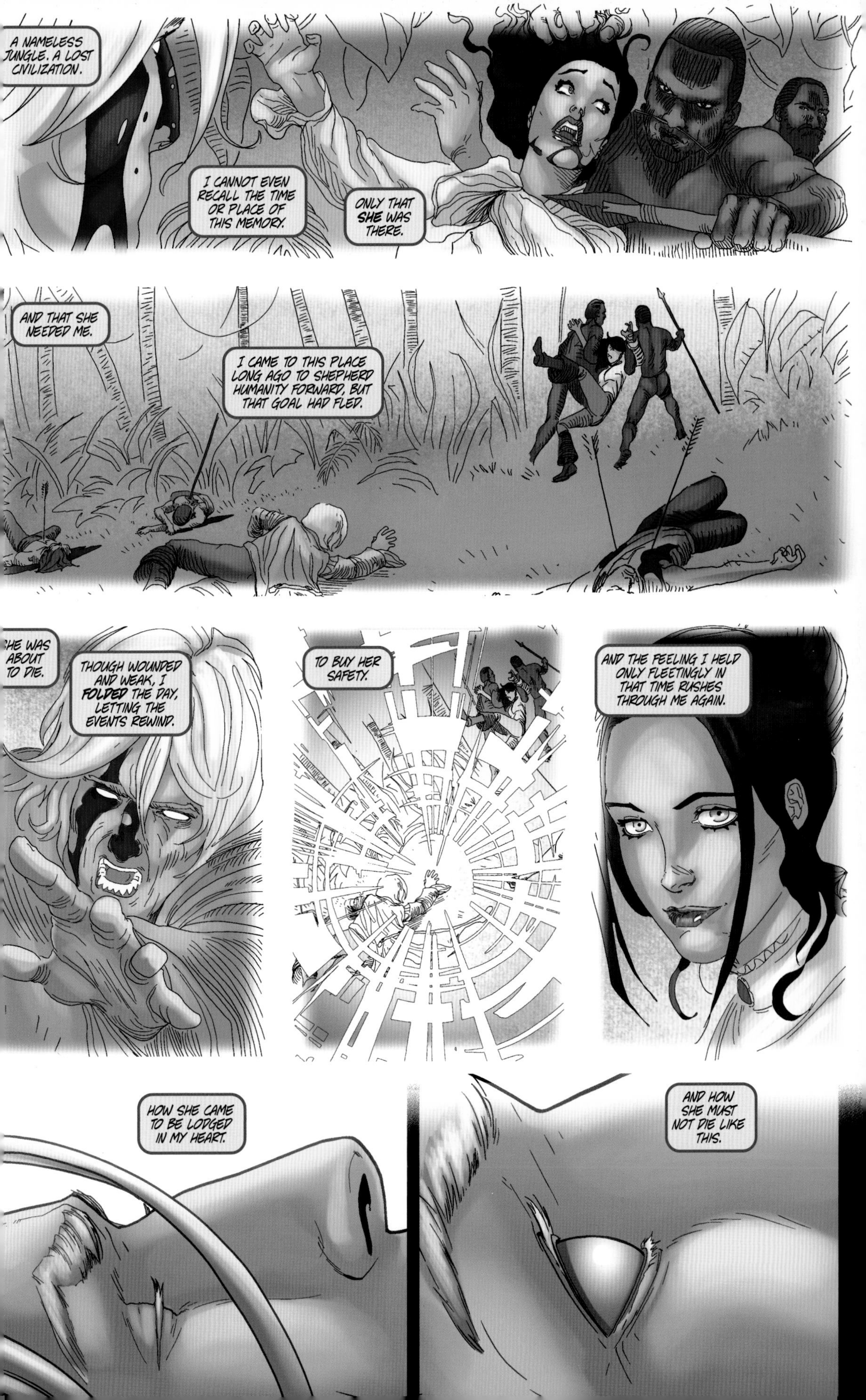
A NAMELESS JUNGLE. A LOST CIVILIZATION.
I CANNOT EVEN RECALL THE TIME OR PLACE OF THIS MEMORY.
ONLY THAT SHE WAS THERE.
AND THAT SHE NEEDED ME.
I CAME TO THIS PLACE LONG AGO TO SHEPHERD HUMANITY FORWARD, BUT THAT GOAL HAD FLED.
SHE WAS ABOUT TO DIE.
THOUGH WOUNDED AND WEAK, I FOLDED THE DAY, LETTING THE EVENTS REWIND.
TO BUY HER SAFETY.
AND THE FEELING I HELD ONLY FLEETINGLY IN THAT TIME RUSHES THROUGH ME AGAIN.
HOW SHE CAME TO BE LODGED IN MY HEART.
AND HOW SHE MUST NOT DIE LIKE THIS.

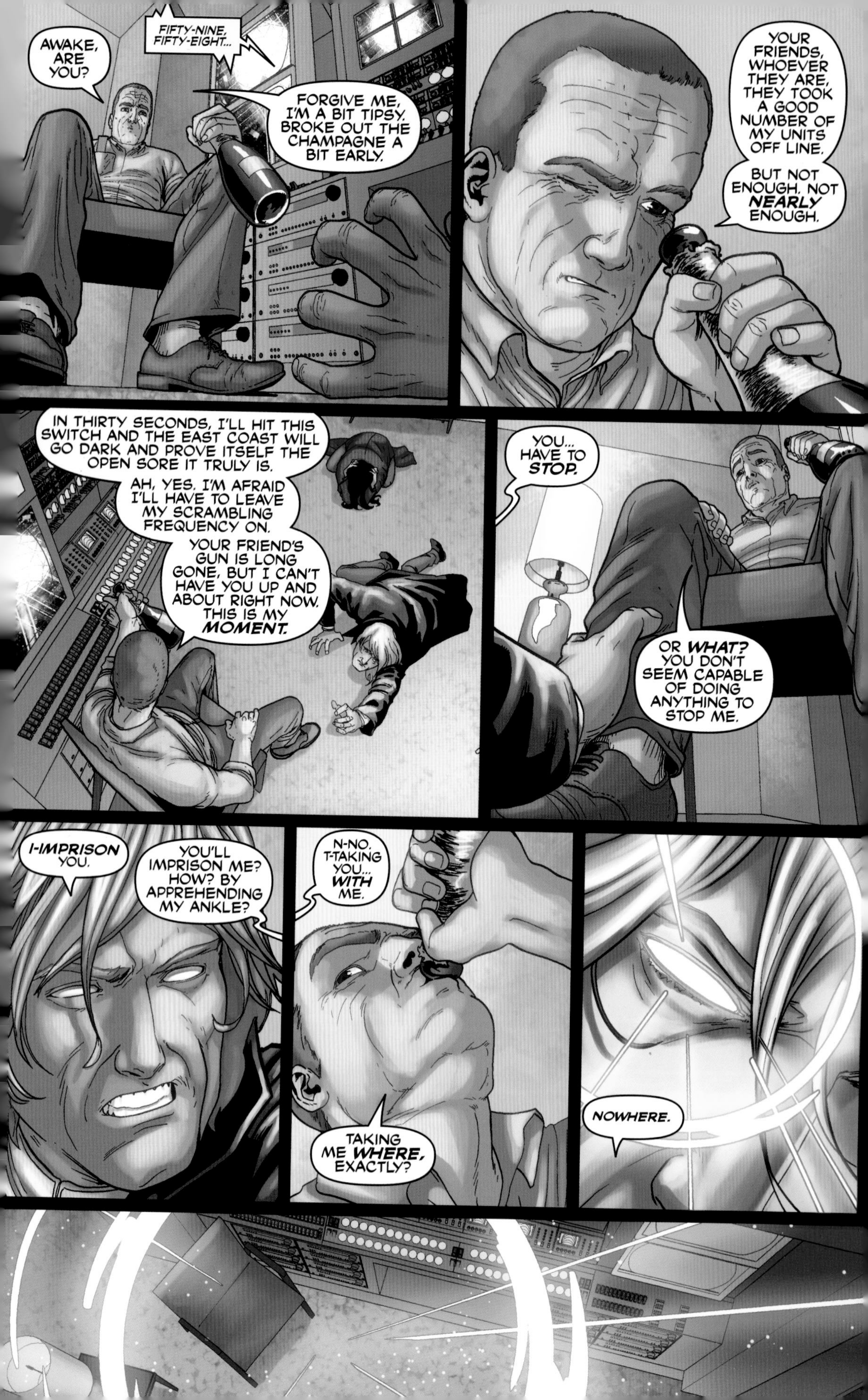
AWAKE, ARE YOU?
FIFTY-NINE, FIFTY-EIGHT...
FORGIVE ME, I'M A BIT TIPSY. BROKE OUT THE CHAMPAGNE A BIT EARLY.
YOUR FRIENDS, WHOEVER THEY ARE, THEY TOOK A GOOD NUMBER OF MY UNITS OFF LINE.
BUT NOT ENOUGH, NOT NEARLY ENOUGH.
IN THIRTY SECONDS, I'LL HIT THIS SWITCH AND THE EAST COAST WILL GO DARK AND PROVE ITSELF THE OPEN SORE IT TRULY IS.
AH, YES. I'M AFRAID I'LL HAVE TO LEAVE MY SCRAMBLING FREQUENCY ON.
YOUR FRIEND'S GUN IS LONG GONE, BUT I CAN'T HAVE YOU UP AND ABOUT RIGHT NOW. THIS IS MY MOMENT.
YOU... HAVE TO STOP.
OR WHAT? YOU DON'T SEEM CAPABLE OF DOING ANYTHING TO STOP ME.
I-IMPRISON YOU.
YOU'LL IMPRISON ME? HOW? BY APPREHENDING MY ANKLE?
N-NO. T-TAKING YOU... WITH ME.
TAKING ME WHERE, EXACTLY?
NOWHERE.

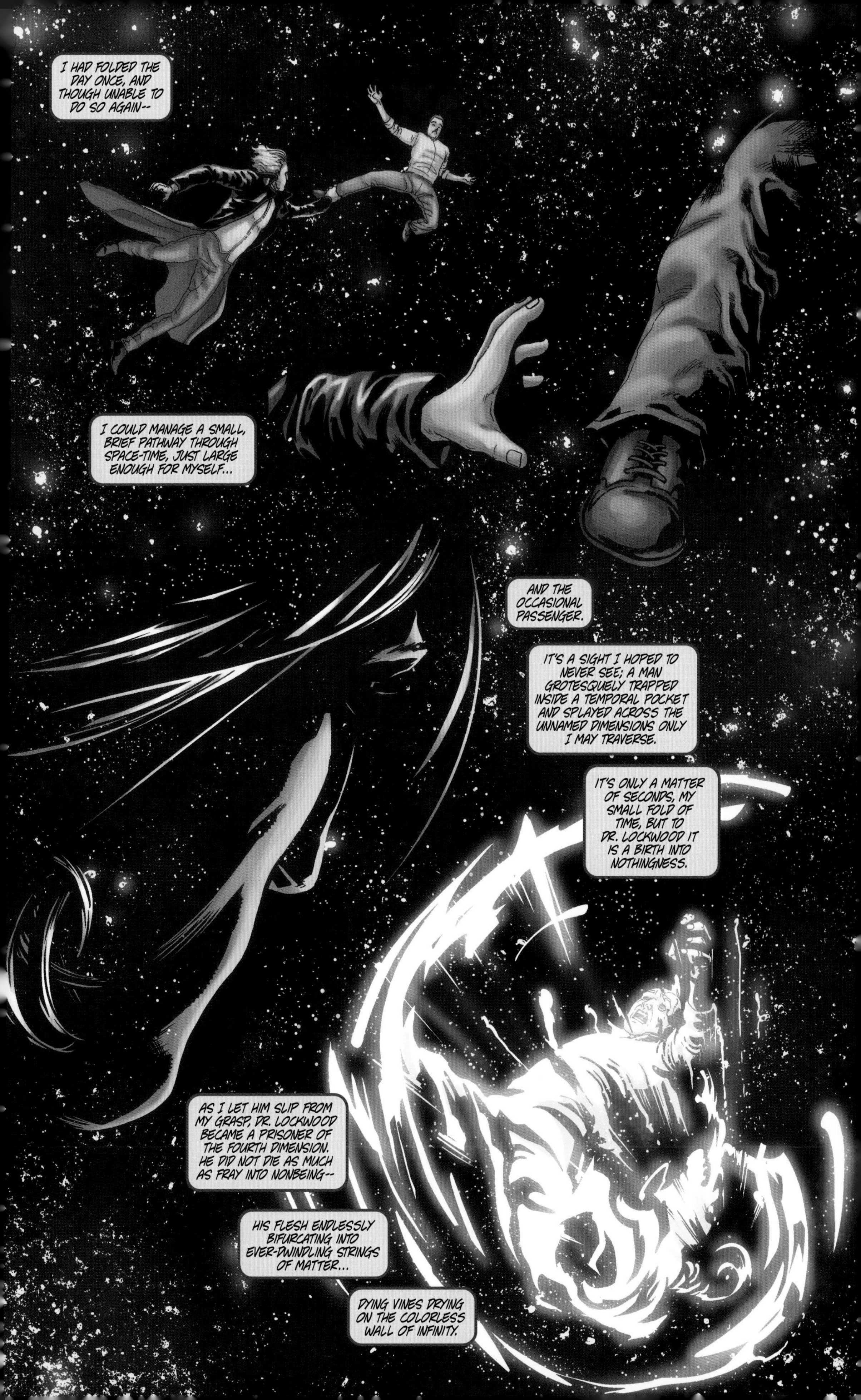
I HAD FOLDED THE DAY ONCE, AND THOUGH UNABLE TO DO SO AGAIN--
I COULD MANAGE A SMALL, BRIEF PATHWAY THROUGH SPACE-TIME, JUST LARGE ENOUGH FOR MYSELF...
AND THE OCCASIONAL PASSENGER.
IT'S A SIGHT I HOPED TO NEVER SEE; A MAN GROTESQUELY TRAPPED INSIDE A TEMPORAL POCKET AND SPLAYED ACROSS THE UNNAMED DIMENSIONS ONLY I MAY TRAVERSE.
IT'S ONLY A MATTER OF SECONDS, MY SMALL FOLD OF TIME, BUT TO DR. LOCKWOOD IT IS A BIRTH INTO NOTHINGNESS.
AS I LET HIM SLIP FROM MY GRASP, DR. LOCKWOOD BECAME A PRISONER OF THE FOURTH DIMENSION. HE DID NOT DIE AS MUCH AS FRAY INTO NONBEING--
HIS FLESH ENDLESSLY BIFURCATING INTO EVER-DWINDLING STRINGS OF MATTER...
DYING VINES DRYING ON THE COLORLESS WALL OF INFINITY.

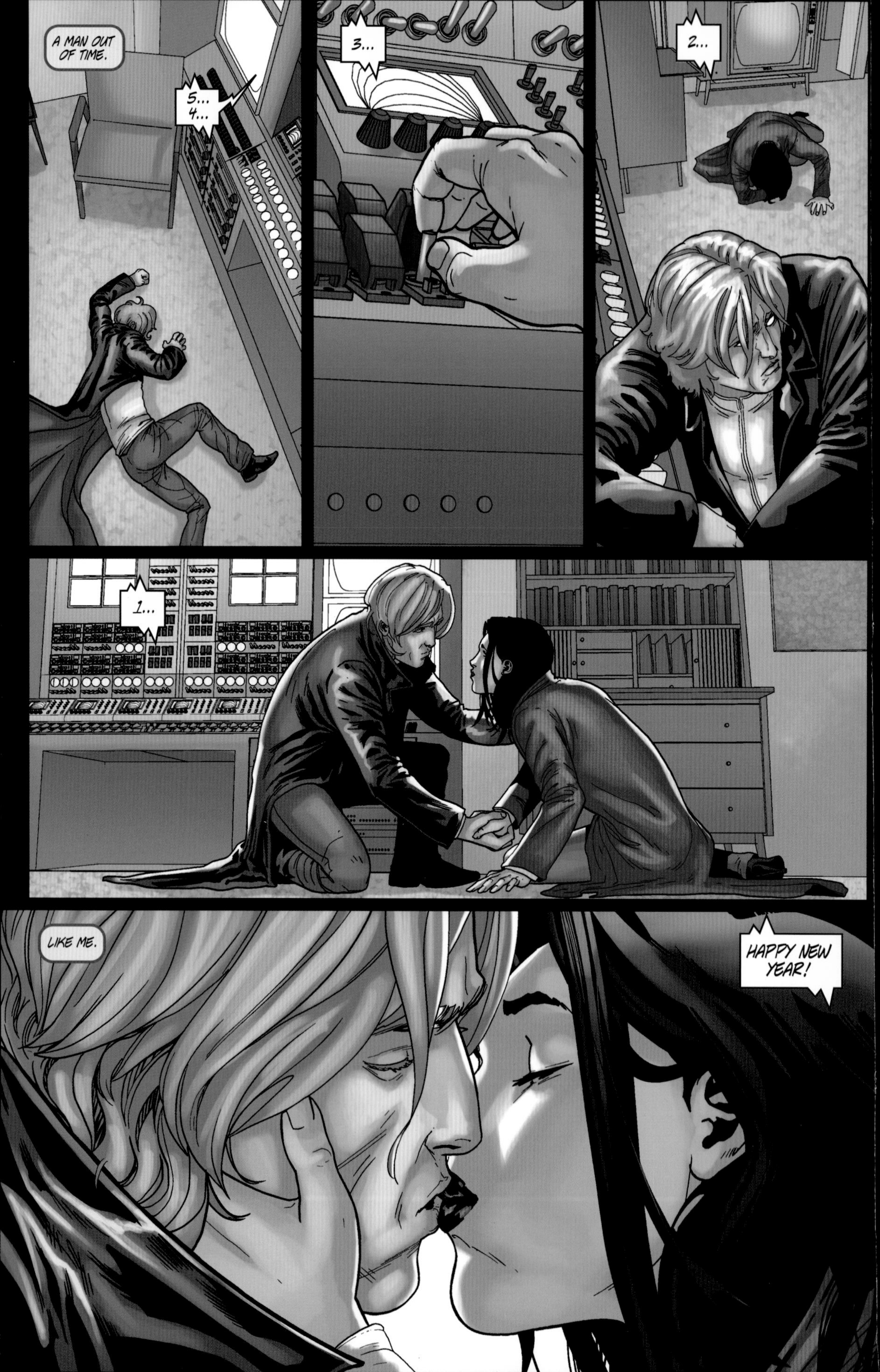
A MAN OUT OF TIME.
5... 4...
3...
2...
1...
LIKE ME.
HAPPY NEW YEAR!

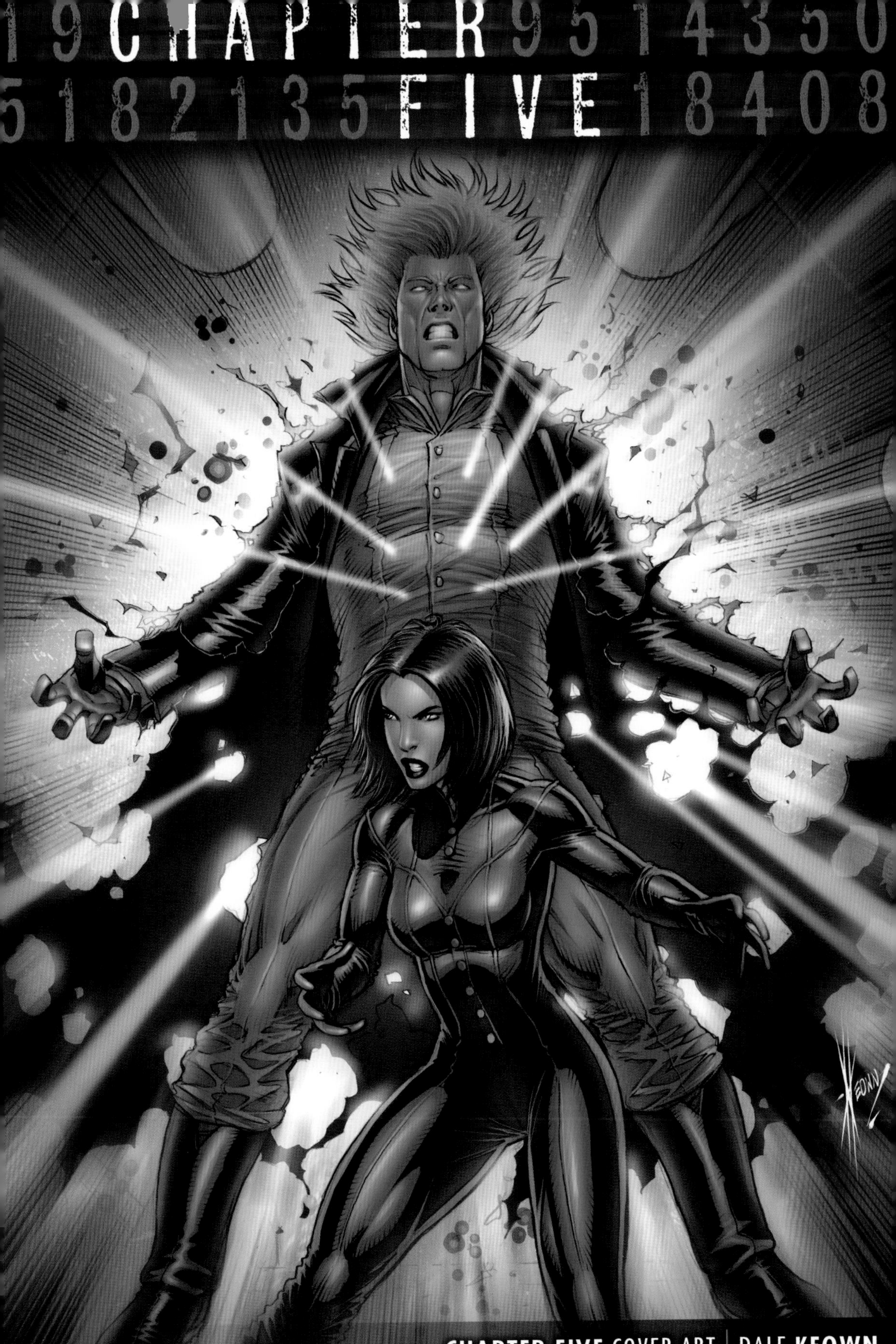
19CHAPTER9514350
5182135FIVE18408
KEOWN

CHAPTER FIVE COVER ART | DALE KEOWN

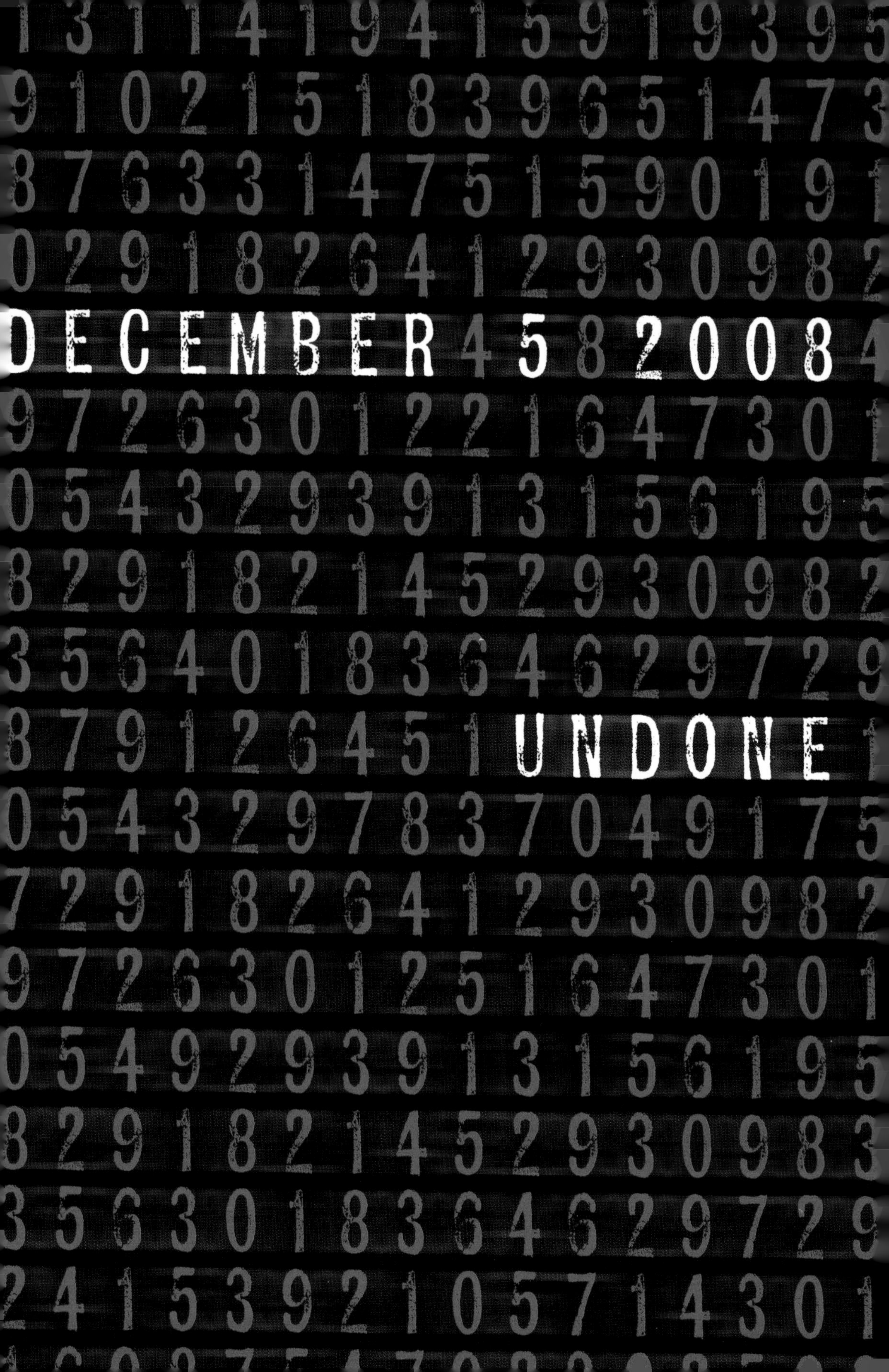
DECEMBER 5 2008
UNDONE

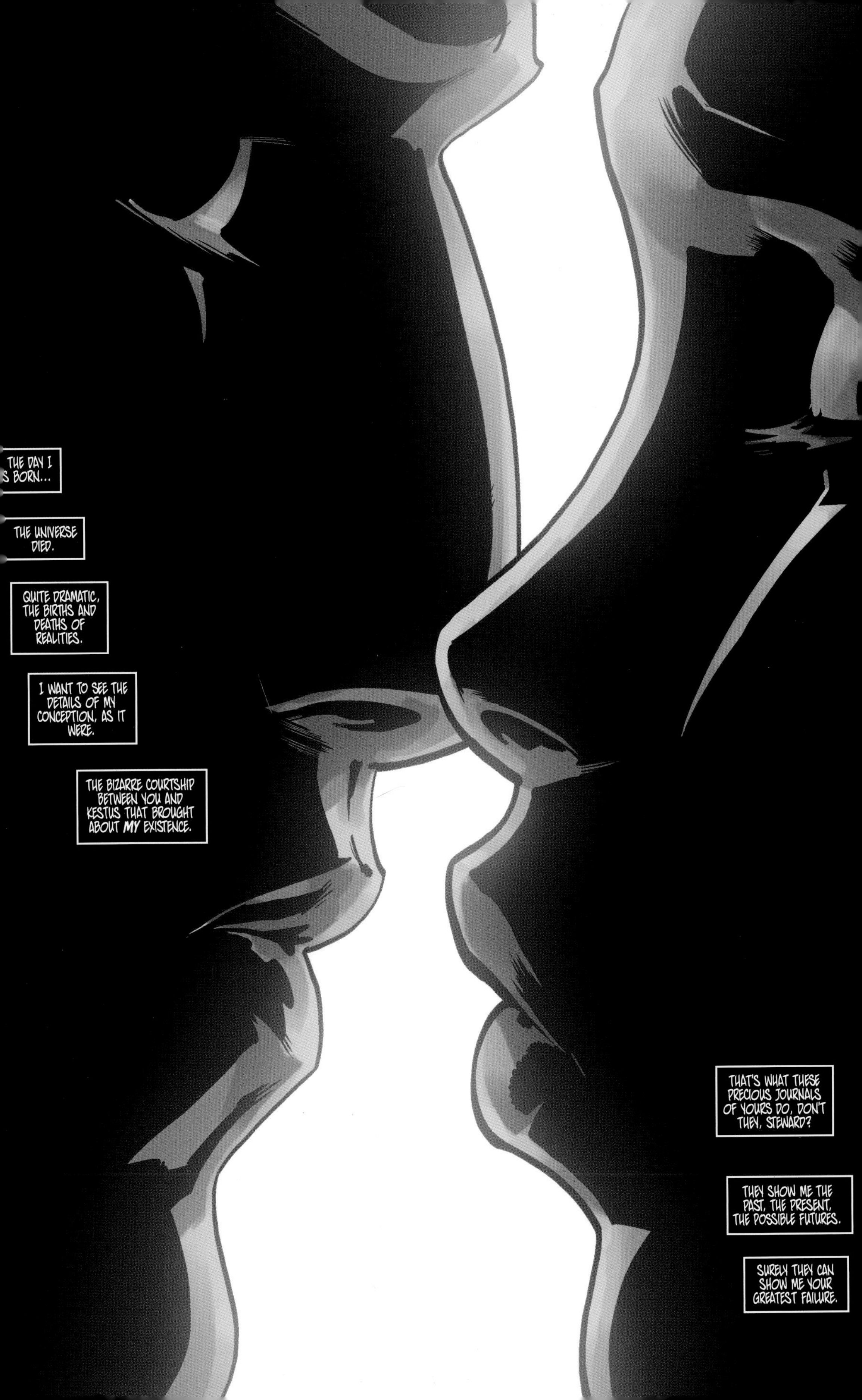
THE DAY I
S BORN...
THE UNIVERSE DIED.
QUITE DRAMATIC, THE BIRTHS AND DEATHS OF REALITIES.
I WANT TO SEE THE DETAILS OF MY CONCEPTION, AS IT WERE.
THE BIZARRE COURTSHIP BETWEEN YOU AND KESTUS THAT BROUGHT ABOUT *MY* EXISTENCE.
THAT'S WHAT THESE PRECIOUS JOURNALS OF YOURS DO, DON'T THEY, STEWARD?
THEY SHOW ME THE PAST, THE PRESENT, THE POSSIBLE FUTURES.
SURELY THEY CAN SHOW ME YOUR GREATEST FAILURE.

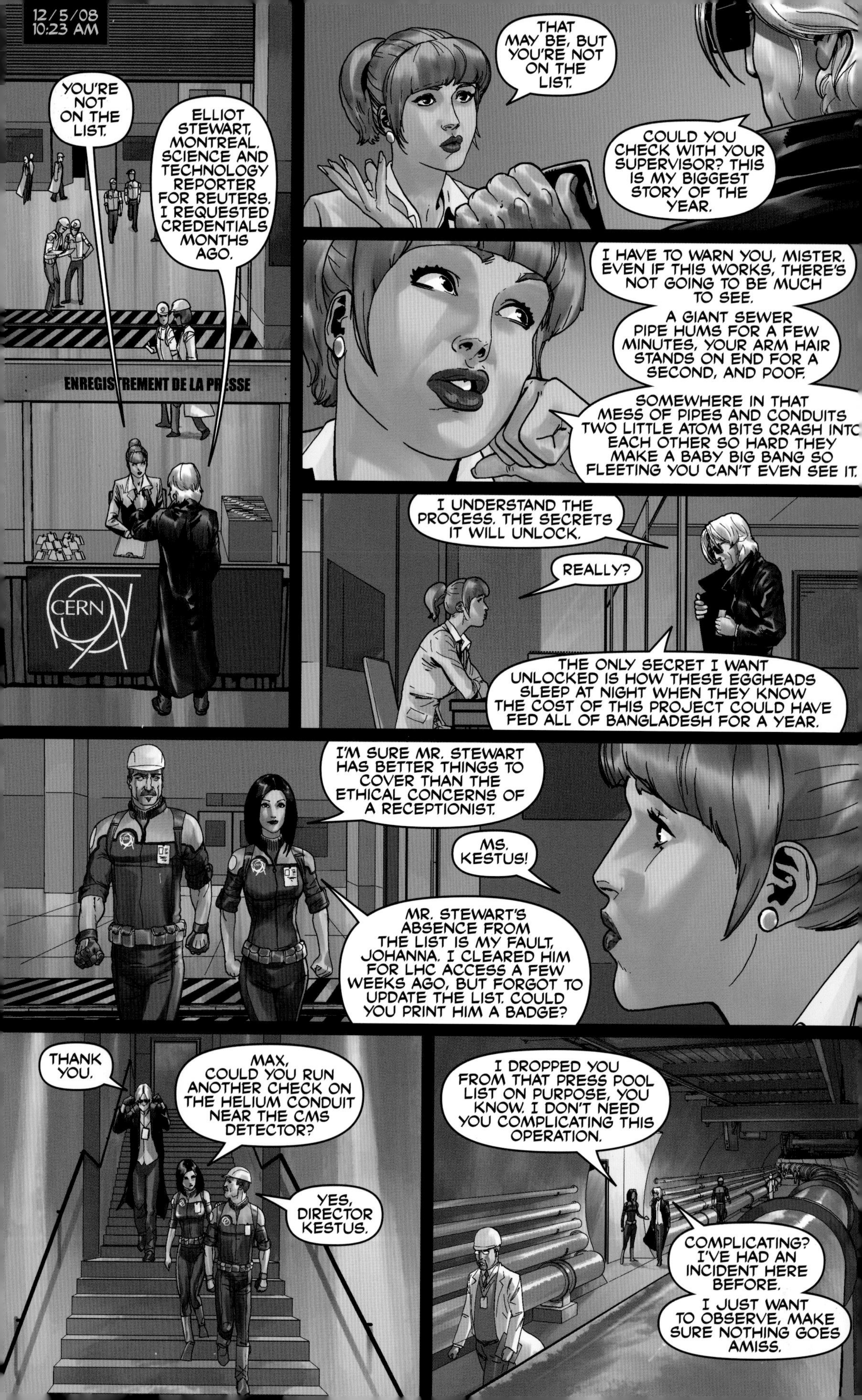
12/5/08
10:23 AM
YOU'RE NOT ON THE LIST.
ELLIOT STEWART, MONTREAL SCIENCE AND TECHNOLOGY REPORTER FOR REUTERS. I REQUESTED CREDENTIALS MONTHS AGO.
ENREGISTREMENT DE LA PRESSE
CERN
THAT MAY BE, BUT YOU'RE NOT ON THE LIST.
COULD YOU CHECK WITH YOUR SUPERVISOR? THIS IS MY BIGGEST STORY OF THE YEAR.
I HAVE TO WARN YOU, MISTER. EVEN IF THIS WORKS, THERE'S NOT GOING TO BE MUCH TO SEE.
A GIANT SEWER PIPE HUMS FOR A FEW MINUTES, YOUR ARM HAIR STANDS ON END FOR A SECOND, AND POOF.
SOMEWHERE IN THAT MESS OF PIPES AND CONDUITS TWO LITTLE ATOM BITS CRASH INTO EACH OTHER SO HARD THEY MAKE A BABY BIG BANG SO FLEETING YOU CAN'T EVEN SEE IT.
I UNDERSTAND THE PROCESS. THE SECRETS IT WILL UNLOCK.
REALLY?
THE ONLY SECRET I WANT UNLOCKED IS HOW THESE EGGHEADS SLEEP AT NIGHT WHEN THEY KNOW THE COST OF THIS PROJECT COULD HAVE FED ALL OF BANGLADESH FOR A YEAR.
I'M SURE MR. STEWART HAS BETTER THINGS TO COVER THAN THE ETHICAL CONCERNS OF A RECEPTIONIST.
MS. KESTUS!
MR. STEWART'S ABSENCE FROM THE LIST IS MY FAULT, JOHANNA. I CLEARED HIM FOR LHC ACCESS A FEW WEEKS AGO, BUT FORGOT TO UPDATE THE LIST. COULD YOU PRINT HIM A BADGE?
THANK YOU.
MAX, COULD YOU RUN ANOTHER CHECK ON THE HELIUM CONDUIT NEAR THE CMS DETECTOR?
YES, DIRECTOR KESTUS.
I DROPPED YOU FROM THAT PRESS POOL LIST ON PURPOSE, YOU KNOW. I DON'T NEED YOU COMPLICATING THIS OPERATION.
COMPLICATING? I'VE HAD AN INCIDENT HERE BEFORE.
I JUST WANT TO OBSERVE, MAKE SURE NOTHING GOES AMISS.

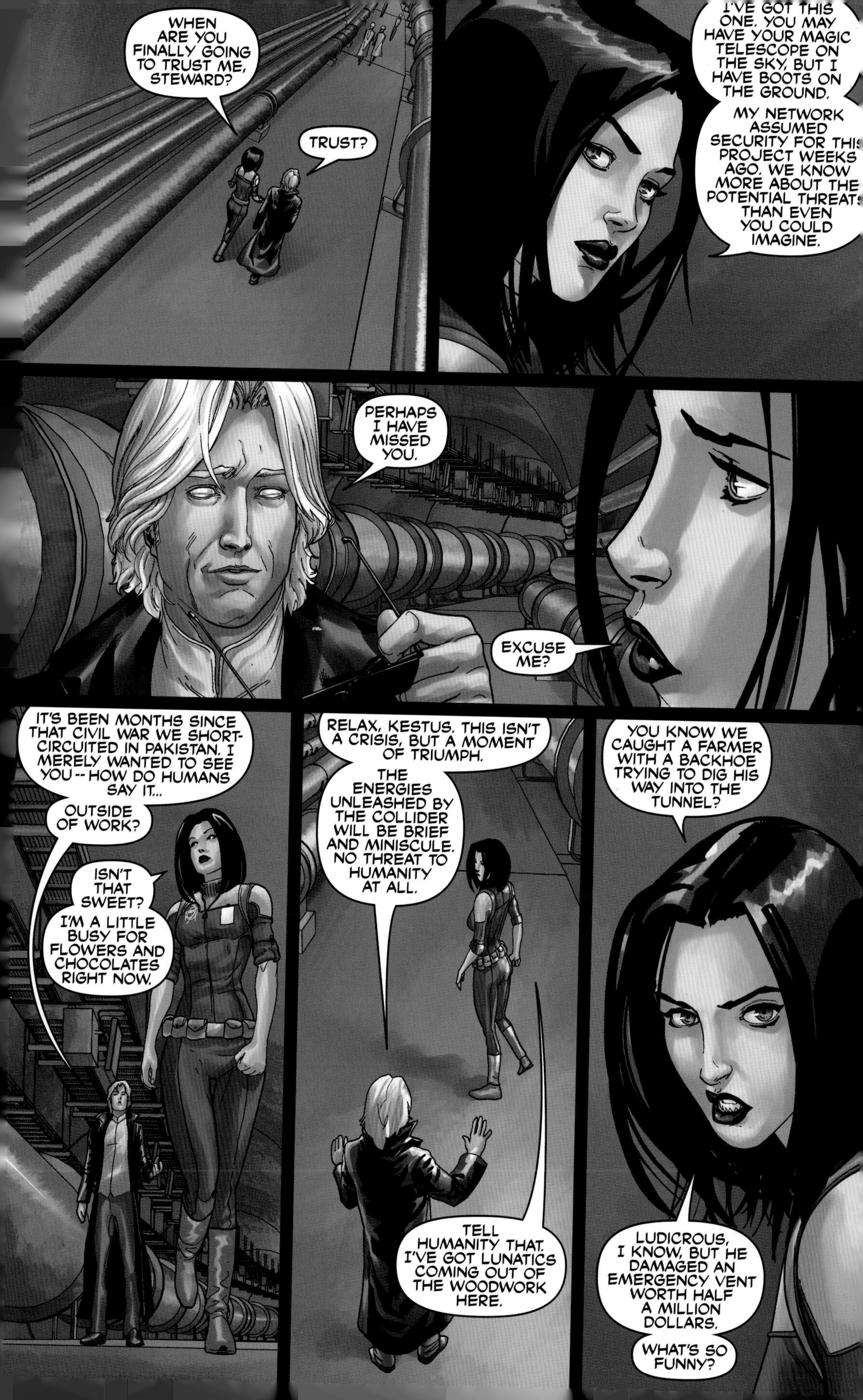
WHEN ARE YOU FINALLY GOING TO TRUST ME, STEWARD?
TRUST?
I'VE GOT THIS ONE. YOU MAY HAVE YOUR MAGIC TELESCOPE ON THE SKY, BUT I HAVE BOOTS ON THE GROUND.
MY NETWORK ASSUMED SECURITY FOR THIS PROJECT WEEKS AGO. WE KNOW MORE ABOUT THE POTENTIAL THREATS THAN EVEN YOU COULD IMAGINE.
PERHAPS I HAVE MISSED YOU.
EXCUSE ME?
IT'S BEEN MONTHS SINCE THAT CIVIL WAR WE SHORT-CIRCUITED IN PAKISTAN. I MERELY WANTED TO SEE YOU -- HOW DO HUMANS SAY IT...
OUTSIDE OF WORK?
ISN'T THAT SWEET?
I'M A LITTLE BUSY FOR FLOWERS AND CHOCOLATES RIGHT NOW.
RELAX, KESTUS. THIS ISN'T A CRISIS, BUT A MOMENT OF TRIUMPH.
THE ENERGIES UNLEASHED BY THE COLLIDER WILL BE BRIEF AND MINISCULE. NO THREAT TO HUMANITY AT ALL.
TELL HUMANITY THAT. I'VE GOT LUNATICS COMING OUT OF THE WOODWORK HERE.
YOU KNOW WE CAUGHT A FARMER WITH A BACKHOE TRYING TO DIG HIS WAY INTO THE TUNNEL?
LUDICROUS, I KNOW, BUT HE DAMAGED AN EMERGENCY VENT WORTH HALF A MILLION DOLLARS.
WHAT'S SO FUNNY?

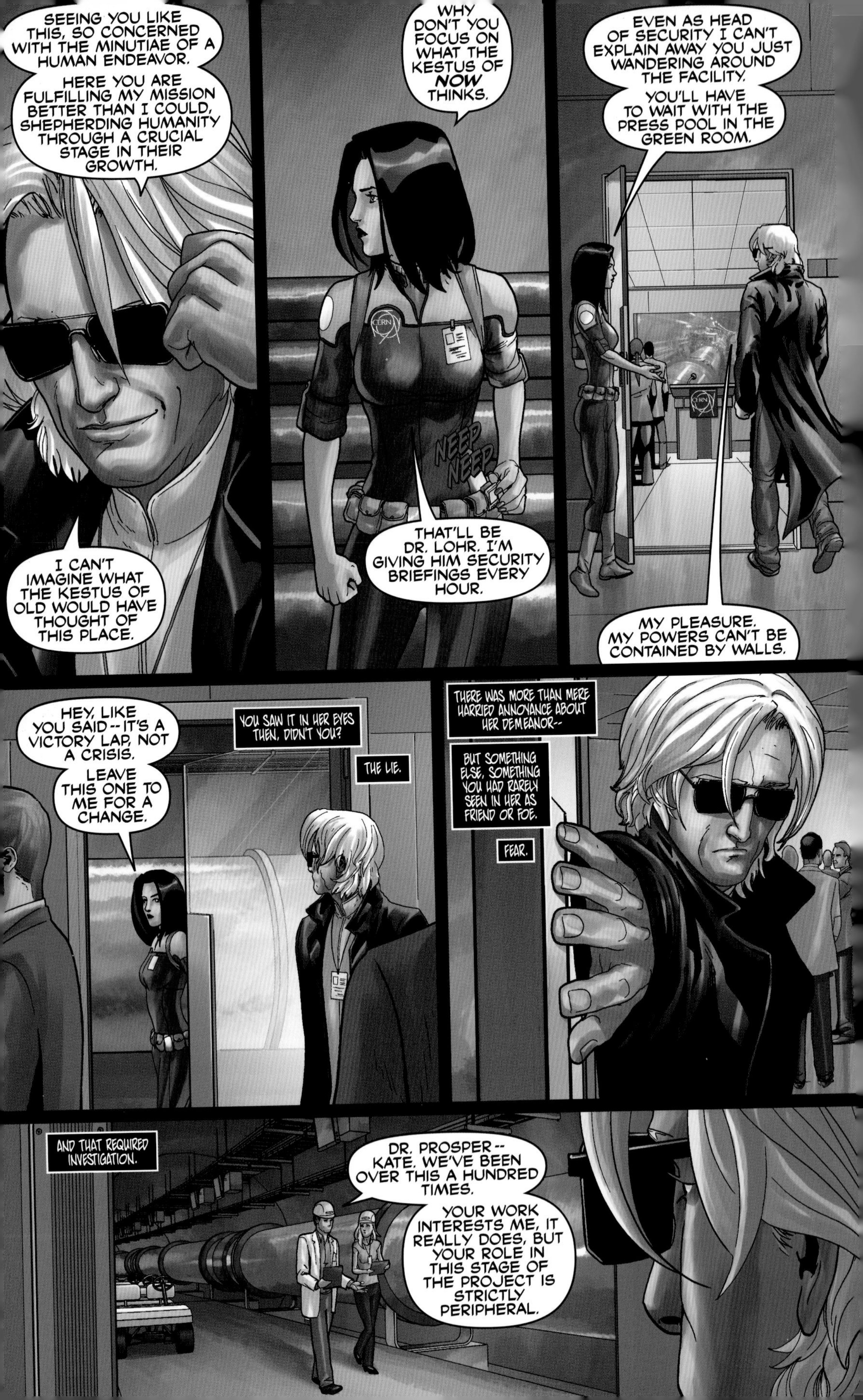

SEEING YOU LIKE THIS, SO CONCERNED WITH THE MINUTIAE OF A HUMAN ENDEAVOR.
HERE YOU ARE FULFILLING MY MISSION BETTER THAN I COULD, SHEPHERDING HUMANITY THROUGH A CRUCIAL STAGE IN THEIR GROWTH.
I CAN'T IMAGINE WHAT THE KESTUS OF OLD WOULD HAVE THOUGHT OF THIS PLACE.
WHY DON'T YOU FOCUS ON WHAT THE KESTUS OF *NOW* THINKS.
CERN
NEEP NEEP
THAT'LL BE DR. LOHR. I'M GIVING HIM SECURITY BRIEFINGS EVERY HOUR.
EVEN AS HEAD OF SECURITY I CAN'T EXPLAIN AWAY YOU JUST WANDERING AROUND THE FACILITY.
YOU'LL HAVE TO WAIT WITH THE PRESS POOL IN THE GREEN ROOM.
MY PLEASURE. MY POWERS CAN'T BE CONTAINED BY WALLS.
HEY, LIKE YOU SAID--IT'S A VICTORY LAP, NOT A CRISIS.
LEAVE THIS ONE TO ME FOR A CHANGE.
YOU SAW IT IN HER EYES THEN, DIDN'T YOU?
THE LIE.
THERE WAS MORE THAN MERE HARRIED ANNOYANCE ABOUT HER DEMEANOR--
BUT SOMETHING ELSE, SOMETHING YOU HAD RARELY SEEN IN HER AS FRIEND OR FOE.
FEAR.
AND THAT REQUIRED INVESTIGATION.
DR. PROSPER--KATE. WE'VE BEEN OVER THIS A HUNDRED TIMES.
YOUR WORK INTERESTS ME, IT REALLY DOES, BUT YOUR ROLE IN THIS STAGE OF THE PROJECT IS STRICTLY PERIPHERAL.

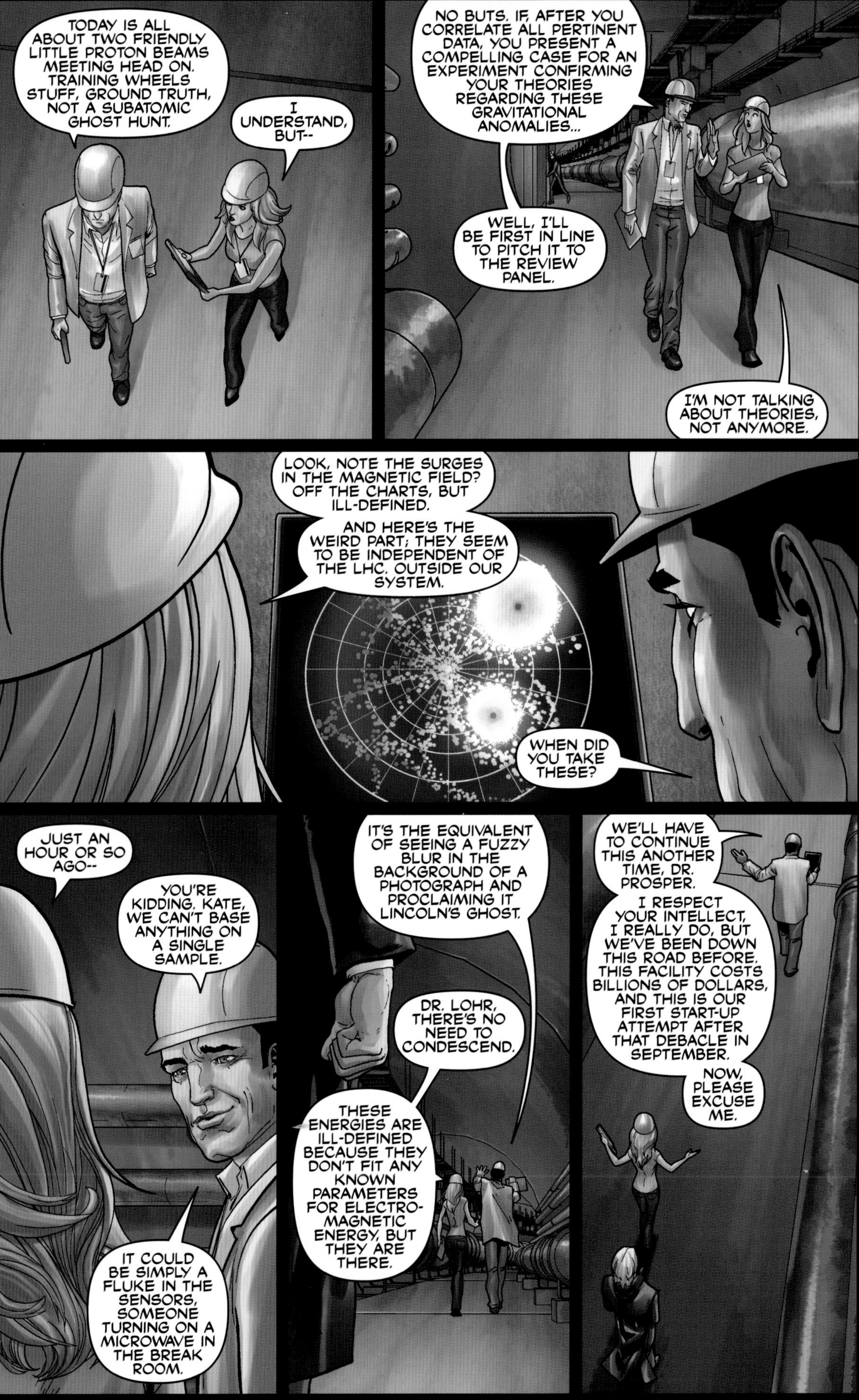
TODAY IS ALL ABOUT TWO FRIENDLY LITTLE PROTON BEAMS MEETING HEAD ON. TRAINING WHEELS STUFF, GROUND TRUTH, NOT A SUBATOMIC GHOST HUNT.
I UNDERSTAND, BUT--
NO BUTS. IF, AFTER YOU CORRELATE ALL PERTINENT DATA, YOU PRESENT A COMPELLING CASE FOR AN EXPERIMENT CONFIRMING YOUR THEORIES REGARDING THESE GRAVITATIONAL ANOMALIES...
WELL, I'LL BE FIRST IN LINE TO PITCH IT TO THE REVIEW PANEL.
I'M NOT TALKING ABOUT THEORIES, NOT ANYMORE.
LOOK, NOTE THE SURGES IN THE MAGNETIC FIELD? OFF THE CHARTS, BUT ILL-DEFINED.
AND HERE'S THE WEIRD PART; THEY SEEM TO BE INDEPENDENT OF THE LHC. OUTSIDE OUR SYSTEM.
WHEN DID YOU TAKE THESE?
JUST AN HOUR OR SO AGO--
YOU'RE KIDDING, KATE, WE CAN'T BASE ANYTHING ON A SINGLE SAMPLE.
IT COULD BE SIMPLY A FLUKE IN THE SENSORS, SOMEONE TURNING ON A MICROWAVE IN THE BREAK ROOM.
IT'S THE EQUIVALENT OF SEEING A FUZZY BLUR IN THE BACKGROUND OF A PHOTOGRAPH AND PROCLAIMING IT LINCOLN'S GHOST.
DR. LOHR, THERE'S NO NEED TO CONDESCEND.
THESE ENERGIES ARE ILL-DEFINED BECAUSE THEY DON'T FIT ANY KNOWN PARAMETERS FOR ELECTRO-MAGNETIC ENERGY, BUT THEY ARE THERE.
WE'LL HAVE TO CONTINUE THIS ANOTHER TIME, DR. PROSPER.
I RESPECT YOUR INTELLECT, I REALLY DO, BUT WE'VE BEEN DOWN THIS ROAD BEFORE. THIS FACILITY COSTS BILLIONS OF DOLLARS, AND THIS IS OUR FIRST START-UP ATTEMPT AFTER THAT DEBACLE IN SEPTEMBER.
NOW, PLEASE EXCUSE ME.

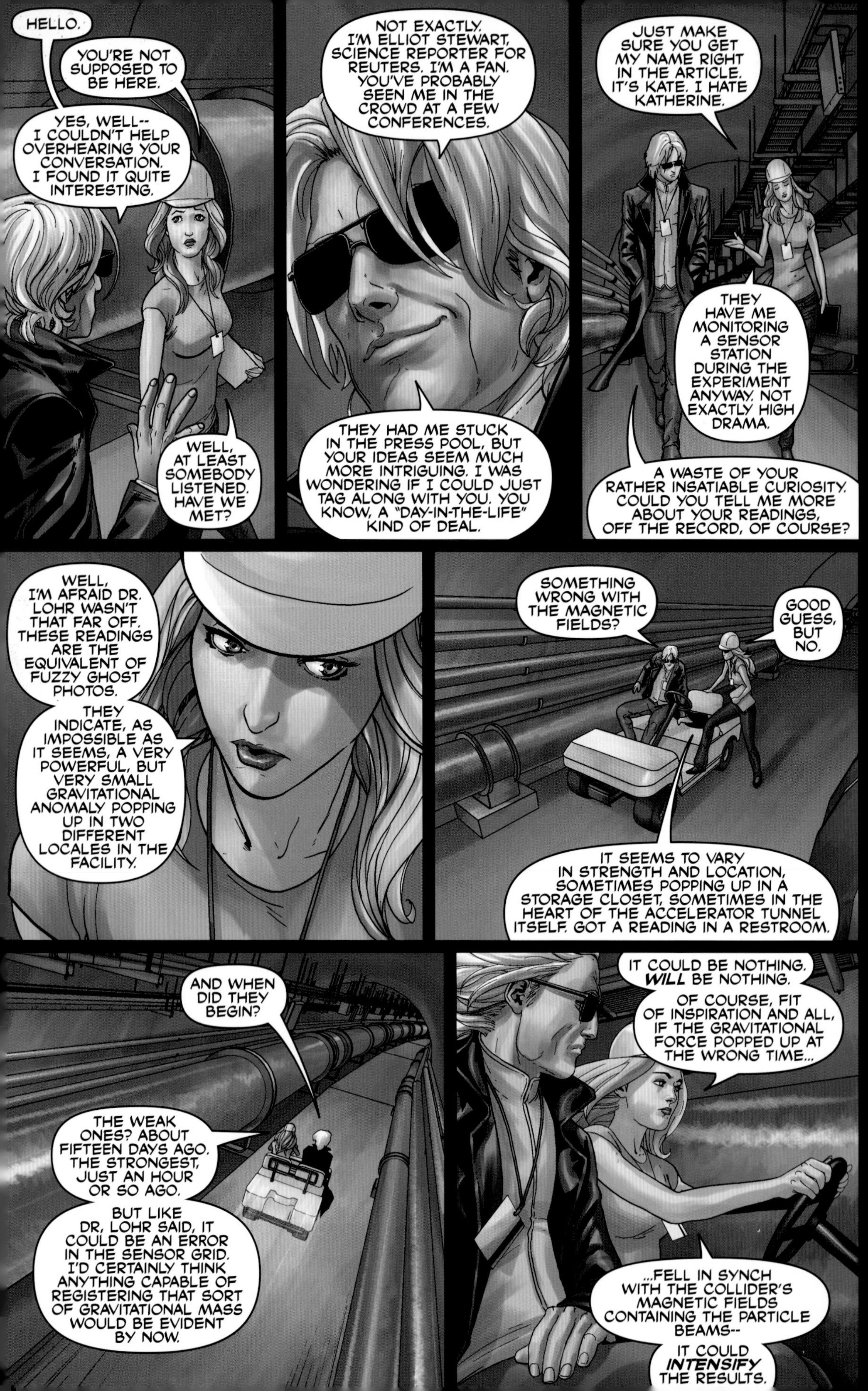
HELLO.
YOU'RE NOT SUPPOSED TO BE HERE.
YES, WELL-- I COULDN'T HELP OVERHEARING YOUR CONVERSATION. I FOUND IT QUITE INTERESTING.
WELL, AT LEAST SOMEBODY LISTENED. HAVE WE MET?
NOT EXACTLY. I'M ELLIOT STEWART, SCIENCE REPORTER FOR REUTERS. I'M A FAN. YOU'VE PROBABLY SEEN ME IN THE CROWD AT A FEW CONFERENCES.
THEY HAD ME STUCK IN THE PRESS POOL, BUT YOUR IDEAS SEEM MUCH MORE INTRIGUING. I WAS WONDERING IF I COULD JUST TAG ALONG WITH YOU. YOU KNOW, A "DAY-IN-THE-LIFE" KIND OF DEAL.
JUST MAKE SURE YOU GET MY NAME RIGHT IN THE ARTICLE. IT'S KATE. I HATE KATHERINE.
THEY HAVE ME MONITORING A SENSOR STATION DURING THE EXPERIMENT ANYWAY. NOT EXACTLY HIGH DRAMA.
A WASTE OF YOUR RATHER INSATIABLE CURIOSITY. COULD YOU TELL ME MORE ABOUT YOUR READINGS, OFF THE RECORD, OF COURSE?
WELL, I'M AFRAID DR. LOHR WASN'T THAT FAR OFF. THESE READINGS ARE THE EQUIVALENT OF FUZZY GHOST PHOTOS.
THEY INDICATE, AS IMPOSSIBLE AS IT SEEMS, A VERY POWERFUL, BUT VERY SMALL GRAVITATIONAL ANOMALY POPPING UP IN TWO DIFFERENT LOCALES IN THE FACILITY.
SOMETHING WRONG WITH THE MAGNETIC FIELDS?
GOOD GUESS, BUT NO.
IT SEEMS TO VARY IN STRENGTH AND LOCATION, SOMETIMES POPPING UP IN A STORAGE CLOSET, SOMETIMES IN THE HEART OF THE ACCELERATOR TUNNEL ITSELF. GOT A READING IN A RESTROOM.
AND WHEN DID THEY BEGIN?
THE WEAK ONES? ABOUT FIFTEEN DAYS AGO. THE STRONGEST, JUST AN HOUR OR SO AGO.
BUT LIKE DR. LOHR SAID, IT COULD BE AN ERROR IN THE SENSOR GRID. I'D CERTAINLY THINK ANYTHING CAPABLE OF REGISTERING THAT SORT OF GRAVITATIONAL MASS WOULD BE EVIDENT BY NOW.
IT COULD BE NOTHING. WILL BE NOTHING.
OF COURSE, FIT OF INSPIRATION AND ALL, IF THE GRAVITATIONAL FORCE POPPED UP AT THE WRONG TIME...
...FELL IN SYNCH WITH THE COLLIDER'S MAGNETIC FIELDS CONTAINING THE PARTICLE BEAMS--
IT COULD INTENSIFY THE RESULTS.

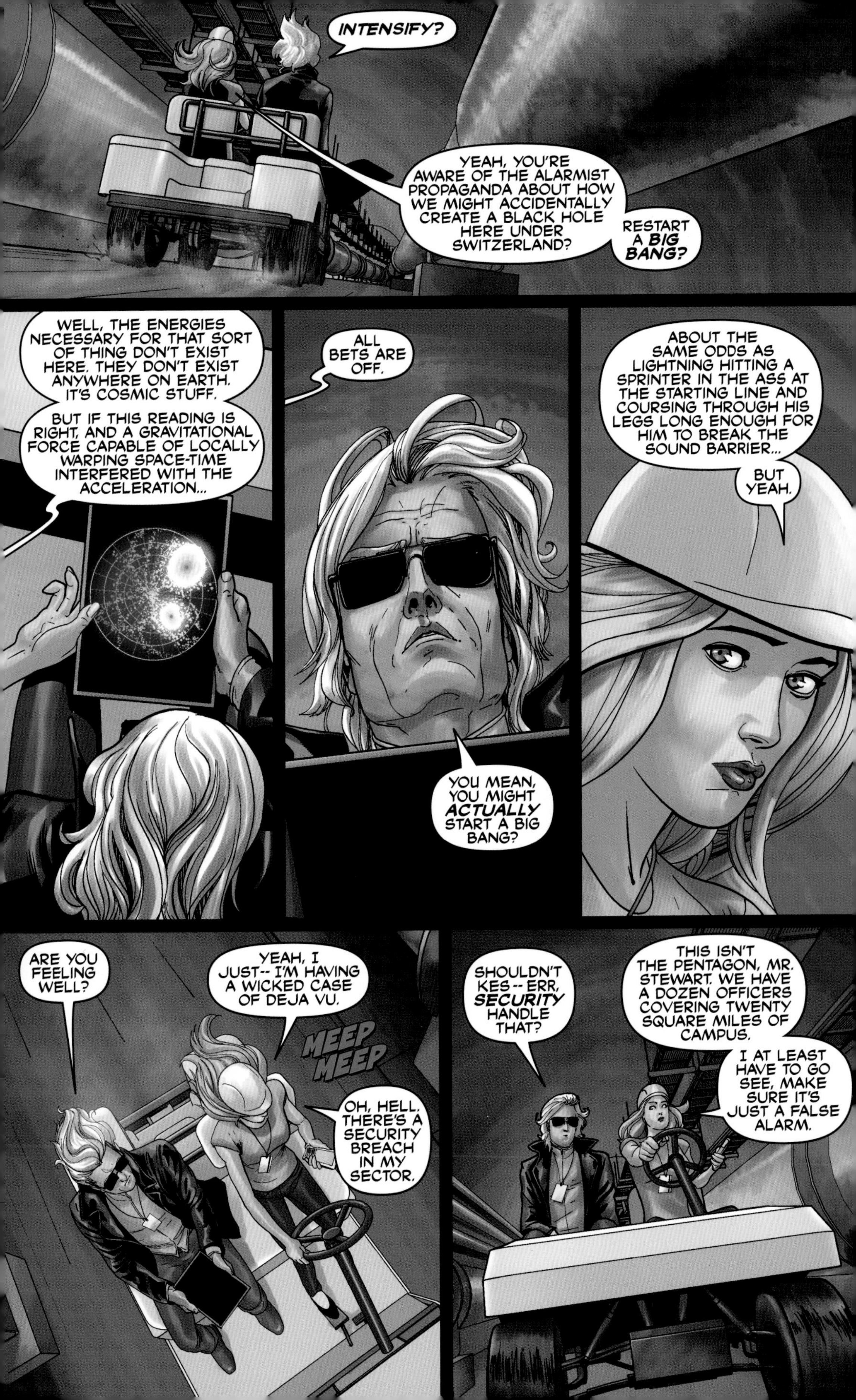
INTENSIFY?
YEAH, YOU'RE AWARE OF THE ALARMIST PROPAGANDA ABOUT HOW WE MIGHT ACCIDENTALLY CREATE A BLACK HOLE HERE UNDER SWITZERLAND?
RESTART A *BIG BANG?*
WELL, THE ENERGIES NECESSARY FOR THAT SORT OF THING DON'T EXIST HERE. THEY DON'T EXIST ANYWHERE ON EARTH. IT'S COSMIC STUFF.
BUT IF THIS READING IS RIGHT, AND A GRAVITATIONAL FORCE CAPABLE OF LOCALLY WARPING SPACE-TIME INTERFERED WITH THE ACCELERATION...
ALL BETS ARE OFF.
YOU MEAN, YOU MIGHT *ACTUALLY* START A BIG BANG?
ABOUT THE SAME ODDS AS LIGHTNING HITTING A SPRINTER IN THE ASS AT THE STARTING LINE AND COURSING THROUGH HIS LEGS LONG ENOUGH FOR HIM TO BREAK THE SOUND BARRIER...
BUT YEAH.
ARE YOU FEELING WELL?
YEAH, I JUST-- I'M HAVING A WICKED CASE OF DEJA VU.
MEEP MEEP
OH, HELL. THERE'S A SECURITY BREACH IN MY SECTOR.
SHOULDN'T KES-- ERR, *SECURITY* HANDLE THAT?
THIS ISN'T THE PENTAGON, MR. STEWART. WE HAVE A DOZEN OFFICERS COVERING TWENTY SQUARE MILES OF CAMPUS.
I AT LEAST HAVE TO GO SEE, MAKE SURE IT'S JUST A FALSE ALARM.

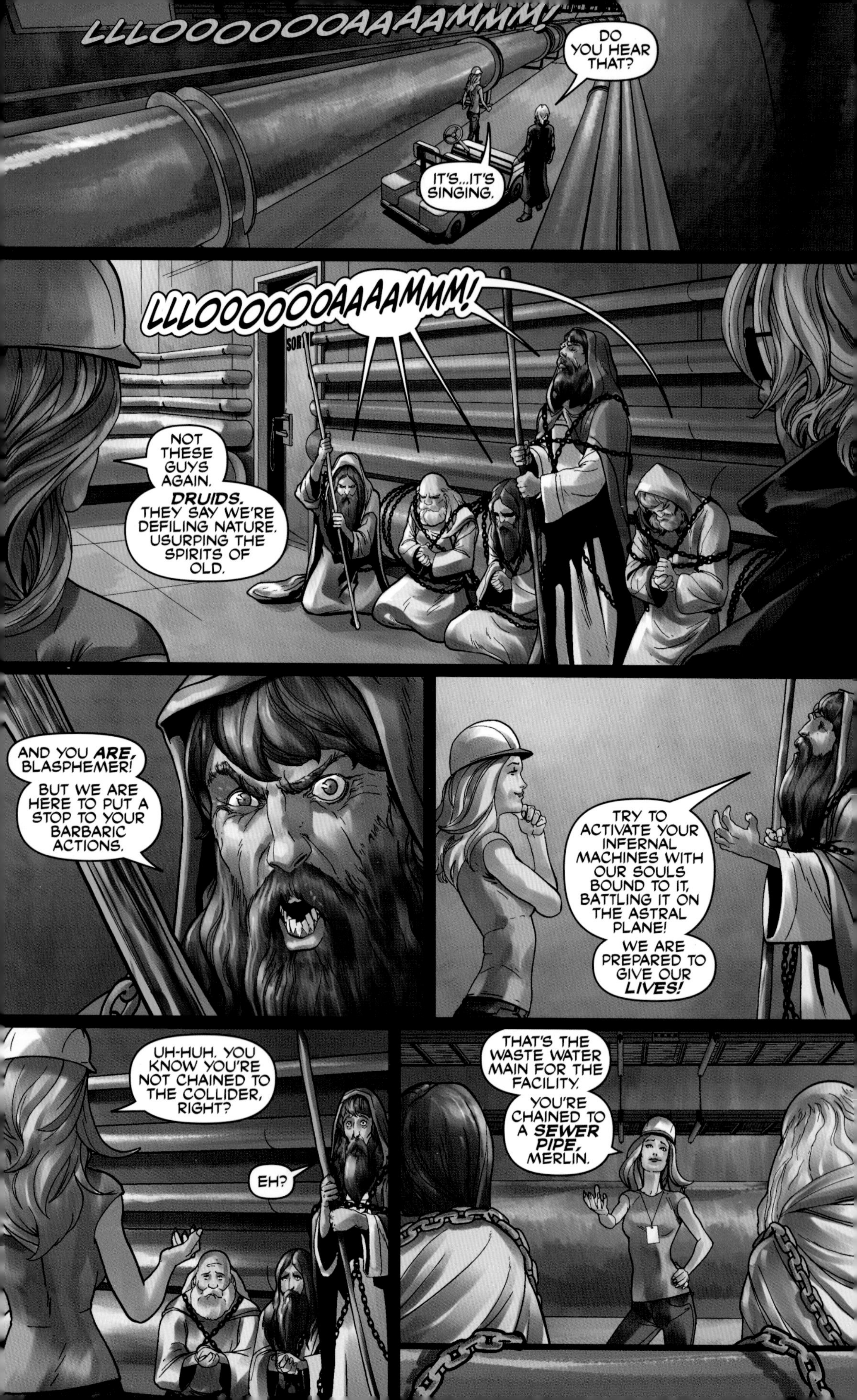
LLLOOOOOOAAAAMMM!
DO YOU HEAR THAT?
IT'S...IT'S SINGING.
LLLOOOOOOAAAAMMM!
NOT THESE GUYS AGAIN.
DRUIDS. THEY SAY WE'RE DEFILING NATURE. USURPING THE SPIRITS OF OLD.
AND YOU ARE, BLASPHEMER!
BUT WE ARE HERE TO PUT A STOP TO YOUR BARBARIC ACTIONS.
TRY TO ACTIVATE YOUR INFERNAL MACHINES WITH OUR SOULS BOUND TO IT, BATTLING IT ON THE ASTRAL PLANE!
WE ARE PREPARED TO GIVE OUR LIVES!
UH-HUH. YOU KNOW YOU'RE NOT CHAINED TO THE COLLIDER, RIGHT?
EH?
THAT'S THE WASTE WATER MAIN FOR THE FACILITY.
YOU'RE CHAINED TO A SEWER PIPE, MERLIN.

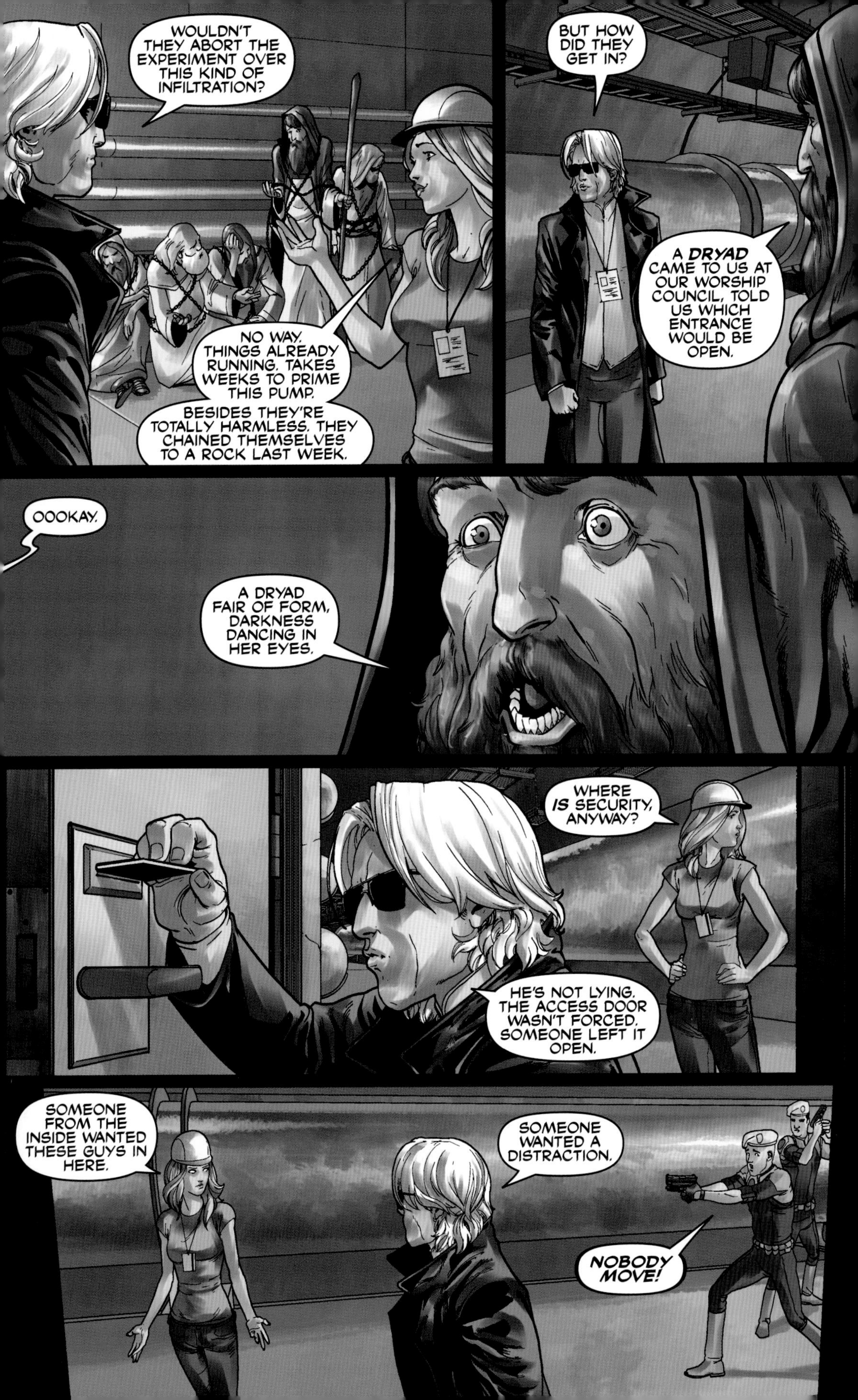
WOULDN'T THEY ABORT THE EXPERIMENT OVER THIS KIND OF INFILTRATION?
NO WAY. THINGS ALREADY RUNNING. TAKES WEEKS TO PRIME THIS PUMP.
BESIDES THEY'RE TOTALLY HARMLESS. THEY CHAINED THEMSELVES TO A ROCK LAST WEEK.
BUT HOW DID THEY GET IN?
A DRYAD CAME TO US AT OUR WORSHIP COUNCIL, TOLD US WHICH ENTRANCE WOULD BE OPEN.
OOOKAY.
A DRYAD FAIR OF FORM, DARKNESS DANCING IN HER EYES.
WHERE IS SECURITY, ANYWAY?
HE'S NOT LYING. THE ACCESS DOOR WASN'T FORCED. SOMEONE LEFT IT OPEN.
SOMEONE FROM THE INSIDE WANTED THESE GUYS IN HERE.
SOMEONE WANTED A DISTRACTION.
NOBODY MOVE!

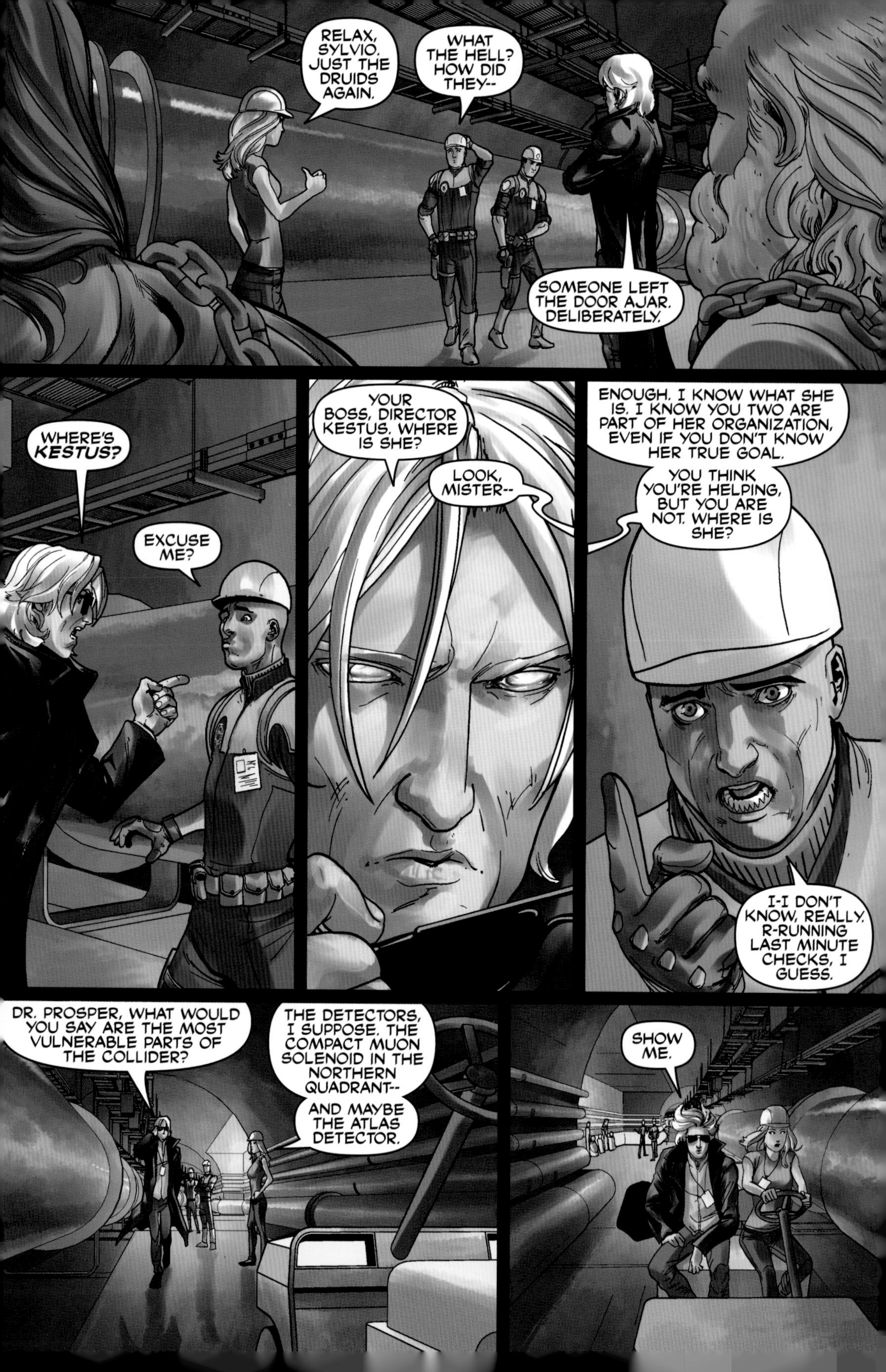
RELAX, SYLVIO. JUST THE DRUIDS AGAIN.
WHAT THE HELL? HOW DID THEY--
SOMEONE LEFT THE DOOR AJAR. DELIBERATELY.
WHERE'S *KESTUS?*
EXCUSE ME?
YOUR BOSS, DIRECTOR KESTUS. WHERE IS SHE?
LOOK, MISTER--
ENOUGH. I KNOW WHAT SHE IS. I KNOW YOU TWO ARE PART OF HER ORGANIZATION, EVEN IF YOU DON'T KNOW HER TRUE GOAL.
YOU THINK YOU'RE HELPING, BUT YOU ARE NOT. WHERE IS SHE?
I-I DON'T KNOW, REALLY. R-RUNNING LAST MINUTE CHECKS, I GUESS.
DR. PROSPER, WHAT WOULD YOU SAY ARE THE MOST VULNERABLE PARTS OF THE COLLIDER?
THE DETECTORS, I SUPPOSE. THE COMPACT MUON SOLENOID IN THE NORTHERN QUADRANT--
AND MAYBE THE ATLAS DETECTOR.
SHOW ME.

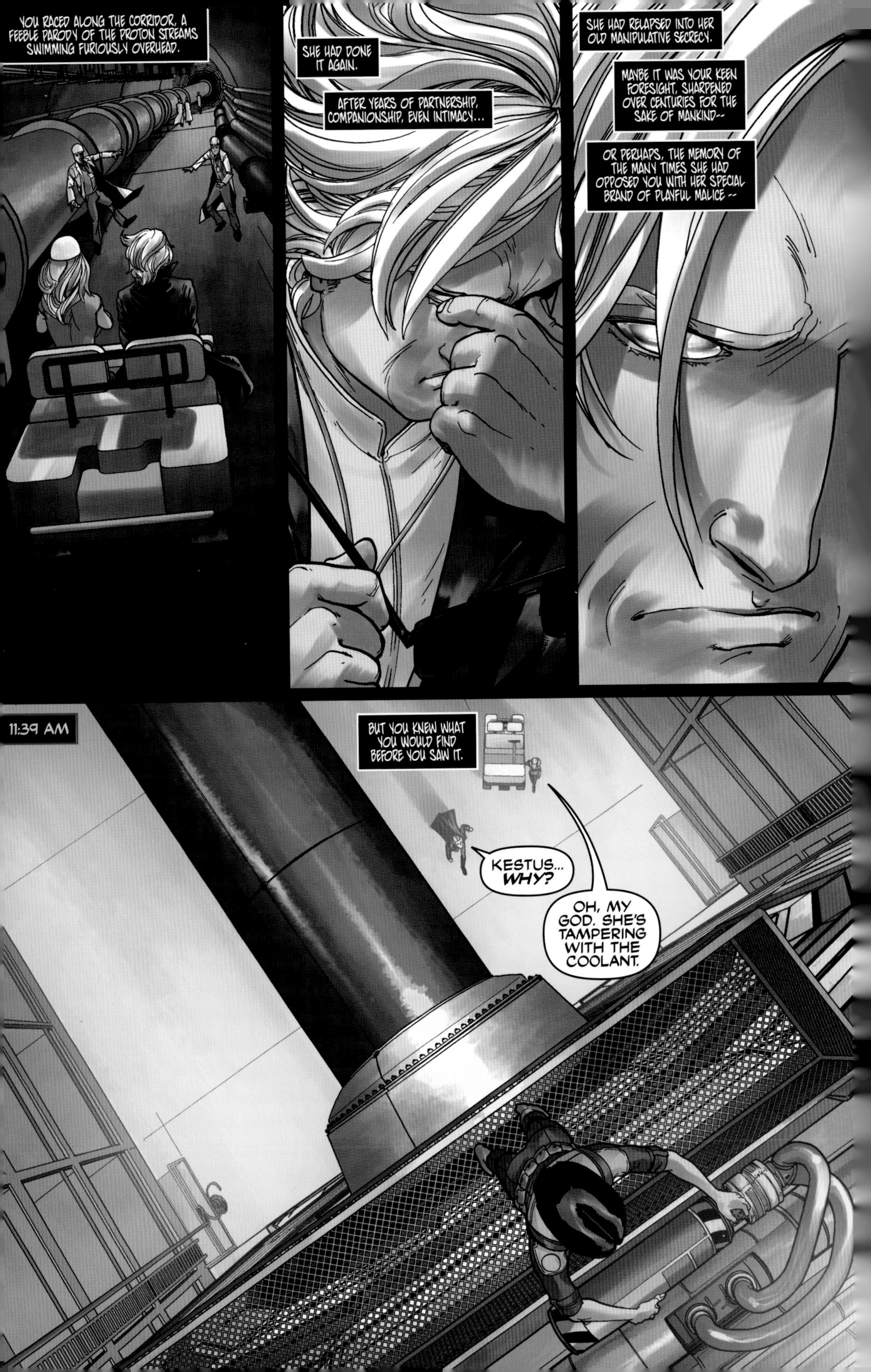

YOU RACED ALONG THE CORRIDOR, A FEEBLE PARODY OF THE PROTON STREAMS SWIMMING FURIOUSLY OVERHEAD.
SHE HAD DONE IT AGAIN.
AFTER YEARS OF PARTNERSHIP, COMPANIONSHIP, EVEN INTIMACY...
SHE HAD RELAPSED INTO HER OLD MANIPULATIVE SECRECY.
MAYBE IT WAS YOUR KEEN FORESIGHT, SHARPENED OVER CENTURIES FOR THE SAKE OF MANKIND--
OR PERHAPS, THE MEMORY OF THE MANY TIMES SHE HAD OPPOSED YOU WITH HER SPECIAL BRAND OF PLAYFUL MALICE --
11:39 AM
BUT YOU KNEW WHAT YOU WOULD FIND BEFORE YOU SAW IT.
KESTUS... WHY?
OH, MY GOD. SHE'S TAMPERING WITH THE COOLANT.

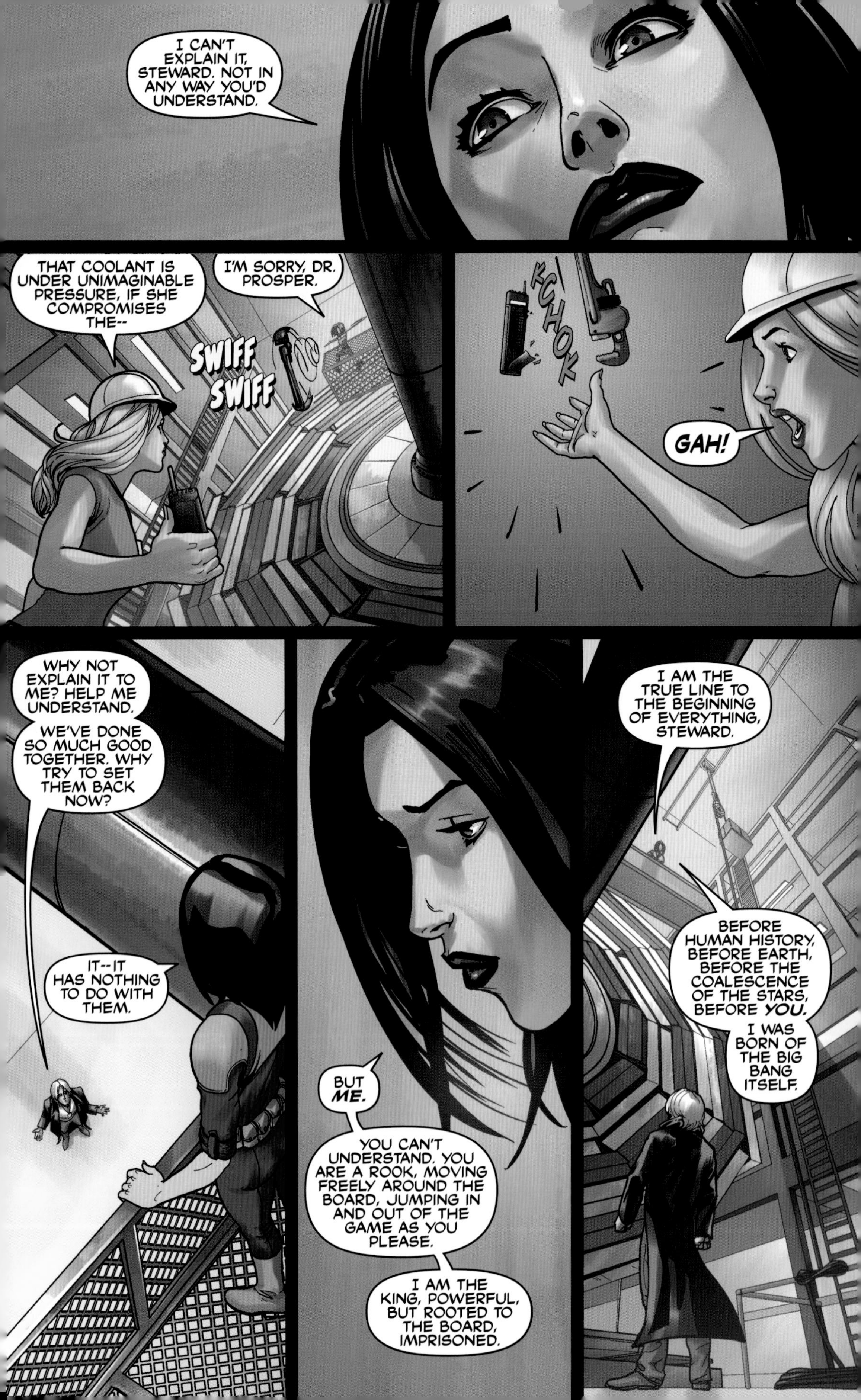
I CAN'T EXPLAIN IT, STEWARD. NOT IN ANY WAY YOU'D UNDERSTAND.
THAT COOLANT IS UNDER UNIMAGINABLE PRESSURE, IF SHE COMPROMISES THE--
I'M SORRY, DR. PROSPER.
SWIFF SWIFF
KCHOK
GAH!
WHY NOT EXPLAIN IT TO ME? HELP ME UNDERSTAND.
WE'VE DONE SO MUCH GOOD TOGETHER. WHY TRY TO SET THEM BACK NOW?
IT--IT HAS NOTHING TO DO WITH THEM.
BUT ME.
YOU CAN'T UNDERSTAND. YOU ARE A ROOK, MOVING FREELY AROUND THE BOARD, JUMPING IN AND OUT OF THE GAME AS YOU PLEASE.
I AM THE KING, POWERFUL, BUT ROOTED TO THE BOARD, IMPRISONED.
I AM THE TRUE LINE TO THE BEGINNING OF EVERYTHING, STEWARD.
BEFORE HUMAN HISTORY, BEFORE EARTH, BEFORE THE COALESCENCE OF THE STARS, BEFORE YOU.
I WAS BORN OF THE BIG BANG ITSELF.

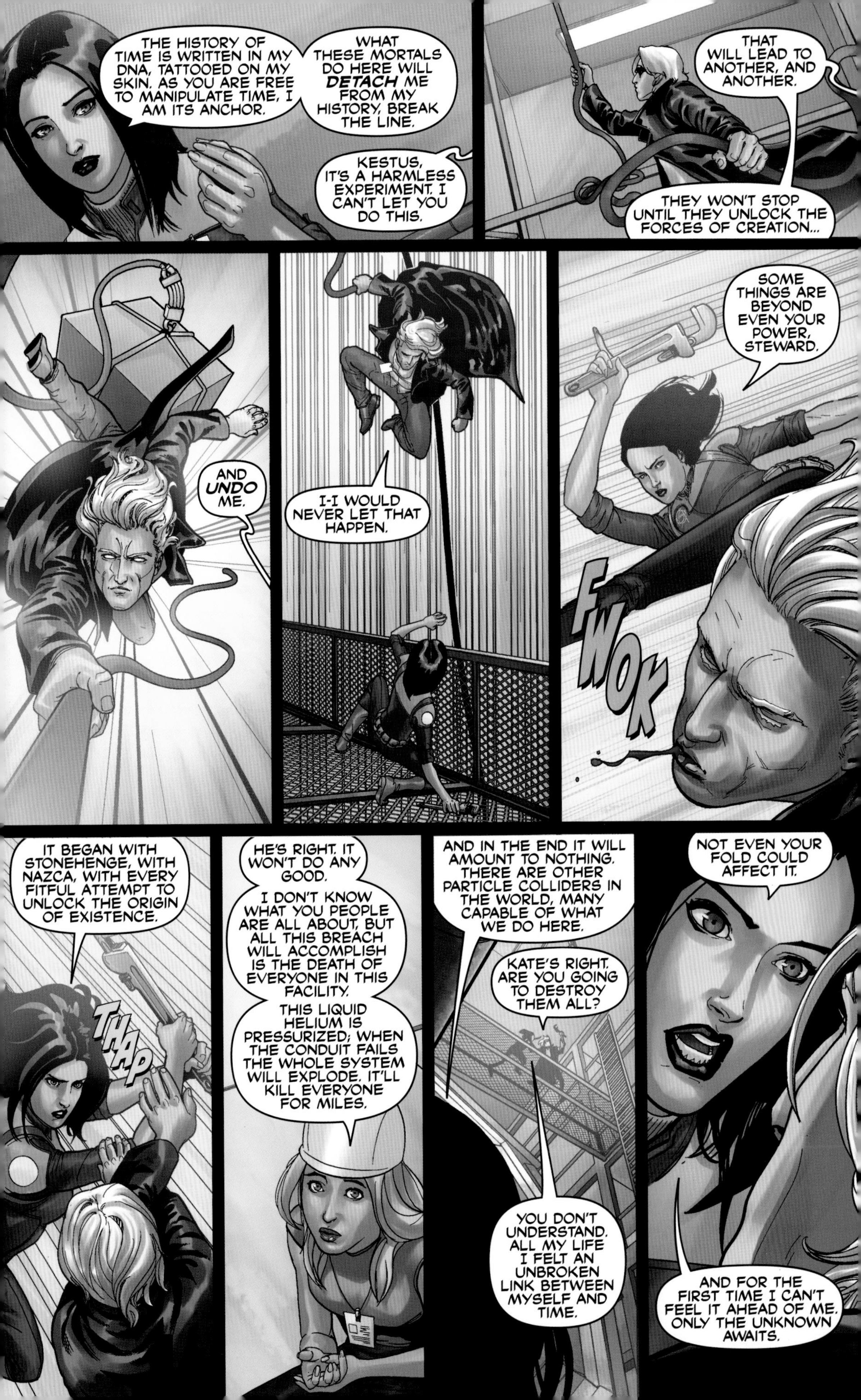
THE HISTORY OF TIME IS WRITTEN IN MY DNA, TATTOOED ON MY SKIN. AS YOU ARE FREE TO MANIPULATE TIME, I AM ITS ANCHOR.
WHAT THESE MORTALS DO HERE WILL DETACH ME FROM MY HISTORY, BREAK THE LINE.
KESTUS, IT'S A HARMLESS EXPERIMENT. I CAN'T LET YOU DO THIS.
THAT WILL LEAD TO ANOTHER, AND ANOTHER.
THEY WON'T STOP UNTIL THEY UNLOCK THE FORCES OF CREATION...
AND UNDO ME.
I-I WOULD NEVER LET THAT HAPPEN.
SOME THINGS ARE BEYOND EVEN YOUR POWER, STEWARD.
FWOK
IT BEGAN WITH STONEHENGE, WITH NAZCA, WITH EVERY FITFUL ATTEMPT TO UNLOCK THE ORIGIN OF EXISTENCE.
THAP
HE'S RIGHT. IT WON'T DO ANY GOOD.
I DON'T KNOW WHAT YOU PEOPLE ARE ALL ABOUT, BUT ALL THIS BREACH WILL ACCOMPLISH IS THE DEATH OF EVERYONE IN THIS FACILITY.
THIS LIQUID HELIUM IS PRESSURIZED; WHEN THE CONDUIT FAILS THE WHOLE SYSTEM WILL EXPLODE. IT'LL KILL EVERYONE FOR MILES.
AND IN THE END IT WILL AMOUNT TO NOTHING. THERE ARE OTHER PARTICLE COLLIDERS IN THE WORLD, MANY CAPABLE OF WHAT WE DO HERE.
KATE'S RIGHT. ARE YOU GOING TO DESTROY THEM ALL?
YOU DON'T UNDERSTAND. ALL MY LIFE I FELT AN UNBROKEN LINK BETWEEN MYSELF AND TIME.
NOT EVEN YOUR FOLD COULD AFFECT IT.
AND FOR THE FIRST TIME I CAN'T FEEL IT AHEAD OF ME. ONLY THE UNKNOWN AWAITS.

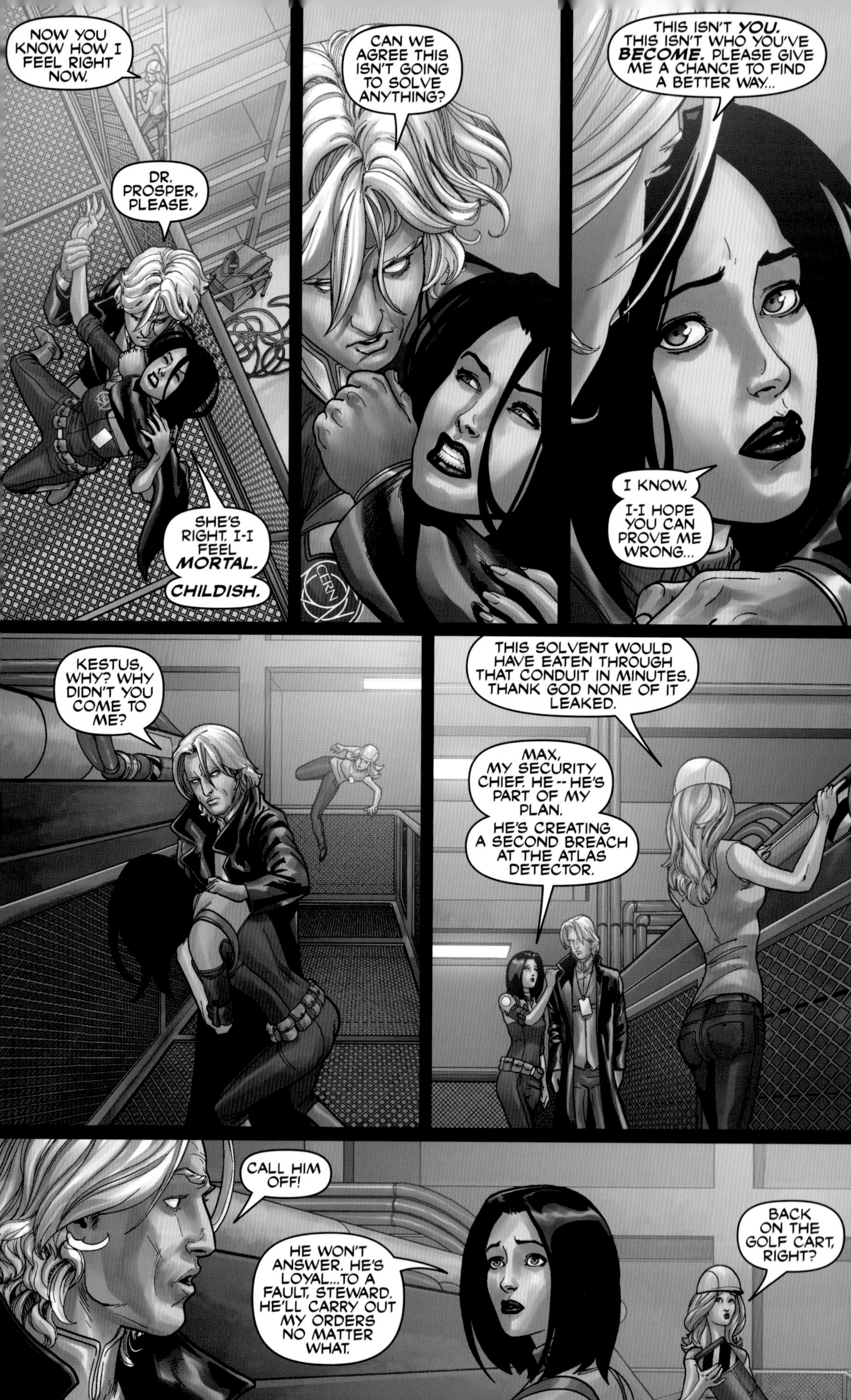
NOW YOU KNOW HOW I FEEL RIGHT NOW.
DR. PROSPER, PLEASE.
SHE'S RIGHT. I-I FEEL MORTAL.
CHILDISH.
CAN WE AGREE THIS ISN'T GOING TO SOLVE ANYTHING?
CERN
THIS ISN'T YOU. THIS ISN'T WHO YOU'VE BECOME. PLEASE GIVE ME A CHANCE TO FIND A BETTER WAY...
I KNOW.
I-I HOPE YOU CAN PROVE ME WRONG...
KESTUS, WHY? WHY DIDN'T YOU COME TO ME?
THIS SOLVENT WOULD HAVE EATEN THROUGH THAT CONDUIT IN MINUTES. THANK GOD NONE OF IT LEAKED.
MAX, MY SECURITY CHIEF. HE -- HE'S PART OF MY PLAN.
HE'S CREATING A SECOND BREACH AT THE ATLAS DETECTOR.
CALL HIM OFF!
HE WON'T ANSWER. HE'S LOYAL...TO A FAULT, STEWARD. HE'LL CARRY OUT MY ORDERS NO MATTER WHAT.
BACK ON THE GOLF CART, RIGHT?

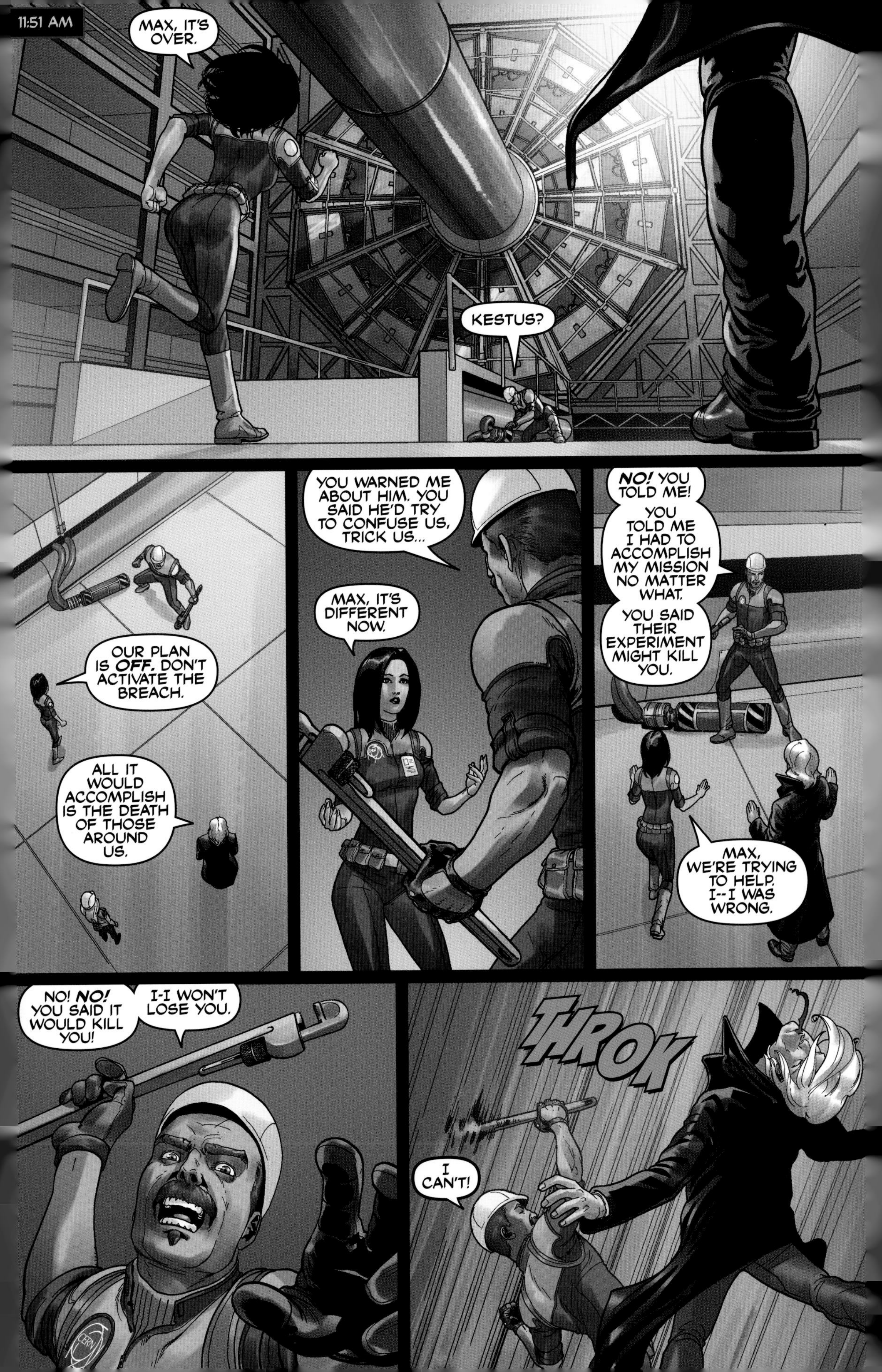
11:51 AM
MAX, IT'S OVER.
KESTUS?
OUR PLAN IS OFF. DON'T ACTIVATE THE BREACH.
ALL IT WOULD ACCOMPLISH IS THE DEATH OF THOSE AROUND US.
YOU WARNED ME ABOUT HIM. YOU SAID HE'D TRY TO CONFUSE US, TRICK US...
MAX, IT'S DIFFERENT NOW.
NO! YOU TOLD ME!
YOU TOLD ME I HAD TO ACCOMPLISH MY MISSION NO MATTER WHAT.
YOU SAID THEIR EXPERIMENT MIGHT KILL YOU.
MAX, WE'RE TRYING TO HELP. I--I WAS WRONG.
NO! NO! YOU SAID IT WOULD KILL YOU!
I-I WON'T LOSE YOU.
THROK
I CAN'T!

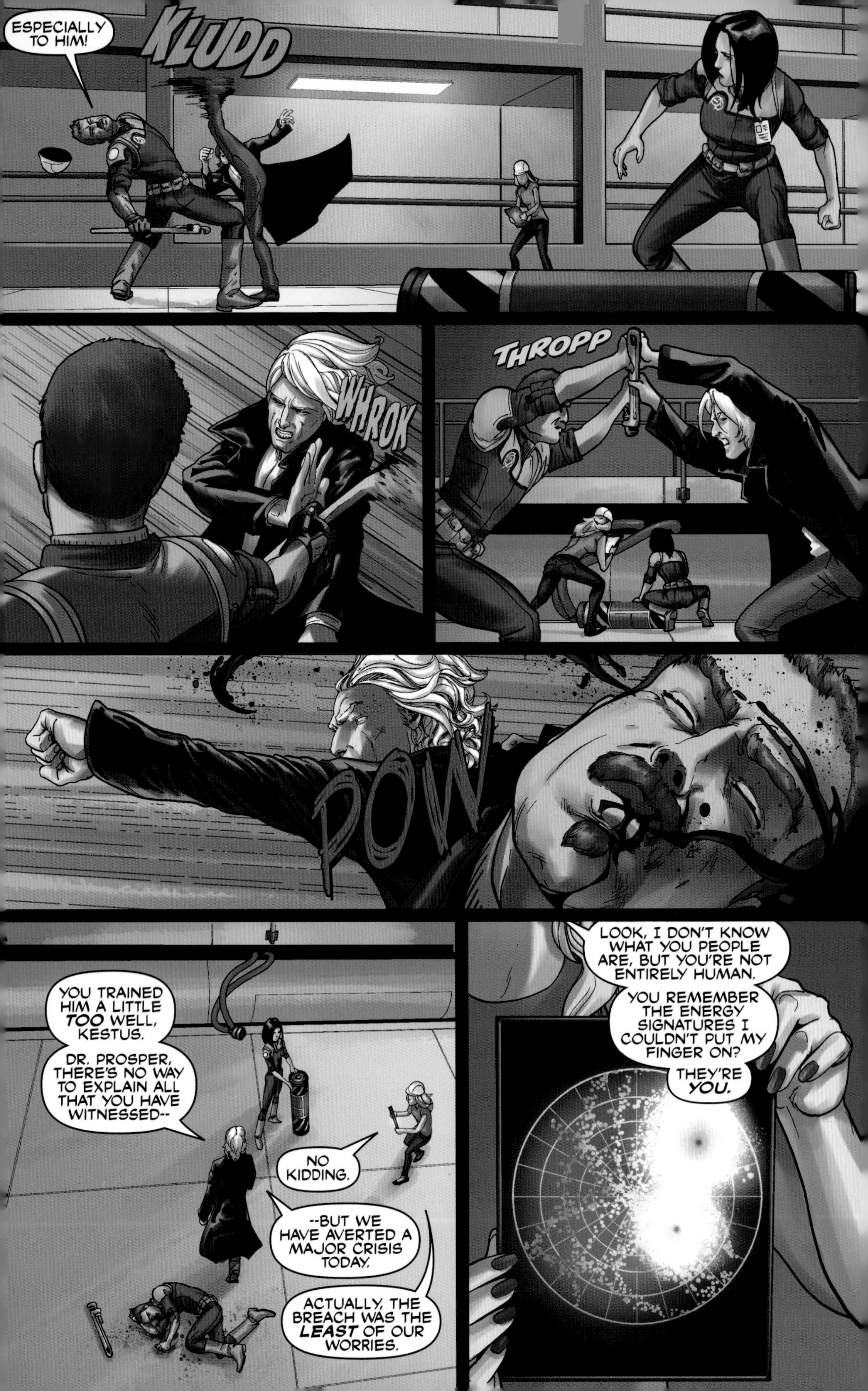
ESPECIALLY TO HIM!
KLUDD
WHROK
THROPP
POW
YOU TRAINED HIM A LITTLE TOO WELL, KESTUS.
DR. PROSPER, THERE'S NO WAY TO EXPLAIN ALL THAT YOU HAVE WITNESSED--
NO KIDDING.
--BUT WE HAVE AVERTED A MAJOR CRISIS TODAY.
ACTUALLY, THE BREACH WAS THE LEAST OF OUR WORRIES.
LOOK, I DON'T KNOW WHAT YOU PEOPLE ARE, BUT YOU'RE NOT ENTIRELY HUMAN.
YOU REMEMBER THE ENERGY SIGNATURES I COULDN'T PUT MY FINGER ON?
THEY'RE YOU.

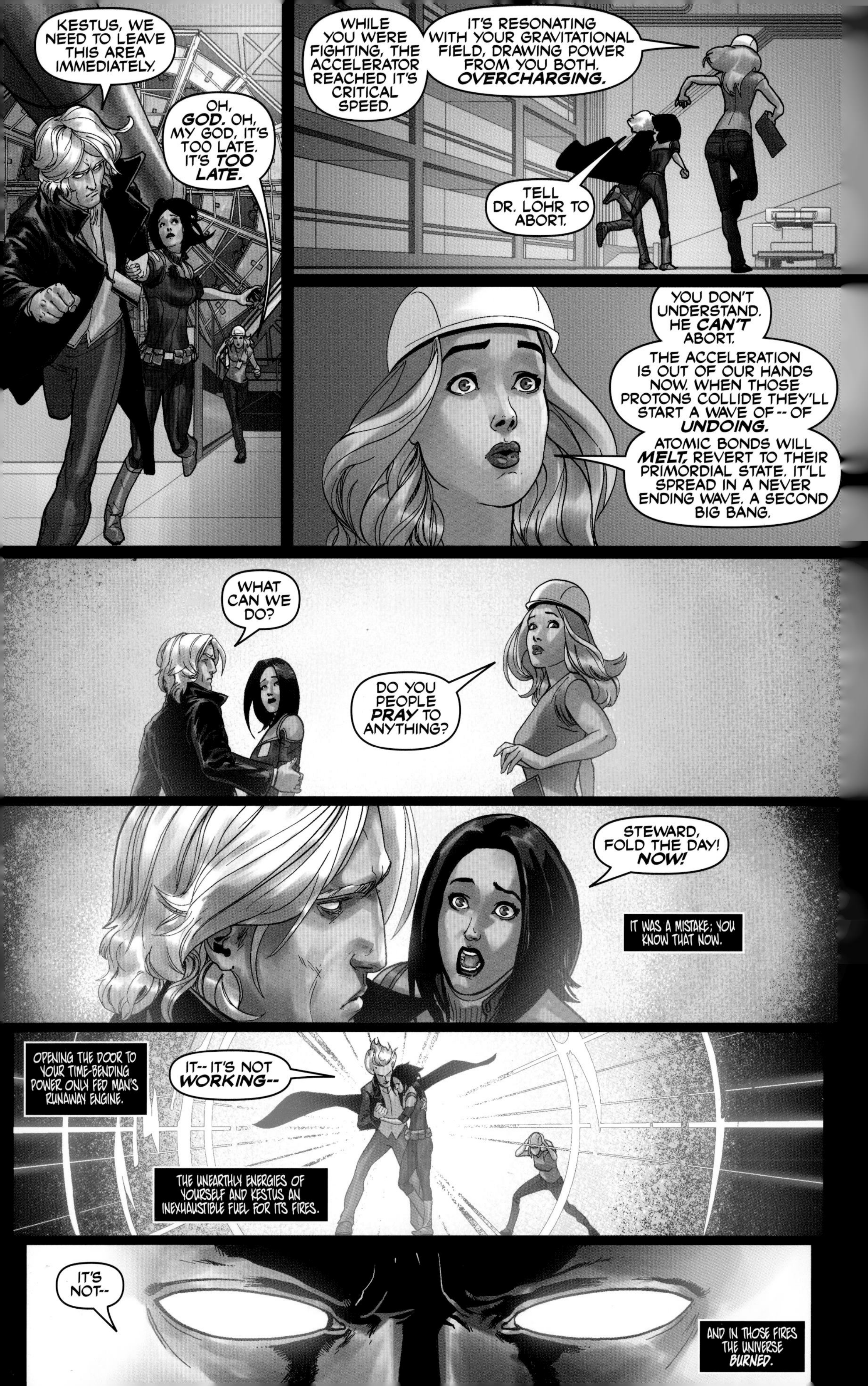
KESTUS, WE NEED TO LEAVE THIS AREA IMMEDIATELY.
OH, GOD. OH, MY GOD, IT'S TOO LATE. IT'S TOO LATE.
WHILE YOU WERE FIGHTING, THE ACCELERATOR REACHED IT'S CRITICAL SPEED.
IT'S RESONATING WITH YOUR GRAVITATIONAL FIELD, DRAWING POWER FROM YOU BOTH. OVERCHARGING.
TELL DR. LOHR TO ABORT.
YOU DON'T UNDERSTAND. HE CAN'T ABORT.
THE ACCELERATION IS OUT OF OUR HANDS NOW. WHEN THOSE PROTONS COLLIDE THEY'LL START A WAVE OF -- OF UNDOING.
ATOMIC BONDS WILL MELT, REVERT TO THEIR PRIMORDIAL STATE. IT'LL SPREAD IN A NEVER ENDING WAVE. A SECOND BIG BANG.
WHAT CAN WE DO?
DO YOU PEOPLE PRAY TO ANYTHING?
STEWARD, FOLD THE DAY! NOW!
IT WAS A MISTAKE; YOU KNOW THAT NOW.
OPENING THE DOOR TO YOUR TIME-BENDING POWER ONLY FED MAN'S RUNAWAY ENGINE.
IT-- IT'S NOT WORKING--
THE UNEARTHLY ENERGIES OF YOURSELF AND KESTUS AN INEXHAUSTIBLE FUEL FOR ITS FIRES.
IT'S NOT--
AND IN THOSE FIRES THE UNIVERSE BURNED.

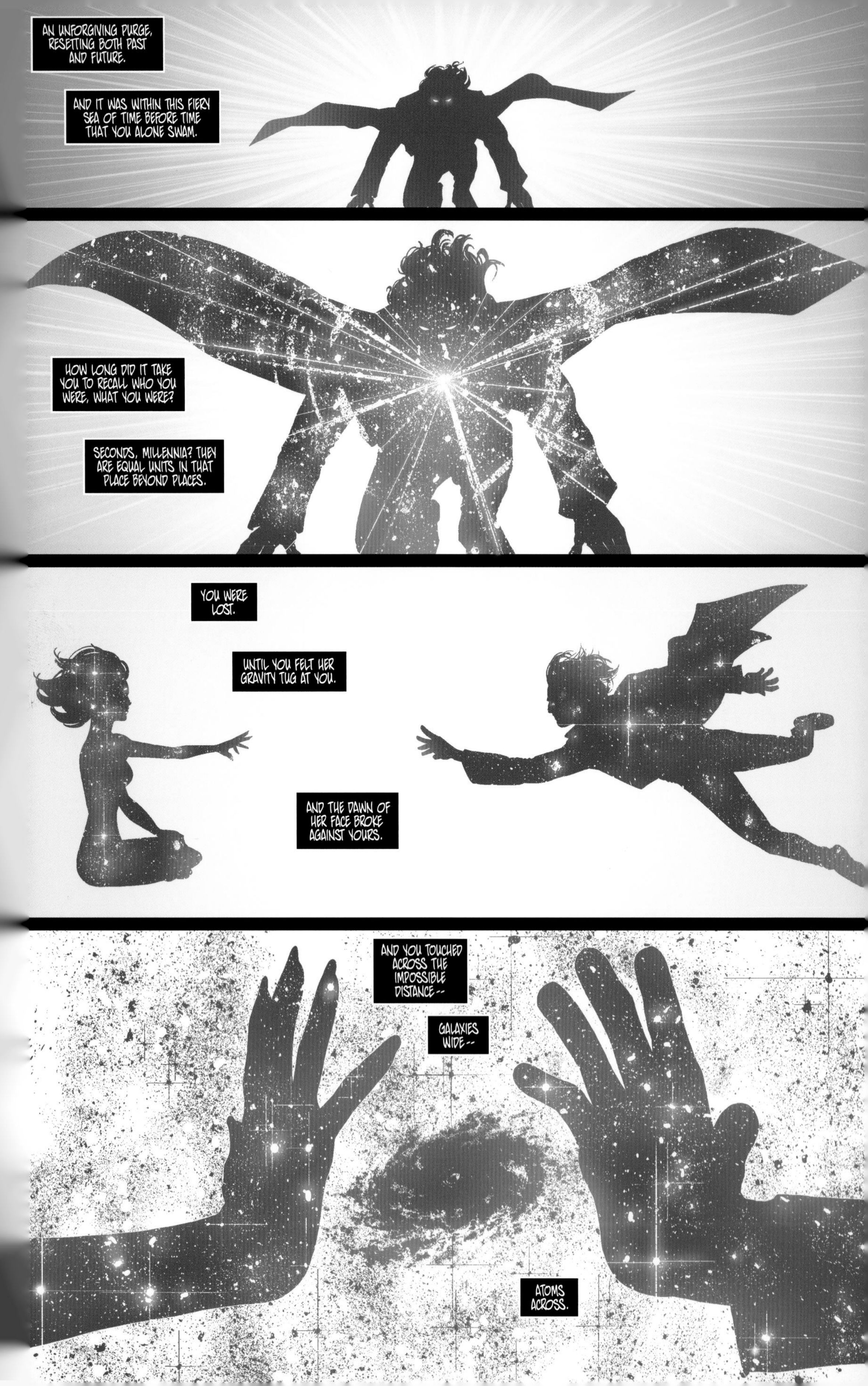

AN UNFORGIVING PURGE, RESETTING BOTH PAST AND FUTURE.
AND IT WAS WITHIN THIS FIERY SEA OF TIME BEFORE TIME THAT YOU ALONE SWAM.
HOW LONG DID IT TAKE YOU TO RECALL WHO YOU WERE, WHAT YOU WERE?
SECONDS, MILLENNIA? THEY ARE EQUAL UNITS IN THAT PLACE BEYOND PLACES.
YOU WERE LOST.
UNTIL YOU FELT HER GRAVITY TUG AT YOU.
AND THE DAWN OF HER FACE BROKE AGAINST YOURS.
AND YOU TOUCHED ACROSS THE IMPOSSIBLE DISTANCE--
GALAXIES WIDE--
ATOMS ACROSS.

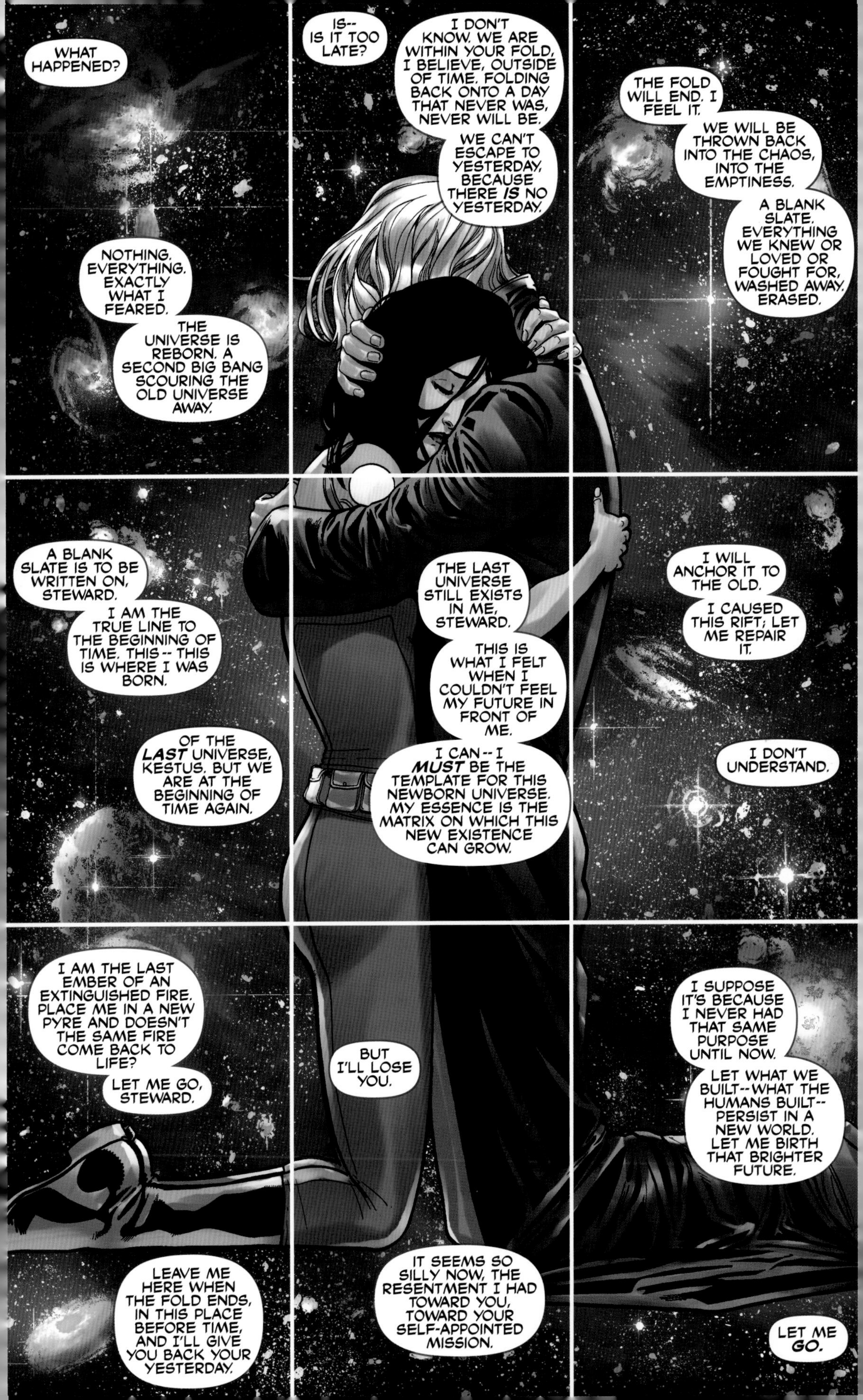
WHAT HAPPENED?
NOTHING. EVERYTHING. EXACTLY WHAT I FEARED.
THE UNIVERSE IS REBORN. A SECOND BIG BANG SCOURING THE OLD UNIVERSE AWAY.
IS-- IS IT TOO LATE?
I DON'T KNOW. WE ARE WITHIN YOUR FOLD, I BELIEVE, OUTSIDE OF TIME. FOLDING BACK ONTO A DAY THAT NEVER WAS, NEVER WILL BE.
WE CAN'T ESCAPE TO YESTERDAY, BECAUSE THERE *IS* NO YESTERDAY.
THE FOLD WILL END. I FEEL IT.
WE WILL BE THROWN BACK INTO THE CHAOS, INTO THE EMPTINESS.
A BLANK SLATE. EVERYTHING WE KNEW OR LOVED OR FOUGHT FOR, WASHED AWAY. ERASED.
A BLANK SLATE IS TO BE WRITTEN ON, STEWARD.
I AM THE TRUE LINE TO THE BEGINNING OF TIME. THIS -- THIS IS WHERE I WAS BORN.
OF THE ***LAST*** UNIVERSE, KESTUS. BUT WE ARE AT THE BEGINNING OF TIME AGAIN.
THE LAST UNIVERSE STILL EXISTS IN ME, STEWARD.
THIS IS WHAT I FELT WHEN I COULDN'T FEEL MY FUTURE IN FRONT OF ME.
I CAN -- I ***MUST*** BE THE TEMPLATE FOR THIS NEWBORN UNIVERSE. MY ESSENCE IS THE MATRIX ON WHICH THIS NEW EXISTENCE CAN GROW.
I WILL ANCHOR IT TO THE OLD.
I CAUSED THIS RIFT; LET ME REPAIR IT.
I DON'T UNDERSTAND.
I AM THE LAST EMBER OF AN EXTINGUISHED FIRE. PLACE ME IN A NEW PYRE AND DOESN'T THE SAME FIRE COME BACK TO LIFE?
LET ME GO, STEWARD.
BUT I'LL LOSE YOU.
I SUPPOSE IT'S BECAUSE I NEVER HAD THAT SAME PURPOSE UNTIL NOW.
LET WHAT WE BUILT--WHAT THE HUMANS BUILT-- PERSIST IN A NEW WORLD. LET ME BIRTH THAT BRIGHTER FUTURE.
LEAVE ME HERE WHEN THE FOLD ENDS, IN THIS PLACE BEFORE TIME, AND I'LL GIVE YOU BACK YOUR YESTERDAY.
IT SEEMS SO SILLY NOW, THE RESENTMENT I HAD TOWARD YOU, TOWARD YOUR SELF-APPOINTED MISSION.
LET ME ***GO.***

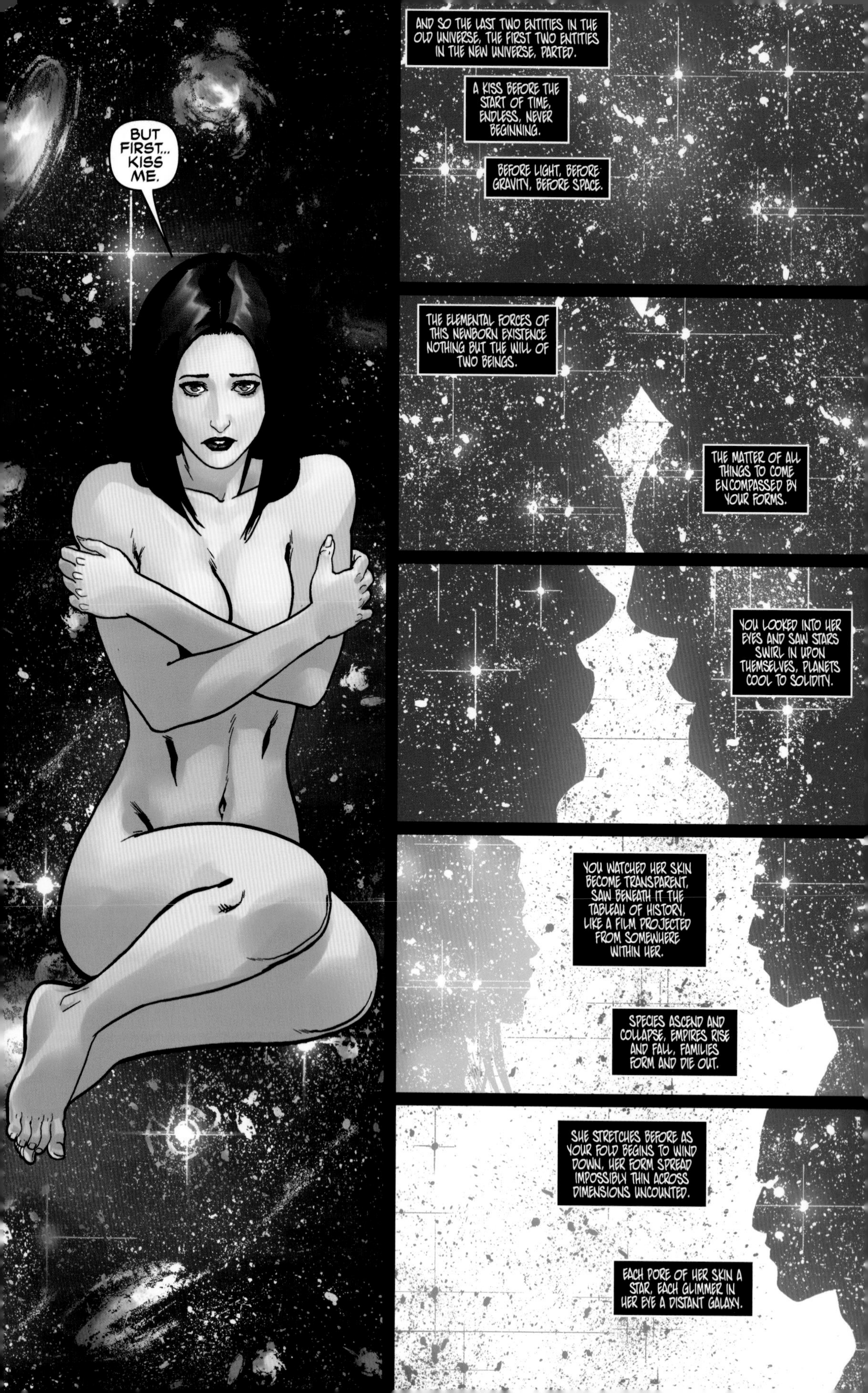
BUT FIRST... KISS ME.
AND SO THE LAST TWO ENTITIES IN THE OLD UNIVERSE, THE FIRST TWO ENTITIES IN THE NEW UNIVERSE, PARTED.
A KISS BEFORE THE START OF TIME, ENDLESS, NEVER BEGINNING.
BEFORE LIGHT, BEFORE GRAVITY, BEFORE SPACE.
THE ELEMENTAL FORCES OF THIS NEWBORN EXISTENCE NOTHING BUT THE WILL OF TWO BEINGS.
THE MATTER OF ALL THINGS TO COME ENCOMPASSED BY YOUR FORMS.
YOU LOOKED INTO HER EYES AND SAW STARS SWIRL IN UPON THEMSELVES, PLANETS COOL TO SOLIDITY.
YOU WATCHED HER SKIN BECOME TRANSPARENT, SAW BENEATH IT THE TABLEAU OF HISTORY, LIKE A FILM PROJECTED FROM SOMEWHERE WITHIN HER.
SPECIES ASCEND AND COLLAPSE, EMPIRES RISE AND FALL, FAMILIES FORM AND DIE OUT.
SHE STRETCHES BEFORE AS YOUR FOLD BEGINS TO WIND DOWN, HER FORM SPREAD IMPOSSIBLY THIN ACROSS DIMENSIONS UNCOUNTED.
EACH PORE OF HER SKIN A STAR, EACH GLIMMER IN HER EYE A DISTANT GALAXY.

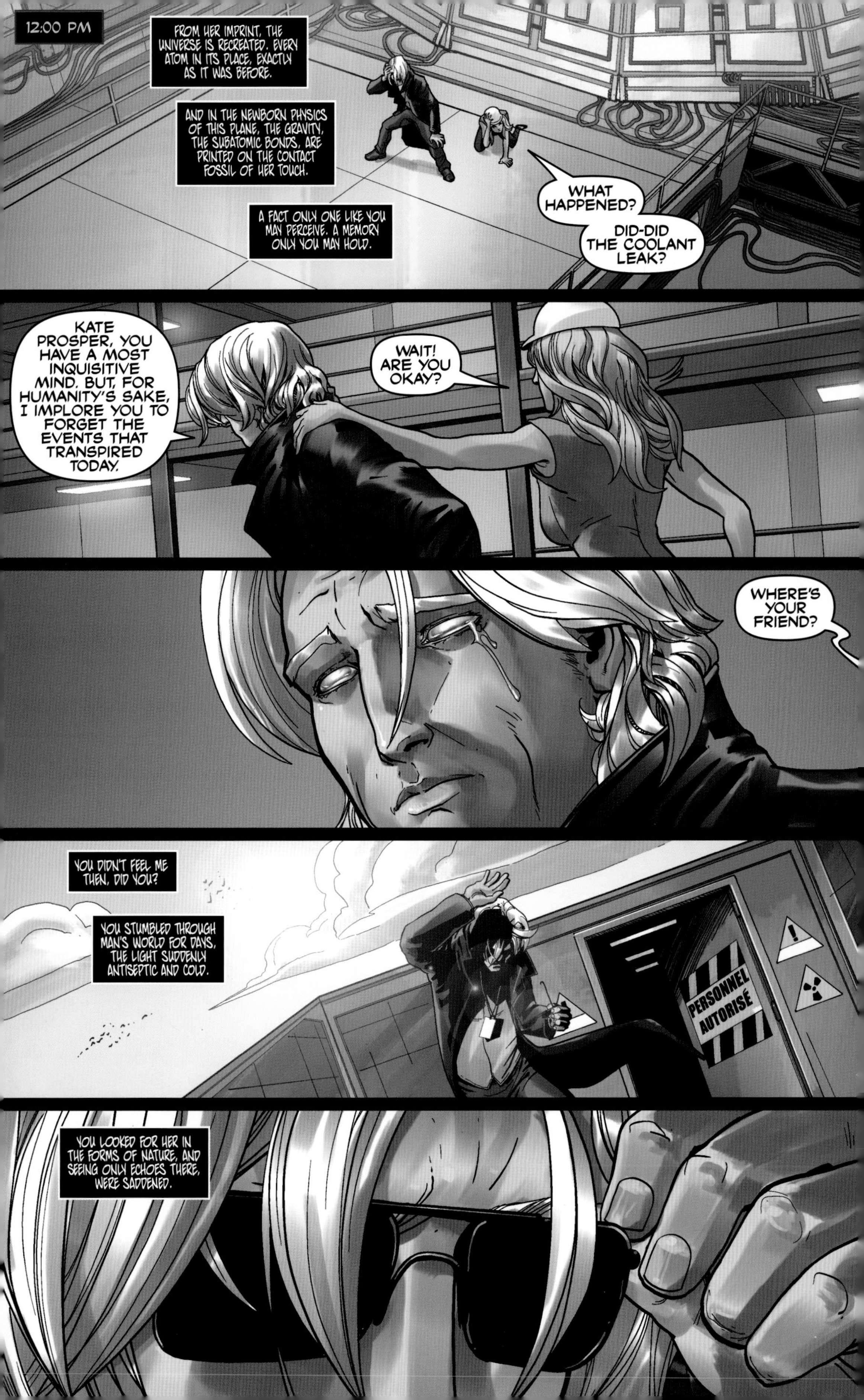
12:00 PM
FROM HER IMPRINT, THE UNIVERSE IS RECREATED. EVERY ATOM IN ITS PLACE, EXACTLY AS IT WAS BEFORE.
AND IN THE NEWBORN PHYSICS OF THIS PLANE, THE GRAVITY, THE SUBATOMIC BONDS, ARE PRINTED ON THE CONTACT FOSSIL OF HER TOUCH.
A FACT ONLY ONE LIKE YOU MAY PERCEIVE. A MEMORY ONLY YOU MAY HOLD.
WHAT HAPPENED?
DID-DID THE COOLANT LEAK?
KATE PROSPER, YOU HAVE A MOST INQUISITIVE MIND. BUT, FOR HUMANITY'S SAKE, I IMPLORE YOU TO FORGET THE EVENTS THAT TRANSPIRED TODAY.
WAIT! ARE YOU OKAY?
WHERE'S YOUR FRIEND?
YOU DIDN'T FEEL ME THEN, DID YOU?
YOU STUMBLED THROUGH MAN'S WORLD FOR DAYS, THE LIGHT SUDDENLY ANTISEPTIC AND COLD.
PERSONNEL AUTORISÉ
YOU LOOKED FOR HER IN THE FORMS OF NATURE, AND SEEING ONLY ECHOES THERE, WERE SADDENED.

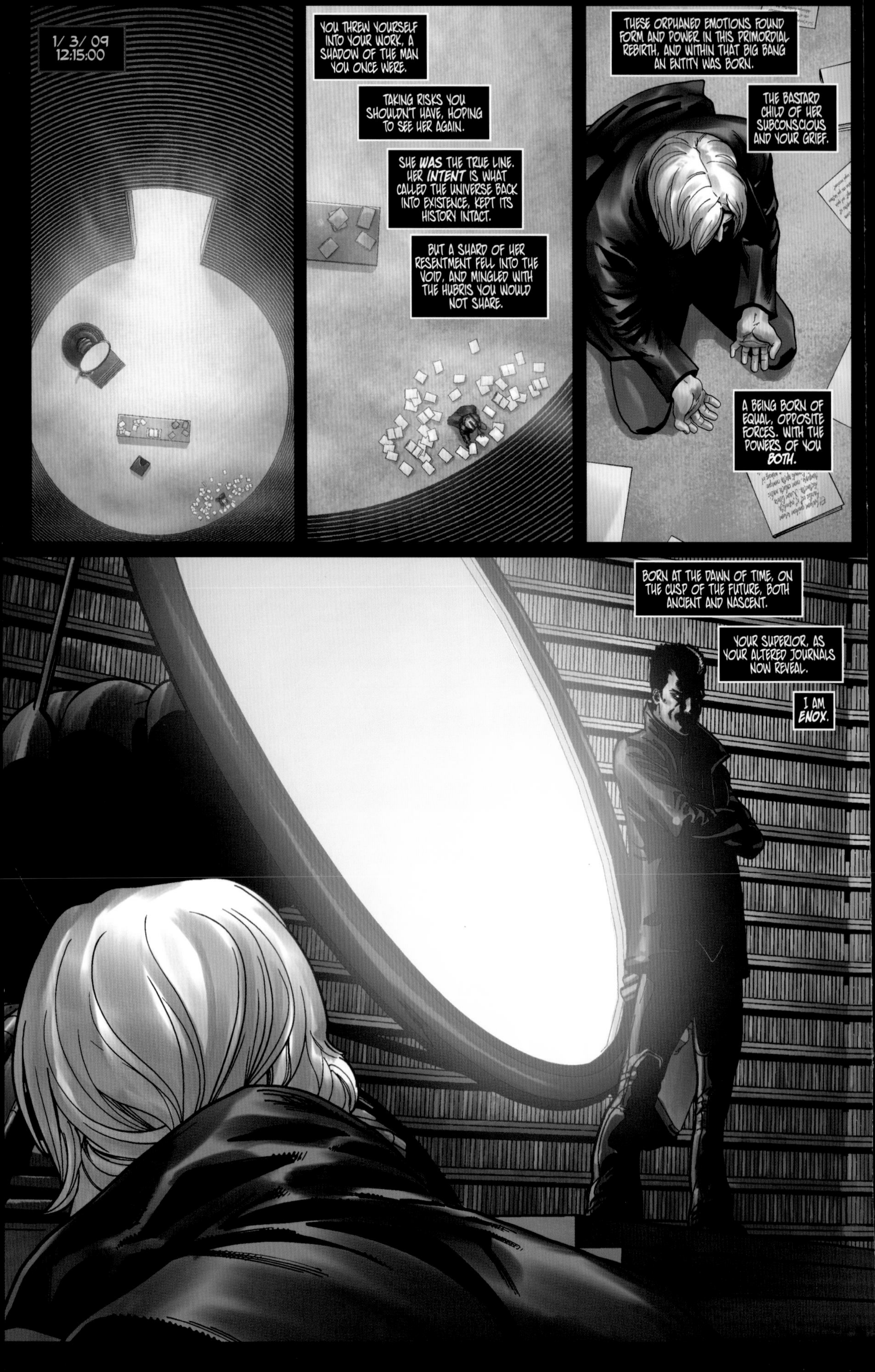

1/ 3/ 09
12:15:00
YOU THREW YOURSELF INTO YOUR WORK, A SHADOW OF THE MAN YOU ONCE WERE.
TAKING RISKS YOU SHOULDN'T HAVE, HOPING TO SEE HER AGAIN.
SHE WAS THE TRUE LINE. HER INTENT IS WHAT CALLED THE UNIVERSE BACK INTO EXISTENCE, KEPT ITS HISTORY INTACT.
BUT A SHARD OF HER RESENTMENT FELL INTO THE VOID, AND MINGLED WITH THE HUBRIS YOU WOULD NOT SHARE.
THESE ORPHANED EMOTIONS FOUND FORM AND POWER IN THIS PRIMORDIAL REBIRTH, AND WITHIN THAT BIG BANG AN ENTITY WAS BORN.
THE BASTARD CHILD OF HER SUBCONSCIOUS AND YOUR GRIEF.
A BEING BORN OF EQUAL, OPPOSITE FORCES. WITH THE POWERS OF YOU BOTH.
BORN AT THE DAWN OF TIME, ON THE CUSP OF THE FUTURE, BOTH ANCIENT AND NASCENT.
YOUR SUPERIOR, AS YOUR ALTERED JOURNALS NOW REVEAL.
I AM ENOX.

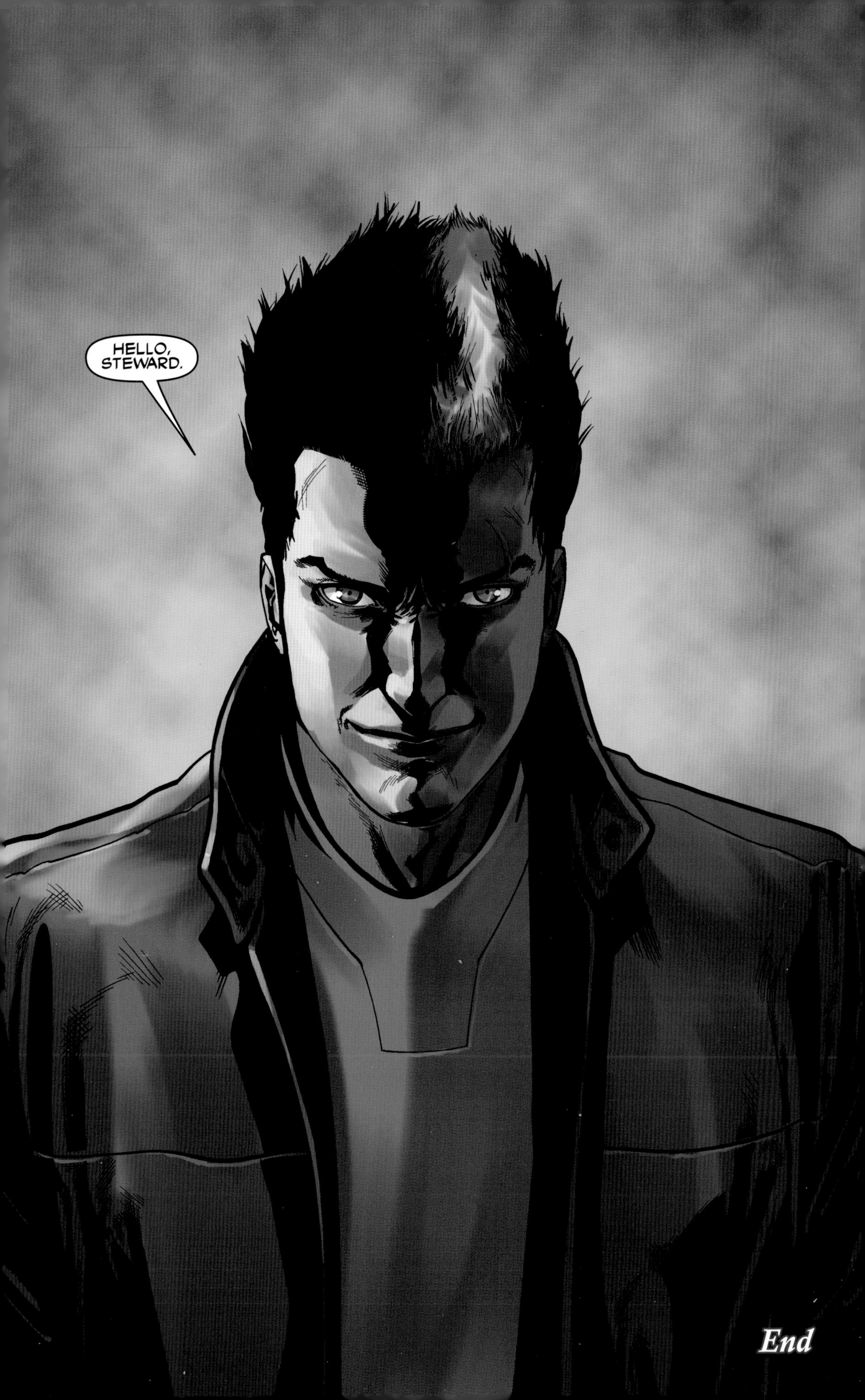
HELLO, STEWARD.
End

CHARACTER RETROSPECT | KESTUS

Age
Immortal

Height
5' 5"

Hair Color
Jet Black

Weight
121 lbs

Eye Color
Ice Blue. Like the waters of the Great Barrier Reef and the sky it reflects.

Origin
Kestus is a child of the Big Bang. She was forged at the same time as our universe, over 13.7 billion years ago. Upon her birth, Kestus acquired consciousness, but was without form. However, once earth's inhabitants evolved to the point of having a sophisticated enough cerebral structure, Kestus took shape, attaining her human physique. Having witnessed the entirety of human creation and experienced Earth's journey into maturation, the immortal Kestus has garnered more knowledge than any single living being, even The Steward.

Motivation/Mission
Unlike The Steward, Kestus has no library, no haven of solitude, no rest from mankind. She lives among us. Her perspective and her approach to humanity have been ever defined by this fact.

Kestus began her earthly existence optimistic about humanity. During our earliest stages, she saw our potential and our appreciation for her planet's bounty. However, this changed quickly. We changed quickly. Kestus came face to face with our ugliest elements too many times for it not to have had its effect. Years of witnessing the darkest sides of human behavior took its toll on her emotions. Her inability to escape humans' affliction on the planet, and each other, left her incapable of remembering the beauty of the human condition.

Grown <u>over centuries of</u> time, Kestus' resentment for Earth's leading species transformed into stoic indignation. She sees humans as simple-minded beings set on Earth to serve her and bend to her will. We are pawns in Kestus' singular mission--to accumulate wealth, power and influence.

Powers
Kestus is imbued with the power of total recall. She is the only known being whose power lives on the same plane as that of The Steward. Her ability lies in the realms of time and space, however, its manifestation is almost completely contrary to his. As opposed to folding away time and extracting memories, Kestus can remember every moment of her existence with complete clarity and detailed recollection. In a world where The Steward represents the potential for bending and making crooked time's linear structure, Kestus is the straight line. She symbolizes its restoration, at least within a single being.

Additionally, Kestus has taken advantage of her eternal life by mastering the arts of language, fighting tactics, history, psychology and the like. As with The Steward, the display of this vast knowledge and experience would appear to be a power to a human observer.

Weaknesses
Given her immortality and inhuman powers, it's somewhat ironic that those traits that could be labeled as weaknesses are the very same that tie Kestus inextricably to human beings, with no chance of escape. Unlike The Steward, Kestus bound to live among Earth's inhabitants. She cannot find reprieve from the species that has come to dishearten her.

As well, since she has taken human form, Kestus, whose original design included no shape, cannot return to her original state. A singular choice, made eons ago, further tethers Kestus to a planet and a species from which she often wishes to be free.

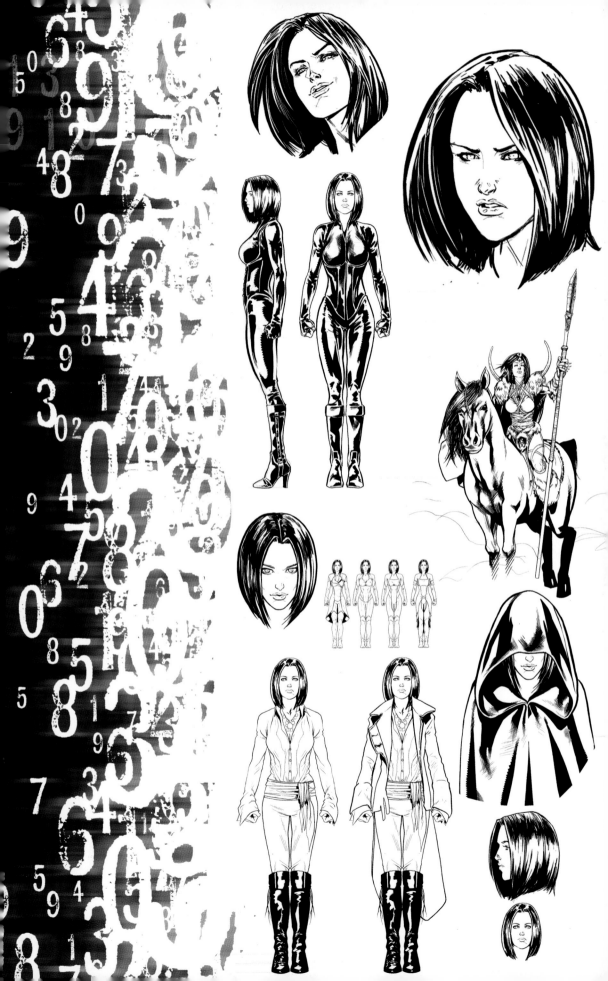

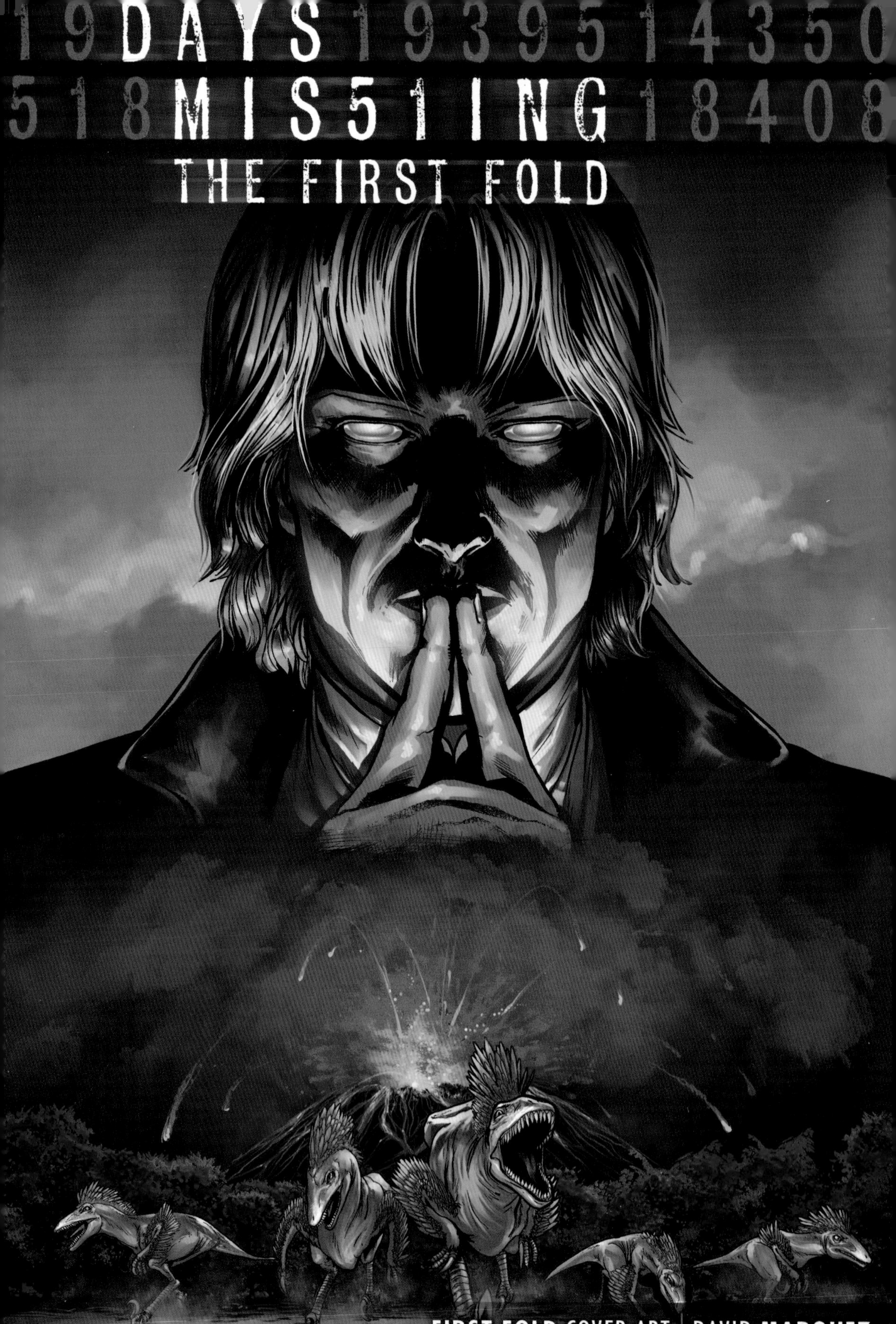
19DAYS1939514350
518MIS51ING18408
THE FIRST FOLD

FIRST FOLD COVER ART | DAVID **MARQUEZ**

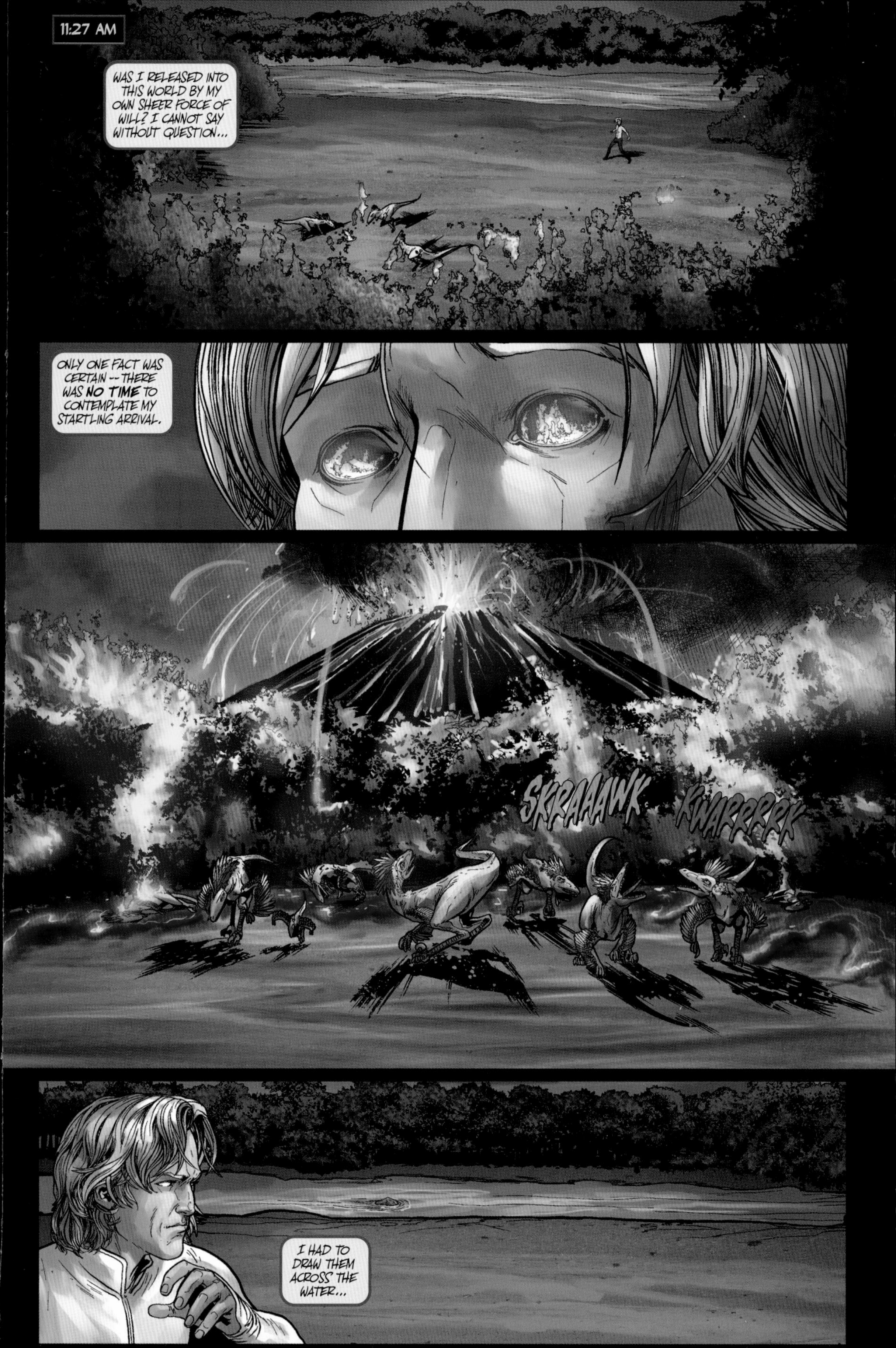
11:27 AM
WAS I RELEASED INTO THIS WORLD BY MY OWN SHEER FORCE OF WILL? I CANNOT SAY WITHOUT QUESTION...
ONLY ONE FACT WAS CERTAIN -- THERE WAS NO TIME TO CONTEMPLATE MY STARTLING ARRIVAL.
SKRAAAWK
KWARRRRK
I HAD TO DRAW THEM ACROSS THE WATER...

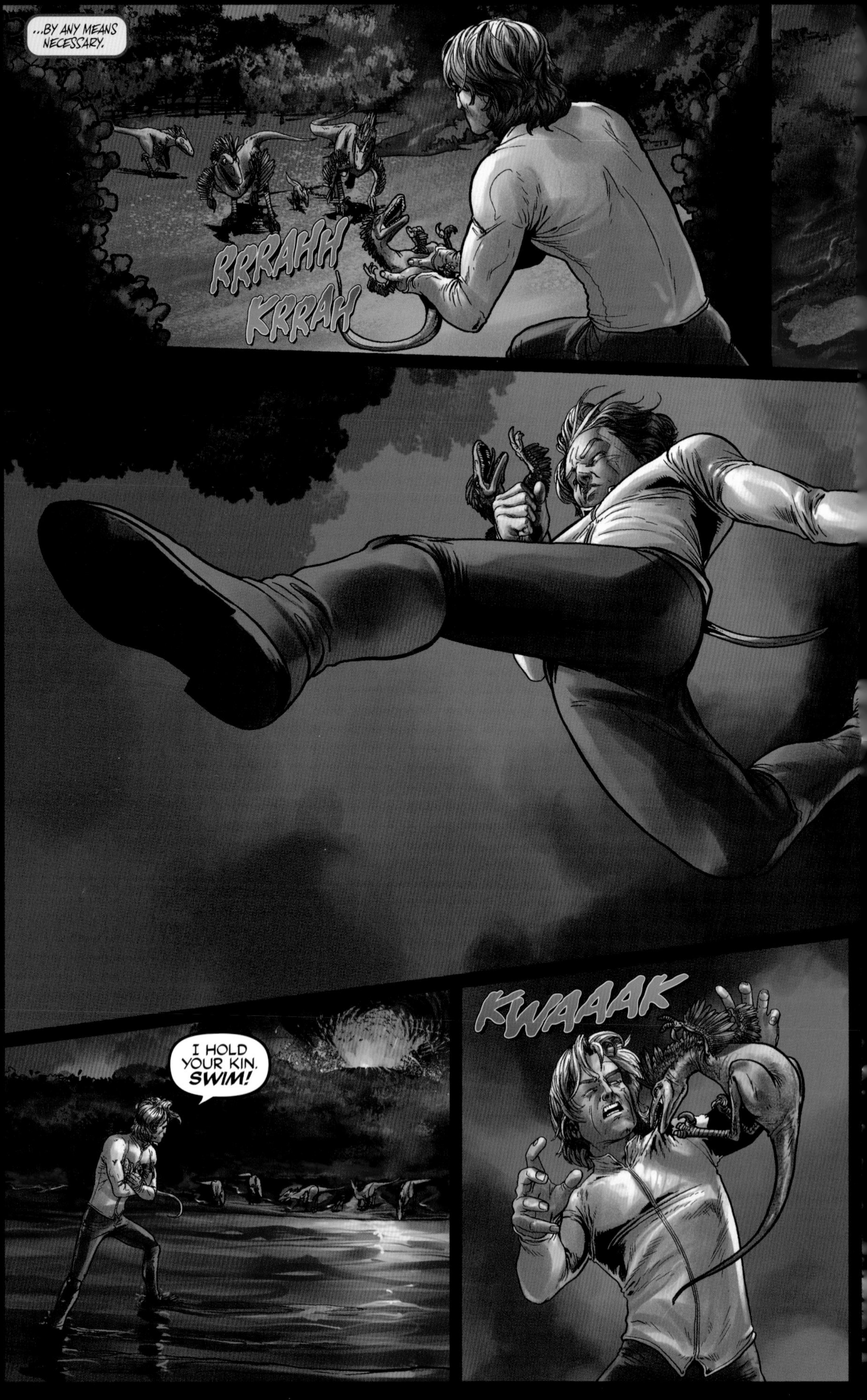
...BY ANY MEANS NECESSARY.
RRRAHH
KRRAH
I HOLD YOUR KIN. SWIM!
KWAAAK

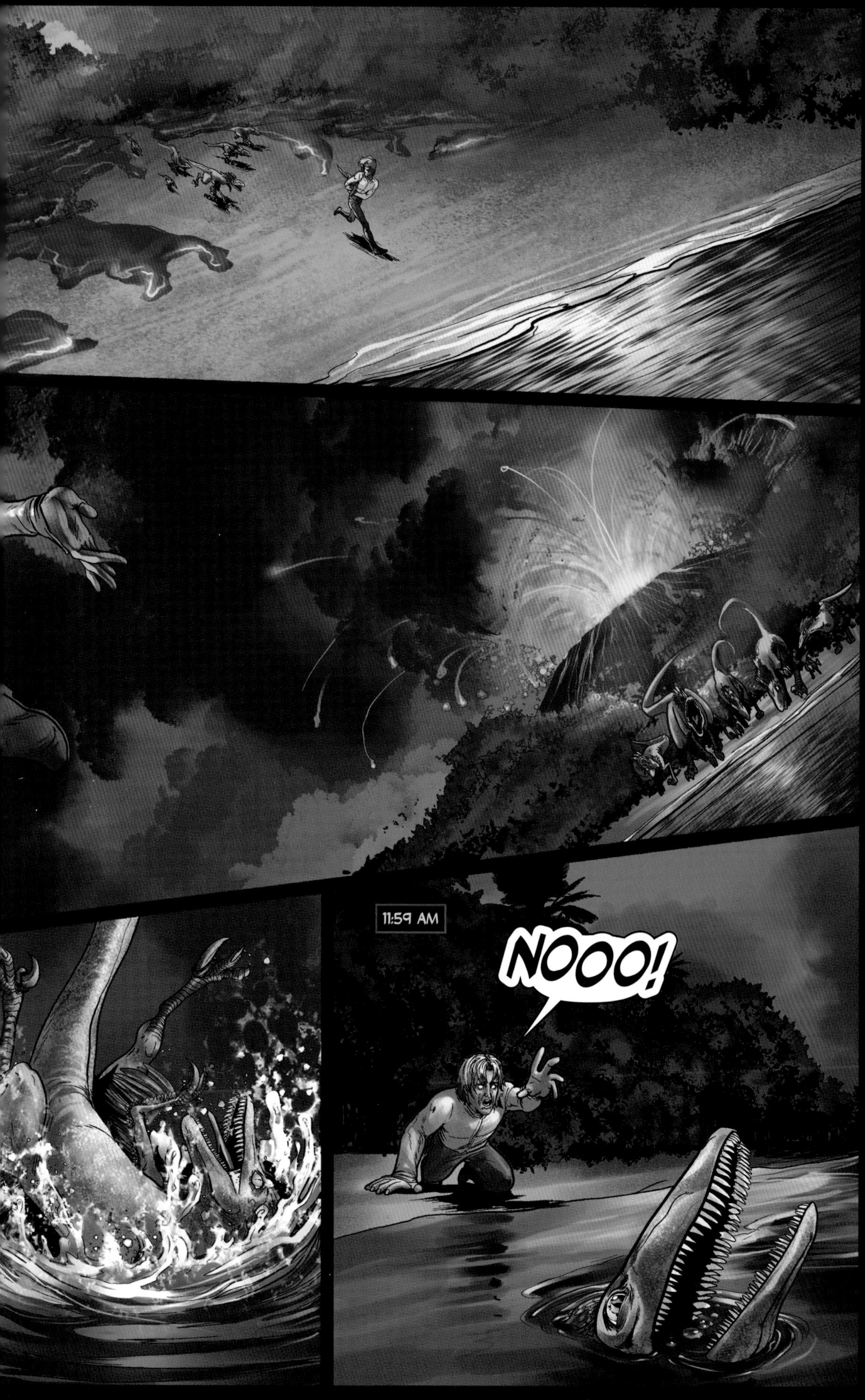
11:59 AM
NOOO!

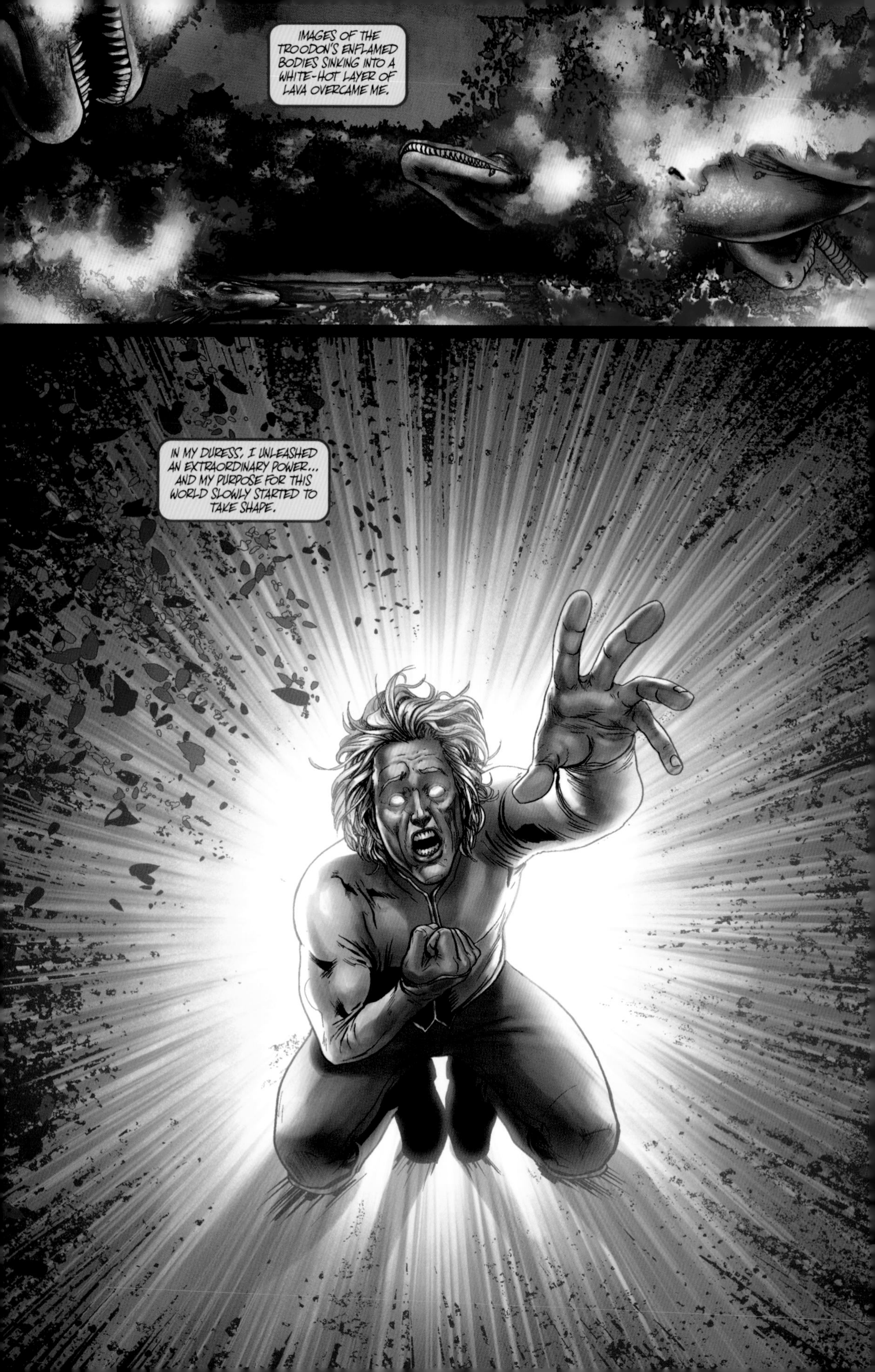
IMAGES OF THE TROODON'S ENFLAMED BODIES SINKING INTO A WHITE-HOT LAYER OF LAVA OVERCAME ME.
IN MY DURESS, I UNLEASHED AN EXTRAORDINARY POWER... AND MY PURPOSE FOR THIS WORLD SLOWLY STARTED TO TAKE SHAPE.

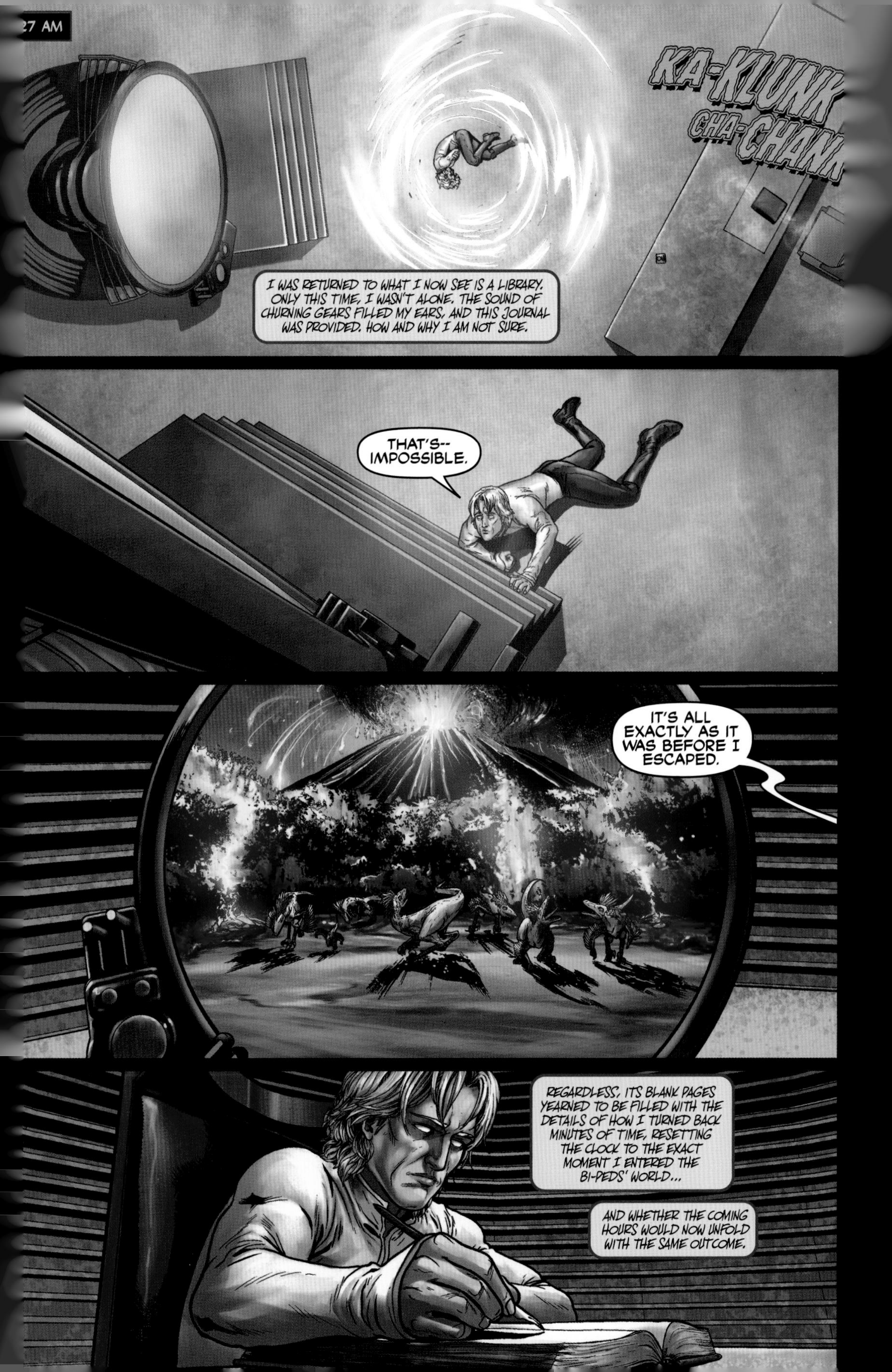
27 AM
KA-KLUNK
CHA-CHANK
I WAS RETURNED TO WHAT I NOW SEE IS A LIBRARY. ONLY THIS TIME, I WASN'T ALONE. THE SOUND OF CHURNING GEARS FILLED MY EARS, AND THIS JOURNAL WAS PROVIDED. HOW AND WHY I AM NOT SURE.
THAT'S-- IMPOSSIBLE.
IT'S ALL EXACTLY AS IT WAS BEFORE I ESCAPED.
REGARDLESS, ITS BLANK PAGES YEARNED TO BE FILLED WITH THE DETAILS OF HOW I TURNED BACK MINUTES OF TIME, RESETTING THE CLOCK TO THE EXACT MOMENT I ENTERED THE BI-PEDS' WORLD...
AND WHETHER THE COMING HOURS WOULD NOW UNFOLD WITH THE SAME OUTCOME.

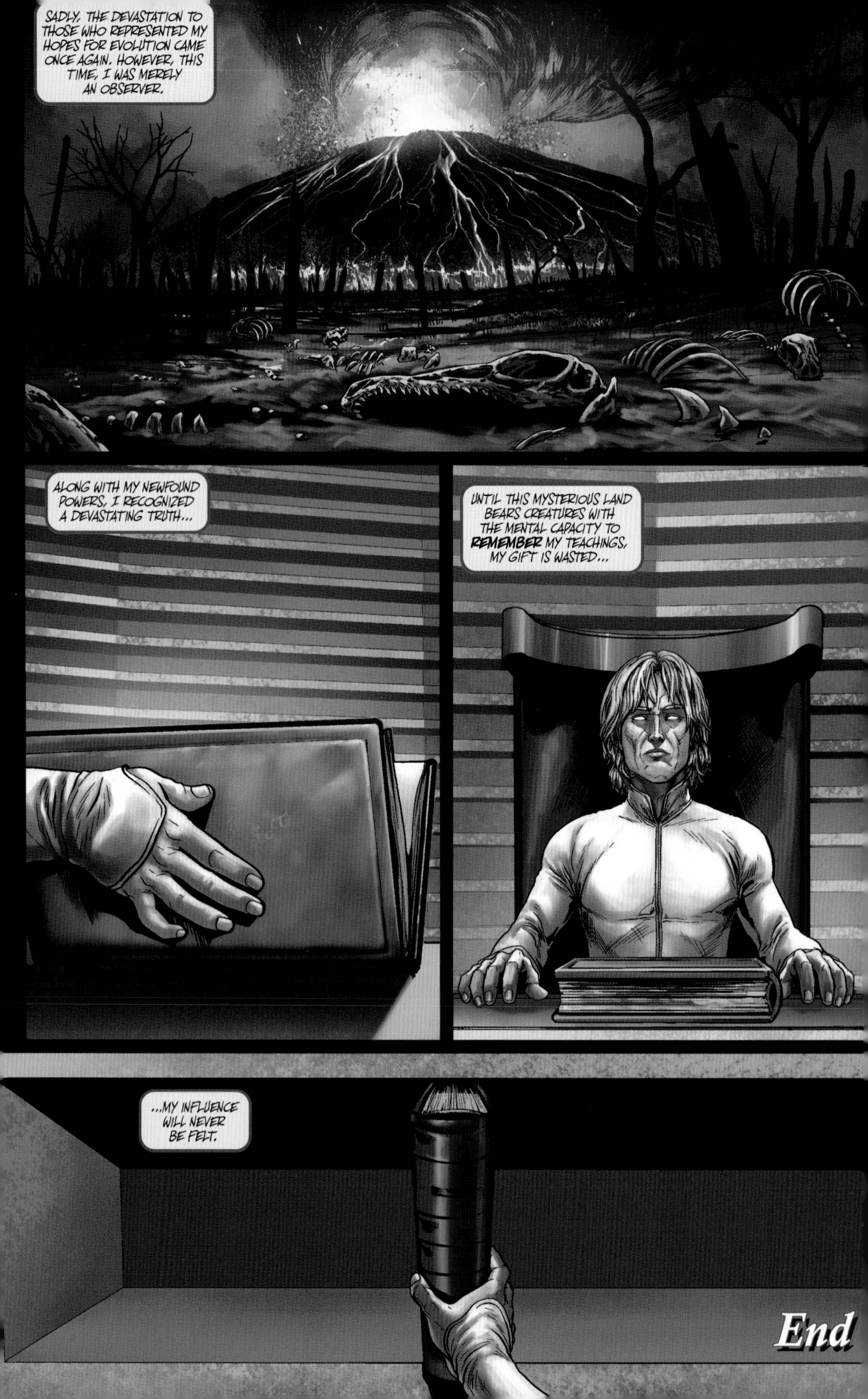
SADLY, THE DEVASTATION TO THOSE WHO REPRESENTED MY HOPES FOR EVOLUTION CAME ONCE AGAIN. HOWEVER, THIS TIME, I WAS MERELY AN OBSERVER.
ALONG WITH MY NEWFOUND POWERS, I RECOGNIZED A DEVASTATING TRUTH...
UNTIL THIS MYSTERIOUS LAND BEARS CREATURES WITH THE MENTAL CAPACITY TO **REMEMBER** MY TEACHINGS, MY GIFT IS WASTED...
...MY INFLUENCE WILL NEVER BE FELT.
End

AFTERWORD | TREVOR ROTH

With *Days Missing* Volume One, the intent was simple–introduce our hero, explain his circumstances and take the reader on incredible journeys through time that showed how integral The Steward has been throughout human history. It was challenging, but we got the job done. It's a spectacular book and I am proud of the results. But the bar was definitely raised with respect to what we set out to accomplish in the second series.

We concluded Volume One with a strong, compelling revelation–The Steward is not alone. By following it with the introduction of a being who lives on a comparable plane as The Steward, we provided a more textured insight into our protagonist, while simultaneously heightening the stakes of each day's story. In order to further develop the complexity of The Steward's character, we needed to create a counterpart with her own dimension–someone who lives in the grays. Kestus plays the role of nemesis, but she's also the only being who has ever satiated The Steward's hunger for companionship. I wanted The Steward to look on the day he met Kestus as the best and worst day of his life.

The biggest challenge with Volume Two was the intricacy with which we needed to intertwine the "days" missing in *Days Missing* Volume Two and the overarching story of The Steward and Kestus. Thank you, Phil Hester and Dave Marquez, for your brilliance. Phil's writing in chapters one and five of Volume One was spot-on and he didn't disappoint in this book either. His capacity for vividly delivering each of the historical days included in the second series, for getting to the heart of the characters, and for weaving the centuries-long relationship between The Steward and Kestus through it all, is nothing short of remarkable. This book wouldn't be what it is without his magic pen.

Further, I can't say enough about the extraordinary abilities of newcomer Dave Marquez, the gifted artist of *Days Missing: Kestus*. We would never have been able to make the story of Kestus as accessible and believable without his talents. As opposed to using different artists for each chapter, as was done for Volume One, we realized that a strong, steady, singular hand was the only way to bring this particular narrative to life. Dave provided that and more. World, look out for this guy.

Stepping back for a moment, it's clear that developing a follow-up to a critically acclaimed graphic novel, produced by the likes of Ian Edginton, Dale Keown, Matz, Frazer Irving, Phil Hester and others, was a fantastic challenge. We were determined to surpass what we accomplished with Volume One by making *Days Missing: Kestus* a great step forward for an already beloved franchise. Thanks to the help of talented people like Phil and Dave, our editors at Archaia and the dedicated production team at Roddenberry, I am proud to say I think we accomplished that goal. I hope that you, the readers, agree.

I can't wait for you to see what we have in store for you next!

— Trevor Roth

ABOUT THE CREATORS

PHIL HESTER has been making comics for over two decades, beginning while a student at the University of Iowa. He spent many years on the indie comics scene, culminating in his Eisner Award-nominated series *The Wretch*. Phil broke into the mainstream with a long run as penciller on DC's *Swamp Thing*. He also drew Kevin Smith's revival of *Green Arrow* with long-time inker Ande Parks. He created *The Coffin* with artist Mike Huddleston, and *Firebreather* with artist Andy Kuhn, now a television feature for Cartoon Network. Phil lives in rural Iowa with his wife and two children.

TREVOR ROTH has played an integral role in pushing the Roddenberry legacy into the 21st century. Roth has developed innovative science-fiction entertainment properties that remain true to the traditions of the late Gene Roddenberry, creator of *Star Trek*. He created the highly successful web-comics *Rod & Barry* and *Gene's Journal*. Roth is a producer of the upcoming documentary *Trek Nation*, and is slated to be an executive producer for the television series *Questor*. He is also the creator of the critically acclaimed comic book series *Days Missing*.

DAVID MARQUEZ graduated from the University of Texas at Austin with degrees in History and Government, but chose to take a risk to pursue his passion for illustration. He auditioned for an animation position on Warner Independent Pictures' *A Scanner Darkly*, and was immediately hired. After Scanner, David worked on a variety of small press and creator-owned comics projects, culminating in the summer of 2010 with the release of his first major project, *Syndrome*, a graphic novel from Archaia Entertainment. David has also illustrated projects at Top Cow and Marvel Comics.

EUGENE "ROD" RODDENBERRY carries the torch left to him by his father, the iconic visionary *Star Trek* creator Gene Roddenberry. As the only son of Gene and Majel Barrett Roddenberry, Rod is continuing in their footsteps, seeking to make the utopian Roddenberry vision a reality. As CEO of Roddenberry Productions, Rod as returned the company to its original mission, creating thoughtful and inspiring content.

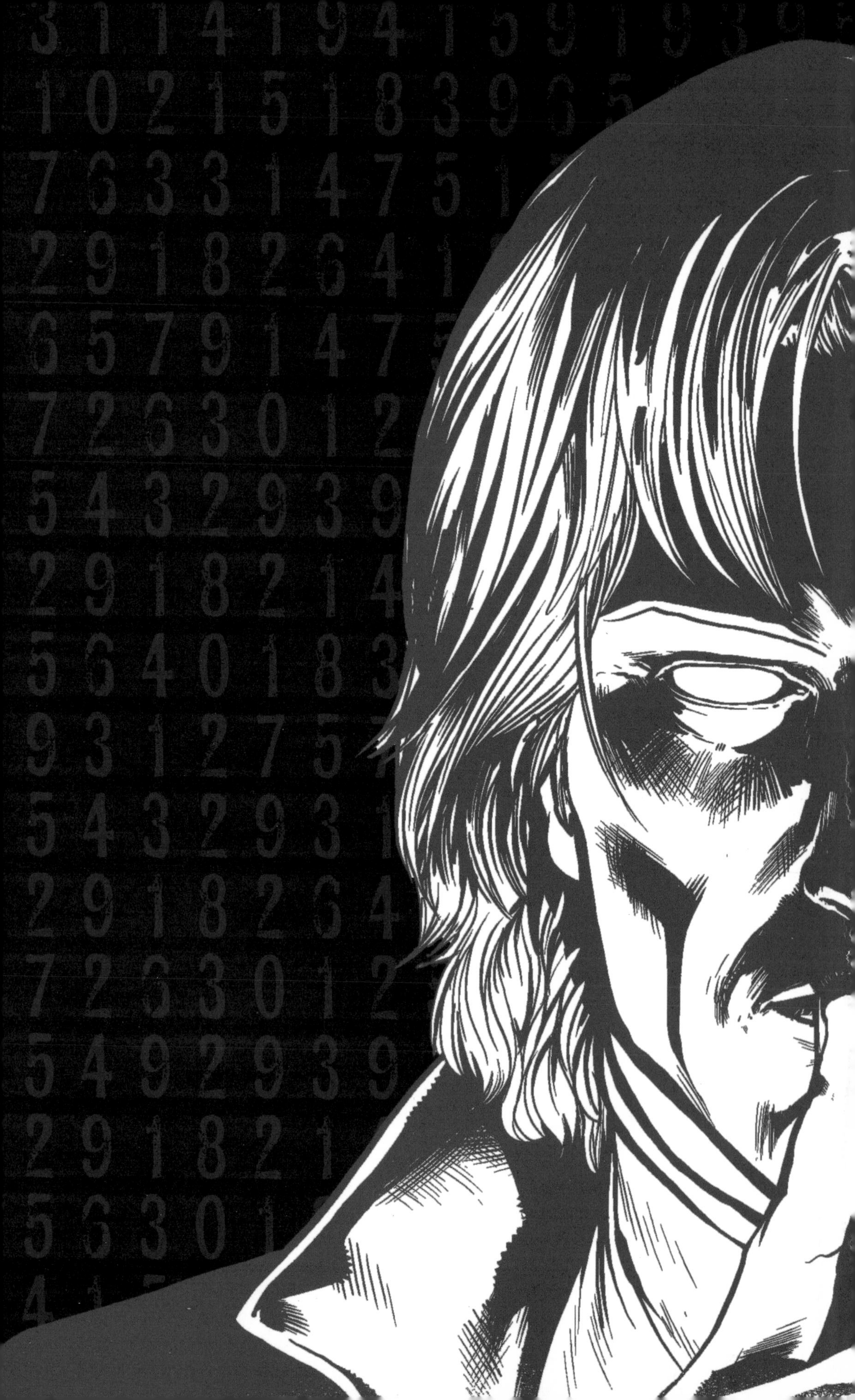